CRYSTAL'S HOUSE OF QUEERS

BROOKE SKIPSTONE

Skipstone
PUBLISHING

ISBN: 978-1-7370064-2-8

Cover design by Cherie Chapman © ccbookdesign
Line drawings © maharanicandra
Watercolor paintings © Arju

First edition

"We all need to be held and loved. Why do people take issue with who does the holding?"

— CRYSTAL ROSE

NOTE

Full color versions of the watercolor paintings used in this novel can be found at www.brookeskipstone.com

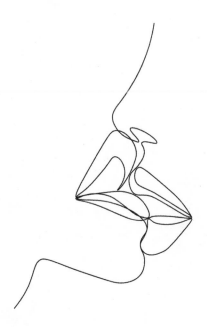

CHAPTER 1

*C*rystal lies naked on her back, watching Haley remove three wet fingers from between her plump lips then slowly insert them into Crystal's mouth.

"Get them wet. Very wet," Haley purrs as her green eyes fix on Crystal's browns. Haley lies against Crystal's left side, propping her head on her right arm.

Crystal wiggles her tongue around each digit while sucking breath in through her nose.

Haley removes her fingers. Her voice sultry and teasing, "Now stretch your arms behind your head. All the way back."

Crystal reaches to touch the headboard, heart pounding in her chest

Haley raises her brows, licks her lips, and says so slowly, "Spread."

Crystal separates her legs.

"You must always look at me." Haley's left hand inches down Crystal's stomach, sending electric jolts through her skin. She groans and twists. With gentle admonishment, Haley says, "No, no, no," and lifts her hand. "You cannot move. Or I stop. Got it?" Haley smiles then licks Crystal's lips.

Crystal reaches with her tongue to touch Haley's as she pulls away. "I won't move. Touch me. Please."

"Look at me always." Their eyes lock together. Haley slides her fingers between Crystal's legs. "You may groan."

Crystal gasps then hitches in a breath, eyes tightening on Haley's. Crystal's arms stiffen, pressing her hands hard against the headboard as Haley's fingers move in circles, faster and faster.

Deep groans roll out from Crystal's belly, spasms convulse her insides, her skin flushes with sweat, but always she sees Haley's shining eyes, and she does not move . . . until . . .

Crystal jerks to a sitting position in her bed, gasping for breath. Slowly, her eyes open to the red numbers on her alarm clock—3:00 am.

She's had another dream of sex with Haley. The second time this week after in-person school started on Monday, September 14, when she saw her senior classmate for the first time since the March lockdown. Crystal shivers as the sweat evaporates from her bare skin. She grabs her pillow and hugs it to her chest.

Years ago near the end of fourth grade, Haley spent the night and slept in this bed. Crystal woke in the early morning with Haley snuggled up against her back, an arm thrown over her side. Crystal tried not to move so Haley would stay glued to her. But she did reach ever so slowly for her hand and brought it to her lips. The next morning, Crystal awoke in the same position with Haley. Crystal wasn't sure, but she sensed Haley was awake, and either they were both too nervous to change position, or too reluctant to end the contact.

Crystal's grandmother knocked. "Are you two girls going to sleep all morning? I've got breakfast ready."

Both girls snapped up, disentangling from each other with nervous laughs. "We're up."

That was the last time Haley slept over. Crystal never understood why.

Now, 18-year-old Crystal lies back down, hugging her pillow, replaying the dream in her mind until exhaustion pushes her into sleep.

Just before the alarm rings, Crystal flings her legs off the mattress and stands. She has a weird feeling that something is amiss. She pulls on jeans, a scoop neck t-shirt, and a gray cotton jacket, left unzipped. After lifting her pack onto her shoulder, she walks down the hall into the kitchen, where she finds no one. Normally, she'd be met by Summer with a plate of eggs, toast, and sausage, but today there's a square of cinnamon swirl coffee cake on a napkin.

Crystal sets her pack on the oak table, stuffs the cake into her mouth, and heads toward the sunroom at the other end of the house. She needs to find something to draw today in art class and record it in a photograph or video. She opens the door onto the deck, letting in cool, moist air. A bank of fog drifts near a narrow pond along a trail leading into the woods behind her house.

All of her senses prickle. Something moves toward her.

She takes out her phone and starts a video as she sits on a fat stump near the woodshed. Her nose and throat fill with the scent of freshly split spruce and birch.

"I wonder if all special needs kids have special powers. I know I do." There's a muffled stamping and the brittle snap of leaves along the path. She holds her breath a moment, worried that even the slightest sound will be too loud.

"I know when animals are watching me. I can feel their eyes on my skin and hear their hearts beating." She stands and strains to find the brown mass she knows moves toward her, an absence of light in the woods which would otherwise glow on this chilly morning in Clear, Alaska.

"With my pen I can draw the shape of anything with a single, continuous line—face, body, raven . . ." She hesitates slightly, lowers her voice even more, and moves her lips closer to the phone. "Or moose. But above all, I have no fear—not of the dark or whatever danger lurks around the next corner."

The fog dissipates, revealing a moose twenty feet away, its breath erupting in bursts of steam through its massive nose tilted straight down, huge black eyes—orbs of pure darkness—fixed on Crystal, who calms her beating heart and does not move. Even when she notices the calf standing behind its mother, shaking its head and twisting its Mohawk bristles along its spine, she remains in control. Crystal knows she's too close, but this view and this intimacy with such a magnificent animal are priceless and worth any risk. She's seen a cow charge her younger brother, JD, when he emerged from the trees into a clearing, but that moose snorted and screeched before moving. This one stands still and silent except for pushing air out of its nostrils in a steady, menacing rhythm. Maybe she senses that Crystal has no fear.

She continues recording. "Who else would stand this close to a thousand-pound cow and her baby with nothing but a camera? Only me." A smile quivers in the corners of her mouth. "Sometimes I'm magic." She barely lifts her right foot and inches it backward. "I'll draw you both later."

She stops the video and walks away from the animals, keeping her gaze fixed on the mother for any sign of a charge. The cow would protect its child at all costs for a year. But after that, she'd drive it away or just leave.

Crystal knows what that feels like. Her mother left her and JD with her grandparents, Mac and Summer, fourteen years ago then disappeared. According to them, her mother and father died in a car wreck a few years later. His fault, of course. They hated Eugene and blamed him for all of Maya's problems.

For years she had wanted to know why her father drove the car drunk, why he flipped off the road into a tree, killing her mother and his irresponsible self. Why he kept her hooked on drugs and alcohol. Why Crystal lost her mother at the very edges of her memory.

Crystal has some recollections of them, like mist along the pond— there one minute and gone the next. Or flitting like redpolls swarming from tree to tree. What Crystal remembers and what Mac and Summer told her were often different. Like when Mom supposedly ran away from her evil husband and flew to the Alaskan village where her grandparents taught, promising to enter rehab and never return to Eugene, the dope dealer.

But Crystal remembers her father driving them to the airport, helping Mom wheel the bags and carry JD while she held Crystal's hand as they stood in line. They were four and three at the time. Dad had even kissed Mom before she left him at the bottom of the escalator to go through security. At least, that's what Crystal saw. She'd asked JD several times about the car ride and the kiss, but he barely knew his name back then.

Doesn't matter anyway. The fact is, Mom left them fourteen years ago and never returned. And Crystal is sure she'd always intended to leave them. Dump the kids and have fun again.

Crystal turns around to look for the moose as she steps onto the deck at the back of her house, but they are gone. Faded into the trees. But not from her phone where they'll live forever. The greatest thing about photographs and her drawings is their permanence. Stuff stays put.

Crystal opens the door and hears the phone ringing in the kitchen. Mac keeps a landline so when the power goes out and the Internet is down, they'll still have a way to make phone calls. Cell phone coverage can be spotty in their area.

Seeing no one nearby to answer, Crystal runs and grabs the phone on the fourth ring. "Hello?"

"I'm looking for Mac Rose," a man's voice says.

Crystal covers the mouthpiece and hears Mac coughing upstairs. "He can't come to the phone right now. Can I tell him who's calling?"

"No . . . that's all right. I'll call back another time. Are you Cr . . .?" He stops.

"Sorry?" Crystal is sure he was about to say her name. Why did he stop?

"Ah, nothing."

"Can I give him a name or number?"

"No. No, I'll call back later. You . . . you seem like a nice girl."

Crystal wonders why he said that. "You were expecting something different?"

"No. Never mind. Sorry to bother you." He hangs up.

What the hell? Mac coughs again and Summer says something to him.

JD opens the bathroom door behind her. They both hear more coughing. "Mac is sick," says JD. His steady eyes meet hers. "Could be Covid." He sucks in his lower lip.

"What's wrong?" she asks, as cold fills her belly.

"Fever. And he keeps sucking on his inhaler."

Her little brother is six foot three with massive shoulders. He dwarfs Crystal by more than a foot and a hundred pounds, which would be scary, but he is the sweetest brother anyone could hope to have.

He walks past her into the living room with his staggered gait. He's been disabled his whole life. His hips are deformed, so he walks with a rolling limp, like he's always skating up an imaginary little hill with his left foot first. He fails every academic subject at school. And he's teased a lot. Mac and Summer doubt he will ever be able to live by himself, but Crystal thinks otherwise. He can hunt and fish, build anything, and he cherishes his girlfriend, Gena. How many skills does he need to raise a family in nowhere Alaska? He's seventeen and ready to find a job. School is doing him no good.

One night many years ago after JD had gone to sleep, Crystal went to her grandparents' bedroom and asked why her brother had so many problems. Mac whipped off his glasses and blurted, "Whiskey." Summer slammed her book shut and tried to shush him, but he wouldn't stop. "Jack Daniel's to be specific. Old No.7. Your mother practically bathed in the stuff. Your brother was drunk when he was born, and so were his parents. They'd just come off a weekend binge, so they called him JD." Until then, Crystal hadn't known his real name was Jack. Or why.

She had never told her brother the truth. Or that their last names used to be Rock before Mac and Summer Rose adopted them. If anyone asks him what the J and D stand for, he says, "They stand for me. I'm JD." He likes making the rhyme.

Crystal finds the self-portrait drawing she finished last night unmoved on the kitchen table. Usually Summer says something nice about her art pieces at breakfast.

She picks up the paper and once again loves the fact her name is Crystal Rose rather than Rock.

A perfect name for an artist because she can draw a beautiful, one-line rose at the end.

At first Crystal had trouble keeping her pen moving on the paper without trying to fix the mistakes. But her teacher told her to "embrace the imperfections" and let them "add a little character to the final result. Just let your talent flow." Crystal practiced over and over until she filled dozens of sketchpads, and she finally realized she had embraced her own imperfections through her art.

She rolls up her drawing and pushes it into a tube she carries in her pack.

Her grandparents come down the stairs, both wearing masks. Mac sits at the table as Summer offers him two pills and a glass of water. After he lifts his mask and gulps them down, she places a wet cloth on his forehead.

"Are you sick?" asks Crystal.

"Maybe. Probably just a cold," says Mac, wrapping his big arms around his chest to stop shivering.

"You two need to wear your masks in the house from now on," says Summer.

"In the house?" asks JD. "Why?"

Summer clenches her jaw and sighs before speaking with more impatience and volume than normal. "Because you're mingling with the whole town at school every day. Who knows how careful any of them have been?"

Crystal watches JD's eyes widen. She knows he's confused by Summer's tone.

Very firmly with a sharp look at both of them: "Put. On. Your. Masks."

Crystal pulls hers out of a back pocket and fastens the straps behind her ears. JD searches his pockets then, finding nothing, stares meekly at Summer, who shakes her head slightly before pulling another mask out of a drawer.

Sweat gathers on her brother's forehead. JD tries hard to not disappoint his grandparents, and she knows he believes he just did.

Summer hands the mask to JD. "Please keep those on all day."

JD puts his on. "Does Mac have Covid?"

Mac pulls his mask down and smiles. "I'm not dead yet, JD. You can ask me."

Summer pulls Mac's mask back to his nose. "Keep it on, Mac."

"Do you?" asks JD, a little quiver in his voice.

"Probably not. I can still smell and taste. Just a cold. Can't anyone catch a cold anymore without everyone freaking out?" He tries to laugh but ends up coughing. Summer pats his back as he props his head on the table.

Mac is still a big, strong man, but now Crystal sees wrinkles and wispy hair and a heaving chest. How sick can he be? She feels a pain and realizes she's been twisting her fingers.

"No one is freaking out, Mac," says Summer. "The cases are increasing all over the country. Over 200,000 people have died, and our governor is doing nothing. Most of the people in this town think Covid is a hoax. But I don't. We're both too old to get this." She looks at JD and Crystal. "Keep your masks on. You don't want to spread it to your friends, and you don't want to bring it home to us. Do you understand?"

Crystal nods.

JD mumbles, "Yes."

This is the first time since the pandemic began they have been told to wear masks in the house. Is Summer blaming them for Mac's illness? How could they be the cause? Crystal's heard nothing at school about anyone—student or parent—being sick.

Summer scans Mac's temperature again. "I don't know why you two have in-person school now anyway. Cases are going up in the borough, not down. You spent the first three weeks at home using your computers. Why'd they have to change?" She looks at the number on the probe.

"Same?" asks Mac then pulls a dose from his inhaler.

"A little higher."

Crystal and JD are very happy to be back in school. They'd been online from mid-March through May and then from late August until Monday, two days ago. During that time, Crystal had seen virtually none of her classmates. She'd never been very social, but she had missed seeing her art teacher and especially Haley. They'd been close friends in the elementary grades but had drifted apart in high school.

Crystal unties her hair and shakes her head. "One reason we went back this week is that special needs students don't learn as much in remote learning."

"Who said that?" asks Summer.

"SPED teacher." Crystal bends over the table to grab her computer and feels her grandmother's eyes searching her, just like she felt the moose eyes earlier.

"Crystal, why aren't you wearing a bra?"

She lifts her eyes to Summer, who signals to hold her shirt against her chest. "Why are you looking?" She stays bent as she shoves books and her computer into her bag. "No one cared about me wearing a bra before. What difference does it make now?"

"Crystal, we've talked about this. You developed over the summer. You can't be flashing everyone."

"Am I flashing, or are you making a special effort to look down my shirt?" She feels blood rushing to her face. Her eyes throb.

"Please stand up straight."

Crystal finishes stuffing her pack without hurrying, drags the zipper closed then swings her pack onto her shoulder as she stands. "Better?"

"Please put on your bra."

Mac coughs. "Just don't bend over in front of the boys, Crystal, and keep your jacket zipped."

Crystal cocks a brow. "Because it'd be my fault if they stared at my boobs?"

JD laughs. "Gena calls them boobs too. A lot of my friends call them tits."

"JD!" Everyone flinches when Summer slaps the table. Crystal can remember only one or two other times when she screamed at JD. He now stands with his mouth open, breathing noisily. His eyes bulge. "There's no need to be crude. Why are you and Gena talking about her . . . breasts?"

Because they've been having sex for the past six months, thinks Crystal so loud she wonders whether anyone hears her. "C'mon, JD. We need to go." Crystal pushes a chair farther under the table and heads for the door.

Summer grabs her arm. "Why are you being so defiant about this?"

"I've gone my whole life without my chest being strangled and bound. No one cared. Now if I don't crush my boobs all day and much of the night, there's something wrong with me. Guys go shirtless at PE all the time. Why can't the girls?"

"That'd be embarrassing," laughs JD as he moves through the door. "Hope you feel better, Mac."

Summer releases Crystal's arm and wrings her hands. "Now you want to go topless? Where are you getting these ideas?"

"Why do I have to *get* them from somewhere besides my own head? Cause I'm too dumb?" Her heart pounds in her chest and lips tighten against her teeth. She wants to say much more but is afraid to start another argument. She tries to slow her breathing. "Hope you feel better, Mac." She exits the house and heads toward her Honda 4-wheeler where JD sits sideways behind the seat.

"I think it's my turn to drive," he says, just like every morning.

Crystal straddles the seat and starts the motor. "It's not your turn until you're older than me."

"And what day will that happen?"

"Exactly." She zips up her jacket, shifts gears, and races away from the house down her long driveway, bordered by spruce and aspen.

Last weekend, Kato told her she needed to wear a bra when she returned to school. He said he didn't want guys staring at her all day. They'd been best friends their whole lives and had never even kissed. Then her boobs grew over the summer, and he couldn't keep his hands off her. He complained she was teasing him, being coy, making him think dirty thoughts. All during July and August, she'd felt excited and confused, sometimes angry. Before this past weekend, they'd only kissed, and honestly, she'd never wanted to do anything more.

But she finally relented. The experience wasn't very exciting, certainly nothing like her dreams of girls. Or kissing Haley in fifth grade.

At first, the dreams bothered her. Could something more be wrong with her brain beyond what school told her? She's never fantasized about a boy. After Saturday's session with Kato, she believes she understands why, but doesn't know what to do or who to tell.

Maybe Haley?

What's the worst that could happen?

She could laugh. Walk away. Tell others.

What's the best she could say?

Me too.

How amazing would that be?

When the best option offers so great a reward, Crystal always ignores the danger. Witness—her encounter with the moose this morning.

Maybe she'll talk to Haley today.

CHAPTER 2

*B*oth siblings remove their masks as Crystal drives down D Street where a few rabbits line up at the edges, trying to be perfectly still, thinking if they don't move, people won't see them. Then when they realize that isn't working, they scamper into the willows. Yesterday, both of them saw a lynx stalking along the road and heard coyotes yip-howling at night, which explains why the number of rabbits has steadily declined.

Just another sign of change and loss. Along with the bigger patches of yellow leaves in the trees, the blood red fireweed, and the whitening of the rabbits' ears and feet—all warning of the long, hard winter to come. Mid-September and already their thoughts turn to winter. Crystal wishes something in her life would stay the same. Or grow to something better rather than fade away.

And now Mac could have Covid. Maybe they all do.

Their school backs up against a stretch of spruce forest between the town and the river park. By far the largest building in town, it is one story except for the gym, which rises in the back, sporting a new brown metal roof. The park, the school, a DMV office/city building, volunteer fire station, and assorted houses, modified trailers, and shacks make up the town of Clear, eighty miles south of Fairbanks along the Parks

Highway. Many of its 120 students live within ten minutes of the K-12 building, and most have attended every grade before graduation. Teachers and principals change frequently, but most classmates grow up together.

A crowd of unmasked students have gathered near Crystal's usual parking spot, laughing as they watch something on Laura's iPad. Mike is poised smugly in front of Crystal as she drives slowly toward him.

Crystal stands in the foot wells, still able to hold the handlebars without bending over. "Excuse me, Mike." She doesn't stop. Fortunately, he jumps out of the way at the last second.

Mike puffs out his chest and flicks a comb through his gelled, blond hair to make sure it's still swept up from his forehead. "Careful, Twig."

JD jumps off the back and walks to Mike, smiling. "How's your day been going?" JD looms over him by six inches and fifty pounds.

Mike shakes his head. "Same question every time, JD. Don't you know anything else to say?"

JD lowers his head and throws a punch at Mike's shoulder, stopping it just before contact. Mike flinches and yelps. "Got you, didn't I?" JD laughs and turns around, looking for Gena, Kato's sister. Crystal takes a quick look and is relieved Kato hasn't arrived yet to drop her off.

"Let Crystal see the video," orders Mike, flashing his blue eyes. The crowd opens while Laura holds the iPad for Crystal to see. Mike is doing a pole dance while wearing only a thong. He's obviously drunk as is everyone else gathered at the nearby gravel pit. The crowd chants *Take it off, Mike*, drowning out the music until he releases the pole, turns his back to the camera and slides off the thong. Gyrating his hips and thrusting his pelvis, he faces the camera, revealing his nude body to screams of appreciation. All Crystal can think of is Summer's order to wear a bra and keep her shirt from revealing too much skin.

"It was a great party," says Mike. "Everybody got laid."

"Too bad you had to settle for that pole," answers Crystal. Some girls laugh and a few guys taunt Mike.

"You're just jealous," he says.

"Of the pole? Which one? The big one at the side of the rock grinder? Or the smaller one between your legs?" She raises her brows and smiles.

"Not much smaller!" He laughs and high fives a couple of guys.

She remembers seeing Kato's boner for the first time, which initially made her blush but later became a pain—literally. She knows seeing Mike naked—he is handsome, after all—should be exciting, but it isn't. All she feels is confusion—and regret.

Laura, a pretty brunette senior with glossy lips and tight jeans, flips the cover over her iPad. "Crystal, you can come to my party tomorrow night. Everyone would love to see you there."

Is she serious? Crystal's never hung out with her classmates outside of school.

Mike snorts a laugh. "Yeah, but wear something low-cut so we know which sex to pair you up with," says Mike, proud of himself. A couple of guys laugh.

Crystal is tired of being demeaned for her size, especially now that she has filled out. She unzips her jacket. "My boobs have grown. You just haven't noticed. Want to see them?" She grabs the bottom of her t-shirt.

No one speaks. Just open mouths and gaping eyes.

Mike fidgets. "What?"

"Guess not." She releases her shirt and shoulders her pack.

"Hey, Crystal." Mike pleads. "Sure. We'd love to see them."

"Too late. Maybe next time." She turns and walks quickly toward the school entrance. Once again, she's been called Twig. She's always been measured by numbers—test scores, grades, height, cup size. She was declared Special Needs years ago, but her needs have nothing to do with numbers or letters, though she isn't yet sure what they are.

She hears the scraping of shoes on gravel behind her and realizes she is walking too fast for JD to follow. She stops and turns. "Sorry, JD. I wasn't thinking."

"You don't have to wait, Crystal." His grin makes his cheeks ball up and his dimples deep. "Would you have done it?"

"Lifted my shirt?"

"Yeah."

"If he had said 'Sure' or 'OK,' I would have. If he can flash his dick to everyone, why can't I flash my boobs?"

"I don't know. Why couldn't you?"

"Because of stupid rules. If I had, I'd be sent home while Mike could talk about my chest all day."

"Hey, JD!" yells Gena as she hops off Kato's Honda and runs toward JD. Dark hair, big black eyes, always happy and laughing. JD lifts her high off the ground as she raises her arms above her head and squeals, "Circle. Circle."

JD turns around slowly several times as she leans her head back and beams at the sky, arms spread wide. He lowers her carefully then they hug. "How's your day been going, Gena?"

"Really good."

"Hey, Crystal," says Haley with a smile as she hurries to keep up with her boyfriend, Dylan.

Crystal's heart skips as a blur of red-auburn hair brushes past her. "Hey, Haley." She lifts a hand to wave, the same hand that Haley touched as she hustled past her. It didn't seem accidental. Crystal felt a little squeeze of her fingers.

Something similar happened yesterday. Crystal stood in front of her open locker next to Haley's. She was trying to remember what class she had next when she felt Haley stumble into her.

Haley laughed. "Oh, my gosh! I didn't know you were standing there. I just turned and started walking. I'm so sorry, Crystal," she said as she held Crystal's arm.

"That's OK. You can bump into me any time." And she'd meant it. Haley had accidentally held her stomach and butt, and Crystal still thinks their faces touched.

On Monday, their first day back at school, Haley came right up close to her and said, "Crystal, you've grown since I last saw you," with such a big smile.

Crystal gulped, glanced around quickly to see how close anyone else was, and said, "You're as pretty as you've always been, Haley. I'm happy to see you." Maybe Crystal misremembers, but she thought Haley stared at her lips just a little too long.

"I'm happy to see you too. See ya." Then she turned and walked away. Crystal couldn't help watching her gorgeous butt swaying to the rhythm of "look at me, look at me, look at me." Crystal had to close her eyes and lean back against her locker for a full minute before she could go to class.

Crystal has dared to think all this is on purpose, that Haley wants to signal Crystal. Maybe she should make her own effort. What's the worst that could happen?

They move toward the entrance where Mr. Rathbone—tall, butch haircut, jeans, and a dress shirt—reminds them to put on their masks. Laura, Mike, and the others hustle over, fumbling with their face coverings. "Hurry up, people," scolds Rathbone.

Kato stands next to his Honda. It still seems odd to her he just watches everyone else enter. She hasn't gotten used to the fact he graduated last May. He thumbs his phone. Hers dings with a message: *Call me. Please. Can I see you at lunch?*

"Are you coming in, Crystal?"

She turns toward Rathbone, nods, slips on her mask, and ducks through the doors. She doesn't know what to feel about Kato. She knows she's hurting him but can't seem to care enough to talk to him.

"Social distance, people," bellows Rathbone as he watches students move to their lockers. No one makes an effort to distance. JD and Gena hold hands next to her locker. Crystal's is around the corner near the gym where she finds Dylan and Haley maskless.

He's pressing her against her open locker door, his left beefy arm pushing on Crystal's locker while grasping her arm, his right hand playing with the increasing gap between her shirt and leggings. Crystal sees the stud in her belly button. His face hovers half an inch from Haley's, wearing a sneer. He pushes fingers down into her leggings. Her eyes widen, she gasps, and her free hand grabs his until he orders, "Don't." She jerks her hand away.

Crystal's muscles quiver as her blood pressure soars.

Dylan has flaunted his ownership of Haley before, but this is the worst. He's the biggest guy in school, and the most volatile. Crystal can't understand why Haley puts up with him other than fear he'll beat her up. Why would any girl or woman want to be pawed, especially in public?

Dylan grinds his pelvis against hers as his hand moves inside and up her shirt. Crystal slaps the locker next to her. "Hey, asshole. Back off!"

Haley turns her head, eyes pleading. Crystal takes out her phone and starts the video. "This is going to the principal, Dylan," angry she didn't think of her phone sooner.

Dylan turns his eyes toward Crystal. "Go ahead. Just necking with my girlfriend. She likes it, don't you Haley?"

"Dylan," Haley whimpers, "Rathbone is coming."

"So?" He presses his lips against hers.

She pushes his chest with her free hand. "C'mon, Dylan, let's go to class."

Dylan grabs her other arm and holds it above her head. "When I'm ready." He forces his tongue into her mouth.

"Dylan Whitley!" Rathbone walks up behind Dylan, who releases Haley's arms. "Think you two need to get to class."

Haley ducks under his shoulder and runs into the bathroom down the hall. Dylan slams her locker shut.

Crystal holds up her phone. "Do you want to see Dylan molest Haley, Mr. Rathbone? I've got the video."

"Molest?" barks Rathbone, glaring at Dylan.

Dylan's veins bulge from his biceps. "Crystal, you could've been next." He sneers and stares at her chest. "Looks like you finally got some boobs."

"Dylan!" snaps Rathbone.

Rathbone glances at her shirt. She looks down and sees her erect nipples pushing against the cloth. "You ever come near me, Dylan, and I'm going to punch you in the balls. If I can find the little things."

Dylan grins and starts to unzip his jeans. "You're welcome to search." He hasn't stopped staring at her chest.

"Dylan, that's enough!" shouts Rathbone.

She looks at Rathbone just as he turns his head away from her shirt and scribbles something on a post-it. "Send your video to Ms. Trimble's phone." He hands her the note. "Dylan, come with me."

"Why?"

"Because you need to explain your behavior to Principal Trimble. And put on your mask, son."

"And if I don't?"

"You'll be suspended. You know the rule."

"Fuck the rules!" he yells then fastens his mask around his chin.

Crystal runs to the bathroom where she finds Haley putting drops into her puffy eyes. She's hitching breaths and her cheeks are wet. "Are you OK?"

Haley tosses the bottle into the sink and rushes to hug her. "Thank you, Crystal. That was so brave." Her hands clutch Crystal's back and head, pushing her face into the flesh above Haley's cami top.

The scent of Haley's milk-white skin and her hair and her clothes startles Crystal as she hesitantly moves her arms around Haley, sending a flush of warmth into her stomach. She breathes in all of Haley's aromas—powerfully sweet, zesty, rich roses—before replying, "Rathbone took Dylan to Trimble. He might be sent home."

Haley squeezes harder. "Now I'm worried about both of us." Her voice is slow, alluring, and breathy with a touch of southern lilt.

Crystal's heart keeps skipping. "We can find a trooper. I'll help you."

The bathroom door opens, and Laura walks in. "Oh. Did I interrupt something?"

Haley quickly squeezes Crystal and lets go. "Dylan was practically raping me by my locker, but Crystal stopped him."

Crystal drops her hands and turns around, trying to slow her breathing. Haley wears no bra. Surely she noticed Crystal wears nothing under her shirt.

"You stopped Dylan?" asks Laura with her hand on her hip.

Crystal offers a slight grin. "Yeah. I threatened to punch his balls."

"Oh, I missed that part," laughs Haley, as she retrieves her eye drops from the sink. She grabs Crystal's arm and pulls her out of the bathroom. "We're late for English. Tell me what happened after I left."

Crystal gasps out the details as they retrieve their computers then hurry down past the commons area outside the main office.

Principal Trimble stands by McHenry's room. "Crystal, Mr. Rathbone told me you have a video?" She's very nice with a round face, hair in a bun, wearing pants and tennis shoes. Trimble's always treated her kindly.

"Oh, yes. Sorry." Crystal pulls out her phone, types in Trimble's number, and sends the evidence to her.

"Thank you for being brave enough to do this for Haley."

Crystal nods.

Trimble continues, "Haley, do you want to talk to me about what happened?"

Haley lowers her eyes. "Not really."

"You sure?"

"It's just not worth it, Ms. Trimble."

"I'm sorry to hear that. Please put your masks on, girls."

"Yes, Ma'am," they reply as they pull up their masks and move into the room.

"Sit by me," says Haley.

Crystal follows her to the back row near the windows looking out onto the sport field, bordered by yellow/orange poplars, aspen, and dark green spruce. This is Crystal's favorite season of the year—no bugs, a beautiful variety of colors, and cool days. She wishes she could roam the woods and river with her camera, but she wants to sit with Haley more.

"I haven't sat next to anyone but Dylan in months, even before this pandemic." Haley moves close to Crystal, leaning her shoulder into Crystal's back. "It's a pretty day. Look." She points to the sky. "Open the window."

Crystal cranks the handle until they can hear the geese honking and chortling.

A long V of maybe fifty birds flies over the field heading southeast, then swirls in a cacophony of squawking, arguing about which direction to take. Crystal has seen this happen many times, but usually after a minute, the geese suddenly form another V and move away. Now they can't seem to make up their minds: churning, confused, breathless.

Just like Crystal.

CHAPTER 3

*L*adies," shouts McHenry. "Please close the window and take your seats. Everyone should have their mask on." He walks around the room handing a paper to each student. A recent transplant to Alaska—for the scenery and animals, he often exclaims—he wears a polyester, multi-pocketed vest over a Henley shirt, cargo pants, and trail-runner sandals. His Oakleys hang from a Croakie. He often shares his surprise that no one else in town dresses like him.

Crystal closes the window and sits at the nearest desk. Haley sits, smiles at Crystal, and winks. "Can't wait to find out what our assignment is." She pulls a file from her pack and works on her nails.

For years in Lower School, Crystal and Haley played together at recess until one day in fifth grade Crystal watched Haley lift up her shirt to Tommy under the new play center, showing off her young breasts. His eyes nearly popped out of his head before he ran off to tell his friends. Haley called Crystal over. "Tommy liked my boobs. Wanna see? They're Bs. Almost C." Haley lifted her shirt. Crystal stared in amazement. "Show me yours."

Crystal's face flushed red.

"C'mon Crystal. We're best friends."

Crystal lowered her head and slowly lifted her shirt. "I don't have any." She pushed her shirt down.

"That's OK. Yours will grow. Tommy wants me to kiss him after school." She scooted closer to Crystal. "You think I'm ready?" Haley puckered and pushed her lips against Crystal's. The two had been practicing kissing for months, always leaving Crystal breathless. Haley claimed she'd heard older boys make fun of girls who were bad kissers, and she didn't want that happening to her.

"You're a great kisser," said Crystal.

"Thanks! Wish me luck." Since Haley had left Crystal under the play center, she had pursued and caught whichever boy she wanted.

Then came Dylan.

Haley has been voted the most beautiful, best dressed, most popular, and most photogenic for the past three years. She makes good grades, and teachers like her. Her two best days of the year are when the Superlative Page winners are announced and when the yearbook appears in May, containing a two-page spread of Haley photos posing beautifully for each "most" and "best" award. She does not play sports, nor is she the top student. She is simply beautiful, perfectly made-up, perfectly proportioned in her leggings with sweeping hole patterns, very nice, and owned by the biggest blowhard, and possibly the crudest guy in school.

Her mother, Maya, was gorgeous too. Her photos are all over the house. None include Eugene. But one day years ago, Crystal found a man's picture hidden in one of her mother's frames. Shirtless, hairy, bearded, proud of his beer gut, sitting on a horse, holding up two fingers like a fake gang sign. She'd always wondered why her mother found him attractive—if that was her father in the photo.

Why would two beautiful girls stay with guys like Eugene and Dylan? Crystal had been told her father lured her mom with drugs. Maybe Dylan does the same.

After handing his last paper to Haley, McHenry strides to the front of the room. "Yesterday we discussed how to write a persuasive essay. Here is your topic: Should changes be made to the high school schedule to foster increased learning, better attendance, and more participation in school activities? You can consider reducing or increasing the number of school days per week, start and finish times, length of class periods, and anything else to make your case, just so the number of instructional hours per week doesn't change. This is due by the start of class tomorrow. Whatever you don't finish in class today, you have to do for homework. Any questions?"

Hands shoot up. Someone shouts, "Would this class count as an instructional hour even if we don't learn anything?"

Another asks, "Who besides you is going to read these opinions and ignore them?"

Giggles and comments flutter around the room. McHenry tries to speak above the din, reminding them that this is a major assignment, and grade checks for cross-country and wrestling are due next Wednesday.

"I really don't want to do this," says Haley as she flips up her computer lid.

Crystal flips up her lid just as McHenry approaches. "I sent you the audio file, Crystal."

"Thank you. I see it." She feels uncomfortable because Haley is listening. She'll know about Crystal's accommodations. In most classes, Crystal sits in the front on the end so any discussions with teachers are relatively private. Most students pay no attention to her and have no idea she doesn't write essays or take the same tests or complete the same assignments.

McHenry sits on the windowsill near her. "You want to try to actually write a paragraph or two? I'd be happy to help you."

A surge of heat pushes through Crystal's skin as she impales him with her large brown eyes. "We both know what's in my IEP."

"Yes, but I thought you might want to try . . ."

"Breaking the law? Don't think so."

He tightens his lips, gives a slight nod, and walks back to his desk where he supposedly monitors student computers from his screen.

"Wow," says Haley. "What's that about?"

Crystal swallows. "I'm SPED, so most of my assignments are different than yours."

"How?"

"Well, for instance, I don't actually write this essay. I can make a film, real or animated. I can make a comic book. Or add narration to a series of photos or images."

"Really? Why?"

"Because I have trouble reading, which is why my instructions are in this audio file. And I can't write for shit."

Haley smiles.

"But I can draw. I'm great with contour lines."

"What are those?"

Crystal pulls her sketchbook from her pack and flips to her *Crystal with the rose* signature then unrolls her self-portrait. "This is me, if you can't tell."

"That's amazing, Crystal." She turns toward Crystal, holding the sketch next to her face. "This is a perfect match, and I love your signature. Can I see?" She holds her hand out for the sketchbook.

"Sure." She watches Haley's face as she flips through the pages. Her mask doesn't hide Haley's expressions. Crystal can almost read her thoughts through the changes in her amazing green eyes. She'd love to draw those eyes. Or anything Haley.

"You're like a genius with that pen."

"Thanks." Crystal always receives compliments for her drawings. But this one feels better than most. She hesitates before asking then takes a deep breath. "Can I draw your face?"

"When?"

"Right now." Crystal finds a blank page and her thin marker pen, turns sideways in her desk, and props her pad on her knees.

Haley blushes. "What do you want me to do?"

Crystal glances toward McHenry, who's talking with a student. "Take off your mask and tilt your face toward me."

"OK." She removes the mask and fluffs her hair. "Should I touch up anything?"

"No, you're perfect as is."

Crystal can now focus on Haley's face without having to turn away or pretend she's not looking. The line flows on the paper, forming the shape of her head, then locks of hair on the right side of her face, her chin, plump lips, and nose, the hair below her chin and the left side of her face, ending with her left eye. Crystal picks up her pen and smiles at the drawing then at Haley. "That's pretty damn good, if I say so myself."

"Let me see."

Crystal carefully removes the paper and hands it to Haley.

"Oh, my god!"

Heads turn. Even McHenry looks up.

Haley quickly replaces her mask then gawks at the image until she scrunches her forehead. "Is that one line?"

"Yes." She scans the room then secretly shows Haley her phone. "Let me take a picture." Haley holds up the paper and faces Crystal while she shoots. "OK. That's yours if you want it."

Haley's eyes bulge then she reaches out her hand to grab Crystal's fingers. "Thank you. I really mean it. Like the best gift ever. You make me look so pretty."

"I just draw what I see." Crystal sees the shine in her eyes as she hands Haley a rubber band. "Roll it up so it doesn't get damaged."

Haley does.

Crystal realizes she hasn't felt this good for ages. She's happy. Warm and fuzzy happy.

"Ladies," says McHenry. "Please get to work."

Haley puts the drawing in her pack. She whispers, "Now I *really* don't want to write this thing." She places her fingers on her keyboard, looks at the instructions, then types a few words.

Crystal can't stop looking at her. She watches her hands and listens to her decorated nails click on the keys. Haley flicks strands of hair back then Crystal notices all the curves in her ear punctuated by three silver hoops.

Haley smiles as she stares at her screen. "You're staring at me, Crystal. Are you drawing another picture of me?"

"No, I'm trying to figure out why someone as amazing as you hangs with Dylan." Haley stops typing and closes her hands. "He pinned you to your locker, pushed his hand down your pants and up to your boobs, then stuck his tongue down your throat. In front of anybody who wanted to see."

"That's one way to look at it."

"There's another way?"

She faces Crystal. "He thinks I'm so desirable he can't keep his hands off me."

"Or he doesn't care about your feelings because you're just an object that makes him look powerful."

She arches an eyebrow. "You wouldn't want someone who thinks you're hot and wants to touch you all day?"

"Maybe, but touching is supposed to be mutual. I've never seen you take the same interest in him as he does you. Not in public, anyway."

"Interesting observation, Crystal. And it's very true." She types.

"Do you even like him?"

Haley stabs the delete key several times. "I try not to ask myself that."

An ache grabs Crystal's throat as she realizes the depth of Haley's sadness. "Why don't you leave him?"

"And then what? Who would want to be with me? He scares everybody, including me."

"Take a break from guys for a while."

She turns to Crystal with raised eyebrows. "What, and try girls? I have truly considered it, but please keep that to yourself."

"Why? Because that would be more embarrassing than what he does to you every day?" Crystal reaches over and hooks her pinkie with Haley who lowers both hands to her lap. "How about being with a friend?"

Haley rubs and squeezes Crystal's hand. Crystal feels the muscles in Haley's leg tense as her hand is pushed harder against her leggings. "And do what? All there is to do in this town is party and have sex." She releases Crystal's hand and flicks more hair behind her ear.

Crystal still touches Haley's leg then slowly pulls it away, trying to hang on to its warmth.

Haley clears her throat. "What do you do every night, Crystal? What wild, exciting things occupy your nights? Maybe I should hang with you later."

Crystal's scalp tingles. "I'd like that."

Their eyes lock again. "And do what?" asks Haley.

"I could make more drawings of you. Different poses. Even teach you how."

Haley sucks in her lips.

Crystal smiles. "Maybe you can show me how to do my eyes like yours."

"You like them?" Haley bats her lashes.

"Love them."

Haley reaches over and touches Crystal's eyebrow. "Do you ever use makeup?"

"No." Her heart skips.

"Do you have any?"

"Just ChapStick."

Her eyes grin. "Well, I can fix that. You'd be gorgeous with some makeup." She stares. "I mean you're pretty without it but . . . I could make your eyes pop."

"Cool."

Crystal realizes that one good thing about wearing masks in class is they hide lips moving. Before today, she never had to worry about getting caught talking with another student because she had no one to talk to. As soft as they are speaking, no one would know they aren't working. Most students have their ear buds in anyway.

Haley whispers, "Do you have any weed or beer?"

Crystal's feels dizzy. "Is that what Dylan gives you?"

She blows out a breath. "Pretty much all I want."

Her breath catches. "Could you deal with him without it?"

"Never tried. Or going home every night. Can't imagine being in my house sober for more than ten minutes with the lunatics." She lifts her eyes to the ceiling and hugs her shoulders.

"Mac has some beer and whiskey. I'm sure JD has some weed. Enough to take care of your needs."

Haley sighs. "All of them?"

"I don't know what they are. But I think we can both use a friend."

Haley glances around the room. "You have a boyfriend?"

"Kato and I are friends."

"But you've never . . ."

Crystal hesitates. "Once."

Haley crosses her legs. "Doesn't sound like it sent you to the moon and back."

"Not even off the ground." Crystal leans toward Haley. "Has Dylan done that for you?"

"Has any boy?" She files her nails. "As long as they get their rocks off. That's all that matters."

"To them. What matters to us?"

Haley flicks her hair back. "Getting wasted and forgetting. How about you?"

"Something different. I just don't know what it is yet."

"Let me know when you find it." She faces her computer screen and types.

Crystal tries to sense Haley's feelings, to see inside her. She believes she can do this with animals, but she thinks she has more trouble understanding people. Of course, that could be because she's normally by herself. JD, on the other hand, knows exactly what is going on inside anyone. He can enter a room and immediately feel tension or happiness or anger in others. It's almost freaky.

She knows she can connect sometimes, like this morning. She remembers her moose video and decides to upload it to her Instagram account. She pulls out her phone and starts the process.

"Crystal," says McHenry, pointing to her phone, which according to school policy is not supposed to be used in class. But Crystal's IEP makes an exception.

"For my project." He nods and looks back to his computer. "Haley, check out @crystalmrosealaska on Instagram."

"I never knew you had a middle name. What is it?" Haley types in the URL.

Crystal clears her throat. "It's just an initial." Her stomach drops. She's never told this story to anyone.

Haley's eyes sparkle. "But what name does it stand for?"

Crystal sighs. Her ears feel impossibly hot. "According to Mac, my parents used a lot of meth. He cooked it and sold it. I was born premature, very small, screaming for meth." She swallows a few times. "My father wanted to name me Crystal Meth Rock, but Mom talked him into using just the initial, so that's on my birth certificate. After Mom abandoned JD and me, Mac and Summer adopted us and changed our last name to Rose."

Haley's eyes widen above her mask. "Wow. I'm so sorry."

"I had to use the 'm' because someone else had already taken @crystalrosealaska. Otherwise, I never mention it. So now you know the big secret, check out the video I shot this morning."

Crystal watches as Haley opens her account, plugs a bud into her ear, and clicks on her latest post. Her stomach flutters as she watches Haley's reactions while she replays the video three times then clicks on other posts. She seems mesmerized. Crystal wishes she could see Haley's lips. Is she smiling?

After several minutes, Haley turns to Crystal. "Girl, you are amazing."

Crystal's blood rushes to her face, and her legs tingle.

"You are so talented. 'Girls' bodies are not responsible for boys' thoughts.' I love that. Who knew you're such a feminist?"

"Not very many. I have, like, twenty followers. I find sayings and things from other sites and change them a little. But all the drawings and photos and videos are mine."

"Can't believe you posted these nude drawings." She points to a post on her computer. *Each of these girls is equally beautiful.* I love it. Which one is you?"

"All of them. Spring. Summer. Now."

Breast size does not equal happiness or beauty. Each of these girls is equally beautiful.

"You look so poised and graceful. You know, the face looks a little like me, don't you think?"

Crystal's breath catches in her chest. She was worried Haley would notice, but hoping she might. "I altered my face a little so people wouldn't think I was flashing everyone."

Haley raises her brows. "The body does too."

"Which one?" Crystal bites her lip.

Haley blushes. "The fourth one. With bigger boobs." They laugh. "Do you remember that time under the play center?"

"Sure. That was the last time you kissed me."

Haley covers her face and peaks at Crystal between fingers. "Have you ever told anyone?"

"No. That's just between us."

Haley looks at Crystal's chest. "Well, you've certainly grown since then."

"Finally. I was so embarrassed when you made me lift my shirt."

"Made you? I just asked."

"I would've done anything you asked." Their eyes meet again.

Haley clears her throat. "When can I come over?"

"Are you serious?"

"Yeah."

Crystal's head buzzes. "Lunch? After school? Anytime."

Haley's eyes twitch, and she looks away. "I'm sure Dylan's expecting me to drive home with him for lunch. My phone's been vibrating constantly with messages. All from him, I'm sure."

"Then after school. I can pick you up. I'll threaten to punch his balls again."

"Don't think that will work outside this building. He can be a badass when he wants to be. I'll just have to see how he's reacting to everything. I'm sure Trimble sent him home, so he's going to be a mess."

"We can contact a trooper."

"I don't know. Maybe I'll think of something." She stands and folds her computer. Other students do the same and move toward the exit.

McHenry stands. "Make sure you've completed this by start of class tomorrow." The clock dings. Class is over. McHenry follows a group out his door and strides toward the teacher's lounge.

Crystal stands. Before she can lift her pack, Haley moves closer until their legs touch.

"Thank you for being my friend, Crystal." She stares at Crystal's lips.

Almost shuddering, Crystal leans into her. "I hope we can see each other later." She watches Haley lick her lips.

"I'd like that." Haley lifts her hand to touch Crystal's cheek.

Crystal pants in short breaths as she presses Haley's hand against her face. "I've dreamed about you." Crystal feels wetness dripping between her legs.

Their eyes meet for several seconds.

"Really?" Haley shifts her stance until she straddles Crystal's hip. "What were we doing?"

Her heart racing, Crystal kisses Haley's palm. "More than this."

Haley flashes her eyes and touches Crystal's lips with her fingers. "Did you like it?"

"So much."

Haley moves her hand lower. Just before Haley's fingers reach below her waist, Crystal notices a girl she's never seen before standing in the doorway, looking at them. She can't see the girl's smile, but she knows it's there. Crystal tenses and grabs Haley's hand. "We better go."

Haley flinches, snaps her head around then pulls her hand away from Crystal's. She stares at Crystal wide-eyed, clutches her pack to her chest, and walks away, ducking her head as she passes the girl in the doorway.

The girl stares at Crystal and lifts her hand in a wave. Flustered, trying to remember to breathe, Crystal gathers her things. When she turns to walk out of the room, the girl is gone.

CHAPTER 4

*C*rystal can't decide whether to hurry and catch up with Haley or linger behind and try to calm down before heading to art class. She watches Haley's butt shimmy away quickly as she holds a phone to her ear. Talking to Dylan, no doubt. No point in running after her now.

Crystal stops in the commons area, trying to determine if she has time to duck inside the bathroom. She notices Trimble talking to the girl who spied on her and Haley. *What did she see?* A younger girl stands near, holding some papers. Trimble takes them and then notices Crystal. "Crystal Rose," Trimble calls. "I want you to meet someone."

"Shit," Crystal mumbles. She rats on Dylan molesting Haley, and now this girl rats on Haley molesting . . . was she? Or did Crystal start it by grabbing Haley's hand? Either way, neither of them wanted it to stop. What would have happened if this girl hadn't looked into the room? The thought is both scary and tantalizing.

"This is Payton Reed," says Trimble, "and her sister Sydney."

Payton offers her hand. "Hi, Crystal. Love your name." She's a few inches taller than Crystal with a silvery, sincere voice.

"Thanks." Crystal shakes her hand and wishes she could see the girl's lips. Is she smiling? Does it hide a secret or is it merely friendly?

Payton's hair is a short and shaggy dirty blonde, unevenly cut, hanging in different lengths—streaked with different shades of blue—around and on her chiseled, lean face. Right now, Crystal sees only one large gray eye. Her loose tunic has been painted with various designs and figures and hides what appears to be a thin body. Crystal thinks she has to be super interesting. And if she's the artist who designed her shirt, she is excellent.

Trimble offers both girls a squirt of hand sanitizer. "Shaking hands is an old tradition we need to discard."

Sydney waves her hand. "Hi."

"Hi, Sydney. How old are you?" asks Crystal.

"Twelve. I'm in seventh grade."

"Then you'll have Ms. Perry. She's very nice. She taught my brother." Sydney is all arms and legs and very thin with long hair. Her eyes are hollow, perhaps from lack of food?

"Payton is a senior," says Trimble. "She loves art, so she'll be with you this period and in some afternoon classes. I'm hoping you'll show her around and introduce her to everyone."

"Sure. I'd be happy to."

Trimble places her hand on Sydney's back. "I'll show you where Ms. Perry's room is." They walk toward the middle school wing.

Crystal points down another hallway. "We're going that way."

"Lead on."

A couple of guys glance at Payton's hair and tunic as the girls walk.

"I think you're attracting attention," says Crystal.

"Not trying to. Just being me."

Crystal gives her a skeptical look.

Payton continues, "I wouldn't care if no one looked twice or paid any attention. In fact, that's what I'd prefer."

Just like I'd prefer no one care whether I wear a bra or not, thinks Crystal.

They reach an empty area where Payton stops. "Are you wondering what I saw between you and that other girl?" She unhooks her mask from one ear. "I hate these things."

Crystal sees very full lips, a square chin, and a button nose. She's beautiful. Crystal steadies her voice. "What was there to see? We were just talking." She can hear her heart pound.

Payton grins. "OK. But if one of you was a guy at the back of that empty classroom, who would care? You're worried because you're both girls, which in this little town, I imagine, would cause a scandal. Yes?"

"Maybe."

"But since I'm gay, what I saw is no big deal. Do you like her?"

Crystal tries to swallow while her stomach flips. "I . . . I don't know." She whispers, "You're a lesbian?"

"Very much. Is that cool?"

"Yeah." Crystal's eyes roam her entire face.

Payton's lips stretch into a smile as she gently nods her head.

Crystal glances down the hallway. "Why'd you look in the room anyway?"

"Because Trimble told me you were there, that you are an artist, just like me. I wanted to meet you."

Crystal smiles.

"Hey, no worries. What would've happened if I hadn't stuck my head in?"

"I don't know." She lowers her head. "It's probably better you did."

Payton chuckles. "Maybe not. You'll probably be wondering the rest of the day."

"Longer than that." Crystal looks around, checking if anyone can hear them then whispers, "Do you worry about being . . . gay? Or people knowing?"

"Used to. But trying to pretend I'm straight was worse." Payton leans her face toward Crystal then says quietly, "I got tired of whispering. Don't you ever?"

"What?"

Louder, "Get tired of whispering? Where's the art room?"

"Oh. Over there. We better go."

Payton pulls on her mask, and they walk quickly into the room where four other students sit before easels.

Crystal smiles when she sees Diana, who is fresh out of college and serves as an itinerant art teacher for the district. She's painted her nose, mouth, and chin on her mask using various weighted lines since drawing is the focus of the first quarter. Crystal only sees her twice a week, but she loves these days. When Diana sees both girls, she moves toward them. "Who's this?"

"Payton Reed," says Crystal. "Just enrolled. Sorry we're late, but we were talking to Ms. Trimble."

"No problem," says Diana as she eyes Payton's shirt. "Did you do this?"

"Yes," answers Payton.

"You are very talented. I love your shading and color choices."

"Thanks. I like your mask. Maybe if I add designs to mine, I'd want to wear it."

Diana's eyes shine. "I'll bring you a blank mask next week that you can decorate. I also need to find another easel for you. Would you mind sharing with Crystal today?"

"I'd love to," says Payton.

"Crystal, you know what to do. Welcome, Payton."

Crystal walks toward an empty easel in the back corner of the room. Payton pulls a chair over and sits while Crystal clamps her phone to the top of the drawing pad.

"Are phones allowed in class?" asks Payton.

"No, but we were supposed to take a picture of something to draw for class today. I shot a video this morning of a cow and calf." She starts the clip then worries what Payton will think about her narration. The first sentence about special needs plays, and Crystal reaches to hit the volume button.

Payton stands and stops her hand. "Please. It's beautiful. Let me hear."

Crystal watches Payton's eyes as they move toward the screen, their hands still touching. Just before Crystal says, " . . . whatever danger lurks around the next corner," she pulls her hand away from Payton and hits pause on the video just when the calf's head emerges from the back of its mother.

"That's what I want to draw," says Crystal. "At first I didn't see the calf because I was watching the mother so closely. But right then, the baby stuck its head out."

"You wrote the narration?"

"Didn't write it. Just said it."

"I love it." She turns her head so she's face to face with Crystal. "We all have special needs and special powers, don't you think? Finding out what they are has to be our life's mission."

"Are you SPED?"

"No, and neither are you. What does that even mean? Who else in here could've said those perfect words while looking at fog turn into a moose?"

Crystal's body flushes with pride, something she doesn't feel very often except with Diana. This new girl is passionate and confident. She confessed to being gay without any hesitation or fear, while Crystal worries about her thoughts, wondering why she couldn't feel the same desire that Kato felt for her—the same she felt today for Haley. That was the problem with Kato last weekend. He gasped at seeing her body and touching her breasts, but she felt no fascination touching him. Everything just seemed wrong.

"You're a poet," says Payton.

"No, I'm not. I can't even understand poetry."

Pointing at the phone, "That's spontaneous poetry. The best kind."

"I don't know what that means."

"Let me see you draw the moose."

"OK." Crystal takes her marker and starts on the left of the cow's body, up through the ears, then down the right side which flows into the calf from his chest to his nose and eye, then over his ears to the mane along his back. She then completes the cow's face with a series of loops.

"How'd you do that?" asks Payton. "It's like you're dancing with your marker."

"I just look very closely at the edges and try not to think too much."

"Show me some of your drawings," says Payton.

Crystal removes her sketchbook from her pack and unrolls the self-portrait she made last night.

"That is amazing. Do you know where the watercolor paper is?"

"Sure." Crystal opens a nearby drawer and pulls out several sheets to clip onto the easel.

Crystal steps back while Payton slides between her and the easel. Payton finds Diana and asks her for watercolor paints. After a few minutes, they return with brushes, a small palette, paint tubes and water.

"Oh, Crystal, that cow and calf are beautiful," exclaims Diana. "So effortless. Show me your photo."

Crystal plays her video while Payton mixes colors on her palette. "Oh my goodness, I love your video. Was that this morning?"

"Yes. And here's my self-portrait."

Diana holds the drawing and shakes her head. "You have progressed so quickly." She holds out her fist to bump. "Amazing!"

Crystal blushes with pride and bumps Diana's fist.

"Crystal," says Payton, "can you redraw your portrait on the watercolor paper?"

"Sure." Crystal clips a fresh paper onto the easel and draws, starting her line at the top of her head. After finishing in about fifteen seconds, she turns and sees Payton and Diana looking at each other with wide eyes.

"That was amazingly quick, Crystal," says Diana.

"I've drawn this so many times, it's like automatic."

"I want to show these to the others," says Diana. She moves to the other side of the room.

"Can I paint it?" asks Payton.

"Sure."

Payton quickly adds colors to Crystal's drawing—pink, green, sienna, yellow, red. Some overlap forming texture and depth while others add isolated accents.

Crystal is awe-struck at how her 2D drawing comes alive. Realistic yet abstract. "That is so cool!"

Payton uses the marker to write her signature—a sweeping P and R then low squiggles after each. "Our first collaboration, Crystal. I could never draw, but I could always see. We make a great team."

Crystal knows she's blushing. She shoots a photo of their creation then Payton holds her own phone out for a selfie with the painting in the background. They kneel and put their heads together before Payton pushes the button. Crystal does the same with her phone.

Diana returns with the drawings. "Payton, where did you learn to paint?"

"At Lathrop High School in Fairbanks before the pandemic. Since then, lots of online lessons. Just left town this morning. We stopped at the first school holding in-person classes. My sister, Sydney, needs to be in a classroom."

"Well, I'm happy you found us. Girls, let me take this to show the others. Why don't you do another?" Diana removes the painting and clips it to another easel across the room. "Come here, class. I want to show you something amazing."

Both girls hear sounds of praise. Blaine turns to look at Crystal, claps both hands to her cheeks and widens her eyes. Crystal bows and laughs.

Payton lowers her mask. "Will you make a drawing of me?"
"Sure."

Payton clips another piece of watercolor paper onto the easel.

Crystal studies Payton's face and shakes her head slightly. "You have such a strong shape. You are so very pretty." Payton removes her mask and ruffles her hair, hiding one eye. Crystal begins on the left side, sweeping up the shoulder and neck, then cheek and jaw to the other side, hair, eye, nose, mouth, then more pointy shags of hair, and a finish on the right shoulder.

"You are a genius, Crystal."

Crystal shakes her head. "No, you are the master of color. Please, I want to watch you."

Payton adds more colors to her palette, including several shades of blue and bright yellow. She adds colors quickly—layering, painting outside the lines, highlighting. Payton's character is revealed by the delicacy and boldness of her strokes—unorthodox, a little wild, defiant.

Payton places her arm on Crystal's shoulder, leaning on her gently as they look at the painting.

"Why did you choose blue for your hair?" asks Crystal.

"Because blue is the warmest color." Payton smiles at Crystal like she just told a joke.

"No, it isn't. Warm colors are red and yellow."

"For me, blue is warm—like the sky."

Payton signs, hands off the marker, and Crystal signs. They take pictures.

Crystal opens her photo of Haley with the drawing. "Can you do one more? Of Haley?" She shows Payton then grabs another piece of paper. "It'll take me just a minute to draw."

Payton smiles. "Sure." She watches Crystal complete the drawing. "Haley is a beautiful girl." She attaches the paper to the easel and mixes various shades of red, pink, and purple. "Can you enlarge the photo?"

Crystal expands the picture and holds her phone just above the paper. After a few minutes, Payton adds some final highlights to Haley's hair.

"Unbelievable, Payton," says Crystal. "Haley will love this." She takes a photo.

"Someday someone will pay money for these," says Payton. "They'll want our earliest projects." She takes her palette and brushes to the sink for cleaning.

Crystal puts away the markers and brings the jars of water. "That's hard to believe."

"Believing is easy. The doing is hard. But everything starts with belief. The trick is to fool yourself into optimism. That something better can be down the road."

"How do you do that?"

"Steal a truck and start driving. Or take your grandfather's old motorhome, extort money to get it fixed then start driving."

"Is that what you did?"

"Part of it. My father killed himself three years ago with a drug over-dose. My mother is now with an abusive man. When I turned eighteen, I went to Child Protective Services and signed up to be my sister's foster parent. My mother can't stay away from the guy. She signed papers so I was able to move Sydney and me to a dry cabin while I collect the foster stipend. But mother and her asshole couldn't stop their drama, so we left."

"Where are you living now?"

"In the motorhome. It's pretty small. After school, we'll go to the park."

"Won't you have to pay?"

"I'm thinking no one will check the campgrounds during the pandemic in September. I have a small generator so we don't have to plug in. I'm sure we can find a hidden site where no one will bother us. We'll be gone every morning."

"What about winter?"

She dries and straightens the brushes. "Hopefully, we'll find a place before then. If not here, then somewhere else farther south."

Crystal watches her from the side, daring to think about the possi-bility of talking and painting with Payton every day. But someone like her wouldn't be happy stuck in Clear. Still, she can't shake the idea out of her head. "Maybe you can stay with us. I can talk to Mac and Summer."

Payton turns around, drying her hands. "Your parents?"

"Grandparents. My parents dumped me and JD fourteen years ago then died in a car wreck."

"Sorry."

"I'm sorry about your shit too."

"Thanks. Friends aren't easy to find." The clock dings to end class. "Where do you go next?"

"Read 360."

"Oh." Payton sighs.

"It's a reading program on the computer."

"I know."

"Where do you go?"

"Math. There's no calculus class here, but Trimble said I could sit in on Algebra II and get help when I need it."

Crystal shakes her head in amazement. "Calculus? Isn't that really hard?"

"Yeah. I can use it to figure out the volume inside your moose, but it can't help me draw one. What you do is much harder. You just don't know it yet." She grabs Crystal's hand and pulls her back to the easel where they gather their things.

Diana brings Crystal's painting back to them and notices Payton and Haley's portraits. "Goodness, those are wonderful! You two are quite the pair. Let them dry and come back after school to get them. I'm very glad you're here, Payton. I know Crystal is too."

The girls leave the room, walk down a short hallway, and find Haley standing at her locker. She turns just as Crystal opens her locker and sees Payton. Her eyes nearly pop.

"Haley, this is Payton."

"Hi, Haley." Payton chuckles softly, grabs Crystal's shoulder, and says, "I'll see you later. I need to get something from my truck." She walks away.

Lowering her voice, Crystal says, "Nothing to worry about, Haley. Payton's cool. What about Dylan?"

"They sent him home, but he wants to pick me up for lunch and then he gets to come back to classes."

She grabs Haley's arm. "Come back?"

"His mother is the mayor, and the video didn't show the worst parts. He and his girlfriend were just being affectionate, he says. Besides, his mother thinks Covid is a hoax and masks are ridiculous. So why should her son be in trouble for expressing his first amendment rights?" She rolls her eyes. "Dylan has gotten away with everything his entire life."

"What are you going to do?"

"I don't know. Hide maybe." She closes her locker a little too hard. "Where is Payton from?"

"Fairbanks. Drove down with her sister this morning. She was looking for me in the room because Trimble told her I'm an artist. She is too. I took her to art class."

Haley looks down then into Crystal's eyes. She whispers, "Did she say anything about us?"

Crystal almost says Payton is gay but stops herself. She knows Payton wouldn't care, but would Haley want to know that someone thinks she's gay? Then again, what if Payton says something to Haley? Crystal needs to make sure that doesn't happen. "She won't say anything, Haley. She did ask if I liked you."

Haley pauses then breathes out her words. "What did you say?"

Crystal lied when she told Payton she didn't know. What's the harm in telling Haley the truth? "Yes. And I would love to see you outside of school."

Haley looks around then at Crystal. "I'll try."

Crystal moves a little closer to hide her contact with Haley's hand on the locker. She holds Haley's fingers briefly before pulling her hand away. "Thanks," says Crystal before she hurries down the hall. She needs to ask Payton to pretend she didn't see Haley touching her.

CHAPTER 5

*F*linging open the glass door, Crystal emerges from the school into the parking lot, hitting a wall of sunlight. She removes her mask, shades her eyes, and finds the motorhome on the far side near a line of trees. Just as she starts walking that way, a blue pickup truck with a large slide-in camper starts up right across the street. A man wearing sunglasses and a cap hangs his arm out the window as he drives slowly past the school, looking directly at Crystal even as his truck leaves her behind. Crystal turns around to see if there is something else he might have been looking at.

Nothing. Weird.

Payton jogs over from her motorhome. "Do you know that guy?"

"No."

"He sure seemed interested in you."

"Probably a pervert. I should've flipped him off."

Payton puts her hands on Crystal's shoulders and gazes into her eyes. "Just for looking? He didn't whistle or say anything. Don't you ever look?" She grins.

"Sometimes. But I don't hang out a window and stare." She walks toward the school.

Payton jumps in front of her, walking backwards. "So you cruise around town on your Honda, looking at guys?"

Crystal laughs. "Haven't tried that yet."

Payton stops. "Or maybe girls?"

Crystal barely stops in time before bumping her. They smile, nose to nose. "Did you get what you needed from your motorhome?"

"Yeah. My vape." They walk together.

Sweat moistens Crystal's forehead, and her stomach flips. Her nerves crawl under her skin as she walks back to the entrance.

"How's Haley?" asks Payton.

"Worried about what you saw and thought."

"She doesn't want anyone talking about her touching another girl."

"That's understandable, isn't it?"

"It shouldn't be," says Payton. "Over five percent of the adult population in this country identifies with LGBTQ. That's a lot of people. Girls touching girls shouldn't be treated like alien sightings."

Crystal stops. "If she asks, which I don't think she will, what will you say?"

"I won't say anything."

They walk.

"Is that the first time you've touched a girl?" asks Payton.

"Yes. I mean, no. Haley and I used to practice kissing back in fifth grade. She wanted to be good for the boys."

"And you?"

Crystal aches to talk to someone about her feelings. Can she trust Payton? Will she tell others about being gay? Why should she care? Hiding is causing her heartburn. "I don't know. It was confusing. I liked it but I thought it was wrong too."

"And then today in the classroom. How'd that happen?"

"Haley's boyfriend was molesting her by my locker this morning. I told him to stop. He does it to her all the time, but she won't leave him. We hugged in the bathroom then talked during English. I grabbed her hand when she said she'd considered trying girls because boys are such assholes."

Payton reaches for the door. "Yes, they are." She pulls, but the door is locked. "What the hell?"

"The doors lock automatically except during lunch. Each door has a video camera connected to screens in the main office. The secretary has to let you in." Crystal pushes the entry button, and soon after they hear a click.

The girls enter the building. "Where's the math class?" asks Payton.

"First door to the right."

"Talk to you afterward?"

"Sure." Crystal jogs down the hall and enters the SPED Resource room where Ms. Bryant helps Sydney log on to a computer. If she saw a dinosaur in the room, Crystal wouldn't be more surprised. She stands near the door, hand raised to her chest, feeling her heart pound. Payton, the genius, has a SPED sister.

"Hey." The girl waves.

"Hey, Sydney."

Ms. Bryant asks, "You know each other?"

"I met her an hour ago. Her older sister went to art with me."

"OK, Crystal," says Ms. Bryant. "You know what to do. I'll need to spend time with Sydney today."

Crystal sits, logs on, and remembers Payton's reaction when she said Read 360. Now she understands why Payton seemed sad because her sister needs the same help. How must Payton feel to be going to calculus while her sister is SPED? She replays Payton's comments about special needs and wanting to find an in-person classroom for her sister. At the time, Crystal thought she was angry about the whole idea of SPED, but now she thinks she's angry about her sister's condition.

Years ago, Summer had tried to explain why some kids don't learn as easily as others, that it's not always caused by drinking and drugs. Crystal knows that parents often feel guilty for their kid's condition even when they've done nothing wrong.

Does Payton feel guilty about her sister? Maybe because she couldn't get her away from her Mom's boyfriend earlier?

Did Payton pump Crystal with praise because she honestly believes

Crystal has talent, or because she needs to convince herself that Sydney can rise above her limitations? Or both?

Crystal's brain hurts trying to understand why life can be so unfair. Or why everyone has to feel pain or regret or longing for something else. The only one she knows who seems continually happy is JD. She has trouble watching his limp, but he never complains. He always stands up straight and tall as he hobbles along, like he has no idea what anyone would be looking at. If someone teases him, JD blows it off because that someone must be having a bad day. He can't read well enough to use the Read 360 program, so he often sits in Ms. Bryant's room with the second and third graders. No matter. He helps them or they help him. He's happy either way. He can shoot and hunt better than anyone in town, and that's enough for him.

Crystal asked him once why he's never frustrated about school or his condition. He said everyone's got problems, and his aren't that bad. "Besides," he said, "Gena and me can make each other feel real good." He winked. "You should try it with Kato. He wants to." Then he shuffled out of her room.

A few months later, she did try, and how did that work out?

Now she wonders whether she's gay and desperately wants to find out. But everything is complicated. Haley's worried about her image and scared of her boyfriend. Payton just rolled into town and may leave tomorrow if the school shuts down again.

Crystal starts the program and tries to improve her reading for the next forty minutes. About two minutes before the clock dings, she tells Ms. Bryant she needs to pee and can't wait. Crystal leaves the room and stands near the school entrance, hoping Haley hasn't already left. She thumbs through her phone, looking at her recent photos, then on a whim posts them to her Instagram account— the photo of Haley holding Crystal's drawing, Haley's painting, and the photos of Payton and her in front of the paintings. She smiles, looks up to the trees, and watches a raven land on the highest branch.

Dylan drives his black jeep toward an open slot in the teacher parking area, shooting her the finger through his open window until he disappears behind another car. Shit. Now she's going to have to be in

49

Rathbone's history class with him after lunch. Crystal moves back inside the school to look for Haley.

Payton and Sydney head toward her. "Sydney says she stole all your teacher time."

"That's OK," answers Crystal. "I actually made some progress today."

"What are you doing for lunch?" asks Payton. "You're welcome to join us in our mobile mansion."

Sydney laughs. "It's a dump, Crystal. Don't let her fool you."

"Shhh!" says Payton, nudging her sister.

"Thanks," says Crystal, "but I have to go home and check on my grandfather. He was feeling sick this morning."

"Bad?"

"Not sure. Hey, I posted our photos on my Instagram."

Payton beams. "Really?"

"Yeah. Go to @crystalmrosealaska."

"Hey, Crystal," says JD, holding hands with Gena as they walk toward her. "Kato's mom made doughnuts. Wanna come?" The couple stands next to Payton. "Never seen you before. Are you new?"

Crystal sees Haley waiting by the water fountain behind them and moves toward her as JD and Payton make introductions. Haley clutches her pack to her chest. "Have you decided?" Crystal whispers.

"He's waiting outside."

"I know. He shot me the finger before he parked."

"He's pretty mad at you. I don't think it's a good idea for me to ride home with you. Maybe after school?"

"Sure." Crystal notices JD holding the door open for Gena, Payton, and Sydney as they exit.

Haley moves closer and lowers her head. "Maybe you can bring me back a shot of Mac's whiskey. I think I'm going to need it."

"Are you serious?"

"God, yes. I'll meet you in the bathroom before class. I better go. Wish me luck."

"I wish you didn't have to feel scared." She holds out her fist. "Be safe." Haley bumps then fast walks to the front door. By the time Crystal moves outside, she sees Dylan's car back out and his passenger door fling open. Haley ducks into her seat, and Dylan spins his tires before she closes her door. He roars away down First Street.

"Crystal," says Kato, leaning against the outside wall behind her.

She jerks in surprise. He takes a step toward her—tall, handsome, slender, with long black hair in a ponytail, and a Native Pride cap. "Hey, Kato. What's up?"

"She speaks." Long, deep dimples crease his cheeks. "You know, those are the first words you've spoken to me in days."

Crystal sees JD and Gena sitting on Kato's Honda, waiting for donuts. Payton stands outside her motorhome, eating something, looking her way. "Sorry, Kato. Too many things going through my head right now."

"That's when you used to talk to me the most."

"I know. I'm sorry." She takes two steps toward the parking lot. "Mac was sick this morning, and I need to check on him."

"Before you run off, I have to tell you something." He moves in front, head lowered. "Mom wants to go back to the village. She's been talking about it for days. She doesn't want to miss whaling season."

Crystal tries to swallow but can't. It's one thing to avoid talking to Kato for a while; it's quite another to never see him again. "When?" Her stomach rolls.

"Soon. Her sister is doing a cakewalk to raise money. Her family wants her home." Kato's people live in the same Iñupiat whaling village where Mac and Summer taught before returning to Clear. His family are the only Natives in town.

Kato stares at her like he's expecting her to say something. Pain and confusion brew in his eyes.

"Does JD know?" She knows he wouldn't stay here if Gena moves away.

"He's heard Mom talk, but he thinks she's just kidding. She made the donuts to celebrate, but she never said why. I think she's going to tell us at lunch. You sure you don't want to come?"

A wave of dizziness washes over Crystal. Her brother snuggles with Gena on the Honda, Payton watches her from afar, Haley went back to her shit boyfriend, and Kato—dear Kato who helped her get through many problems in the past—is about to fly away. Everyone could be out of her life any second.

And Mac is sick. She pulls her hair back from her face and stares at the sky.

Kato points his thumb over his shoulder. "Who's that girl?"

"What?"

"That girl by the motorhome who's been staring at you."

"Payton. She enrolled today."

He thumbs his phone and shows her the screen. "I saw your posts. You two seem pretty happy in the photos. Like you've been buddies for years. You just met today?"

"Yeah."

"Really?" He swipes to reveal another photo. "And when'd you get to be friends with Haley, of all people?" His neck tenses. "Anything you want to tell me?"

Crystal wonders why he's angry until it dawns on her that he's jealous of Haley. Or angry she didn't break down about him going to the village.

"And when did you post these nudes?" He holds out his phone to her like he doesn't want the pictures near him.

Her head spins. "Last night . . ."

"Since when are you an exhibitionist? You're posing naked to the entire world." He stuffs his phone into his back pocket.

"I have twenty followers, Kato. And who else besides you is going to know any of the drawings are of me? They're drawings, not photos. Why are you acting like you're my father?"

"Someone needs to. You're out of control, Crystal."

"You're the only one here throwing a tantrum." She pushes past him and stomps to her Honda. As she backs up, Payton opens her door and offers sanctuary. Kato watches, shaking his head in, what . . . disgust?

She revs her engine until her tires spit gravel before they catch, making her escape.

CHAPTER 6

*A*fter several minutes of kicking up dust along the roads and cutting across corners, Crystal turns into her long driveway. Streaks of green, yellow, and orange whip by in her periphery, like all the events of this morning rushing through her mind. Kato had no desire to have her eat at his house. He just wanted an excuse to start a conversation then tear into her. His manhood was offended when she didn't relish his lovemaking skills. He took her rejection of him afterward as a shot at his inadequacy. Now she's posting nudes and drawing her girlfriends. She's out of control? Meaning, she's out of *his* control.

Damn right.

She parks, turns the key, and bolts off the Honda. She needs to calm down before entering the house or else she'll have to explain her anger. Parched, she pulls a water bottle out of her pack and drains most of it. The rest she pours onto her neck before entering the kitchen.

Years ago, Mac and Summer had bought a very small house, but over time he'd added a sunroom, more bedrooms, a screened back porch, and a second floor, which is where her grandparents must be now. The wood creaks above her. Quickly, she finds Mac's whiskey bottle, pours some into her bottle, which then disappears inside her pack. Summer has left two plates of sandwiches and chips on the table. Crystal grabs a half and walks into the living room where the walls are full of Summer's photographs—bears catching fish by a waterfall, polar bears in the ocean, and JD and her exploring the wilderness. She taught Crystal everything she knows about cameras.

Crystal lifts one of her mother's photos from the top of the roll top desk. Maya had been gorgeous. Another photo shows her holding JD and Crystal in the village. They never got around to taking a family photo before Maya left, a regret that has ached in Mac and Summer for years. That was the last time any of them saw her and the last photo they took of her.

Summer lugs a suitcase down the stairs then moves to Crystal's side. "You know, you are looking more and more like her. You've become a beautiful woman just like she was."

Crystal knows the real beauty in the room, however, is Summer. She had been gorgeous in her teens: dark hair, huge brown eyes, high cheeks, and a very full mouth. Over the years, Crystal had seen many men just stare and sigh at her. After a very long winter when the snow refuses to melt even into May, and then the trees green up in a few days, the feeling that everyone experiences when the birds fill the branches and the lupine and bluebells burst out of the ground, that pent up joy is finally expressed by one word—summer. She is aptly named.

Crystal sets the photo back on the desk. "Neither of us could ever be as pretty as you, Summer. But that's Mac's fault."

Summer laughs at the old joke. Crystal always thinks of wind chimes at the sound—soft, light, musical—even through a mask.

"Where's JD?"

"At Kato's with Gena eating donuts. Kato says Lena wants to go back to the village."

Summer winces. "Oh no. Does JD know they're leaving?"

"He will by now."

They both hear a wracking cough. "Get your mask on, Crystal. I'm taking Mac to Fairbanks. He needs to see a doctor." She wheels the suitcase into the kitchen.

Crystal's shoulders tighten and her throat is suddenly dry. "Are you staying the night?" She follows Summer.

"I'm sure they'll check him into the hospital. His fever is high, and he's having trouble breathing." She faces Crystal, her eyes watering. "I think he has Covid. And I'm starting to feel achy myself."

Mac lumbers down the stairs, wheezing. He stops after the last step and tries to catch his breath. As he walks to the kitchen, his hands grab onto anything to keep him from falling.

Crystal's hands shake as she watches her grandfather come toward her with a blank expression, air moving in and out of his mouth as fast as he can manage. She reaches for his arm. "Oh, Mac. C'mon, big guy. You have to hang in there."

The landline phone rings. Mac grabs the handle. "Hello?"

"Let me have the phone, Mac," orders Summer.

Mac's eyes widen in terror. He swings his arm at both of them. Growling, "Go to the screen room." He coughs. "Now!"

Summer and Crystal do not move.

Mac turns away from them. "When hell freezes over! And they're not your kids!" Again, he tries to signal to Summer to take Crystal outside.

Crystal's heart leaps into her neck and flutters.

Mac turns around, lowering his voice but not its intensity. "No, you cannot see our kids! If you come anywhere near them or our house, I will shoot your ass!" Mac slams the handle into the base.

"Was that my father?" asks Crystal.

"He's not your father. Just a sperm donor." Mac collapses into a chair at the table, holds his head, and tries to breathe.

Crystal gasps. "He's alive?"

"Is he coming here?" asks Summer, her neck tense.

"You heard what I told him. He'd better not."

"But he wants to?" asks Summer.

"That's what he said."

"Why do you get to decide?" asks Crystal. "You knew he's alive?"

When Summer puts her hands on Crystal's shoulders, she jerks away. "Crystal, we weren't sure. He called us right after we returned from the village and told us Maya had died in a car wreck. We wanted proof. A police report, something. He never answered our calls. We never heard from Maya after she left the village. We thought maybe he'd killed her. We called the police where they lived last, but they knew nothing of a wreck. We hired a private investigator, but he came up with nothing. If they were alive, they didn't want us to know it."

Every muscle tense, Crystal shouts, "Why did you lie to us?"

Mac slaps the table with both hands. "We were trying to protect you!" He pushes the chair back and stands with a stagger. "You were abandoned by your mother. Eugene told us she died. We didn't know any different. Even if we found her, we couldn't make her come home. We thought it was better for you and JD to believe they had died rather than wonder why your parents never wanted to see you."

Crystal feels a surge of heat rush up her legs. "Mom could still be alive!"

Mac grabs the back of a chair. "Maybe. Who knows? Probably not."

"Why all of a sudden does he want to see us?"

"Now that's the best question you've asked. Why? Because he suddenly feels remorse and wants to be a father? Bullshit! He's always been a lying sonofabitch, Crystal. And a con. You can't trust him."

She feels a pounding in her ears. "If he decides to come here, you can't shoot him."

He looks directly at Crystal with a sneer. "Watch me. I should've done it years ago." He shuffles toward the door. "We need to go, Summer. I feel like crap." He stumbles through the mudroom and hangs on to the porch railing as he walks down the steps toward their truck.

Summer reaches out her arms. "I'm sorry, Crystal."

A cold fury fills her gut. "Do you think maybe it would've been better to tell us the truth than to find out this way?"

"We never thought we'd hear from him."

"My mother, your daughter, could drive up to this house tonight. What would you do? Scream at her? Tell her you'll shoot her if she doesn't leave?"

Tears flood Summer's eyes. "I'd hold her and never let her go. I've hoped . . . dreamed that I'd look out the window one morning, and there she'd . . ." She pushes her fists into her eyes while her body spasms in pain.

Crystal runs to her and holds her. "If she's alive, Eugene would probably know where she is. Right? So maybe we ought to talk to him."

Summer shakes her head. "He's evil, Crystal. You can't trust him. He can never come into this house. He's stolen from us before, not just Maya. Money, credit cards, checks, guns. All for drugs. What kind of man abandons his children and never contacts them?"

"If Mom's alive, then she did the same. What kind of mother won't leave an abusive man and forces her daughters to live on their own?"

"Who are you talking about?"

"A girl I met today. And Haley, who won't leave her asshole boyfriend Dylan? This happens all the time, Summer."

"I don't know what you're talking about, Crystal. I'll call you later. I'm not sure when I'll be back. Should be tomorrow. I've wiped down everything I could. You should leave the windows open as long as you can and please use the sanitizer. I've got to go." She grabs Crystal one more time before leaving the house. Crystal looks through the window as they back up then drive away.

Crystal lifts the phone off its hook. She knows it's too old to save phone numbers. There's no redial button. Just a relic from a past when people valued their privacy. Or didn't want to be found. The man who called this morning had to have been Eugene. Maybe he'd call again, but she'd be at school and couldn't forward anything.

Would she talk to him? What if he drove up right now?

Caution screams in her mind. She remembers all the stories Mac and Summer have fed her. But if they've lied about her parents dying, they could've lied about everything else.

Why would they want to? Why was Eugene always the evil one? What if her mother made all the bad choices?

Parents are reluctant to believe bad things about their kids. If someone accused JD of stealing, Summer would never believe it. And if for some reason he were involved in a robbery, it'd be because someone had forced him to go along, or tricked him. Wouldn't Mac and Summer believe the same about their daughter?

Maybe Maya was the asshole.

If so, she'd be the exception. Crystal knows too many examples of boys and men taking advantage of girls and women. Haley and Dylan, Payton and her mom's boyfriend, Kato's mom—Lena—and countless men who've tricked her into having sex. The only exceptions she knows are JD, who'd never mistreat or abandon Gena, and Kato, at least the version Before Sex. Maybe "BS" always stands for bullshit. Once Crystal grew her boobs, Kato became just another horny boy who couldn't understand why she wasn't eager to spread her legs for him.

Crystal picks up another half sandwich and pushes it to her mouth before stopping. She goes to the counter and squirts gel into her hands before handling the food again. She pulls a few Clorox wipes from the tube and wipes the table, phone, doorknobs, chair—anything she remembers Mac and Summer touching. She can't get sick right now.

She stuffs food into her pack and sees her bottle containing the whiskey. That gets wiped, along with Mac's whiskey bottle. She takes a sip, wrinkles her nose, and swallows the bitter liquid, coughing as it burns her chest on the way down. Not her first drink, but one of a very few.

She thinks of JD—should she call to tell him about Eugene? What would be the point? He's dealing with Gena leaving town right now. No need to add to his burden. It could wait until after school.

How is she going to sit through history with Dylan next to Haley? And Payton will be there too. She takes another sip then bolts out of the house and onto her Honda. Soon she turns onto First Street with the school just down the road.

Crystal shoulders her pack and hustles inside where she sees Payton talking to Trimble through the glass walls of the main office. What's that about?

As Crystal walks past Rathbone's room, she turns her head to see if Haley sits with Dylan in the back corner of the room, their usual hangout. She's there, flashing scared eyes as she notices Crystal pass the doorway, heading for the bathroom around the corner.

Crystal enters, wondering if Haley will follow. They have four minutes before class. The door swings open, Crystal inhales and tenses, then relaxes when she sees Payton enter and remove her mask. Then she smears neon orange lipstick onto her lips.

Crystal smiles into the mirror. "Hey. I love the color."

"Are you surprised?"

Crystal gestures to her painted shirt and blue hair. "Why would I be? In fact, I'm surprised they're only one color."

"That's an idea." She pulls out another tube and adds pink to her bottom lip then puckers. "Who wouldn't find these lips attractive?"

Crystal cracks a smile and faces the mirror. "I can think of a few people."

Payton leans over the sink and plants a kiss on the mirror. "That should start an interesting conversation."

"I saw you talking to Trimble."

"Yeah. Just trying to give her a heads up."

"About what?"

"Dylan."

They lock eyes in the mirror. The door swings open, and Haley starts to enter, sees Payton, and turns to leave.

"Haley," blurts Crystal. "Please."

Payton winks at Crystal then moves through the door. "I'm just leaving."

Haley walks back in and takes a deep breath. "I heard her say, 'Dylan.'"

"She didn't explain."

Haley's eyes move to the lipstick smudge on the mirror. "That girl is odd."

"She's an artist." Trying to change the subject away from Payton, she pulls her bottle out of her pack. "I brought you something."

Haley's eyes widen. "Is it?"

"Yeah." She pulls up the spigot and pushes the bottle into Haley's hands.

She drinks and closes her eyes. "Thank you." After another sip she says, "You posted my picture."

Crystal smiles. "Yes. I love it."

"And more with Payton."

Crystal's stomach drops.

Haley hands back the bottle. "I'm sorry, Crystal. I wasn't thinking. Please don't be mad at me."

"Why would . . ."

Haley plants a quick kiss on her cheek then bolts out of the room.

"What the hell?" It's obvious to her that Haley's jealous of Payton. How crazy is that?

And what is she apologizing for?

CHAPTER 7

*C*rystal zips her pack and walks to Rathbone's classroom, entering just as the clock dings. She catches Haley staring at her from beside a glowering Dylan. Crystal sits in the front row next to Payton.

Rathbone is an institution at the school, a no-nonsense teacher who accepts no off-task behavior in his class. He posts his bachelor's, his master's, and his teaching certificate very prominently behind his desk. He has several times expanded his collapsible pointer and slapped each of these documents when a student challenges his expertise.

His daily assignment is to explain an important current event. Most students spend two minutes before class searching Google News to grab a story. Most are not called to report, but no one can guess who he'll choose.

"Fred," says Rathbone. "Please share your current event with the class."

Fred stands. "Yes, sir. According to various websites, Black Lives Matter is funded by George Soros and is run by Marxist pedophiles . . ."

"Stop right there, Fred. Is your story that these claims are true or that this nonsense is being spread online?"

Fred seems confused. "Well, sure they're true. I've read this information in several places."

"Tell you what. By tomorrow, you need to turn in a report citing specific evidence from reputable sources that your claims are true."

Fred groans.

"Specific evidence, Fred. Not 'he said,' 'she said.' You need to learn the difference between gossip and evidence."

"I have another news story," whined Fred.

"No, I think doing this research would serve you well. By tomorrow at the beginning of class. You may sit."

Fred flops into his seat.

"Crystal. What news event can you share?"

Crystal's mind races. She forgot to look up a story. She could talk about Alaska's first place rank in sexual assault as evidenced by Dylan this morning. She looks at Fred, and an idea hits her.

"To follow up with the need for evidence to back up a claim, my brother and I were told that my parents died in a car wreck about thirteen years ago. However, there was never a report of a wreck or a death certificate. During lunch my father called Mac today, so evidently he's not dead. I'm not sure about my mother. My . . . grandparents said they lied to JD and me to protect us and that my father is an evil man, but I have no evidence of this other than he abandoned my brother and me fourteen years ago and has never tried to see or talk to us until now. Of course, my mother is guilty of the same, but if she died in a wreck, that would be an excuse for her not trying to call or see us."

Crystal bites her lip and hopes the tears welling in her eyes won't drip.

"I'm so sorry, Crystal," says Haley from the back of the room.

Payton grabs Crystal's hand, squeezes, then lets go.

"That's too sad," says Laura.

"This happened today at lunch?" asks Rathbone, gently. Crystal nods. "I'm very sorry. I hope things work out. Thank you for sharing."

Crystal sits.

"Haley, do you have a story to share with us?"

"I have one, Mr. Rathbone," shouts Dylan as he leaps up from his seat.

The ache in Crystal's throat intensifies. She turns her head and sees a terrified Haley staring at her.

"I called on Haley," says Rathbone.

A siren wails in the distance, moving closer.

"We worked on one together. It's about the evils of social media. We just found an important example."

"You need to sit down, Dylan," barks Rathbone.

"No, sir. This is important. All you have to do is check out the Instagram account @crystalmrosealaska to see what I'm talking about."

Crystal tries to stifle a gasp as her muscles tense.

Dylan holds out his phone, showing Crystal's drawings. "She's posted nude drawings of herself with three different breast sizes." A few guys say, "Whoa!" Several students flip up their computer lids. A few pull out their phones. Haley has slumped into her chair, covering her face.

Payton stands. "She's an artist, you dipshit! They're drawings."

"Who are you, freak?"

"The girl who called a trooper twenty minutes ago."

Rathbone slams his whiteboard with his pointer. "Sit down, Dylan! The rest of you, stash those phones or lose them, and close your computers."

Dylan moves to the middle of the room. "She's trying to convince girls that bigger boobs equal happiness. Shame on you!"

Crystal jumps up. "That's the opposite of what I said, you moron!"

Rathbone slams his pointer closed. "Give me your phone, Dylan. Now!"

Dylan smiles maliciously. "You want my phone? Here it is. Come take it." He holds his phone shoulder-high in his left hand and makes a fist with his right hand near his pocket.

The siren stops just outside.

Everyone freezes. Rathbone drops his pointer on his desk and smiles at Dylan. "You know the rules, Dylan. Hand me your phone and you can pick it up from Principal Trimble after school."

"Fat chance, Rathbone. C'mon, Haley. Let's get out of here." He reaches down to grab her arm. Haley looks horrified, not expecting to be included in this scene.

She looks up and pleads quietly. "Dylan, please."

But the caveman will not back down. "Let's go!" he says, grabbing her arm.

Haley jerks it away. "No, Dylan." Her scared eyes find Crystal's, then turn hard. "No, Dylan." She leaves her seat and walks toward Rathbone.

"Really?" An evil smile creases his face as he mocks her: "'Dylan, please.' You'll be saying that a hundred times before tomorrow, bitch."

"Dylan, you will have to say much more than 'please' before you return to my classroom. We need to see Mrs. Trimble." Rathbone walks toward the door. "C'mon, Dylan. Let's go."

"I ain't going anywhere with you, Rathbone." He shoves past the man, almost knocking him down, and starts to open the door just as Trimble on the other side knocks and pulls the door open. Standing with Trimble is Brian, a state trooper, a very large version with a wide-brimmed hat shadowing his eyes.

Trimble folds her hands and steels her voice. "Dylan, you need to—."

"I need to get out of here," Dylan says as he tries to walk past the trooper, who puts his hand on Dylan's chest.

"Son. Hold on."

Dylan glares at the trooper, who glares back, a head taller than him.

From behind this standoff, Rathbone speaks. "Dylan needs to be suspended, Ms. Trimble. He's been disruptive, threatening, and abusive toward Haley and Crystal."

"Officer," says Trimble, "Dylan needs to leave school, and you, young man, need to return after school with your parents." Her voice quavers, even though she's trying so hard to show strength.

"Oh, no! I'm already peeing in my pants."

Trimble's eyes go wide as Dylan laughs.

The trooper takes Dylan's arm and leads him away from the classroom as he talks into his radio.

Dylan shouts, "You will regret this, Haley! You too, Crystal!"

Crystal runs to the doorway, ready to shout something back.

"That's a threat, son," says the trooper. "Perfect evidence for them to get a restraining order. Not your smartest move." They exit the building.

Crystal shakes her head. Maybe Dylan will suffer consequences for once.

Haley bolts out to the hall and heads for the bathroom. Crystal gestures to Rathbone, he nods, and she follows.

As she opens the door, Crystal hears retching sounds. She finds Haley kneeling in front of a toilet, puking.

Crystal pushes the girl's hair behind her head. "I'm here, Haley." She pulls paper from the roll and gently wipes Haley's face.

"It's all my fault," she gasps then lurches again, partially missing the bowl.

Crystal rubs her back and keeps her hair up. "Nothing's your fault. Dylan's an asshole." She wipes Haley's mouth then pulls a small bottle of sanitizer out of her pack.

"I was in his car when I noticed you had posted our picture. I loved it." She holds out her hands while Crystal squirts. "Then I saw the two you made with Payton, and I said, 'Shit' or something stupid. He wanted my phone. I tried to keep it from him, but he twisted my wrist and took it away. He looked through your account and got angrier and angrier. He said you were a pervert, that the only reason you yelled at him this morning was because you were jealous."

Crystal barks a laugh. "Jealous of him? He's a Neanderthal."

"Jealous of me." She fixes her eyes on Crystal. "He said you'd do the same to me if you had the chance."

Crystal can hardly breathe. "I'd never do anything you didn't want me to do."

"I know. He wrote ugly comments on your nude posts."

"I saw his comments during lunch," says Payton, the door swinging shut behind her.

Haley's eyes widen and she tries to push herself up. Crystal lifts one arm while Payton reaches for the other. Haley flinches. "It's OK, Haley," says Payton. "I'm on your side. You were brave as hell in there." Payton offers a gentle smile.

Haley blinks back a tear and flashes a quick smile. "Thanks."

Crystal pulls towels from the dispenser. "I'll clean up."

Payton takes the papers. "Let me. I've had a lot of experience." She runs water on the towels then pulls out more fresh ones before dropping to her knees in the stall.

Haley brings a handful of water from the sink to her mouth. "You called the trooper?"

"Yeah," answers Payton, as she wipes the floor. "I heard him scream at you as you got into his car. Then it looked like he hit you."

"He shoved me against the window."

Crystal wraps her arm around Haley, who leans against her. She won't let anyone hurt her again.

Payton wipes the toilet seat. "About ten minutes later I saw his comments and tried to warn Trimble that Dylan would cause a problem. I called the trooper and told him a girl was being threatened and there was going to be a fight."

"How did you know?" asks Haley.

Payton stands. "Because my mother's boyfriend is a guy like Dylan. I can always tell when Harold's about to explode."

Payton flushes the toilet with her shoe, dumps wads of paper into the trash can, then washes her hands.

"Thank you," says Haley.

"That's OK. I've done that many times for my mom."

"Why does your mom stay with Harold?" asks Haley.

"Because he has a job and an income; she doesn't. He keeps her supplied with booze and then makes her cry because she's a drunk. He likes being in control of people. It makes him feel better about his sorry life. Where's the nearest courthouse?"

"Nenana," says Crystal. "About thirty miles from here. Why?"

"Because you both need to have Dylan served with a restraining order."

"He won't like that," says Haley.

"Tough shit," says Payton. "That way, if he shows up within fifty feet of you, he's in trouble."

"In trouble with who?" asks Haley. "It usually takes an hour for a trooper to respond to a call. You were lucky Brian got out here in twenty minutes."

Payton folds her arms and furrows her brows. "What's the alternative? He keeps harassing you? In person and online? By the way, Crystal, you should delete the post he ruined and turn your account to private. A lot of his dick friends added crap comments."

Crystal pulls out her phone and opens her Instagram account. She changes the settings to private then struggles to read through a few comments before deleting several posts.

Haley brushes her hair. "This is a very small town, Payton. If I start a war with Dylan, I won't be able to go anywhere in Clear or hang with anybody."

"Except me," says Crystal.

"And me," adds Payton. "I have a gun in my motorhome."

Haley pulls hair from her brush. "That's great, but Dylan has twenty guns and lots of friends, including my brothers and parents."

Payton sits on the counter. "Do you have any relatives outside of town or know anyone else you can live with?"

"You can stay with me," says Crystal. "My brother's probably going to be leaving with his girlfriend soon, so that's one empty bedroom. My grandparents will be in Fairbanks for at least one night. I have plenty of room."

Haley squeezes her arm. "Thank you, Crystal. The only reason you're in this mess is because you helped me with Dylan this morning. Why did you do that?"

Crystal's muscles tighten. "Because no one helped my mother. She was beautiful, and Eugene wouldn't leave her alone. He gave her drugs and convinced her she was the most important thing in his life. Until she wasn't. I don't want the same thing to happen to you."

Haley swallows. "Is your mother alive?"

She shakes her head. "I don't know. And I'm not sure if I care."

"I'm so sorry." Haley pushes hair out of Crystal's face before pressing her cheek against it and pulling Crystal's body against hers. Heat surges between them.

Crystal's hands clutch and pull. When her fingers feel the soft skin barely exposed between her pants and cami, she gasps and runs her hand up Haley's back.

There's knocking on the door. "Girls, are you in there?" asks Trimble before she walks into the bathroom.

Crystal snaps her face back and sees Payton move behind Haley, blocking her from Trimble's view, and spreading her arms around both girls.

Payton squeezes the girls. "We're just having a group hug, Ms. Trimble."

Crystal and Haley separate after clutching each other's hands. Payton turns around. "I'll bet we need to return to class, don't we?"

"Yes, please."

"We'll be right out," says Payton as she actually walks the woman toward the door. "Just one more minute, we promise. Thank you, Ms. Trimble."

Crystal watches Payton pull the door closed and face Haley and her as they hold hands.

"I know I'm new here," says Payton, "but I don't want to see either of you hurt or unhappy. I'll do anything I can to help both of you. Haley, you can hide in my motorhome if you want. I'm going to park it in a site by the river out of view. I'll drive you both to Nenana to the court. I'll even drive you to Fairbanks if you want. You two ought to have a chance to be with each other without having to worry about shits like Dylan. He doesn't own you."

"Thank you, Payton," says Haley. "I'm just nervous." She reaches out her hand to Payton who takes it in hers. "You painted Crystal's drawing of me?"

"Yes."

"I love it. Thank you. I'm sorry . . ."

Payton squeezes her hand. "Hey, no worries."

"Why don't you two leave first, so we don't make a grand entrance into Rathbone's room. That will give me time to fix my face a little." She releases both hands and turns to the mirror.

Payton catches Crystal's eye and nods toward the door.

"See you in a bit, Haley," says Crystal just before they exit.

A few steps into the hall, Payton stops. "Why did she throw up?"

"I don't know. Nerves? She's pretty scared of Dylan." She searches Payton's eyes. "I gave her a shot of Mac's whiskey just before class. Maybe she drank more than I thought."

Payton sighs and shakes her head. "Don't give her any more whiskey, Crystal. Please." She walks ahead.

Why does Payton seem angry?

CHAPTER 8

*H*aley enters Rathbone's classroom and walks quickly back to her seat by the window. A pain fills Crystal's chest as she realizes why Haley never looked her way. In his post on her three nudes photo, Dylan wrote, *The ONLY reason u draw ur tits is to show Haley. Then you draw her picture once you got me suspended. Dyke!*

Haley's afraid of being called a lesbian.

What about Crystal? How many students in Rathbone's room think she's gay? Does she care? What if Haley will only be with her in bathrooms or away from school? Would that matter to her? Before today she was basically alone and invisible, afraid people would see only her flaws. She rejected herself before others could.

But now things are different. She has special powers. She's not stupid. Not abandoned. Not a twig.

For the first time in her life she feels desire, an aching need, a constant thrill at the possibility of loving and being loved.

Crystal turns her head and finds Haley looking at her before she jerks her head toward the window.

She realizes she feels sorry for Haley. Before this morning she was the superlative queen with her own two pages in the yearbook. Yes, that came with a cost, the biggest being Dylan. Still, everyone liked her, thought she was the most beautiful. She actually enjoyed making guys' eyes bulge.

Then Crystal had to throw a fit in the hallway, and now her world is destroyed.

But it was really never happy. Haley never felt love, never returned his attention. She hides her misery with beer and weed. Pretends she enjoys sex. Doesn't want to be at home or with Dylan.

Has anyone besides herself held Haley so tight with so much desire? Has Haley's heart ever beaten as fiercely as it did when she hugged Crystal?

She needs to ask Haley. When? In the bathroom?

As the class exits, Payton moves her mouth close to Crystal's ear. "Do you want to see my mansion?"

Crystal laughs. "Said the spider to the fly. Sydney says it's a dump."

"Is there some law against a mansion being a dump?"

"You need your vape again?"

"Maybe. Don't you have any bad habits?"

"Not yet, but the day is young." Crystal sees Lena down the hall, removing her cleaning cart from a closet. No matter how rocky Crystal's relationship with Kato is now, his mother has always been nice to her. "Hey, save me a seat. I need to talk to someone."

"Sure."

Crystal turns away, calls to Lena, and waves. They hurry toward each other.

Lena crushes her with a hug. "Crystal, I've been worried about you."

"Why?" Lena always smells like cigarettes, wine, and cheap perfume.

"All that crap Dylan's writing on Facebook. Such shit," says Lena. She spends most of her time scrolling through her phone, checking on local conversations, as well as all the drama from the villages where she has hundreds of relatives. Lena wears hoop earrings and keeps her eyes heavily lined; her long black hair is kinked and shiny, hanging down to her waist.

Crystal notices a new tattoo on her right arm and hand—a Native design of dots and lines. "I don't do Facebook," says Crystal. "He's blaming me for getting suspended?"

"Yeah. And other things." She pulls a baggie from her jacket. "I brought you a donut. It's fresh."

Crystal has always loved her donuts. "Kato told me you baked today."

"Why didn't you come?"

"I had to check on Mac. Summer took him to Fairbanks because he's sick."

"Oh, I'm so sorry. All that and this Dylan stuff." She strokes Crystal's hair. "Maybe it's too much for you."

"And you're moving back to the village." Crystal hopes Lena says this isn't true.

Suddenly Lena smiles. "My sister sent me some beluga! I never had it for how many years. Not since the village. They caught five in the lagoon this weekend. And one of the crews already caught a bowhead. I can't wait to get back. *Arigaa!*"

Crystal feels an ache in her throat. "When are you going back?"

"Two days."

"That soon? And Gena's going?"

"Yes and JD."

Crystal feels dizzy. "How can he? Didn't he just find out?"

"I told him for sure today, but he knew it would happen. Just not the day. Gena bought his plane ticket."

Probably using the dividend she gets every six months from her Native corporation, thinks Crystal.

Crystal wrings her hands. "But he hasn't said anything to Mac or Summer. Or to me."

"He's been nervous, Crystal. They want to get married. He didn't want Mac and Summer to scold him. He hates disappointing them."

Crystal's stomach clenches. "But they're so young."

"Seventeen is not so young. Besides, I think she might be pregnant." She flashes her eyes and smiles.

The clock dings. Now she's late.

Crystal's breathing stops. She tightens her eyes. "When did Kato know you were leaving?"

"For weeks. He hoped you might want to go with him, but now he says you two are fighting, so I guess not?"

Which is why he increased his efforts to have sex with me. "Kato's my friend, Lena. But that's as far as it goes." She sees the disappointment on Lena's face. "I'm late for class." She runs down the hall toward her science class.

Fortunately, Ms. Deena is with another student across the room and doesn't notice Crystal's entrance. Payton waves her over.

"What are we doing?" asks Crystal.

"A quick experiment then we'll watch a video. You're supposed to have notes from yesterday."

Crystal opens her computer and finds yesterday's results—observations about rocks subjected to freeze and thaw and weights of chalk, pumice, limestone, and granite prior to soaking in water all night.

"Can you do this, Payton? My mind is a mess right now."

"Sure." While Payton removes rocks from tubes for weighing, she asks, "What's going on?"

"Not much. My brother has probably gotten his girlfriend pregnant, and they're moving to a village in two days where they'll be married. And the reason I had to practically force Kato to wear a condom last Saturday was because he was hoping I'd get pregnant."

Payton blots water from a piece of chalk. "You had sex with Kato?"

"Yeah. A total snore."

"First time?"

Crystal nods.

"Regrets?"

"Too many to count."

She drops the chalk on the digital scale. "You know one of the best things about having sex with girls is no one gets pregnant." She glances at Crystal. "Just saying."

"*One* of the best? What are others?"

Payton blots the pumice and whispers, "You actually get to have orgasms. I'm assuming you didn't."

"Not even close."

Payton records the weight. "Amazing," she smirks. "Water makes rocks heavier." She rolls her eyes. "Who would've guessed?"

"You already know everything, Payton. Why are you in school?"

"I'll ask you a better question. Why are you pining over Haley when she'll be back with Dylan within a week? If not sooner."

"How do you know?"

"Because I've seen it before. Many, many times."

Crystal turns her head, looking for Haley. She finds her laughing with Laura, but after a few seconds, Haley steals a glance at Crystal and raises one brow. Crystal smiles, and Haley looks away.

Payton weighs the granite. "I'm sure she's aching to kiss you as much as you want her, but she will leave you for Dylan."

"Because of your mom?"

"And your mom. And over half the women in Alaska who put up with crap because they fear the unknown."

"And what's that?"

Payton moves her lips to Crystal's ear. "The feel of a woman's lips between their legs."

Crystal closes her eyes and tries to steady her breathing. All she can see in her mind are lips—pressing together, opening, and squeezing tongues.

"Do you ladies have your data?" asks Ms. Deena.

Crystal nearly jumps out of her skin.

"Were you asleep, Crystal?"

"No, ma'am." Crystal sits up in her chair.

Payton hands Deena her data chart. "I'd just described my favorite dessert to her, and she was eating it in her mind."

Crystal stifles a shriek then coughs.

"It must've been delicious," says Deena. "You'll have to describe it to me sometime." She walks away.

Crystal claps her hand over her mouth, a hot blush flooding her face. Payton grins while Deena describes the video on rock weathering they are about to take notes on.

Crystal pulls a marker and her sketchpad out of her pack. She looks at Payton. "Write for both of us? I have something to draw."

Deena drops the lights and starts the film. Crystal props her feet on another stool and angles her pad to catch the light from the window behind her. She sees large, sensuous, puffy lips in her mind. And tongues. She glances at Payton's mouth, now half open. Quietly, she says, "Can you pucker just a little?"

Payton gives her a side-glance and puckers. Then licks her lips.

After a few minutes and a couple of discarded pages, Crystal looks at her picture and

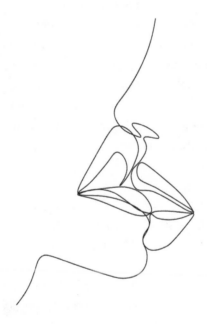

thinks—could she please be on either side of that action? Or both? She is always amazed at how a single, plain line can turn into anything. With just a slight bend or tiny loop or sweeping curve, she can create a personality, a desire, or the special needs of two people, who, though unaware of such a truth, are connected as one.

She nudges Payton. "Would you like to paint this?"

Payton looks at the paper then smiles at Crystal. "Dylan was right. You are a pervert. But in a good way."

"You like?"

"Almost as good as the real thing. I'll paint it."

"Cool." Crystal closes her pad and watches the last thirty seconds of the video.

After a few minutes, Payton and Crystal lean against a wall in the commons area when Haley approaches Crystal's left side. "I saw you drawing in class. Can I see?"

"Sure," says Crystal, glancing quickly at Payton. She opens her pad, holding the cover up to block any view from the front.

Haley gasps as her eyes stay fixed on the image. "Whose lips?"

"Whose do you want them to be?" asks Crystal.

"You're the artist." She touches the paper and traces the line with her fingertip. "That's one line, isn't it?"

"Yes. One line with a few kinks and curves that made you gasp."

Haley looks at Crystal. "Tell me."

"The lips on the left are yours. The ones on the right aren't Dylan's."

Haley gazes at Crystal's lips. "Can I take a picture?" She pulls her phone from her leggings. "Maybe if I look long enough, I'll figure it out."

"Sure."

Haley's phone clicks. "Thanks." Crystal watches her walk to her locker, hypnotized. Haley shakes her hair.

Payton drapes her arm over Crystal's shoulders. "You are gawking, Crystal. And she knows it."

Crystal gasps and turns her face toward a smiling Payton.

"And you know those lips are mine." Payton points to the drawing. "They posed for you."

"I know. You both have amazing lips."

Payton touches the mouth on the right side of the drawing. "These lips are luscious. Just starting to open, like it's her first time."

Crystal flips the cover and swallows then finds Payton's eyes. "It would be. Well, since fifth grade." Crystal clutches her pad and walks away.

For the next hour, Ms. Bryant helps Crystal and other SPED students with math, her weakest subject. When the clock dings, she feels a rush of relief, but as soon as she enters the hall, she feels the weight of so many issues—Haley/Dylan, JD leaving (did he even return to school after lunch?), Payton, her father, and Mac/Summer. And her mother?

Her phone dings and she sees a text from Summer. *Hospital is admitting Mac. We were both tested for Covid but no results until two days or longer, but they believe he's positive. I'll call you later when I have a few minutes. I spoke to Ms. Trimble and told her you and JD have likely been exposed, so don't expect school to be open tomorrow.*

Shit! Crystal's first thought is the possibility that both her grandparents could die. But Mac wasn't sick yesterday. How could it get this serious so quickly?

Her second is Payton driving south to find another school.

"Hey," says Sydney as she grabs Crystal's hand. "What's your name again?"

"Crystal." She looks at a longhaired version of Payton with the same gray eyes.

"Oh yeah."

"How was your day?"

"Great. I love it here. Where's my sister?"

"Let's go find her."

JD used to have trouble remembering names, but he learned to repeat a new name in his head twenty times. He still forgets sometimes, but he doesn't meet new people very often.

Except now he'll meet an entire village. Crystal wonders if anyone there will remember JD as a three-year-old. She and her brother arrived in the village in September, seeing whales butchered on the beach and shared in whaling captain's homes open to the entire community. She remembers kissing her mother good-bye before Mac took her to the runway where she boarded a plane for Fairbanks. There she was supposed to meet a woman from the rehab center, but her mother boarded another plane for Seattle instead. And then another and another to Mississippi where she disappeared. JD would now return during the same whaling season, probably eliminating any chance of seeing his parents. Would he care? Should she even tell him about Eugene's call?

"I was looking for you, Sis," says Payton, kneeling before her sister. "You were supposed to meet me in your classroom."

"I saw . . . um . . . Crystal, so I went with her."

"OK, let's find our campsite." She holds Sydney's other hand as the three make their way out of the building. "I got our paintings from Diana."

"Good. You can hang onto them."

They scan the parking lot. No Dylan, no Kato, no JD or Gena. Crystal wonders if she'll see her brother again. Surely he'll come back to the house for his things. Unless he already did. He wouldn't leave without seeing her. He wouldn't.

The school bus pulls away from the front entrance and heads to First Street. Crystal watches as the last remaining students leave in their trucks or walk away down the road.

"Are you looking for Dylan?" asks Haley as she stands next to Crystal.

"And my brother, but they're not here. How are you getting home? I can give you a ride."

Haley shades her eyes. "I thought about that, but Dylan would push us into a ditch. I called my brothers to take me home."

Crystal wrinkles her brow. "Will you stay there tonight?"

"I don't want to." She hesitates. "Does your offer still stand?"

"Sure." Crystal's limbs tingle. "Give me your number, and I'll pick you up."

Payton pulls out her phone. "Give me both numbers. I can pick her up and take her to your place. Don't think Dylan can push me into a ditch."

"Thanks, Payton," says Haley.

After the girls exchange numbers, Payton walks her sister to their motorhome.

"We may not have school tomorrow," says Crystal.

"Why?" asks Haley.

"Because Mac is in the hospital. He probably has Covid and Summer told Trimble."

"Great. At least school lets me escape my house and Dylan for a few hours. He's suspended for three days. Where's JD? Don't you always drive him home?"

"He went to Gena's for lunch and didn't come back. Lena's moving back to her village, and JD's going with his girlfriend."

Haley twists a lock of hair around her finger. "You're going home to an empty house?"

"Looks like it."

Haley smiles and touches her top lip with her tongue. "I know who the other lips belong to. What made you think of drawing that picture?"

Flutters tickle her stomach. "It was either do that or watch a video about rock weathering."

Haley tilts her head. "That's the only reason?"

"Actually, that's all I've been able to think about since this morning."

"Really? Drawing it . . ." She flashes her eyes then whispers, "Or doing it?"

Payton waves at both girls as she exits the parking lot. They wave back.

Crystal welcomes the interruption. She can't tell whether Hayley is enjoying her embarrassment or signaling the same desire Crystal can't get out of her head.

"When will you tell me about the dream I was in?" asks Haley.

"Whenever you want."

A loud, vintage Mustang with painted flames on the hood and sides rumbles toward the parking lot.

Right afterwards, the blue camper truck drives past the school with the same man looking out the window at Crystal. *What the hell?*

Haley rolls her eyes. "My favorite brothers. Jesus, I hate that car."

Danny's arm hangs out the window when the car stops. "Your chariot arrives. Jump in." He opens the door and leans the seat forward.

Nick exits the driver side. "Hey, Crystal. I've heard a lot about you today."

"If it came from Dylan," snaps Haley, "it's bullshit."

Both brothers, identical twins, have spiked hair and their racecar numbers tattooed on their arms. They obviously think they're hot commodities, smiling and posing for imaginary cameras.

"Are you calling your boyfriend bullshit?" asks Danny.

"He's not my boyfriend."

"Is *she* your girlfriend now?" taunts Nick.

"Fuck you, Nick." She glances at Crystal. "I'll call you later."

Crystal tenses as she hears warnings in her mind. "You sure you want to go with them?"

Haley laughs. "They're harmless. All bark and no bite." She pushes the seat hard onto Danny then plops in the back.

Nick spits into the gravel. "See you around, Crystal. I enjoyed looking at your boobs, the bigger ones, that is." He laughs, sits inside, and slams the door.

Crystal shoots them the finger as Nick does a perfect bootleg turn before rumbling out onto the road.

Crystal stands in the parking lot feeling lonely. She knows her house will be empty. How will she stand being alone all night? If Haley can't get away, which seems unlikely after seeing her brothers, maybe she'll drive to the park and visit Payton.

She jumps on her Honda, turns the key, and hits the starter button. Nothing. She tries again. No sound, no clicking. She gets off and looks at—what? She knows nothing about mechanics. She considers trying to get help from a teacher, but the school is locked, and no one will be in the office to let her through the video surveillance system. The staff always meets after school. Two days ago she forgot her pack in the office. It took her twenty minutes to find someone to let her in, and he was pissed. She could call Kato but doesn't want to deal with his questions. Payton would come if she called, but then there'd be no reason for her to go back to the campground. She'd park in Crystal's driveway and visit her house.

Then how could she ever be alone with Haley?

She'll have to walk home.

CHAPTER 9

*C*rystal shoulders her pack and walks away from the school as yellow and red leaves dance across the road, pushed by a cool breeze. The feathery foxtails along the shoulder glisten iridescent pink. The sky peeking through the clouds is a deep powder blue, and the tops of mountains in the distance are dusted with snow. Normally, Crystal would enjoy this walk, stopping frequently to take pictures, but her heart is heavy and her brain is swirling.

As she passes the city building, she sees the blue camper truck backed in at the side near the access ramp. Now she notices that it's a rental RV from Northern Skies in Fairbanks. The man sits behind the wheel, holding up a map in front of his face. She wants to say, "Hey, douchebag, the park is down the road. Just follow the signs," but she doesn't and keeps walking. After another ten seconds, she thinks she hears a baby crying. She stops. Houses face her on either side of the street with windows open. She turns around and sees the man still sitting behind a map.

After another minute, she takes a right on D Street while replaying the scenes with Haley, wondering if she could've been toying with Crystal, flirting to evoke a response. In years past, she'd seen Haley flash her smile or expose some skin in front of guys just for the pleasure of their reactions. She seemed to enjoy controlling them, but now Dylan controls her. Haley would not flirt with guys now. But maybe she would flirt with Crystal, out of sight, to get that same rush of excitement.

Maybe she's playing Crystal for a fool.

As she steps onto Second Street, she hears shouting in the direction of an abandoned house with a faded "For Sale By Owner" sign in the overgrown yard full of dead cars and trucks. JD has told her some kids use it as a party house.

Something bangs then a voice shouting, "Dylan. Stop!"

Crystal grips her straps and starts walking hard toward the house. That sounded like Haley.

"I don't want to!"

She sprints across the road, her heart pounding. What is he doing to her?

As she enters the yard, she hears guys laughing. She drops her pack and she notices the Mustang nearby.

The front door is partially open. Crystal quietly slides through, hearing gagging sounds then some guy moaning. The place is trashed. Empty bottles litter the carpet. Sofa and seat cushions are thrown around the floor. Ashtrays are full. The place smells like sweat, cigarettes, and weed.

Crystal moves quietly down the hallway until she can see an open door. Dylan leans against a wall, looking down at Haley kneeling, her back toward Crystal, arms tied behind her. He grips her hair as he viciously humps her face, snarling and grunting. Haley gags.

"Hey!" shouts Crystal, running toward Dylan, heat flushing through her body. Haley tries to turn her head, but Dylan forces it back against his groin. Just as Crystal passes the kitchen, Danny steps in front, arms out, hands crashing into her shoulders.

"Hello, Crystal," says Danny. "Come to join the party?"

Crystal turns and sees Nick standing behind her, sneering. She tries to suck air into her lungs. She wants to scream at them but can't make her voice work.

Dylan erupts in explosive grunts then pushes Haley away. He notices

Crystal staring at him, his pants below his knees. "When did she get here?"

"Just now," says Nick.

Dylan smiles as he pulls his pants up slowly. "Mike told me you offered to flash your tits this morning. I'm thinking you'll want to do the same for us."

"Hey, I vote for that." Nick puts his hand on her hips to pull up her shirt, but Crystal whips around and flails at his face.

"Get away from me!"

"Crystal?" yells Haley. "Is that you?"

"I'm here, Haley!" Crystal jerks around to face Danny and sees Haley struggling to stand. Crystal takes a step toward him. "You let that shit do this to your sister? What kind of brothers are you?"

Danny holds up his hands. "She's not hurt. She made a deal with Dylan."

Dylan pushes Danny to the side and moves toward Crystal. "I think I've figured you out. This morning, you weren't jealous of me. You were jealous of Haley. You wanted me to do that to you. Well, now's your chance."

"You're crazy, Dylan. Haley, let's get out of here."

Dylan laughs and grabs the bottom of Crystal's shirt with both hands and rips upwards. She clenches her arms and twists away from him. Dylan moves closer, leering, as she backs up into Nick. After she elbows him in the stomach, Nick grabs her arms. She stomps on his feet then he snarls and shoves her toward Dylan.

Haley stands. "Leave her alone!"

"Anyone here?" A voice yells from the front of the house. Everyone looks toward the sound.

"Yes," Crystal yells. "Back here!"

"Who the hell is that?" growls Dylan, as he jerks his head toward the front door. Nick and Danny disappear down the hall.

"Who are you?" says Nick, out of sight.

"I saw the 'For Sale' sign outside. I'm looking for a house." The voice comes closer.

Crystal pushes past Dylan toward Haley. She unties her hands, Haley grabs her pack, and they both run out of the room, only to be stopped by Dylan, glaring at both girls.

"Hey, mister," shouts Crystal. "We're trapped back here!"

Dylan tightens his eyes at Crystal. "You'll get yours."

Crystal's lips tighten against her teeth. "Already got her, dickhead."

"What's going on here?" yells the man.

Crystal pulls Haley past Dylan until they both see the man—the same one who had stared at Crystal earlier in the day, still wearing shades and a cap.

Nick and Danny stand with folded arms, blocking the hallway. "You need to leave, mister. Who the hell are you?"

Dylan joins the brothers. "You're trespassing."

The man smiles, staring hard at the boys. "The sign said 'For Sale.' I heard a girl yelling. Thought I'd check that out." The man lifts his right hand, which holds a mini baseball bat. "Maybe you should let the girls go." The man has a slight grin on his face, like he has no fear at all and is just waiting for an opportunity to crack their heads.

"The girls were having fun with us, old man," says Dylan. "Just having a party with our girlfriends."

"We're not your girlfriends," barks Haley as she and Crystal push through the boys and walk quickly to the man who sweeps them behind him.

"Sorry to break up your little party, fellas," the man says. "Don't like the house, now that I see the inside. Looks like it's been trashed by a bunch of punks. See you around."

Crystal watches the man keep his eyes on the boys, like he hopes one will try to take him on. Once they're outside, he says, "Get into the truck, girls."

Crystal retrieves her pack and looks at Haley. "Maybe we should just walk away."

"We need to get out of here," says Haley, gasping for breath.

The man opens the passenger door of his truck. "Look, I'm not going to hurt either of you. I'll take you home or wherever you want to go. Get inside before they decide to do something stupid." He walks around to the driver's side. Crystal climbs in first. Haley closes the door. The man starts the truck and pulls out of the driveway.

Haley hugs Crystal. "How many times are you going to save me today?"

Crystal holds Haley's head against her chest, trying to keep from crying. "I hope that's the last time I need to."

"I'm done with Dylan."

"Good."

"Which way?" asks the man.

"My Honda won't start at the school. Can you fix it?"

"Sure." He speeds down Second Street without turning on D.

"Hey!" Crystal yells. "This is the wrong way. Stop! C'mon, Haley." She starts to open the door as Haley sits up, looking terrified.

"Close the door, Crystal," the man says. "I'll get your Honda started."

Crystal freezes. The bottom of her stomach seems to disappear. "How do you know my name?"

He stops at the intersection of Second and A Street and turns to Crystal. "You always looked like your mother. Fourteen years doesn't change that. I guess it's harder for a four-year-old to remember what her father looks like." He removes his glasses.

Crystal stares at him. In the only picture she had found, he had a beard and long hair, and a beer gut. This man is shaved and lean. But his face is the same. She sees JD's eyes and mouth.

"You're Eugene Rock?" Crystal asks.

"Yes, I am. We spoke on the phone this morning. I know how to get to the school." After a couple of minutes, he pulls into the school parking lot and parks by her Honda.

Crystal scoots closer to Haley. "Mac said he would shoot you if you tried to see me."

He looks at Crystal. "Maybe he'll think different after you tell him I rescued you and your friend."

Haley stares at Eugene. "This is your father?"

Crystal's skin prickles, all her senses on alert. "Guess so."

He stares back. "And you are?"

"Haley. The big ugly oaf is my former boyfriend, and the other two losers are my brothers."

"Brothers? Great family you have."

Heat surges through Crystal's skin as she reaches past Haley to pop the door. "You're one to talk about great families." The girls exit the truck. Crystal slams the door and talks through the open window. "Why are you even here?"

The two stare at each other until Eugene sighs. "God, you look like Maya." He breaks the stare and looks out the windshield.

Crystal slaps the door. "Who ruined JD's life forever. Who you killed." Half of her is full of bitterness and anger; the other half is desperate for answers and reunion, happy that he rescued Haley and her. She fights to keep her face like stone while those two forces struggle for control.

He opens his door then walks around the back of the truck before bending down to look at her Honda. "I'm sure that's what Mac and Summer told you, but she had the wreck by herself."

"You claimed she had a wreck, but there was no proof. You kept her from going to rehab."

He grabs a wire on the Honda. "Somebody disconnected your solenoid." He holds out the wire. "At least they didn't cut it." He reattaches the wire.

After all these years of never talking to her, Crystal can't believe he's ignoring her now. "And dealt drugs and fed her addiction!" Haley hugs her from behind.

After a good pause, he looks up at Crystal. "And who saved your ass from three boys who would still be having their fun with you two if I hadn't come around." He glares at Crystal. "That true or not true?"

Crystal hesitates. "Probably. Thanks for saving us."

He nods, tightens the last screw, and stands.

A gust of cool wind comes from the west, bending the trees and smelling like rain. Crystal sees a bank of dark clouds moving toward them and across the sun.

Still standing behind her, Haley pulls Crystal's hair out of her face. "Why did you come by that house, Eugene?"

"When I drove into town, I saw Crystal standing outside the school. I knew it was her and that she didn't recognize me. I didn't know whether to get out and say hi or wait. So I pulled up at that city building and just hung out in my camper. Thought I'd wait until she drove home. Then the trooper came by and took that ugly oaf . . ."

"Dylan," says Haley.

"OK. He took Dylan to his patrol car for a while then I saw him walk off down D Street talking on his phone. I got bored and drove around the park and to the river. Then through town looking at houses I remembered from years ago." He smiles. "Me and Maya lived here for awhile, months before you were born, Crystal."

"Yeah," says Crystal. "That didn't work out very well. Mac said you both stole from him, and he ran you off."

He removes his hat and scratches his head. "There's always two sides to every story."

Panic rises like bile in Crystal's chest. "Did you go by my house?" She doesn't want him to know Mac and Summer are gone.

"No. Just down Second and Third. I turned back toward the school and saw that Mustang. And then it went down D Street. A little bit later, I saw you walk by and turn down D. I wondered, what the hell everybody's going down D Street for?" He tries to chuckle.

Crystal senses he's lying. "Why didn't you say something when I walked by? Were you just stalking me?"

"Actually, I was trying to figure out how to talk to you. Look, I was nervous about how you'd react. I knew Mac would've filled your head with crap about me."

"Like they'd have to make up anything."

"Yeah, well, like I said before—two sides to every story." He pulls out a cigarette. "For instance, your mother abandoned you so she hook up with her latest guy." He lights and takes a puff. "I tried to talk her into going to rehab then bringing you both back, but she had other ideas." He spits onto the gravel. "Look, I was no saint, but your mother wasn't either. We both made bad decisions. But I didn't dump my kids. You were fortunate to have Summer and Mac to take care of you." He nods his head several times. "They were better parents to you than we could have been." He leans back against the camper and folds his arms.

The idea that he just delivered a memorized speech crosses Crystal's mind. "How could Mac and Summer have been worse? Mom damaged both of us, especially JD. You named us after drugs and alcohol."

"Look, Crystal," he spits out a piece of tobacco. "I'm not going to justify what we did or try to minimize it. You have every right to be angry."

She feels her head will explode. With her arms spread wide, she blurts, "Thanks. I wouldn't want to be angry without the right to do so."

Eugene leans his head forward and lowers his voice. "Maybe at some point we can talk about the past, and I'll do a better job. I hope we have that chance."

"Did she prevent *you* from coming back to JD and me? You blame the dumping on her. You just let her do it?"

Eugene pulls his ear and shuffles his feet. "It's complicated."

Haley hooks arms with Crystal and stands by her side. "You haven't answered why you went to that house."

He takes a deep breath. "After Crystal walked down D Street for a block, I followed her. When I saw her run toward that house, I sped up. Then I heard the shouts."

Haley shakes her head. "What would you have done if she hadn't run to the house? Or what if she'd turned around and seen you?"

Eugene scratches his neck. "I don't know. I was nervous and wasn't sure what to do."

Haley chortles, "You'd rather Crystal think you're a stalker than her father?"

Eugene folds his arms and looks at his shoes.

Haley moves toward the Honda. "Why did you disconnect Crystal's solenoid?"

Crystal's head snaps to Haley. Eugene stands up straight. "What the hell are you talking about, girl?"

"My brothers fix and race cars. I've seen them work on all kinds of ATVs. If they were trying to figure out why Crystal's Honda wouldn't start, they'd check several things—the battery, the fuse. But most of all, they'd try to start it themselves. You went straight to the loose wire. I think you disconnected it."

He pulls another draw on his cigarette then stomps it into the gravel. "You're full of shit, Haley."

Crystal takes the key out of her pocket. "No, she's not. Wouldn't you ask me for this?"

"Hey, I saw the wire and I fixed it. You're making a mountain out of nothing."

Crystal tightens her eyes. "And the bigger question is—why did you come back to Clear?"

Eugene squirms. "Already said—to see you and JD."

Crystal scoffs, "So just out of the blue one day you decide to see your kids after fourteen years?"

Eugene stares hard at her, breathing deeply.

Crystal glares back. "Is my mother alive?"

Eugene turns his face away. The two girls look at each other.

Crystal folds her arms. "Simple question, Eugene. Is Maya alive?"

No answer.

Haley shakes her head. "She didn't die in the wreck, did she?"

Eugene tightens his jaw. "No."

Crystal's stomach twists and knots up. "Then why did you tell Mac and Summer that she did?"

Eugene steps away from his truck, leaning toward the girls. "Because Maya told me to."

"Why?"

"She wanted her parents to think she was dead."

"And her kids."

"Yes."

A light turns on in Crystal's head. "You didn't come here to see me or JD, did you? You're trying to find Maya and you think she'll come here." All her muscles tingle. "You *were* stalking me. You think she'll try to find me, and you want to be there when that happens. Or you wanted to talk to me to see if she's already here." Thoughts race inside her mind. "The reason you stared at me while driving by is because if I'd reacted to seeing you, that would prove Maya had already come home and warned us you were after her." Warmth floods her body. "And you thought if you drove by again after everyone had left the parking lot, I might wave you down and ask for help with my Honda. But Nick and Danny blew that idea." Crystal glares at Eugene and speaks slowly. "Why would my mother want to come home?"

Eugene fidgets.

"I notice you don't deny anything I just said," Crystal says.

Haley moves back to Crystal. "Maybe she's trying to get away from you. Isn't that right? Like I want to get away from Dylan, she wants to get away from you. And maybe for the same reasons."

Eugene shakes his head. "She didn't run away from me."

Haley's top lip curls back from her teeth. "What are you going to do when she shows up? Will there be a happy reunion? Or will you punish her? You assholes are all the same. If Dylan can't have me, he'll make sure no one else can. Even if it means hurting me. Are you planning to hurt Crystal's mother?"

He shakes his head, glances at the girls then averts his eyes. "No, I'd never hurt her."

Crystal jabs her finger toward him. "You've spent half your life hurting her. Tell you what, if she shows up, we won't tell you. If you show up, we've got plenty of guns."

Both girls stab Eugene with their eyes while he leans back against his truck with a half-grin on his face, snorting air through his nose.

"C'mon, Haley. I'll take you to my house." Crystal lifts the bungee cord on the rear bumper and snaps it onto both their packs then straddles the seat. She starts her Honda while Haley jumps on behind her.

Eugene takes a step toward them. "Maybe I should follow you home to make sure those boys . . ."

Crystal looks straight ahead, stone-faced. "Those boys better hope we don't see them." When Crystal feels Haley holding her hips, she twists the throttle and kicks gravel at Eugene's truck, crossing First and racing down A Street.

She feels abandoned again, except this time it hurts even more. Her father returned to her life just to flaunt his indifference, just to say, "I didn't come here to see you. If I thought your mother would go somewhere else, I wouldn't have bothered disturbing your life."

At the intersection of Second and A, she stops, wind tears dripping from her cheeks.

Her parents are alive, yet all she feels is anger and pain. Her father is an asshole. Could her mother be the same?

"What's wrong, Crystal?" asks Haley.

Her chin quivers as she closes her eyes. "I need someone to hold me. To want me."

Crystal feels Haley kiss the back of her neck and move her arms around her stomach. Crystal huddles inside Haley's warmth, her pain draining from her.

"I want you, Crystal Rose. More than anything," whispers Haley.

CHAPTER 10

A few drops of rain hit Crystal's arms and face as she turns off the road and onto an old overgrown trail. A father and son used to clear trails around the town in early summer, but they moved to Anchorage some years ago. No one else took up the task. Now wild animals and wandering pets are the only ones who know this path leads to the Rose residence on the north edge of town.

The girls bend low to avoid leaning trees as Crystal maneuvers her Honda through the Feather Creek fen before finding higher ground. Now she makes her way through young spruce, fallen logs, and leafless primrose. Shriveled rosehips still hang on the spiny branches, which try to scrape the girls' legs as they push by.

Haley pulls Crystal tighter against her chest. "Why are we going this way, Crystal?"

"Because only me and JD and maybe a few other people in town know this is a back way to my house. Dylan and your brothers wouldn't expect us to use this trail."

Crystal sees the flash of lightning above them and waits for the thunder. Just a few hundred yards to go as the rain splatters down. Haley lifts the back of Crystal's jacket and burrows her head underneath. The crushing slap of thunder echoes in their chests, and a few pieces of pea-sized hail hit their heads.

"Almost there," shouts Crystal. She sees the woodshed through the trees and the stump where she videoed the cow and calf this morning. She shifts into second now and hops over the railroad ties bordering the old fort and swing set.

The sound of the deluge pounding on the metal roof is deafening, like a train bearing down on them. Protecting her head with her arm, Crystal races up next to the back deck and stops her Honda. "Grab the packs!" She hops off the machine and digs in her jeans for the key. A torrent of hail crashes onto the cedar planks, hiding the house behind a roaring blur.

"Open the freakin door!" yells Haley, ducking under the packs draped across her back as Crystal tries to find the lock on the handle. "Fuck, I'm cold. Hurry!"

Crystal finally pushes the key in and flips the lock. As she steps inside, Haley pushes from behind. They fall into the sunroom on top of each other. Hail bounces off the deck into the house as the two girls laugh and slip and finally get up. Crystal shuts the door, and they look at each other—soaked to the bone, hair plastered to faces and necks, Haley's makeup running down her cheeks.

"I'm not sure this is the first date we had in mind," laughs Haley.

"No, but we'll never forget it." She wipes water off Haley's face. "Even wet and half frozen, you are beautiful."

She tries to cover her face. "I look like a drowned cat."

"A beautiful drowned cat." Crystal kisses her forehead. "I owed you one. From the bathroom before Rathbone's class."

Haley nods then shivers. Crystal rips off her wet jacket, drops it, and throws her arms around Haley's back, trying to warm her up.

They both vibrate against each other as the puddles beneath their feet spread wider.

Haley barks a laugh. "Jesus, girl, your nipples are stabbing me. I've got dents in my boobs!" She pushes Crystal back and looks at her soaked, now see-through t-shirt. "You're either very cold or very aroused."

Tingles crawl up her skin. "Both."

"My God, they're staring at me!" Haley cups Crystal's breasts. "I don't like being stared at."

Crystal presses Haley's hands against her chest. "Not true. You love it. Let's get some towels to dry off." She pulls one of Haley's wrists and leads her back to the bathroom. Crystal turns on the space heater and pulls two towels off the shower rod. "Here." She offers the towel to Haley, who has raised her arms above her head, facing the mirror.

Haley flashes her brows through the glass. "A little help? My clothes are too wet for me to take them off myself."

Crystal can't breathe as she stares. "You want me to take off your shirt?"

"And my pants. I want to take a shower." Haley bites her bottom lip.

A tongue of heat slithers up the back of Crystal's neck. "I've always done what you asked." She stands behind Haley, works her fingers inside the bottom of her shirt then pulls up, revealing the belly button stud she saw this morning. The wet material clings to the underside of Haley's breasts, pushing them higher as Crystal inches the shirt up, revealing the impossibly white skin rarely exposed to view. Crystal stands mesmerized as the breasts plummet and bounce slightly off Haley's ribs.

"Keep pulling, Crystal. I'm smothering in here."

Crystal snaps her eyes away from Haley's breasts and sees the shirt bunched around Haley's head. She yanks it off and drops it to the floor.

The girls' eyes meet in the mirror before Crystal's wanders down to the dark pink nipples pointing at her.

"You like?" Haley purrs, shaking ever so slightly.

"Yes," Crystal gasps. "You said you might be drawing number four, but I'm thinking five at least." Crystal lowers her fingers to the girl's hips.

Haley blushes. "Well, if you can stop staring, you can remove my leggings. I think you'll have to peel them off. They feel glued to me."

Crystal kneels as she works her fingertips between the clammy leggings and wet hips. Slowly, she pulls down her pants until Haley's butt cleavage shows. Feeling deliciously dizzy, Crystal presses her cheek against Haley's hip as she pulls then pushes the fabric to the floor. Haley lifts each foot out of each leg. Crystal sits back onto her calves and gazes at the perfect round cheeks cuddling the top of Haley's legs.

Crystal's lips part as her lungs empty. Her heart skips and squeezes as her skin heats. She wants to touch, to devour, yet to gaze forever. Inside her mind an animal and angel wrestle for control.

Haley turns around and Crystal gasps.

"No one has ever looked at me like you do now, Crystal." She steps closer and reaches for Crystal's face. "Your eyes burn my skin."

"I don't ever want to close them." She clutches Haley's waist and pulls her stomach to her lips, kissing around her navel then lower until she feels the tiny stubble on Haley's pubis. She kisses lower, summoning a moan from Haley.

Haley kneels and clutches Crystal's head. "Have you done this before?"

"No. Have you?"

She shakes her head. "But I want to."

Crystal bends her neck and moves her open lips to Haley's, urgent to kiss. Neither mouth closes as they share tongues and drink each other's breath.

The kitchen phone rings twice before the girls separate their mouths. Two more times before both girls can stand, and once more before Haley pulls off Crystal's shirt.

"I had to see them before you go," says Haley. "You're gorgeous." Crystal doesn't move as Haley pulls the shower curtain back and puts one foot into the tub. "Go, silly. Answer the phone." Haley steps behind the curtain and pulls it closed.

Crystal rushes out of the bathroom and lunges at the phone. "Hello."

"Crystal?" asks Summer. "I've tried to call your cell several times. Are you all right?"

Crystal tries to block the nude images of Haley from her mind. "Yes. We had hail and got caught in the rain. Sorry."

"You and JD? Is he home?"

"No. He's still at Gena's."

"Then who were you . . .?"

"It's a long story. How's Mac?"

"Not good. They've put him on oxygen. He's . . . he's not doing well, Crystal. They're very worried about him." She coughs.

Crystal's chest tightens. "How can he be that sick? He was fine yesterday."

"No, he wasn't. He's been feeling bad for a few days, but he kept it to himself."

Crystal rubs her eyes. "How are you feeling?"

"They don't want me to go anywhere. My oxygen level is under 90. I'm sure they'll admit me. Crystal, I'm so worried."

Her insides quiver. "Can you see Mac?"

"No. He's isolated."

Crystal sees the etching of a wolf on a window Mac did years ago. And all the fancy woodwork around the door jamb. Everywhere she looks, she sees Mac in this house. How can he not be here? "Does he have his phone?"

"Honey, he can't do anything now except try to breathe."

Crystal feels a knot tightening at the base of her throat. Guilt pushes tears from her eyes. "Did JD and I get you both sick?"

"Don't worry about that. Mac and I went to the store this weekend. We could've caught something there."

A memory of Kato convincing her to sneak them into her bedroom just after her grandparents left on Saturday flashes through Crystal's mind. She shivers and catches her reflection in the window glass— topless in sopping wet jeans. She remembers her argument with Summer this morning and cringes. There was no need to start something, but she couldn't have imagined what would happen today.

Still, there has been so much unsaid in this house. JD would never talk to Summer about his relationship with Gena. Crystal could never discuss her sexuality. And how could she ever explain Haley and what's already happened in her own bathroom?

Crystal shivers. She's going to get sick herself unless she changes clothes. She puts the phone on the table and starts to remove her jeans.

"Are you still there, Crystal?" asks Summer.

"Yes. Just trying to dry off a little." Should she say anything about

Eugene or JD moving and getting married? Or keep that to herself? She steps out of her jeans. "I'll be back in one minute."

She runs to the hall closet and grabs a towel to blot her skin. From her drawers she pulls sweatpants and a robe, is about to leave when she thinks of Haley. She finds more sweats and runs back to the kitchen. While she pulls on her pants, she bends over and talks into the phone. "I'm back, Summer. I had to get a towel."

She hears the shower stop and worries that Haley will call out. Dumping the robe onto the phone to muffle the sound, she picks up the other set of sweats and goes to the bathroom. She knocks lightly and pushes the door open only to find the room filled with steam. Haley, like an angel in the mist, stands naked in the tub, rubbing her hair with a towel, her breasts swaying in concert.

Stunned and momentarily speechless, Crystal stands and gawks. Haley lifts her head, smiles, and says, "Yes?"

Crystal swallows and whispers, "I'm on the phone with Summer. She doesn't know you're here." She leaves the sweats on the vanity and closes the door.

Picking up the robe and phone, Crystal says, "I'm back. Sorry."

"Is everything all right? You seem distracted."

Damn right, she thinks. How to answer? "Why shouldn't I be distracted? Both my grandparents are probably sick with Covid in another town where I can't see them."

"I'm going to call Kathy and ask her to pick up groceries for you when she goes to town."

"We're fine, Summer. We have plenty of food." She doesn't want to worry about more people coming to the house. The list is already long —Eugene, Dylan, Danny, Nick, Kato—and that doesn't include her brother who she wants to see.

"Did anything happen at school today?"

"Why do you ask?"

"Ms. Trimble said I should be proud of you. Something about Dylan."

Her stomach sinks. What did Trimble tell Summer? "I stopped him from bothering Haley, that's all."

"She made it sound more than that."

"Well, he is a hot head."

"Did he threaten you?"

What should she say? That he wants to *do* her next, that she'll *get hers*, that he tried to strip off her shirt? "Whatever he said doesn't matter. He's suspended for three days."

"I'm just . . . I'm just worried about you and JD."

Crystal hears Summer wiping her nose. She decides she can't say anything now about Eugene or JD leaving. "We'll be all right. You and Mac will be home soon."

"But maybe we won't, Crystal. We may not." She mumbles something. "I've got to call the bank. I'll talk to you in the morning."

Cold invades her chest. "You both will be all right. I love you."

"And we love you. And JD."

Crystal hangs up the phone. *What if they don't come back? And JD leaves?* Would everyone abandon her? She slumps into the same chair Mac sat in after hanging up on Eugene. Her head spins with worry, but her body feels numb. She stares out the window, seeing nothing.

Snippets of her conversation with Eugene swirl in her mind. Why is her mother coming home? That's the hardest question. Eugene, she can understand—men are possessive and can't stand to lose. But her mother? Does she want to see her parents? Her children? Why? That makes no sense after so many years of absence.

Her father? He won't stay. All he cares about is finding Maya. Why? To get her back or to punish her?

Mac and Summer had told her many times Maya left Eugene to bring them to the village, that he didn't know she was running away that morning in September many years ago. But he *did* know. He came with them to the airport.

Now Eugene claims she hasn't run away from him. If that's true, then why is he looking for her? If he knows where she is, then why does he want to be here before her?

Are they planning something together?

He did say Crystal should tell Mac how he saved his granddaughter.

Why? To convince Mac to let him come to the house? For what? To be there when Maya shows up? Or something else?

She can't figure anything out. Her brain is jammed with too many possibilities, the same feeling she gets when she tries to read. So many words on the page. Change one or two around, and the sentence says the opposite—or nothing at all.

What is she going to do? She leans back in the chair and crosses her arms over her eyes, hoping she can keep from crying.

After another minute, Haley opens the bathroom door and walks into the kitchen.

"Crystal, what's wrong?"

Haley moves quickly to her side.

"Everybody is leaving me."

"I'm not." She touches Crystal's face and kisses her cheek. "How are Mac and Summer?"

"Probably dying." She turns to Haley, now dressed with damp hair draped over her back and shoulders.

"Can you see them? Payton said she'd drive us to Fairbanks."

"No. Mac's in isolation and Summer thinks she'll be admitted soon." Crystal stands and hugs Haley. "Thanks for being with me."

"Thanks for rescuing me. You have a lot of spunk for your size. Have you rescued many girls?" She moves her hands through the robe, around Crystal's waist.

"No. I beat up Louis in Second Grade at recess when he wouldn't stop teasing JD."

Haley laughs. "I remember that. You scared me."

Crystal pushes her fingertips along Haley's hair. "Until recently I didn't think girls had to be rescued. You and Laura and all your friends always seem so sure of yourselves."

"Just a big lie, Crystal. All we ever do is try to look pretty so a guy will like us. Hopefully, a nice one." She touches Crystal's lips and cheek with her fingers. "Maybe we all need to be rescued."

They stare at each other's lips. "From guys?"

"Maybe."

They kiss, their hands caressing each other's breasts, their legs pressing hard against each other. They separate, breathing heavily, their eyes exploring every curve and lash and texture on the other's face.

"Where's your bedroom?" asks Haley.

"Down the hall."

"Show me?"

"I'll show you everything."

The bite of tires on gravel turns their heads to the window where they see a trooper car pulling into the driveway.

"Shit," exclaims Haley.

"Why is he here?"

"I'm guessing Dylan."

CHAPTER 11

They see Trooper Brian exit the car and look at the house and around the yard. Haley ties Crystal's robe. "Let's find out what he wants." They exit the kitchen into the mudroom then out to the porch. "What's up, Brian? Tell me Dylan didn't send you here."

He smiles and tips his hat. "Hello, Haley. Crystal. Where's Mac and Summer?"

Crystal folds her arms. "In the hospital in Fairbanks, but I'd like you to keep that to yourself."

"OK. We had a call from a woman who claims that a Eugene Rock stole money from her and slapped her several times when he was drunk."

Both girls side glance at each other. Crystal wonders if the woman is her mother.

"Mr. Rock mentioned to her before he left that he had something to settle with Mac."

"Who is this woman?" asks Crystal, her heart pounding. She grabs Haley's fingers.

"She wouldn't give her name. She gave us a description of the man and asked us to check with Mac and Summer."

Crystal shades her eyes from the sun behind the trooper. "Does she know them?"

"Claims to, but she didn't explain. We asked her why she didn't report a crime against the man. She said she was too scared. That he's mean."

"Do you have her phone number?"

"No, I don't."

"So Dylan's not involved in this?" snaps Haley.

Brian smiles. "Not the first part, but right after the woman called, Dylan called and reported a kidnapping."

Haley folds her arms. "Kidnapping? Of who?"

"You and Crystal. He said a man with the same description as that woman gave threatened to beat him and your brothers if they didn't release you two girls to him."

Haley throws her hands above her head. "What a pile of shit! That man saved us from being raped."

Brian frowns and pulls out a pen. He opens a pad. "Are you saying Dylan tried to rape you?"

Haley stomps her foot in frustration. "No, but he forced me to suck his dick, and he and my brothers were trying to pull off Crystal's shirt." With more intensity, "They would've raped Crystal for sure if Eugene hadn't showed up."

Brian writes in his pad. "You claim Eugene Rock took you two girls away from the house on Second Street."

"Yes," answers Crystal, "but he didn't kidnap us."

"Do either of you want to press charges against Dylan? How did he force you to have sex?" His pen is poised above the paper.

Haley shakes her head and grits her teeth. "That's why he called you, Brian. He didn't think we were kidnapped. He wanted to make sure I didn't charge him with anything."

"How so?"

"Don't you see? He was afraid we'd call to complain, so he got ahead of the game and called himself, putting the blame on the other guy. Now if I press charges, he'll say, 'Why would I call the troopers if I'd committed a crime?' I already know what he told you. He said we got into an argument at school, that he asked my brothers to bring me to him so he could apologize. Which he did, though he didn't mean it. Then he said we should make up and have sex. Then I gave him head. Am I right so far?"

Brian grins as he writes. "Pretty close, Haley. Pretty close."

"Her hands were tied behind her back," yells Crystal, "and he was fucking her throat. She couldn't breathe!"

Haley turns to Crystal. "But then he's going to say that I've done that before when we weren't fighting."

Crystal feels her stomach drop. "Have you?"

Haley grimaces. "Yeah. How sick is that?"

Crystal wraps her arms around Haley's shoulders. "I'm sorry."

Haley moves an arm around Crystal's waist. "But there's more, right, Brian?"

"Afraid so."

Haley continues. "Then Crystal came into the house in a jealous rage. The reason Crystal lied about Dylan and me at school was because she was jealous and wanted Dylan to herself. Crystal barged in, screamed at me, then started to pull off her own shirt."

Crystal snaps to Haley, her eyes bulging. "Are you kidding me?"

"Hell, I know Dylan and my brothers backwards and forwards. Then my beloved brothers tried to keep you from stripping in front of all of them when the crazy man with the bat came into the house."

Crystal shakes her head. "OK, but why would we leave with him? Someone neither of us knew at the time?"

Haley turns to the trooper. "You want to answer that one, Brian?"

He flips back a few pages in his pad. "Because Crystal didn't want to get into trouble with her grandparents. She didn't want them to know what she was really up to. By leaving with the man, Crystal could pretend she was attacked and Haley went with her because you two are friends."

Haley claps her hands. "Bingo! Perfect." She points her finger at Brian. "And you probably believed every word."

"No, I've had too many dealings with Dylan and your brothers. But what they couldn't explain was why Eugene Rock was there in the first place. And the other problem is why three good-sized men were so cowed by one man and a little bat that they'd let you two be kidnapped without a fight."

Haley raises her brows. "Hmm, because they're lying weenies?"

Brian stifles a laugh. "Do you two want to make an official complaint against them?"

Haley shakes her head. "No, we don't." She looks to the ground. "Not yet anyway."

Crystal reaches for her hand. "Why not, Haley?" Why shouldn't they try to get them arrested? A thought slides through her brain that maybe Haley's not telling the entire story.

Haley looks at Crystal. "Because we already know what they'll say, and how will we refute it?"

"Eugene saw . . ."

"He saw nothing." Haley kicks gravel. "He heard screaming, but he saw nothing. And what kind of screams were they? From fear or from excitement? Hell, we were screaming because we were having fun! I've seen way too many TV lawyers attack witnesses in rape cases. And bring up all their past shit. No, we don't want to make a complaint."

"OK," says Brian. "But maybe you should stay away from Dylan."

"That's what I'm trying to do. And you'd better not tell him or my brothers that I'm with Crystal. If we're kidnapped, we could be anywhere. You tried, and you can't find either of us. You got that?"

"I hear you, Haley. Now, let's get back to Eugene Rock. Do you know who and where he is?"

"Not sure where," says Crystal. "He's my father. Today is the first time I've seen him since I was four years old. Mac and Summer told JD and me he had died." She clears her throat and sucks in her lips. Should she hope? "I'm pretty sure that woman who called was my mother, who also is supposed to be dead. But for some reason, she's trying to come back here. She wanted to see if Eugene got here before her. He's looking for her."

Brian tilts his head. "Why is that?"

"I have no idea, but I think I'll find out pretty soon."

"Where do you think he might be?"

"Close by. He drives a rented blue camper truck. Maybe he's down at the park, but I'll bet he was parked on D Street somewhere hidden where he could view anyone going down my driveway. He saw you coming, and he snuck away. He knows his way around town because he used to live here years ago."

Brian flips his notebook closed and drops it into his pocket. "OK, I'll drive around and see what I find. Is he a danger to you?"

"I don't think so," says Crystal. "Unless I'm hiding my mother from him."

"When are Mac and Summer getting back?"

"I don't know. Mac's real sick. Summer might be in the hospital by now."

"I'm sorry to hear that. You tell them I hope they get better. Always liked your grandparents. Call me if the lying . . . if those boys come here to bother you." He hands Haley and Crystal his card. "I'd check back with you later, but I'm the only officer available today between Nenana and Cantwell. You two stay safe."

In another minute, he drives away.

"Where's my phone?" shouts Haley as she bolts back into the house.

Crystal follows and thinks she'd better look at her own phone. Summer said she'd tried to call her. How long has she not looked at it?

She finds it in her wet, wadded jeans on the kitchen floor. After unlocking, she sees missed phone calls from both Summer and Payton.

"That shit!" yells Haley as she charges out of the bathroom, holding her phone. "Dylan's posted on the town Facebook page that we were kidnapped and everyone needs to find the man in the camper truck. 'Please help me find my girlfriend,' he says. God, I could kill him."

Crystal opens a message from Payton. *Hail damaged my roof. I need some caulk to fix it. Do you have any?* That was an hour ago. "Damn. How can everything be so screwed up at the same time?" She texts back. *Sorry for not answering. Lots of stuff going on. Yes, I'm sure we have caulk. Drive to D Street, turn north. My driveway is at the end. Take a right.*

Payton replies. *OK. Thanks!*

Haley is still flipping through screens, getting angrier every second. "What are we going to do about Dylan and my asshole brothers?"

"Option One." Crystal starts pacing around the kitchen. "We tell the truth—all of it—then order everyone to stay away from my house or we'll call Brian and load our guns."

"I like the guns. Option Two?"

"We say my father thought he was saving me and you from harm, so he took us away. We're safe and there was no kidnapping. No Brian. No guns."

"Still like the guns."

"Option Three. My father wanted me to see my mother who's sick in Fairbanks and I asked you to come with me since I haven't seen my parents for fourteen years. We're somewhere on the Parks Highway. Try and find us." Crystal stops at the sink and fills a glass with water. "Which one do you like best?"

"I think I'd like a beer." She goes to the refrigerator. "Can I?"

Payton's warning about not giving Haley whiskey flashes in her mind. She didn't understand why then and still doesn't. Maybe Payton has something against underage drinking? "Sure. Second shelf." She pulls a bottle opener out of a nearby drawer and tosses it on the counter.

Haley removes a Corona and holds it out. "Seriously? He drinks these during the pandemic?" She opens the bottle and chugs a few swallows.

"Yeah. He thought it would keep him from catching Covid. Fighting fire with fire, so to speak. 'Corona beer will kill the corona virus,' he said many times."

"He should have tried bleach, like Trump said to do. Then Mac would never have caught anything. You think a female president would ever say something as stupid as that?" Haley leans back against the counter.

"Hope we find out soon." She puts the glass down and dries her hands on a towel.

Haley offers the bottle. "You want some?"

"No thanks." She walks to the window and looks outside. "Do you think that woman was my mom?"

"Who else?"

"Why can't she call?"

"Maybe she's scared of getting yelled at. Would you?"

"Yell at her?" Crystal feels pain in her eyes. "No. I'd do what Summer said this morning. Grab her and never let her go." She blinks, trying to keep the tears in her eyes. "I'd like to have a mother."

Haley finishes the bottle. "My mother's worthless. Drunk all the time. Watches the news all day and screams at the TV while she keeps stuffing her face. When I was in eighth grade I told her that Nick and Danny were always peeking through my door trying to see me naked. And they stole my bikini top when I was sunbathing then took a video of me running after them. 'Boys will be boys,' she chuckled. That crap happened all the time. Hell, it still happens. Maybe the mothers you want are the ones who aren't there."

Crystal hugs herself and stares out the window. "Well, if she shows up, I'll hug her and not even ask questions. Maybe she'll hug me back."

Haley holds her from behind, her chin on Crystal's shoulder. "We all need hugs. When we're young, we get hugs all the time. Then we grow up and no one hugs us anymore. Daddy hasn't touched me in years. I guess my boobs and butt got too big for his comfort zone. The only hugs I've gotten in years are from guys trying to feel me up."

Crystal bends down to kiss Haley's arm. "And from me. Will you stay here tonight?"

"Where would I sleep?"

Crystal turns to face her. "With me? If you want."

Haley plays with Crystal's hair as their eyes memorize each other's faces. "Yes. I'd love to." Haley brushes her lips on Crystal's. "Maybe you should change out of that robe."

"Come help me pick out something to wear." Crystal grabs Haley's hand and takes her down the hall.

CHAPTER 12

*C*rystal's room is small with drawings and photos stuck randomly all over the walls—closeups of leaves, flowers, and berries; intricate natural designs created by Labrador tea, spider webs, and lichen; every local animal, including a grizzly sow and two cubs digging through trashcans from this past June; sunrises and sunsets plus northern lights; and, of course, line drawings of her house and family, along with pages of self-portraits. Crystal's entire world greets her every morning and evening. Nothing is ever removed or covered, just added to, now up one corner of the ceiling. A large white board on one wall displays a self-portrait drawing of Crystal sitting.

Haley stands in the doorway, open-mouthed, trying to absorb it all. "Damn, Crystal, you are something. I love this."

Crystal smiles. "I'm glad. So do I." She opens her closet to show Haley her clothing options, including a never-worn pair of stretch jeans Crystal bought at Value Village in Fairbanks—a size too big for her, but a size too small for Haley.

"I'm not sure my butt can fit into these," says Haley, holding the pair waist high. "You'll have fun watching me put these on."

"Oooh, do I get to watch?"

"Certainly." Haley raises a brow and half smiles as she pulls off her sweatshirt.

Crystal's breath catches in her chest as her mouth gapes open.

"Oops! I forgot to pick out a shirt. Can I use your robe until I find something suitable?"

Crystal's face reddens. "Sure." She removes her robe and tosses it to Haley, who then tosses it on the bed. "Now we can stare at each other."

Crystal licks her lips. "You are so evil."

"I'm just getting started." She tilts her head and cocks a brow. "Do you like evil?"

"So far." Though she's afraid her heart will burst, it's beating so fast.

"Great." Haley moves toward Crystal until their chests touch. "I love your drawing on the white board. Would you do another of me? Maybe one of us kissing?" Haley touches her lips to Crystal's.

"Yes." She struggles trying to pull her phone out of her pocket while Haley rubs her tongue tip over Crystal's bottom lip. Gasping for air, Crystal asks, "Do you want me to take a pic or not?" Haley smiles and steps back a little. Crystal props her phone against the mirror on her dresser and sets the timer. "We have five seconds."

Haley moves her hand to Crystal's neck as they kiss. The camera takes the picture, but they don't separate.

After a few more seconds, Haley pulls back just enough to speak. "You are the best kisser. Even in fifth grade I liked kissing you. Think of all that time I wasted."

"We have plenty of time now." She grabs her phone and shows Haley the photo. "I like that. I can draw it now, if you want."

"Yes, please."

"Hold it for me." Crystal takes her drawing pad and pen from her desk and sits in her chair.

Haley holds the phone against her cleavage, her boobs hanging over her arms. "Is that good?"

Crystal stares and shakes her head. "Evil. Pure evil!"

"Just focus on the photo, Crystal." Haley slowly sways her torso, making her boobs jiggle close to Crystal's face. "Can't you focus?" Her voice drips with seduction.

Crystal clears her throat and closes her eyes. "I think I can. I think I can." She takes a deep breath, opens her eyes, and places her pen on the paper. Haley sways faster. Crystal starts a line then runs it off the page. "Can you please stop moving?" she pleads, unable to turn away from Haley's breasts. "Just for a few minutes?" She rips off the page and readies another.

Her voice coy, sweet, and sultry—"As you wish. I'll stand perfectly still." She holds the camera away from her body, partially covering her breasts.

Crystal starts a line under her chin, sweeps down to make hair, then her face and lips before moving to Haley's lips, hair, and then ending with her hand. She stares at the drawing for a few seconds then turns it around. "What do you think?"

"Oh, my god! I love it. We look good together." She gives Crystal a kiss. "Thank you. Thank you."

Crystal removes the page and sets it on the dresser. "We should put our clothes on. Payton should be here soon."

"Payton? Why?"

"The hail damaged her motorhome, and she needs some caulk. I told her I had some." Crystal notices a touch of alarm on Haley's face. "Don't worry about Payton. She's cool. We don't have to act any differently around her than we do by ourselves. She's gay and not afraid to tell anyone. Plus, she can paint this for us. She'd make it even more beautiful."

"OK. But I want you to do one more." Haley pulls off her pants. "I loved the nudes you did of yourself. Can you draw one of me?" Haley lifts her hair behind her head, turns a little sideways and pushes out her tongue, boobs and butt as she does her best Myley Cyrus impression. "How's this?"

Crystal feels dizzy. "We'll have to work up to that pose. Turn around. Let me start with your backside."

"You don't think my back is as sexy as my front?" She turns her back to Crystal, shifts her weight to one hip, swings her right arm back a little, revealing just a hint of her breast.

"Actually, it's more sexy. I love your butt. But I can't possibly stare at your stomach and below without melting into a puddle on the floor. Stay like that."

Crystal starts with her right heel, sweeps up to her hip, then down around the bottom of her cheeks, down her left leg then up to her arm, head, hair, then right arm.

They both hear honking in the driveway.

"Payton's here. Look at this."

Haley turns around as Crystal holds up her pad.

"Does my butt really look like that?"

"Better, but that's close."

"You always make me look so sexy. How?"

"Because you are." Crystal plants a quick kiss on her forehead then grabs a t-shirt out of her drawer and pulls it on. "Get dressed."

"Where's your underwear?"

Crystal pulls open a side drawer. Haley reaches in and pulls out a handful of panties then flashes a coy smile. "You know what I'm going to do."

"You are so evil." Crystal runs out of the room as Haley laughs. She stops in the kitchen and sees Sydney bolt out the passenger door and run toward the swing set and fort with Payton following, carrying her pack and a long-sleeved flannel shirt. She now wears a tie-dyed cropped tank top revealing a lot of skin before the low-rise faded and torn jeans start well below her hipbones. Her arms and abs are tight with muscles.

Sydney climbs the rock wall at the side of the fort and sticks her head out the crow's nest tower. Payton checks the swings and bolts then hangs from the monkey bars, feet tucked back, and pulls herself up several times with little effort.

Crystal watches as she walks toward them. "Are you an athlete?"

"Not anymore," says Payton. "Used to be in gymnastics and did a lot of rock climbing."

Sydney jumps into a swing and kicks her feet to make it move. "Love your swing set . . . uh . . . "

"Crystal," says Payton.

Sydney kicks higher. "Yeah, Crystal."

"Is Haley inside?" asks Payton.

"Yeah," answers Crystal. "She's trying to find some clothes."

Payton smiles, hooking her thumbs in her jeans. "Oh, really? You two must be having fun."

Crystal blushes. "We got caught in the hail and rain. We were soaked."

Payton smiles and nods.

"And I just realized all our wet clothes are still on the floor in three different rooms."

"Sounds like desperation stripping to me. How'd you escape the kidnapper?"

"How do you know about him?"

"It's all over Facebook. It's easy to find this town's pages."

"That was my father. He saved us from Dylan and her brothers, but he's a jerk. Just trying to find my mom who's evidently run away from him. Brian, that trooper who came to the school, came out here looking for Eugene the kidnapper. I wanted to press charges against Dylan, but Haley doesn't want to."

"Whoa, dude. There's a lot happening here. Do Dylan and her brothers know you're here?"

"I don't know. Haley and I were trying to figure out our options, but we're still not sure what to do." Crystal sits on the railroad tie between the play area and the driveway.

"Won't they come?"

"Probably."

"What would they want?"

"I don't know. Maybe to take Haley away from her lesbo girlfriend."

Payton sits down. "They can label you only if you let them. Would they care if you called them unwoke dickheads?"

"They'd laugh."

"There you go. That should tell you something."

"But calling them rapists is different. And that's what they're afraid of."

"Did they?"

"Dylan forced a blow job from Haley, and they all tried to rip off my shirt." Crystal remembers Sydney swinging behind her and stands. "Maybe we should talk somewhere else."

"No need. I don't hide things from Sydney. Isn't that right, Sis?"

Sydney kicks her feet high above their heads. "Why didn't you kick them in the balls? Or shoot them?"

"That a girl," says Payton as she stands.

Crystal scrunches her forehead and looks at Payton. "For one thing, I didn't have a gun at the time."

"That was your first mistake. At least carry Mace. Did any of your options include guns?"

"The first one. Haley liked it best." Crystal notices Haley waving from the front porch. "Speaking of."

Payton waves back. "I've got a couple of ideas we can talk about."

"Great." Crystal watches Haley walk toward them, still wearing sweatpants. "Am I a pervert for loving how she walks? I have to remind myself to breathe."

"Then we're both perverts. She is totally beautiful."

Haley stops in front of both girls. "Hey, Payton. I love your clothes. My God, you have muscles. How do you two girls stay so slender? Crystal, I tried forever to get your jeans on, but my ass is too big."

"And beautiful."

Haley hooks Crystal's arm. "So you say."

"I'll say it too," says Payton.

"Why, thank you."

"I think you're gorgeous," says Sydney, jumping off the swing and running to Haley. "What's your name?"

"Haley Carson. What's yours?"

"Sydney Beck Reed."

"Very nice to meet you, Sydney Beck Reed." They shake hands. "Why don't y'all come inside? I'm starving."

"Great idea," says Payton. "We are too. Just finished our last Cup Noodles an hour ago."

"We have plenty of food," says Crystal. "Summer has been in survivalist mode since March. We're good for months and that includes feeding JD."

Payton picks up her pack and unrolls the three paintings. "This belongs to you."

Haley holds her painting and shakes her head. "You two are amazing. And look at these."

Payton and Crystal hold their paintings.

"Where can we put these?" asks Haley.

"On the refrigerator, of course," says Crystal. "We have lots of magnets."

"Cool," says Haley.

"Race me to the door, Sis?" asks Payton as she picks up her shirt.

Sydney screams and takes off, Payton jogging behind.

Haley leans close to Crystal. "I picked up all our wet clothes and tossed them into the washer. Didn't want our guests to think we're slobs."

"*Our* guests?"

"I think you're stuck with me. Where else am I going to go? What Danny and Nick did today is the last straw."

"How will you get your stuff?"

"I'm not sure."

"Payton said she has some ideas. Did you find some underwear?"

"I'm going commando!" She pulls out the waist of her sweats. Crystal can't help looking. "I read somewhere it's healthier."

"I feel like I've run five miles since you've been here."

"See there. Running is good for you." Haley reaches for the door-knob. "Do you think Mac and Summer will let me stay?"

"Maybe they won't have a choice. But if they knew what your alternative is, I'm sure they'd let you stay. What about your parents?"

"I'm eighteen." She flashes her eyes and opens the door. "They can say whatever they want, but it won't matter."

Payton has opened several packages of food on the counter. "I'm making a snack plate. Lunchmeat, cheese, carrots, olives, crackers, and blue cheese dressing. Is that OK with you two?"

"OK with me. Thanks, Payton," says Crystal.

Sydney rolls turkey around a cheese stick then looks at Crystal with dreamy eyes. "I love these. Thank you, Crystal." She takes a bite, closes her eyes, and chews slowly.

Haley opens the fridge and grabs a Corona. "Sydney, what would you like to drink?" She peers through the shelves. "Coke, milk, orange juice, bottled tea, and water."

"Tea, please."

Haley twists off the cap and hands a tea to Sydney then uses the bottle opener for her beer.

Payton glances at Crystal then at Haley. "How's your stomach been, Haley? Any more puking since school?"

"I gagged at the house after Dylan did his thing." She drinks.

"I almost lost it watching you," says Crystal as she puts the paintings on the side of the fridge.

Payton carries the plate and a roll of paper towels to the table, and they all sit. Hands immediately reach. "Wait, please." The hands freeze. She tears off towels and hands them to each girl. "Let's try to keep the food off Crystal's table."

"Is now good?" asks Crystal, smiling, smoothing her towel on the oak that Mac stained years ago.

"Now is good," answers Payton as she stacks ham and cheese squares between two crackers. During the next several minutes, everyone concentrates on stuffing their mouths.

Crystal watches their faces as she eats and can't remember a time when she had this many visitors. How would this be different if Summer and Mac were home?

Mac would've fixed her Honda at the school, so Haley would've been on her own with Dylan. After Payton's call, he probably would've driven to the park with caulk to fix Payton's roof. And Eugene would still be watching from a distance. JD might still be at Gena's, forcing Crystal to eat a normal dinner with her grandparents, never talking about Haley.

She wants her grandparents home and well, but somehow she needs to feel more comfortable telling them her thoughts and feelings. How? She opened up this morning during the argument about her bra. Actually, she didn't. She was forced to. If Summer hadn't looked down her shirt, scrutinizing her behavior for something to fuss about, no discussion about wearing or not wearing bras would've happened, just like nothing had happened the previous two days when Summer hadn't noticed what wasn't under her shirt.

All this silence promotes secrecy, hiding, and trying to get away with something. Like Crystal is being trained to lie. Maybe Mac and Summer suspect JD has sex with Gena, but they won't say anything (either because they don't want to know or don't want to give him ideas). Their silence implies his behavior is wrong and signals that he needs to hide what he's doing.

And why isn't JD home? Because he knows he'll be scolded if he returns now. JD has no idea Mac and Summer are in Fairbanks. He's applauding his luck that no one has tried to call him. He's thinking he can get away with staying out all night and keeping his fingers crossed while he helps Gena pack.

Crystal learned at a young age to hide the uncomfortable topics, especially anything to do with sex, when they are often the most important topics to discuss.

Does Payton's mother know she's gay? Crystal will have to ask her that later.

Will Crystal ever tell her grandparents she's gay?

She hopes she still has the chance.

CHAPTER 13

*P*ayton stands in the living room while Haley and Crystal watch her from the sofa. Sydney is cleaning up in the kitchen. "Before you go into a danger zone, start the video and slip your phone into your pants with the camera is just peeking out. Do it every time. It will save your ass more than once. Even if someone sees your phone, they'll think that's just where you carry it."

"OK," says Haley, "but neither of us did that before we went into that house."

Payton gives her a sly smile. "But you did. All you need to do is convince Dylan and your brothers you recorded everything."

"How?" asks Crystal.

"First, are any of those guys experienced with Garageband?"

Haley laughs. "No way."

"OK." She removes her school computer from her pack. "Haley, find any videos of your brothers and Dylan talking. I need to know what they sound like."

"OK. Then what?"

"I'm going to record you two reenacting the scene in that house. Just portions of it. I'll play it from my motorhome speakers when they come by then convince them we have the whole video tape which we will post on Facebook before sending it to Brian."

Haley's face lights up. "You're a genius." She pulls out her phone and thumbs through screens.

"Crystal, tell me what you heard and when you heard it as you entered the house. I'm guessing you can remember sounds and dialogue very well."

Her breath hitches on the intake. "How did you know?"

"Because you can feel an animal's eyes on your skin and hear their hearts beating."

Crystal smiles. "The first thing I heard was Haley saying, 'Dylan. Stop!' I walked faster on the road then heard, 'I don't want to!'"

Payton types.

"Then I ran across the road toward the house. I got to the door and heard Nick and Danny laughing."

Payton stops. "Haley, do you have a video of your brothers laughing?"

"Yes," answers Haley. "What do I do with stuff when I find it?"

"Drop them in a new folder." Haley nods and thumbs her screen.

Payton looks at Crystal. "Next."

"I heard gagging and moaning as I walked through the front room. Then I saw Dylan humping Haley's face. Him grunting louder and Haley gagging really bad."

For the next several minutes, Crystal describes what happened until she heard Eugene's voice. Haley airdrops what she found to Payton's computer.

Payton stands. "Now, let's go outside."

The girls follow.

Payton positions Crystal by the motorhome and Haley by the swing set. "Start your video, Crystal, and stick your phone in your waist," directs Payton. "Haley, when I point, you say, 'Dylan. Stop!' When I point again, you yell, 'I don't want to.'"

Haley nods.

"Crystal, we need to hear the gravel sounds. Walk fast then run toward her. Got it?"

Crystal nods. Her mind swirls with the harsh memories. She wants revenge. "Payback time."

"You'll have it when you watch those boys squirm as they hear this. OK, walk." Payton points to Haley who says her line. Crystal walks quicker. Payton points. Haley screams and Crystal runs.

They move back inside and reenact Crystal walking toward a gagging Haley.

"What about Dylan's voice?" asks Haley.

"I'll add that in a minute. You wouldn't have a video of Dylan cumming, would you?"

Haley rolls her eyes. "I'm ashamed to say I do, but you'll be scarred for life." She spends a few seconds searching her files then airdrops it.

After several minutes of recording more of the girls' lines, Payton says, "Crystal, say Danny's line, 'Hello, Crystal. Come to join the party?' as best you can like him.

"OK," she says, "but my voice is different."

"I can adjust the pitch and tempo to sound close to his. I'm a genius with Garageband."

"Have you done this before?"

"Faked a video?"

Sydney stands in the doorway between the kitchen and the living room. "Yes, she has. When Harold tried to catch me in the house. Mom had passed out, and Payton was at work."

Haley frowns. *"Did* he catch you?"

"Yes, but I used my Mace and got away."

"I made a recording," says Payton, "just like I'm doing now. I told him I'd placed cameras in the house and had the whole scene on a flash drive. I played part of an audio clip for him and told him I'd take it to Child Protective Services the next morning unless he gave me the money to fix the motorhome and pay my deposit for the cabin. We left his house a few days later."

Haley walks to Sydney and gives her a hug. "I know how you felt, Sydney. I wish I'd had a big sister like Payton. Would've been nice to have leverage over my brothers."

"When I'm through," says Payton, "they'll be more than happy to get all your things and bring them back here. And Dylan should leave you alone, if he has any sense."

"Don't give him too much credit," says Haley, still holding Sydney. "Aren't they going to realize your audio is different than what actually happened?"

"Why would they remember what happened? The event meant more to you than to them. What they remember would be different than a real video anyway. The idea that we would make a fake audio will never occur to them."

"But won't they recognize the voices are different?" asks Haley.

"Whose? Yours and Crystal's are the same. We've got Dylan grunting and cumming. Even Nick and Danny laughing. Don't worry. This will work. Oh, by the way, how big is Dylan's dick?"

Haley tries to cover Sydney's ears, but she shakes her head in protest. "I know what a dick is."

"OK," says Haley. "Average?"

"It's a little on the small side," says Crystal. "I remember being surprised after he threw Haley to the ground."

Payton smiles. "Big guy with a little dick, which explains why he has to act tough all the time. I'll use that against him. OK, girls, I need some time to put this together."

Haley turns to Crystal. "Let's take Sydney to your room to show her all your pictures. Maybe you can teach her how you draw."

Haley moves down the hall with Crystal following as she wonders what Haley did with her last two drawings. When Sydney opens her door, Crystal sees the drawings on her mirror, their edges slipped between the glass and wood. Should she remove them?

Sydney walks slowly, enraptured by every photograph and drawing. "Whoa! This is cool. Did you do all these?"

"Yes," answers Crystal, moving over to stand in front of her drawing of Haley.

Sydney smiles and reaches for the drawing. "Can I?"

Crystal moves. "Sure."

Sydney touches the line of Haley's leg and follows it throughout the drawing. "Are you worried about me seeing Haley naked?"

"A little," answers Crystal.

"Don't be. I've seen lots of nudes."

"How did you know that was me?" asks Haley.

She points to the other drawing on the mirror. "Because this one is of you two kissing, the face on both is similar, and that can't be Crystal's butt." She giggles. "Sorry, Crystal."

"No problem."

"Does Payton paint many nudes?" asks Haley. "Is that why you seem comfortable looking at them?"

"Payton does, but mostly it's because I've seen all the body parts, for real and in pictures."

Haley and Crystal's eyes meet, amazed at how casually Sydney talks about these topics. "Why?" asks Haley.

Sydney takes a deep breath. "Two months ago, Payton noticed I wasn't talking, that I seemed nervous and scared. I finally told her I had seen Harold naked a few times. I wasn't sure if it was by accident or on purpose. I thought it might even be my fault." She pauses, tightens her jaw twice, then goes on. "Like he'd leave the bathroom door halfway open, I'd open it, and he'd be sitting on the toilet or drying himself after a shower."

"My God," says Haley. "My brothers would do that to me all the time then threaten they'd tell our parents I was being nasty and trying to look at them."

Sydney turns around and crosses her arms. "Payton told me that being shocked made me silent, which made Harold powerful. And once he felt that power, he'd try to use it. If I wasn't shocked by seeing a penis or hearing him and Mom having sex, then I'd keep control. Payton helped educate me."

"You are very lucky to have Payton as your sister," says Haley. "Did you try to talk to your mother about any of this?"

"No. Well, I tried a few months ago, but . . . she made me feel weird."

"What happened?"

"Harold would tease me when I took a long shower. He'd ask, 'What are you doing in there?' And then, 'Did I hear you singing, or were you making other noises?' And then he'd wink, like he thought I was keeping secrets. Then Mom asked me in private if I was doing anything nasty in the shower. I said no, but she kept asking, getting angry. She told me I hadn't put the showerhead back. And was I doing something I shouldn't with the showerhead? We have one with a hose that clips on the top. I finally told her yes, and she got mad. She told me not to do that, and I only had five minutes to shower from then on."

Crystal tightens her face and tries to keep from laughing. "Did that stop you?"

Sydney smiles. "No. Just made me never want to talk to her about anything private."

Sometimes Crystal would panic after leaving the bathroom because she thought she left the shower head hanging. Summer looked at her funny one day when Crystal ran back into the room ahead of her grandmother and raced to get to the showerhead only to find she'd already put it back. "Does Payton know about the shower?"

"Sure. We have one with a hose in the motorhome. Do you have one here?"

"Yes," says Haley, smiling. "It pulses. Really hard. Doesn't it, Crystal?"

Keeping a straight face, she says, "Yes, it's really good for getting the soap out of my hair."

"Oh, I hadn't thought to use it for that. Maybe next time." Haley flashes her eyes, causing Crystal to blush.

"You two seem embarrassed," says Sydney. "Payton says that embarrassment is a choice you don't have to make. You two need to learn to get over it and not be afraid to talk about things."

"That's very good advice, Sydney," says Haley. "You are wise beyond your years."

"Payton knows what you do in the shower," asks Crystal, "and she's OK with that?"

"She does it too. What's the big deal? Payton said she'd rather me explore my own body than let someone else do it."

Crystal shakes her head, realizing the trap that society forces on kids. Most everybody masturbates, but everyone feels guilty and never talks about it. "What's a pain is that you're made to feel ashamed no matter who does the exploring. Which is why everybody tries to keep them secret."

"I don't like having to keep secrets," says Sydney. "Do you?"

Crystal looks at herself in the mirror. "No, I don't." She remembers Summer complaining about Maya always keeping secrets from them, always lying. Mac said she started chasing boys at too young an age and couldn't stand being without a boyfriend. Eugene claimed her mother left him for another man, and he had to save her. Now she's left him again. For another man?

Would Sydney grow up the same way? Maybe not because she can pleasure herself and talk freely with her sister.

But if Sydney had stayed with her mom?

Sydney picks up a drawing from Crystal's desk. "How do you do this?"

"Want me to show you?"

Both Haley and Sydney say, "Yes."

Crystal moves to her desk, opens her pad, and grabs her marker. She shows them different ways to indicate an eye and how to add lashes. Also, how loops can turn into noses. Then she shows them one of her earliest drawings of two faces, each looking in opposite directions, with the chin of one person becoming the nose of the other.

"Oooh, I love this," says Sydney. "It's like one's kissing the other's neck."

"Or two people who can never see each other," says Haley.

Crystal traces the line with her finger. "They don't have to see each other because they are part of one person, inseparable, like lovers." She sighs and licks her lip. "I hope I can feel that way about somebody." She hands Sydney a marker and gives her a new paper. "You want to try?"

"Yes." Sydney fixes her eyes on Crystal's drawing, then holds the tip of her marker over a spot on the page. "I'm afraid I'll make a mistake."

"Learn to love your mistakes. That's what my teacher told me. Just move the pen and see where it goes. If yours is different than mine, that's OK because it's yours. I've got plenty of paper."

Crystal feels Haley resting her chin on her head. Haley hugs her from behind. "I want to feel that way about someone too. Like I don't have to keep doing something to be loved. I just am. And both of us would feel complete with each other."

Crystal hugs Haley's arms as they watch Sydney draw slowly at first, so torturously unsure. Then a little faster until she runs out of paper before she can finish the second pair of lips.

"I messed up," says Sydney, clutching her face with her hands.

Payton enters the room, and Haley turns her head. "Come look. Sydney is drawing."

"That's good, Sis," says Payton bending over her sister.

"No, it isn't."

"Pick up your pen for a sec."

Sydney does while Payton moves the first paper toward the window and adds a new paper underneath.

"Now finish the second face. We can tape it later."

Sydney makes the short curve of the chin and a long, sweeping curve for the neck. Crystal opens a drawer in her desk and takes out double-sided tape, pulls off a piece and gives it to her.

"Payton, can you lift the edge?" asks Sydney.

"Sure." She does and her sister applies the tape.

Payton holds up the drawing. "It's perfect."

"Where can I hang it?" asks Sydney.

"Anywhere you want," answers Crystal.

Sydney takes the paper out of the room. The other girls hear the front door opening then watch her disappear into the motorhome.

"Thanks," says Payton. "She loved doing that."

"She's fun to be with," says Haley.

Crystal stands. "She told us what's wrong with silence and embarrassment and how you two can talk about anything."

"Including shower heads," says Haley with a wink. "By the way, Crystal has a good one in her bathroom. You should try it out." Haley's phone dings. "Oh, surprise. A text from Dylan. *Where are you? Your parents are worried and want me to bring you home.* Imagine worried parents asking someone like Dylan to bring home their daughter. Kinda cringey. What should I say?"

Payton holds up her laptop. "Tell him you're at Crystal's and you're not going home. I've got everything ready. I just need to hook this up to my speakers. And get my gun."

"Gun?" asks Haley.

"Yup. My Smith & Wesson M&P Sport II with a 40 clip."

"You plan to use that?" asks Crystal, squishing her eyebrows together.

"Only to send a message those idiots can understand. And to suspend their disbelief. I don't want them scrutinizing the audio. Send your text then come out to the deck." She leaves the room.

Haley stares at the door. "She is so cool. Like nothing fazes her."

"Lucky for us."

Haley texts. *Dearest Dylan, fuck you. I'm at Crystal's. Where are you?* "I sent Dylan a poem." She shows Crystal the screen.

"He'll like that."

CHAPTER 14

*H*aley! A double rainbow!" Crystal stands on her deck, holding her phone to the pewter sky, accented with diaphanous white streaks. The lowering sun behind her intensifies the colors of the first rainbow. The mirror image rainbow above the first almost fades into the mottled clouds.

Haley presses her chest against Crystal's back. "Those are beautiful," says Haley. She holds her bottle of beer against Crystal's stomach. "Do you want some?"

"Sure." She takes the bottle and tilts it to her mouth, swallows, and hands it back to Haley. "A double rainbow means good luck."

"I thought a rainbow meant gay pride."

Crystal turns around. "Maybe two means lots of pride . . ." Her heart pounds. If Haley can say it then maybe she can shout it. "Or two lovers." Crystal places her hands around Haley's hips.

"Not yet, but soon." She kisses Crystal's eyes, nose, and lips. "Very soon."

Crystal squeezes tighter. "If you were my lover, I would feel like that rainbow, shining across the sky for everyone to see."

"Would you? You wouldn't be worried what others think?"

Crystal holds Haley's face. "Not if you're with me."

"I want to feel like that."

Payton approaches with her AR rifle held back on her shoulder. "Got your cameras ready? I hear a car coming."

Haley and Crystal start their videos and slip their cameras into their waists near their hips.

"Sydney's in the motorhome. She'll start the audio when I signal."

"You're not going to shoot anyone, are you Payton?" asks Haley.

"No people. Just some wood scraps I set up near the shed."

"And you're doing the talking?" asks Crystal, sweat gathering in her armpits.

"I'll start off. You two jump in whenever you want to. Relax, girls. We got this." She steps closer, reaches for Crystal's shoulder, and leans her head between theirs.

Crystal and Haley touch their foreheads to Payton.

"Just have fun and smile," says Payton. "They hate it when girls laugh at them."

The deep rumbling of a supercharged Mustang echoes in Crystal's chest as she sees a car move into the driveway from D Street. Payton turns around and walks casually to the center of the parking area. As soon as the Mustang moves within fifty feet of her, Payton levels her gun at ten o'clock to the car's twelve, and fires three quick shots, knocking small birch rounds into the trees.

The car's tires bite the gravel and skid to a stop. All three boys jump out, glaring at her.

"Hey, freak!" yells Dylan. "It's against the law to shoot within the city limits."

Payton fires once more. Danny and Nick flinch. Dylan stands his ground, glowering. "Then call the trooper. I've got Brian's card in my pocket if you need the number. Crystal and Haley are recording everything. When he shows up we can give him the video."

The girls on the deck smile and wave.

"Along with the video of your assault on Haley and Crystal earlier today."

Payton fires again.

Dylan folds his arms. "No assault and no video."

Payton lays the gun back on her shoulder. "Really? Haley said, 'I don't want to,' as in she didn't want her hands tied while you shoved your little dick into her mouth."

Dylan barks and harrumphs. "It's not little."

"The video doesn't lie, Dylan. We can put a frame up on Instagram with a vote panel, if you want. Big? Or little? Girls, what do you think the vote will be?"

Crystal sticks out her thumb and points it down with a smile. "Little."

Haley points one thumb down. "Below average boner." Her other thumb drops lower. "Tiny otherwise."

Dylan glares at Haley.

Payton fires another shot, causing all three boys to jump. "Any jury watching this video would declare it sexual assault and attempted rape. But you know what's really weird? The sound is much more dramatic." She holds her thumb up, signaling Sydney. "Take a listen."

Speakers in the motorhome pump out a bass-enhanced audio.

A chair is knocked over. Feet scuffle on the floor. "Dylan. Stop!" yells Haley. Steps quicken on gravel.

More banging. "I don't want to!"

Running across gravel. Nick and Danny laugh.

Nick and Danny look at each other with mouths gaping. Dylan stares straight ahead.

Haley gags while Dylan moans. Then he grunts as his pelvis slaps against Haley's face. More gagging.

Crystal yells, "Hey!"

Dylan's grunts get louder just before Danny says, "Hello, Crystal. Come to join the party?" Before Danny finishes his line, Dylan's orgasm drowns him out. Haley is shoved to the floor.

Payton holds up her thumb. The sound stops.

All three boys stare at the horizon breathing heavily.

"But here's my favorite part," says Payton. She gives the signal. If anything, the sound is louder, thumping inside Crystal's chest.

All three boys laugh. Crystal snarls and screams. Nick grunts as an elbow slams his gut. He yelps when Crystal's foot stomps his. Skin slaps as laughter and grunts increase in volume, punctuated by Haley's scream, "Leave her alone!"

A man's voice yells, "Anyone here?"

Crystal yells, "Yes. Back here!"

Payton gives the signal, and the sound stops.

"I'm thinking this will get you five to ten," says Payton. "What do you think, girls?"

"At least!" yells Haley. "The whole town will see this video, Dylan. What will everyone think of your kidnapping story then?"

"I'm going to need years of therapy," says Crystal. "You guys will be paying damages to me your whole life."

Payton fires a shot then moves closer to the car. "This is what you'll do now. Get back in your car, get all of Haley's clothes, makeup, everything that's hers and bring it back here, packed in a suitcase or crates. Neatly. If you're not back here within forty-five minutes, we're calling Brian and we're posting the video on Facebook for everyone to see."

"And my stash of weed, Nick," yells Haley. "With nothing missing."

"You're going to live with these dykes?" barks Dylan, wrinkling his nose against his pinched eyebrows.

"As opposed to living with my invisible parents and lying brothers who let you assault me?"

Dylan's face reddens with splotches. "Where's the video of you begging me for an oxy? You said you'd let me do anything for one."

Heat flashes through Crystal's body. "And, of course, the only thing you could think to do was ram your dick into her throat. Why don't you just buy a sex doll, Dylan? Then you can screw it all you want, even choke and slap it."

A vein engorges on Dylan's forehead. "Shut up, queer!"

Crystal's nails dig into her palms. "If queer and dyke mean the opposite of you, then I'll gladly be both. Who gave you the right to judge any of us? All you want to do is screw Haley. I want to make love to her." She looks back at Haley, standing wide-eyed on the deck. "If she'll have me."

Haley gazes at Crystal, breathing quickly. Slowly her arms reach out, and Crystal runs to embrace her.

Payton fires a shot. "What's it going to be fellas? Do we post the video, or not?"

"OK," says Nick. "If we do what you say, what happens to the video?"

"Nothing," answers Payton. "We'll keep it in case you bother us again, either in person or online. We'd better not see anything criticizing Crystal or Haley on any platform. Got that, Dylan? You don't raise our dyke flag. We raise our own. Nick, you're the only one allowed to come back here with Haley's stuff. If we see anyone else, the video is uploaded. After Nick comes back and leaves, you three can't come here without our permission. Got that?" Payton signals Sydney and the sound sequence starts from the top.

The three boys curse and grind their jaws, but they all climb into the car. Nick turns around and spins his tires, leaving Crystal's house behind.

"Just hold your positions, girls," says Payton. "Let them leave before we react."

After another minute, the dust cloud dissipates from the driveway, leaving no sign of the Mustang. Payton signals Sydney, the sound stops, and turns around. "I think they believed us."

Haley sobs on Crystal's shoulder.

Crystal rubs Haley's back. "It's OK, Haley. They're gone."

Payton jogs to the deck. "What's wrong?"

Haley tries to catch her breath while Crystal gently pushes her hair away from her face. "What Dylan said is true. I wanted him to give me an oxy. He said, 'What would you do for one?' I told him he owed me, that if his apology meant anything he should give it to me. He threw a chair against the wall and said he was leaving. That's when I said, 'Dylan, don't.' Then I told him he could . . . fuck my face."

"But you didn't want your hands tied?" asks Crystal.

"No. He was angry, and I knew . . . he would hurt me. But he wouldn't give me the pill unless I agreed." She covers her face. "You shouldn't want to be with me. I'm as worthless as my mother."

Crystal pulls Haley to her chest. "You are amazing, kind, sweet, loving . . ."

Payton wraps her arms around both girls. "You are both brave . . ."

"I don't deserve you two. I deserve Dylan."

"You deserve this." Crystal kisses her lips.

"We're your friends," says Payton, kissing her forehead. "For as long as you'll have us."

Haley clutches them both, kissing each of their cheeks, and sheds new tears.

"What's going on?" yells Sydney as she runs from the motorhome to the girls. "Why is Haley crying?"

Crystal and Payton move slightly, allowing the little girl to hug Haley's waist.

"Because I was trying to keep a secret." Haley lifts Sydney up for a full hug, the girl's legs wrapping around. "But you taught me how bad that is."

"Well, Payton taught me."

"Yes, your sister is a genius." Haley touches Payton's shoulder. "That soundtrack is brilliant."

"And you're such a badass with that gun," says Crystal. "When'd you learn to shoot?"

"I was also on the rifle team in school." Payton pulls out her phone. "One of you air drop the video of their visit to me. I'll cut the last few minutes out and have it ready to upload if we have to."

Crystal holds her phone and starts the process. "That's right. We said nothing about uploading this video."

"If they call our bluff," says Payton, "we have an actual video to show everyone."

All three phones ding with a message from the school district. Haley sets Sydney down. *Remote instruction will begin tomorrow for all grades and follow the same schedule used last week. Check-in for your first period is at 8:30. All staff and students attending Clear School today were potentially exposed to Covid-19. Everyone should quarantine for fourteen days. Free Covid testing will be available in the school gym on Saturday from 12:00 – 3:00.*

Even though Crystal knew this was coming, dread washes over her as she reads. "This is because of me and JD. We should've stayed home today."

"It wouldn't have mattered," says Payton. "You both were exposed days ago when you went to school. Today wouldn't have changed anything."

Crystal's voice shakes. "Will . . . you drive to another school?"

"How can I? I'm supposed to quarantine. No other school will let us enroll."

Crystal's shoulders tighten. "Would you want to leave?"

"No, Sydney and I'd like to stay here, if you don't mind."

"We'd love you both to stay," says Haley.

"Do you have room?" asks Payton. "The roof leaked around the air conditioner and soaked our bed."

"Yes," replies Crystal. "You two can stay in JD's room. I'll text him now." *Are u staying w Gena tonite?*

JD texts back. *Yes. I'm helping pack. See you AM.*

No school tomorrow. Back to online. Ugh!

Doesnt matter.

??

Will tell u AM.

Crystal decides she won't press him now. She'll give him time to figure out what he wants to say. She knows he'll cry when he tells her he's leaving, and he hates crying. "Bring in your wet sheets," Crystal tells Payton. "I'll put JD's sheets in the washer. You two don't want to go near them until they're clean."

"Ewww!" shouts Sydney as Payton pulls her toward their motorhome.

Crystal hears the inside phone ring and immediately thinks about Eugene. He must've heard the shots and maybe seen the Mustang. What could he want? "I'll get the phone."

"I'll move our clothes to the dryer," says Haley.

They both run into the house.

CHAPTER 15

*C*rystal watches the phone ring a fifth time before taking a deep breath then answering with a lifeless, "Hello."

"I was just about to zip over there and look for bodies," says Eugene with extreme urgency. "Is everyone all right?"

"Why wouldn't we be?" Why does he always sound fake to her?

"I heard a dozen shots then saw those boys tear down D Street."

"A friend of mine shot some targets. Nothing to worry about. And, no, Maya is not here." Crystal hears the dryer door being shut and the cycle start. "Where are you hiding your truck?"

Haley walks into the kitchen and mouths, "Eugene?"

Crystal nods.

"I'm just keeping an eye out for my daughter's safety since Mac and Summer aren't there."

Cold settles into Crystal's chest. Is he bluffing, or does he know? "They went to town and will be back later tonight."

"You sure about that? The school's shutting down because of exposure to Covid. Lots of speculation on Facebook about who's sick. A couple of comments mentioned Mac by name."

"That should make you very happy. Look, I'm real busy . . ." Her lips press into a white slash.

"Don't hang up, Crystal. Hear me out. I could park in your driveway tonight and make sure those boys don't come back."

She rubs her brow to push away a headache. "Stop faking concern, Eugene. The only reason you'd want to park outside is to intercept Maya. And right now I'm rooting for her to sneak in without your knowledge. I'll bet she has some great stories to tell."

Eugene barks, "Look! I saved you and your friend today. I didn't have to do that."

Her body temperature jolts upward. "You didn't have to screw with my Honda, either. If I see your truck anywhere near my house, I'll call the troopers. We have plenty of guns here and people to shoot them."

"Is that a threat?"

"That's a promise!" She slams the phone into the body and shakes her head. "Why do I have to deal with him today? On top of everything else." She flops into a nearby chair and stares out the window.

Haley goes to the table and unzips Crystal's pack. "Is your thermos in here? I think we could both use a shot." She pulls out the bottle and flips up the spigot. "Here."

Crystal takes a sip. "Why is my mother coming here? Or is there some other reason why Eugene showed up?" She takes another sip and gives the bottle to Haley.

"Maybe your mom has had enough of Eugene and wants to come home." She lifts the bottle to her mouth and lets the final drops splash onto her tongue. "Is there more?"

"Yeah. Cabinet to the left of the dishwasher."

Haley gets up and finds the whiskey. "Or maybe she wants Eugene to think she's coming here when she's actually hooking up with another man somewhere else." She fills two small glasses with ice and a little water before pouring a shot of whiskey into each.

"OK," says Crystal, taking a glass from Haley. "But she'd still have to convince Eugene she wants to go home. If there's a possibility of running off with another guy, then why involve her parents?" She drinks.

"Maybe there is no other guy. Maybe a girl." Haley winks at Crystal as she raises her glass. "Wouldn't that be ironic?"

"Yeah, but at least I could understand that." She squeezes the glass until her knuckles turn white. "According to my grandparents, Maya has been with one loser man after another. Seems to me after all of them plus Eugene, she'd try something different."

"Why do you call your mom Maya? And why Mac and Summer? I've always wondered that."

Crystal stirs the ice with her finger. "Because Summer didn't like being called Grandma. It made her seem old, she said. Mac didn't care one way or the other, but if we called him Grandpa, she'd still feel old. So JD and I used their names." She sucks her finger. "Why should I call Maya mom? Whenever Mac and Summer would talk about her, they always used her name. Same with Eugene. You think I'm being rude calling that asshole Eugene instead of Daddy?"

"No." She takes a drink.

"What do you call your father?"

Haley blows out a breath. "We hardly ever talk, but when we do, I call him Daddy."

"Why don't you talk?"

"Because he caught me screwing Tommy in 7th grade. We were totally naked in my bedroom. Daddy walked in and just stared at me, totally disappointed. He said, 'I've raised a slut.' Then he told us both to get dressed and for Tommy to leave. He didn't speak to me for almost a year after that until he saw me with another boy at the carnival. Just holding hands. Later, he asked, 'Is that who you're screwing now?' He knew how Nick and Danny treated me, but he never said anything to them. They have a slut for a sister, after all. Who could blame them?" She finishes her drink. "I've always been a disappointment."

Crystal feels so weighted, so drained. "That sucks."

Her nostrils flare. "Yes, it does. Even though I make all As and always get voted most this and most that, I'm a slut and will always be a slut. Sometimes I say to myself, if he's going to think the worst of me, I might as well have some fun. Why deny myself when everyone thinks I'm doing it anyway?" She stares at her glass, rubbing her finger around the edge.

"What's he going to think of you staying over here?"

"And being a lesbian? Ha, that will be much worse, I'm sure." Her chin quivers. She sniffs and tries to hide wiping an eye. "Not just for him. For everyone." A bitter laugh escapes her throat. "I could stay with Dylan, and everyone would say, 'No problem.' But if I'm caught with you, no matter how sweet you are to me, they'll call me a dyke and much worse. Think I'll get another drink." She hurries to the counter, pours more whiskey into her glass then turns around. "Will the names bother you? When you talk to Summer again, will you feel comfortable telling her I'm sleeping with you? Or if Maya shows up, will you tell her?"

Crystal stands and walks to Haley. "I said if you were my lover, I'd shine like that rainbow for everyone to see."

Haley's face flushes. "Are you sure? After everything you know about me?"

"I'm sure." She touches Haley's face.

"When do we raise our dyke flag?"

Payton and Sydney struggle through the mudroom with armloads of wet bedding and clothes.

"Ask Payton."

Payton drops her pile on the floor. "Ask me what?"

Haley helps Sydney carry her load through the kitchen toward the utility room.

"How did you come out and deal with the consequences?" asks Crystal.

"Not very well, the first time. My parents forced me to talk with a psychiatrist."

"How did that go?"

"All the family shit hit the fan—my parents' drug use, their constant fighting, and on and on. They saw my sexual preference as their fault and that family therapy would fix everything. I was forced to attend sessions with them for a year. After that they realized I was still gay, and they were still unhappily married."

Sydney and Haley return to the kitchen.

"What happened then?" Crystal asks.

"Dad lost his job and his health insurance, so no more therapy. I basically closeted myself and hid my feelings. Then Dad died from an 'accidental' drug overdose and at one point Mom blamed me." She pushes her fingers through her hair. "I realized I was a fool for caring what everyone else thought. I can't control their minds, so I shouldn't try." Payton sighs and swallows. "At least half of my straight friends have major family problems, several are depressed, and lots are bullies or targets of bullies. Their sexuality doesn't cause or prevent anything. Yet many objected when I told them I didn't want to be in their straight club anymore."

"Did they bully you?"

She nods her head. "They tried, but I wasn't the only dyke in that school. When you hide who you are, it's hard to make friends. When you're honest and open, you find others like you. How long have you been hiding, Crystal? And you'd still be alone if you hadn't stood up for Haley this morning or if I had driven to Healy instead of stopping here. But now you have us both."

"And me," says Sydney.

Payton smiles. "Are you a lesbian, little Sis?"

"I don't know yet, but I'll fight like hell to protect all of you."

Payton hugs her. "I know you will." She kisses her forehead. "And I'll do the same for you."

"We all will," says Haley, holding Sydney's shoulders. "I truly like your sister, Payton. I wish I could be her and start all over."

Crystal sits. "Would you have told me you're gay if you hadn't seen Haley and me . . . uh when we were in the classroom . . . doing, you know . . ." She looks at Haley one brow cocked. "How would you describe what we were doing in McHenry's room, Haley?"

Haley's eyes glow with a twinkle of mischief. "I wanted to get inside your pants. I could smell you dripping. I almost swooned."

Sydney covers her face. "Eww!"

Crystal starts to crawl under the table but laughs instead.

Haley wrinkles her nose. "I'm obsessed with aromas. Good ones, sexy ones. Not armpits or toes. Did you know there's a new perfume made to smell like vagina? Mmm."

Crystal tightens her cheeks to keep from laughing. "My original question, Payton, was, would you have told me you're gay if you hadn't seen us?"

"No, but soon after," says Payton. "You look differently at girls than at guys, especially Haley. It's very obvious."

Crystal's ears redden. "To you, maybe."

"And to me," says Haley, placing her hands on the chair arms and bending her face slowly toward Crystal. "I feel your look. Even when I can't see your eyes. I've got burn marks on my butt." Haley wets her top lip.

Crystal feels dizzy. "I didn't see any."

"It's like sunbathing. The burn comes later." Haley watches Crystal swallow rapidly as their eyes lock. "No boy has ever looked at me like you do. You are so obvious."

Crystal sighs. "I can't help it."

"Good." Haley turns around and walks across the room, pulling Crystal's gaze with her.

Sydney clears her throat. "My eyes and ears are burning. Just so you know."

Crystal shakes her head to break the spell. "Payton, why did you tell me you're gay? Were you hitting on me?"

"A little, but mainly to find an ally and to give you one."

Crystal nods. "You were raising your dyke flag."

"On my terms. You and Haley have to learn when to raise yours. You don't have to slap people in the face with it. But you have to raise it when you can't be yourself otherwise."

How would Crystal act differently if everyone knew her secret, and she didn't care? Like she's acting now. Free, without worry. Not like at school or with Summer and Mac. Even JD.

Sydney reaches for part of the bedding pile at Payton's feet. "C'mon, Payton, carry some of this."

They both pick up the rest of the pile and take it out of the kitchen.

"I'll get JD's sheets." Crystal and Haley walk down the hall and open a door opposite Crystal's room. JD's walls are bare except for a few photos of Gena, ptarmigan tail feathers, and some painted burnt wood picture plaques Mac taught him to make.

Crystal strips the sheets from his bed and finds several yellowish stains in the middle of his mattress protector.

Haley chuckles. "Does Gena spend the night?"

Crystal clears her throat, trying to get her voice to work. "Not physically, but evidently in his dreams."

"He must dream a lot," Haley laughs.

Crystal removes the cover while Haley gathers the pillowcases. They throw them in the washer and find Payton and her sister looking through the freezer.

Payton pulls out a small box. "Hey, Sis, do you want a Reese's Klondike bar?"

"Yum!"

Payton holds out the box to Crystal and Haley, who grabs a treat while Crystal shakes her head. "JD's always had the sweet tooth. Not me."

Crystal's phone rings. She looks at the screen, and her heart skips a beat. "It's Summer." She accepts the call. "How's Mac doing?"

"They've put him on a ventilator."

Crystal's mouth slackens as she raises her eyes to the other girls.

"What's wrong?" whispers Haley.

"Who is that?" asks Summer.

"Haley. She's staying with me."

"Because of Dylan?"

"Yeah. I'm keeping her safe."

"Does Holly know she's there?"

"Who?"

"Haley's mother."

"Do you know her?"

"I've lived in Clear for forty years," says Summer. "Certainly I know her. Does Holly know?"

Crystal glances at Haley. "Not yet. Tell me about Mac."

"He can't breathe on his own. I didn't know whether to give permission or not. Neither of us wants to be kept alive by a machine, but this is different."

"Will . . . will he live?"

"They don't know."

Crystal pulls her hair and closes her eyes. "He has to get better." Her chest feels so heavy, she has to bend over.

Payton and Haley grab her arms and lead her to a chair. Payton switches the sound to speaker and sets the phone on the table.

Crystal tries to calm her breathing. "What about you?"

"I'm on oxygen and checked into a room. I tried to call JD, but he won't answer."

"He's at Gena's helping them pack."

"But why wouldn't he answer?"

"He doesn't know you and Mac are in Fairbanks. He's worried you'll tell him to come home. He wants to stay with Gena." Crystal listens to Summer's raspy breathing. "I'll text him in a few minutes."

She sighs slowly, almost whimpering. "He wants to go with Lena to the village, doesn't he?"

"He loves Gena. I'm sure he's torn up about having to choose between us and her. He said he'd come by tomorrow morning."

Summer coughs out a cry. "I don't think I can stand him moving away from us. Or Mac. He might die!" She weeps.

Crystal pushes her fists into her eyes. "He's still a strong man. He'll fight this."

"Right now he doesn't even know he's alive."

"Then someone has to talk to him, tell him he can see Maya."

"What?" Summer blurts. "How do you know?"

"Because Eugene is in town looking for her."

"You saw him? She's alive?"

"Yeah, it's a long story, but he's looking for Maya. She's run away from him, and he thinks she's coming here."

Summer chokes, "My God! My daughter is alive," before collapsing into a spasm of hacking and crying.

Payton grabs a napkin from the table and wipes Crystal's eyes. "You and Mac both need to come home and see her. She's expecting to see all of us."

Payton and Haley hold Crystal's hands.

"Where is Eugene now?"

"Somewhere in town, hiding in a camper truck."

"Are you safe? You should call JD and tell him to come home."

"I'm safe. Payton has a 40 clip AR, and her little sister will fight like hell to protect us." Crystal nods at Sydney, who smiles back at her.

"Who's Payton?"

"A new girl who entered school today with her sister. Their motorhome is parked in our driveway. All four of us stood up to Dylan and Haley's brothers. No man is going to mess with us."

"How long are they staying with you?"

Crystal smiles at the three girls standing in front of her. "I don't want them to go." The idea that any of her friends might leave slams into her chest. She realizes she could easily be talking to Summer from an empty house, worried she won't see either of her grandparents again and her brother only once more.

But she's not alone. She feels more comfort in the presence of these girls than she's ever felt before. She stands and holds out her arms. Payton and Haley slip in on each side while Sydney hugs her waist. "They're welcome to stay with me as long as they want. I love them."

Crystal kisses Sydney's head, then touches Payton's surprised lips, then devours Haley's open mouth. Soon, Crystal tastes Haley's tears until she kisses her cheeks dry.

"Crystal?" Summer asks urgently. "What's going on? Are you there?"

Crystal picks up her phone from the table. She should lie and say she had to wipe her eyes, but she needs to tell her grandmother the truth. She might not have another chance to be open and honest with her. "I'm sorry, Summer. I was kissing Haley." Crystal watches Haley's eyes shimmer. "I know you won't understand now, but when you get home, you *and* Mac, we'll have a good talk. Haley's my girlfriend, and she's sleeping with me tonight. I'll send you pictures of everyone in a few minutes."

Crystal hears nothing but slow breathing through the phone for at least twenty seconds.

Calmly, with just a hint of resignation, Summer asks, "Crystal, are you sure?"

"Yeah. Totally sure. I'm gay and I'm raising my dyke flag." Payton nods and smiles.

"What's a dyke flag? Is that what you called it?"

"Don't worry about that now. It's just an expression. Are you OK?" Summer seemed angrier this morning about Crystal not wearing a bra. She thought Summer would say more than, "Are you sure?"

"I'm OK, Crystal. I just wish we'd been able . . . to talk about this before now."

"We'll have plenty of time to talk when you get home. You make sure a nurse gets the message to Mac about Maya. If my mother shows up, I'll call you no matter when it happens. And as soon as we hang up, I'm calling JD. I want you two home with me, Summer. Got that?"

"Yes, Dear. You'll be receiving an email tomorrow with documents you need to sign."

"What are they?"

"Financial arrangements . . . in case . . . just in case."

A surge of panic rushes up Crystal's neck. "Am I supposed to read them?"

"You can use the text to speech, and you don't have to read it. They told me all you'd have to do is click in boxes that are marked for you."

"OK."

"Please stay safe tonight. I love you."

"I love you too." The call disconnects. Crystal fights to keep the image of Summer in her mind, but it blurs to a swirl of fading colors.

Crystal pockets her phone. "She took that better than I expected."

Haley hugs her. "I've never heard my mother mention Summer. I didn't know they knew each other."

They all hear the Mustang before watching it pull into the driveway.

Nick jumps out the door of his car. "Haley, I got your stuff!"

CHAPTER 16

*I*s anyone else in the car?" asks Haley.

Payton moves closer to the window. "Not unless some-one's in the trunk. Sydney, stay in the house. You can bring the rifle if we need it."

Haley opens the door, followed by Crystal and Payton. "Well, I'm sure you enjoyed going through all my underwear, Nick. Did you take pictures?"

"Cut the crap, Haley," says Nick. He bends his seat forward and pulls out a suitcase and two boxes. He finds two more crates in the trunk. "I didn't bring your photos and certificates on the wall. Mom came back just after I loaded the last crate in the trunk."

"Came back? From where? She hardly leaves the house."

"We don't know. She went somewhere yesterday too." He laughs. "Maybe she found a boyfriend. Are you going to text her?"

"I haven't decided," says Haley. "Maybe she won't notice. Where's my stash?"

Nick unzips a compartment on the suitcase and pulls a baggie about halfway out. "Right here. All of it." He shoves the bag back. His eyes lock onto Payton. "Where'd you come from?"

Payton's gray eyes look especially cold. "Does it matter? I'm here

146

now."

He shakes his head with a slight grin. "Such a tough girl."

"When I need to be. Otherwise, I'm just a pussy."

Haley blurts out a laugh.

Payton tightens her eyes. "You say 'tough girl' like it's an oxymoron. Like if I called you a 'smart guy.'"

Haley laughs again. Crystal doesn't get the joke, but senses Payton is yanking his chain.

Nick sticks his chin out and crosses his arms. "I have no idea what you're talking about."

Payton smiles. "That's exactly my point."

Nick looks hard at her like he's trying to decide whether he should be mad or not. "Oh, yeah," says Nick. "Almost forgot something." He reaches back into his car, pulls a red foil pouch off his dash, and holds it up to Haley. "I found these in the back of one of your drawers."

Haley's face turns red.

Nick shows her the top of the package and sneers. "I noticed it was open. Supposed to be twenty strips, but there's only nineteen. I'm wondering if it was positive or negative."

"Negative, you dipshit." She grabs the pouch.

Crystal's neck cramps as her mind replays Haley puking at school and Payton's warning about giving her whiskey. Did Haley suspect she was pregnant?

Nick puffs out his chest. "I don't know. You've been real moody lately. Like all of a sudden you want to be with Twig 2.0."

"Her name is Crystal."

Nick sneers. "Whatever."

Haley crosses her arms. "Like I'd have to be *moody* to dump such a hunk as Dylan? How about conscious?"

"OK," says Nick. "Dylan can be an ass, but you can have any guy in town, and you've been with most of them. Now you want to be with Crystal? That makes no sense."

"She was the first person I ever kissed." Haley holds Crystal. "I should have stayed with her."

"Yeah, then you wouldn't need to buy a package of test strips. Are you pregnant?"

Crystal's head jerks toward Haley.

Haley throws her hands up. "No! You don't care about me anyway. Why does my relationship with Crystal bother you?"

Nick bites his lip. "Two girls kissing? It's not right."

"But it's right to treat girls like they're nothing more than boobs and a pussy?"

He rolls his eyes. "Which you've been flaunting for years."

Payton slaps the car hood. "Because that's what she was taught all her male-centric life—girls are nothing without their looks."

"You better not have dented my car." Nick squats and scrutinizes the metal.

Payton leans over and places both hands on the fender. "Too late. Your male ego has already been damaged. Nick Carson's sister is a dyke. What will everyone say? Time to climb into your machomobile and rumble on home, smart guy."

Nick glares at Payton and curls his upper lip back in disgust.

Payton's doesn't flinch. "Remember, we have the video. And keep the test strips to yourself."

Nick shakes his head, throws one last glare at Haley, then jumps into his car. With a lurch in reverse and a twist of the wheel, he spins his car ninety degrees, then leaves in a cloud of dust.

Haley covers her face and cries as Crystal walks her back to the door. She hears Payton pick up a box and wheel the suitcase across the driveway. Sydney bursts outside and grunts trying to lift a crate.

Inside the kitchen, Crystal helps Haley into a chair while she pours a glass of water. She offers it to Haley.

"Can I have . . ."

"No. Drink this."

Payton and Sydney drop their loads and go outside for the rest.

Crystal puts the glass on the table then sits in another chair. "Are you taking birth control pills?"

"I was until six weeks ago. I kept getting yeast infections, so I stopped. I'm going to get an IUD."

"When did you use the first strip?"

"About four weeks ago. It was negative. I swear."

Crystal takes the pouch from Haley and looks for directions. She unfolds a paper and tries to read. "Any ur . . .urine spec . . . speci . . ." She holds the paper closer.

"Specimen," says Haley.

". . . the first morning urine . . . speci . . .men is opti . . . opti . . . Fuck!" Crystal rubs her eyes and clenches her jaw. She hates how shitty she is at reading. "Can you read this? Please?"

Haley takes the paper. "It says I'm supposed to use my first pee in the morning and wait exactly five minutes."

"And you did that?"

"Yes."

"Are you supposed to test again?"

"I'll do it tomorrow morning."

Crystal falls to her knees and holds Haley's legs. "I'll help you. All of us will help you. Whether you are or aren't, we'll be with you and love you no matter what. But you cannot drink any more alcohol. That's why JD is so . . . so disabled." Tears pour out of her eyes. "Because Maya drank whiskey all the time. Please. Promise me you won't drink any more. Please."

Haley kneels on the floor and hugs Crystal. "I won't. I promise. But I already have, Crystal." Haley's chest heaves. "I'm sorry."

Payton and Sydney enter the kitchen and carefully set their boxes on the floor.

"What's done is done," says Crystal. "But until you do your test tomorrow, no more. OK?"

"OK."

The girls hold each other's wet faces.

"Will you still . . ." blubbers Haley.

"Yes." Crystal kisses her cheeks. "Yes." She kisses her nose. "I'm pretty stubborn." She kisses Haley's lips.

Payton catches Crystal's eye. "Do you want these in your room?"

"Yes. Please stack them in the corner."

Sydney and Payton move Haley's things down the hall.

The dryer buzzes. Both girls stand, trying to catch their breath, wiping their faces.

"I'll check the clothes and sheets," says Haley.

"OK. I need to call JD."

Haley walks out of the kitchen. Crystal pulls out her phone and moves through the living room. Holding the phone to her ear, she listens to the rings.

Finally, JD answers and asks his standard question that somehow always sounds sincere. He wants to know how others are doing before he burdens them with his problems. "How's your day been going?"

"Like total shit. I need to tell you a few things. Can you talk?"

"Sure. What's up?"

Crystal walks outside onto the deck. "When I went home for lunch, Eugene called the house."

"Eugene?"

"Yeah. Eugene, our supposedly dead father. He told Mac he wanted to see us, but Mac threatened to shoot him. Now Eugene's here in town, trying to find Maya. Our mother is alive, JD. She didn't die in a car wreck. She's trying to come home and get away from that asshole, but I don't know why."

"Wow. Do Mac and Summer know?"

"I told Summer. This is the bad news, JD. Are you ready?"

His voice wavers. "I don't know."

"Mac is on a ventilator at the hospital. He can't breathe on his own. Summer is real worried he might die."

Crystal waits for JD to say something, but all she hears is muffled squeaks and whimpers. After another ten seconds, she hears him sniff and clear his throat.

"JD?"

She hears him inhale in spasms and exhale in stifled sobs.

The words barely escape JD's mouth, "Can we see him?"

Crystal can't remember the last time he cried. "They won't let us in."

"Can we Facetime?"

"He's not conscious. We just have to wait."

"I don't have time to wait," he pleads. "I'm flying out Friday morning. We're going to Fairbanks tomorrow to stay with Lena's friend."

"You're going with Gena to the village?"

"Yes. Can I see Summer?"

"I don't think so. She's in the hospital on oxygen. But I'm sure you can Facetime tomorrow." Crystal hears him trying to clear his throat. "When were you going to tell them about leaving?"

"I was scared to. Gena didn't want to stay here and be away from her family when she had . . . had . . ."

"The baby?"

"How did you know?"

"I talked to Lena today." She tries to sound positive. "You're going to be a father."

He sighs. "I know. That's real scary."

"You'll be a great daddy. JD, you need to make sure Gena doesn't drink or smoke or anything like that."

"We already talked about that. Neither of us is doing anything. We both want our kid to be born healthy. Not like me."

"Or me. I hope I can ask Maya what happened to us. And why. Would you want to see her?"

"Her more than him."

"I know she's around somewhere, or Eugene wouldn't be hiding near our driveway."

JD snorts. "There's lots of ways to get to our house besides down the driveway. Maya would know that. She lived here longer than we have."

"You're right. She'd probably come down the trail behind the wood-shed." The same way she took Haley to her house. Maybe she should go back down that way tomorrow and look around.

His voice quivers as he starts to speak. "Crystal . . ." He swallows and sucks in a shaky breath. "Crystal, do you think Mac's going to die?"

"I don't know." She rubs her neck and shoulder, trying to relieve the building tension. "I asked Summer to make sure someone tells him his daughter is alive. If he knows that, there's no way he's going to leave without seeing her."

JD sniffs. "Mac taught me to hunt and shoot and fix things. Almost everything I know."

"You'll have to do the same for your baby. You and Gena."

"Yeah. We will."

Crystal hears his phone vibrate.

"Hey," says JD. "Gena's calling me. We still have lots to pack. I'll see you tomorrow."

Tears fill her eyes. "OK. I love you, JD. I know I don't tell you that enough. But I do."

"I love you too, Crystal. Bye."

Crystal watches her phone screen turn black and feels her stomach drop. She touches the glass to see her screensaver photo—JD holding up a string of ptarmigan between Mac and Summer. She took that three weeks ago.

JD loves to hunt ptarmigan, which he always shoots in the eye with his .22. Mac counts out the shells before he leaves, then has JD do the math when he returns: how many birds he missed, what percentage of kills he made. JD knows the math is easier if he doesn't miss, so he usually doesn't. He shot that string of eight with seven bullets. Mac was immensely proud of him.

Now Mac might die, along with Summer, and JD will fly hundreds of miles away. How could she stand looking at that photo then?

Crystal sees Payton exit her motorhome with her vape pen. "What's everybody doing?" she asks.

Payton walks over. "Sorting and folding laundry." She takes a quick hit from her pen.

"Why do you vape?"

"I needed to stop smoking. This helps me stay calm."

"Is that why you never seem to get flustered?"

"And painting." She pulls smoke into her mouth and blows it out her nose.

"You don't inhale?"

"No. I'm trying to repair my lungs. Do you think we should hide the alcohol?"

"Haley promised she wouldn't drink."

"Yeah, well my mom promised when she was pregnant with Sydney. She lied."

"We don't even know if she's pregnant."

"She is. She stopped taking birth control pills and she bought test strips. Part of her knows she is, but she doesn't want to face the truth."

Crystal runs her fingers through her hair. "When my mother first got pregnant with me, she told her parents. After another month, according to them, Maya said she wasn't pregnant any more. She didn't eat much so she didn't show. She used drugs and smoked like normal. Mac and Summer thought she must've had a miscarriage. Then I was born premature, like it was a surprise to her." Her stomach aches. "I could never understand how anyone could do that."

Payton takes a hit. "Because having a baby changes your entire life. For a teen, it's scary as hell. Maybe Haley's first test was positive, but she couldn't deal with it. Every option she saw was bad. Then she blocked the truth by acting like she always did."

"My mother did the same. Her Dylan was Eugene. Maya didn't want him."

"And Maya probably thought she couldn't stay home pregnant where she'd be reminded of her failure every day."

The hard pit of anger Crystal has always harbored inside for her mother softens a little. Maybe the baby inside Haley would blame its mother for drinking or using, but Crystal knows what Haley is going through and why she needs to be loved, not blamed.

Payton takes a hit. "You threw her a lifeline today."

"How?"

"If you'd said nothing this morning about Dylan, where would she be? You gave her another option. You'd love her. You'd kiss her. You'd save her."

Crystal watches brown, spotted leaves fall from the alders just off the deck. "And Mom never had another option."

"Maybe she did, but she was scared to take it. A lifeline doesn't work if one side is scared to throw it, or the other is afraid to catch it." Payton takes another hit. "Will Haley being pregnant make you like her less or not want to be with her?"

"No. Why would it?"

"Make sure she knows that."

Thoughts race inside Crystal's head, but they're like hundreds of words on a page she can't read. She looks down the trail behind the woodshed and wishes her mother would appear. She knows one thing for sure now—she needs to talk to her mother.

CHAPTER 17

*H*aley and Sydney burst through the door onto the deck. "You have a keyboard," gushes Sydney.

"Yes," says Crystal. "My grandmother plays."

"Can I learn?"

"Sure, but I don't know much. I could never get the hang of each hand moving in different directions."

"I can play a little," says Haley.

Sydney beams. "Cool."

"I want to send a picture of you three to Summer. Payton, get with them, please." Payton moves between Haley and Sydney and puts her arms around both. "Smile!" She takes several, picks out the best, and sends it to Summer.

The slow puttering of a Honda drifts toward them from the trail curving behind the wood shed. Crystal forgets to breathe as she cranes her neck to see. Could this be her mother? Or Eugene?

Payton pockets her vape pen and takes a few steps toward the sound. Crystal follows her.

The Honda motor stops and both girls hear footsteps shattering the fallen leaves.

Crystal's eyes widen, her heart pounds. "Maya . . ." She starts to run then abruptly stops when she sees a woman with straight, layered hair full of glistening, golden blonde streaks. Who is she? Crystal runs her hands through her hair. Her chest feels like it will burst.

The woman stops. "Crystal?" Her full red lips stretch slowly into a smile. "Is Haley here?"

"Are you Holly?" Panic flutters beneath her skin, just enough to make her worry about an imminent argument and an order to send Haley home.

"That I am." The woman stands two inches taller than Haley, wearing short rubber boots, black leggings, and a gold, sparkly tunic tied at the waist.

"Haley's on the deck. How'd you know to come this way to my house?"

"Back in the day, this is how I came to see your mom when she'd sneak out. My goodness, but you do look like Maya."

Crystal sucks in a quick breath as her heart skips.

Payton approaches them.

"Hi, I'm Holly." She holds out her hand then pulls it back. "I keep forgetting we can't touch each other anymore." She smiles at Payton. "Are you the girl with the AR? My boys were quite impressed."

"Yes, Ma'am."

"Holly's good. I'm trying to avoid 'Ma'am' for a few more years." She heads for the house, leaving Crystal behind, mouth open.

"You knew Maya?" She hurries to catch up, leaving Payton behind.

"She was my best friend for a long time." Holly stops when she sees her daughter glaring at her. "Hey, Haley. You've had an eventful day, haven't you?"

She folds her arms. "Like you care."

"I'm here, aren't I?" She walks onto the deck.

Haley turns away from her. "I'm not going home."

"I don't blame you." She notices Sydney. "And you are?"

"Sydney, Payton's sister." She flings her hair out of her face.

"Nice to meet you. Such a pretty girl." Holly puts her hands on her hips, looks up at the house then around the back yard where the grass is dark green yet covered inches thick in dried, yellow leaves. A spring gurgles into a small pond thirty yards away, spanned by a wooden bridge. "Such a beautiful home and yard." She turns to Crystal. "How are Mac and Summer?"

"They're both in Fairbanks in the hospital. Mac's on a ventilator."

"Oh no. I'm so sorry. Can you talk to either of them?"

"Summer. Not Mac."

"And JD?"

"He's with his girlfriend. They're moving to a village in two days."

"He's leaving?"

Crystal nods.

"You'll be by yourselves for at least a few days?"

"Probably. But we can take care of ourselves."

"It's a shame that you have to. This Covid crap is ruining everything."

"What did Nick and Danny say happened here?" snaps Haley.

"Does it matter? Whatever they said is an exaggeration or a lie." She touches the walls of the sunroom. "This is beveled cedar. It used to be that plastic greenhouse stuff. Mac has done so much since I was here last."

Haley's eyes pop. "When were you here?"

"Twenty-one years ago." She hugs herself and shivers. "Can we go inside? I'm getting chilled." She opens the door and walks into the sunroom, the other girls following, glancing at each other in confusion.

Holly stops in the living room and finds photos of Maya. She picks up one of her standing against a broad spruce trunk with bluebell flowers in her hair. Maya's shoulders are bare. She holds purple lupine in her hands just below her chin, her head tilted to smell them, though her eyes look up at the camera. The corners of her mouth turn up slightly. Holly stares at it, her thumb caressing the glass, her lips parting as her eyes glow.

Crystal stands beside her. "That's my favorite. Such a sexy look."

Holly nods and sighs.

"I've tried to find the tree around here," says Crystal, "but I can't. Do you know where she was in that picture?"

"Exactly where. Just a place we used to run off to."

Haley stands on her mother's other side. "Maya's not wearing a shirt, is she?"

Holly's cheeks tighten and push up against her eyes. "Nope. The only things she's wearing are the flowers in her hair." She laughs. "We'd just smoked a J and were acting silly."

Crystal's eyes widen. "You took the picture?"

"Yes, I did, but Maya told Summer she'd used a tripod. I'd been banished by that time."

"Were you lovers?" asks Payton, leaning against the roll top desk.

Crystal watches Holly's face turn pink after her eyes flick away from Payton's face.

"You certainly jump to crazy conclusions, Payton. I was just a bad influence. Summer suspected me of providing marijuana to her daughter. But it went both ways."

"Why have you never mentioned Maya to me?" asks Haley.

A cloud passes over Holly's face. "Because . . . because she was a childhood friend, and we both moved on. I only saw her a few times after this picture."

"Did you know Eugene?" asks Crystal.

Holly's eyes tense. "Yes, I knew the sleazeball. Sorry to say that about your father, Crystal, but if God ever made a sleazeball, it's Eugene."

"He's in town. Haley and I saw him after school. He's looking for Maya."

"Is he?" Holly returns the photo to the desk.

Crystal is struck by Holly's lack of surprise. "Until today, JD and I were told they both died years ago in a car wreck."

"Yes, I'd heard that story." She finds other photos of Maya as she walks around the room.

"Did you believe it?"

"I wasn't sure. She called me in July 2006 from Mississippi in such despair. She wished she'd never left Alaska. She wanted to come home but couldn't figure out how to do it."

Haley tilts her head. "Why did she call you after so many years?"

Holly shrugs and turns to another photo. "Just wanted to talk to an old friend, I guess."

Crystal moves to Holly's side. "2006 is when she left me and JD in the village."

"I know."

Crystal's eyes probe the woman's face, looking for any reaction. "She was supposed to go to rehab in Fairbanks, but Eugene talked her into flying back to him."

"Is that what Mac and Summer told you?"

"Yes. Isn't that true?"

Holly sighs. "Do y'all have anything to drink?" She moves toward the kitchen.

"Did she want to see you?" asks Payton.

Holly stops in the kitchen doorway and looks back at Payton. "There you go, jumping to conclusions again."

"No need to jump," says Payton. "The story's written all over your face. I think you were supposed to meet in Fairbanks, but something happened."

She scoffs. "*Something happened* is the story of my life." She walks into the kitchen and opens the refrigerator. "You mind if I take one of Mac's beers?"

Crystal calls out, "Help yourself," as she and the other girls follow into the kitchen. Her heart won't stop skipping and racing. She thinks Holly knows where her mother is. And maybe what really happened fourteen years ago. Crystal had been told many times that thirty minutes after Maya arrived in the village, she was on the phone talking to Eugene, that he talked her into flying back. She watches Holly tilt a Corona and chug half of it. "Did Maya call you from the village?"

"Yes, she did."

"More than once?"

"Maybe. Why do you ask?" She drinks more of the beer.

"Because you said she wanted to come home to Alaska but couldn't figure out how. Then she convinced Mac and Summer that Eugene was beating her. They bought her tickets for the village. Except I remember Eugene driving us all to the airport, so she wasn't sneaking out on him at all. I thought her plan all along was to dump JD and me and then go back to Eugene, but I could never understand why Maya called Eugene from the village if he was in on her plan from the beginning."

"Maya was calling Holly," says Payton, fixing her gaze on the woman. "I think someone threw a lifeline but didn't pull it in when the time came."

Holly finishes the beer and stares blankly. "Or never figured out a way to throw it."

"Or backed out at the last minute."

Holly finds Payton's eyes for a few seconds before flinching and turning toward Haley.

"You had all three of your kids by that time," says Payton. "Haley was the same age as Crystal."

Holly stares at her daughter with shiny eyes. "Maya had good options with her kids. I didn't."

Haley crosses her arms. "Maya abandoned her kids, but you wouldn't?"

"No." She shakes her head and tries to smile. "We talked about going to rehab together. That's all. Jack worked nights at the power plant, and neither of us had family nearby to help out if I was away for six weeks."

"Maya went back to Eugene because you couldn't go to rehab with her?" asks Crystal. "Weren't there other options?"

"That's too many years ago, Crystal. It's hard to remember every detail." She opens the refrigerator and pulls out another beer. "I don't think there was a plan for after rehab."

Crystal blows out a breath and notices Haley staring at her with such sad eyes. Crystal hears her heart thud dully in her chest. "Did you see her in Fairbanks?"

Holly takes a long drink. "No. I'd planned to take the kids to town to shop, but my car wouldn't start. And Jack wouldn't get his ass out of bed to help me." She drinks. "It's almost funny looking back on it. And Maya couldn't rent a car because she didn't have enough room on her credit card. We spent a crazy hour screaming and crying, going round and round, trying to figure out how to get one of us on the highway to the other." She drinks. "She'd covered four thousand miles to see me, but we couldn't close the last eighty. That's when I think she started calling Eugene."

While Holly finishes her second beer, Crystal moves to Haley for a hug, burying her face in her chest while Haley rubs her back.

"I'm sorry, Crystal," says Holly, touching Crystal's hair. "Maybe if I'd done more, your mother wouldn't have gone back to that asshole."

Crystal won't speak because she's afraid of what she'll say. Why couldn't Maya have entered rehab by herself? Gotten sober and gone back to her parents and kids? Then they could've all moved back to Clear. Maya and Holly could at least see each other. But they couldn't figure out what to do, their brains distorted by alcohol. Then both women continued to be miserable and drink or use drugs or both.

Holly folds her arms and looks at her daughter. "Haley, you're going to stay here with Crystal?"

"Yes."

"Where? In her room?"

"Yes." The sarcasm drips onto the floor— "Only if that's all right with you."

"Show me, please." Holly starts walking down the hall toward Crystal's room.

Crystal looks at Haley and whispers, "The drawings." Both girls hurry to catch up, but Holly has already found the papers on the mirror when they walk through the doorway.

"You did these, Crystal?" asks Holly, awe coloring her voice.

"Yes."

"They are very beautiful." She holds up Haley's nude and raises her brows. "You know where you got that luscious ass of yours, don't you?"

Haley smiles. "I could take a wild guess."

Holly rolls her eyes. "Of course, at your age I was already pregnant with your brothers, and my figure was starting to . . . well, expand. Hopefully, you can keep yours a little longer."

Crystal watches Haley's smile disappear.

Holly examines the kiss drawing. "When did you two start?"

"Kissing? Fifth grade," says Crystal. "But then we stopped for years until today."

"Does it bother you?" asks Haley.

"Does it matter? Because if you're concerned what others think of you for being attracted to Crystal, you'll stop. And then regret that decision for the rest of your life."

"Like you?" asks her daughter.

Holly raises her hands slightly then lets them fall. She stares at the floor. "I have many regrets. I hope your list never grows as long." She moves to the end of the dresser and grabs it with both hands. "Do you mind helping?"

"With what?" asks Haley.

"Move this away from the wall." The dresser is heavy, but after some grunting and a few profanities, they move it a foot away from the wall. "Crystal, I'm sure you know this was your mother's room and furniture." Holly moves one hand along the back of the dresser, and her fingers pick at brown tape until a horizontal strip is removed. Then she pulls off a vertical strip, revealing a thin piece of cardboard taped against the wood. Now Holly pushes back the open corner slowly until she fastens her fingers on something inside the pouch. She pulls out an 8x10 black and white photograph and props it against the mirror.

All three gaze at a double exposure of Maya and Holly's faces emerging from each other, looking in opposite directions but with all four eyes facing the camera. If one didn't know the age of the photo, one would swear the two girls were Crystal and Haley.

"I was eighteen, she was sixteen," says Holly with reverence. "We worked for hours in the darkroom trying to print this."

"What's a darkroom?" asks Haley.

Holly laughs. "Of course, you wouldn't know. We had a photography class back then where we learned to develop black and white film and to print our own pictures. Our teacher was old school. No Photoshop or digital cameras. The room had an orange safe light on the ceiling. And trays of stinky chemicals along the wall. The rule was that only two girls or two boys could be in it at a time. The teacher knew what would happen if a boy and girl got in there by themselves. You couldn't help but bump into each other . . . or touch. To this day, I can't smell vinegar or see an orange light without thinking of Maya and me in the darkroom."

"Did anyone ever suspect what you two did in there?" asks Haley.

"Suspect what?" Holly bats her eyes. "We completed our projects and both made As."

Haley rolls her eyes. "OK, now I know you're lying. You never made an A in high school. At least that's what you've told me."

Holly flashes a wry grin. "Don't believe everything people tell you. How many times have I told you that? After lots of tries, we finally made this print. I thought after all these years, it would've been lost, but she hid it behind her dresser."

Crystal pulls out her phone and snaps several pictures. "Can I draw it?"

"Sure you can."

Crystal takes the photo to her desk and props it against the window blinds. She studies both faces and decides to start with one side of Maya's nose, then move to her lips, then the other side of her nose to the eye, then the face and hair and finish with her other eye. She starts another line for Holly's nose, then to her eye, lips, face, hair then finishes with the other eye.

"That is amazing, Crystal," says Holly. "Why are you stuck in this shit-hole town?"

"I'm waiting to see my mother." Crystal tries to look through Holly's eyes into her brain. "And you know where she is. Otherwise, how would you know where to look for the photo?"

Holly touches Crystal's hair. "God, looking at you sitting in this room brings back so many memories of your mother." She sits next to her. "What would you do if you saw her?"

Her throat tightens and she swallows. "I'd hold her and never let her go."

Crystal feels Holly's eyes probing her face, trying to see inside her mind. "But she abandoned you," says Holly. "She wanted you to believe she was dead," she says slowly with such a sad tone. "Can you forgive her for that?"

"I've spent many years blaming her, but where would JD and I be if we had stayed with her and Eugene? The only reason JD can do anything is because of Mac and Summer's patience. Maybe Maya knew our only hope was to be with them."

Holly leans over and reaches for Crystal's face. "It always takes time for kids to realize the value of their parents. Hopefully, when they do, the canyon between them isn't too wide to jump over."

Crystal's face flushes with heat. "Can you bring her to me?"

Holly stands up. "Probably, but we have to be careful. Eugene is not a forgiving man." She pulls out her phone. "Can I take a picture of you and that drawing?"

"Yes." Crystal holds the drawing and smiles. "One of you?" Crystal holds out her phone.

"Sure." Holly turns around and fixes her hair in the mirror then smiles at Crystal, who shoots the picture. Holly reaches her hand out to her daughter. "Haley? We haven't taken one together for years. Come."

Haley slides over. Holly wraps her right arm around her daughter's shoulder, while Haley slowly slides her arm around her mother's waist. Crystal takes a few photos.

"Will you send that to Haley, and then," she turns to Haley, "you send me one?"

"Yeah," says Haley.

"Oh, almost forgot," says Holly as she pulls the pouch of test strips out of a dresser drawer. "I found these on the dresser when I walked in."

Haley takes a step backward and lifts her hands to her mouth.

"I figure these aren't Crystal's." She furrows her brow and almost whispers. "Are you?"

Haley closes her eyes, breathes, then opens them. "I don't know. The first strip was negative, but I think it was too early. I'm going to test again tomorrow morning."

"Then I'll come by again in the morning. You'll be all right, Haley, whichever way it turns out. I'll be on your side no matter what. I know you may not believe me because of how I've neglected you for years, but I'm serious. And I'm pretty sure these girls will support you as well. You hear?"

Haley nods quickly as tears drip out of her eyes.

Holly holds out her arms. "Hug?"

Haley almost leaps against her mother.

"I know I've been a shitty mom to you, but maybe I can make up for it now. I do love you, Haley."

Crystal sees Haley's fingers clutch her mother's back as both women cry.

"I love you too, Mom."

Crystal desperately wants to do the same with her mother.

CHAPTER 18

*T*he light wanes as Holly salutes the four girls on the deck before she disappears down the trail. Soon the Honda starts and moves away into the trees. Crystal knows she must have come this way to avoid Eugene. Maya would suspect he'd lurk along the road and driveway. He must not know about Holly and her history with her mother. It's clear Holly came to check things out, to see if the house is safe and welcoming for Maya.

Crystal is tempted to follow Holly back to her mother, but she's worried Eugene will see her and know where she's going. Better to trust Holly to find a way to bring Maya to her.

How did her mother get to Alaska? What did she tell Eugene this time? Did he come with her? If so, how did she lose him? So many questions and only a few answers. It seems like her entire life has been filled with questions about Maya.

Haley hugs Crystal from behind. "Your mother and my mother were lovers, but they both married men and had kids. I kept my mother from being with the woman she loved."

Crystal feels Haley's tears dripping on her shoulder. "Holly already had kids before you came along. The real question is why your mother was banished."

"Mac and Summer thought Mom gave Maya drugs."

"They banished Holly, then Eugene gave Maya drugs. That sure solved the problem."

"Drugs weren't the issue," says Payton. "They were lovers and got caught. Mac and Summer thought the problem would be solved by forbidding the relationship, which resulted in them sneaking out, messing around in the dark room at school, and who knows where else. If the two girls were allowed to be in love, neither one would have used alcohol or drugs to numb their pain."

"Or had us," says Haley. "It's hard knowing you're the reason your mother has been an unhappy drunk most of her life."

Payton shakes her head. "You're innocent, Haley. The world is fucked up. I'm sure Holly and Maya wanted to tell everyone they loved each other but knew they couldn't."

Haley blinks tears from her eyes. "They could have, but they chickened out."

"They had no place to go. Almost half the homeless teens in this country are gay. Where would you both be now if Mac and Summer were still in this house?"

Haley hugs her shoulders. "Maybe with you, Payton. Would you have picked us up?"

Sydney wraps her arms around Haley's waist. "Definitely. I would've forced her to stop."

"Only if they had food," says Payton, smiling. "We were down to our last Cup Noodles."

Crystal pulls out her phone. "Even if Summer were here, I can't believe she'd make the same mistake again." She sends the picture of the double exposure to Summer, along with her drawing and a note—*Holly came by. She knows where Maya is. I think I'll see her soon. This photo was taped behind my dreser. Maya and Holly made the print in high school after u banisht (?) Holly from Maya's life. Do you think now that was a mistake?*

Crystal stares at her phone, hoping Summer will call her. After another minute, she punches Summer's call button.

An unfamiliar muffled voice answers. "Hello?"

Crystal's heart stops. "Where's Summer?"

"I'm her nurse. Your grandmother is having trouble talking right now, but she wanted me to answer the phone."

Crystal exhales, the pulse throbbing in her neck echoes in her ears. "Did she read my message?"

"Yes. Well, I read it to her. She cried a little then said, 'Yes. Tell Crystal and Maya, yes.'"

Crystal squeezes her eyes shut, sending tears down her cheeks. "Is Summer OK?"

"She's on oxygen and her fever has gone down a little."

"And Mac?"

"Still on a ventilator. I'll text you a number to call next time you want information or to send a message to your grandmother. I have to go." She ends the call.

Crystal stares at her phone and wipes her eyes.

"How is Summer?" asks Haley.

"I couldn't talk to her. The nurse relayed a message that Summer made a mistake with Holly and Maya and to tell my mom. I sent her the photograph. Oh, Haley, I'm supposed to send you the drawing." Crystal sends it to Haley then collapses into a deck chair. "How much would've changed if Mac and Summer had accepted Holly?"

Haley sits on the chair arm and strokes Crystal's hair. "How would any other mother in this town have reacted to me leaving home to be with you?"

Crystal leans against Haley. "Is Holly going to care what her friends think?"

"How could she?" asks Payton. "Sounds like she's going to be with Maya, if they can get rid of Eugene."

"Wow," says Haley. "Everyone in Clear will have lots to talk about."

"Good," says Payton. "Maybe people will stop keeping secrets. Do you think we're the only girls in Clear who are gay or bi?"

"Or guys?" asks Crystal.

"For sure, guys," says Haley. "Mike's gay, but he won't admit it."

"Seriously?" asks Crystal, eyes scrunched in disbelief.

Haley gets up from the chair. "He's always stripping or talking about how horny he is. Like he's overcompensating." She walks to the edge of the deck.

Crystal remembers his "everybody got laid" comment. Maybe he said that to hide what he didn't do. "Has he had sex with a girl?"

She throws the comment over her shoulder. "Only one that I know of."

Crystal looks at Haley's back and wonders if she's hiding something. She catches Payton's eye. Crystal shrugs.

"How hard would it be for him to come out?" asks Payton.

Haley turns around to face them. "Really hard. Dylan's already accused him. To his face and to others."

"When did you start thinking about your own preference?" asks Payton.

"Well, kissing Crystal seemed so natural until it didn't, especially after Ms. Cline saw us one day and threatened to tell my mom."

"She did?" asks Crystal. "You never told me."

"I was too embarrassed." Haley stares into the fading sunset past the driveway—streaks of magenta laced with glowing, gray clouds behind the trees. "Now, I wish I'd told her to call. I think the threat made me chase guys even harder. I convinced myself I was just going through a phase with Crystal, and now I'd grown up. My goal in life seemed to be catch and conquer, which meant getting them to have sex with me. I made them feel good and convinced them they did the same for me. But I'd masturbate later watching porn. Which got to be exclusively lesbian porn. Another big secret."

"Did the guys know you were faking?" asks Crystal.

Haley laughs and shakes her head. "Hell no. They bragged about how much I came. How loud and crazy I was. I made them feel like sex gods. But I was faking the whole time. This past summer, I stopped pretending with Dylan, and he didn't even notice."

Payton stands and faces them. "Straight women achieve the fewest orgasms during sex—about sixty percent of the time, but their men believe these women orgasm eighty-five percent of the time. Which means at least a quarter of straight women's orgasms are fake. Lesbians orgasm about ninety percent of the time. No need for faking."

Haley laughs. "Where did you get this information? Personal experience?"

"No. From published scientific studies."

"And your conclusion, Dr. Payton?"

"That's obvious. Girl sex is more honest and fun for everyone involved."

Crystal raises her hand. "How do I get the job of asking people about their orgasms?"

"Go to college and major in women, gender, and sexuality studies. That's my goal."

Crystal tries to smile. "That's a great goal." She looks at the ground, knowing college is not a possibility.

Payton kneels on the deck and finds Crystal's eyes. "There are ways for you to study art after high school. I can help you."

Her spirit stops deflating and starts to fill again. "Really? I'd like that."

Payton stands. "Haley, you'd do great in college."

A smile ripples across Haley's face. "Maybe." She takes a deep breath. "But that takes money."

Payton's eyes flash with hope. "There are lots of ways to get funding. I'm serious."

Haley grabs Payton's hand and smiles. "Says the person who was down to one Cup Noodles."

Sydney stands. "All this talk of orgasms makes me want to take a shower. Does anyone need to pee before I disappear for fifteen minutes?"

Crystal frowns and points her finger at the girl. "Five-minute limit for showers in this house."

"No way!"

"Just kidding. Take as much time as you want."

Haley moves toward the door. "Let me use the potty real quick then you can have it, Sydney." She runs inside.

Payton catches Crystal's eye. "Where are the test strips?"

"On my dresser."

Payton looks through the glass on the door. "She went to your room first."

"Wouldn't you want to know? I'd be going crazy."

"She thinks if she's pregnant, her life will end, but it won't. Her mother will help her. And Maya. And us. She can go to college online. It's not the end of the world."

Crystal shakes her head. Her arms feel heavy. "But to her it would seem that way."

"Payton knows what Haley's going through," says Sydney.

Crystal snaps her head toward Payton who avoids her eyes.

Payton looks through the door. "Haley just walked back into your bedroom. You can take a shower, Sis."

"OK." Sydney goes inside.

"Were you pregnant?" asks Crystal.

Payton turns around and leans against the door. "At fourteen." Tears fill her eyes. "While we were still in therapy. My parents took me to get an abortion."

"Is that what you wanted?"

"It didn't matter what I wanted. I was fourteen. The problem was how I got pregnant. My father told me I was too young to know I was gay. How could I know since I'd never had sex with a boy. He wanted me to try kissing a boy, just make out a little he said. So I did with a boy in my class named Jake after we got off the bus and were walking home. We found an old shed we could sneak into."

"Did he rape you?"

"No. Jake was sweet. He always asked before we went any further."

Payton tries to catch her breath while walking around the deck.

"I thought maybe I could be normal. Maybe then there'd be fewer things to fight about at my house. All I had to do was like having sex with Jake. For several days we went to the shed after school and kept doing more and more until finally he came inside me. I didn't particularly enjoy it, but I convinced myself I could do it. How many other girls have done the same? I rode him every day for a week until some other kids saw us leaving the shed and told my parents.

"My mother was furious with me until I told her Dad wanted me to. He, of course, denied everything. A few weeks later I started puking in the morning. I got tested and then had an abortion.

"I was furious with myself and especially at my father. I refused any more therapy. The fighting got worse. I took Sydney with me to my friend's house almost every night so she wouldn't have to hear them. A few months later, Dad overdosed on heroin."

Payton flops into a chair. "I know what Haley's going through, but I also know she can get through this. She has friends and a mother who's going to support her no matter what Haley decides to do." She stands and looks through the door. "Haley's been in your bedroom for at least five minutes which means she knows the result. Do you want us both to go to her or just you?"

"Both." Crystal runs to Payton and hugs her. "I'm sorry about what happened to you, but I'm glad you're here with us." She kisses Payton's cheek then grabs her hand. "Let's go see her."

They walk through the door, past Maya's picture with the flowers, past Holly and Haley's empty beer bottles, past Sydney "singing" in the shower, until they hear Haley crying.

Crystal knocks gently then opens the door to find Haley collapsed on the bed, her hands clutching her face, weeping. The girls sit gently on either side. "We love you, Haley." Crystal lies down and kisses Haley's hand and face while Payton holds and kisses her other hand. "We love you."

Between gasps for breath, Haley asks, "What am I going to do?"

Crystal kisses Haley's eyes and cheeks, removing her tears. "You don't have to decide that now."

Haley struggles to sit up. "What will I tell Dylan?"

Payton kneels on the floor and finds Haley's eyes. "He doesn't need to know anything right now. Maybe ever. If you decide to keep your baby, then he needs to earn the right to be the father. You don't owe him anything. If you decide not to keep it, then he never has to know."

Crystal leans Haley's head on her shoulder. "We won't let you make the same mistake both our moms made."

The kitchen phone rings. Crystal grits her teeth and looks at Payton.

"You don't have to answer."

"If I don't," says Crystal, "I'll just wonder if my father caught my mother. Hold her."

Payton nods and sits on the bed with Haley. Crystal runs down the hall.

CHAPTER 19

"Hey, Daddy, what's up?" Crystal barks into the phone. "When are you leaving town?"

Eugene's raspy, slurred voice slithers into her ear. "You'd like that, wouldn't you?"

"Sounds like you've been drinking. Must be from missing Mom, huh?"

"Where is she, bitch?"

Crystal's muscles quiver, half in anger, half in fear. This is the voice her mother heard many times, the one that forced Maya to leave home or stay with him. "Now are you saying, 'Where is the bitch?' or 'Where is she, you bitch?' Because that will make a difference in what I say next to you."

"Maya was in my camper when I followed you down D Street. After you left the school with Haley, Maya wasn't there. How'd you manage that, bitch?"

Crystal's brain races to decide whether he's telling the truth or not. Why would he tell her this? Maya was in the camper? Then why did he pretend to be looking for her?

The sounds of him sucking liquid out of a bottle and swallowing gurgle through the speaker. "I figure she must've contacted you before we showed up in town today. You guys had it all planned, didn't you?"

A rolling heat fills her belly. "I don't know what the fuck you're talking about, Eugene. Just so you know, I'm recording this conversation. You better be careful what you say next." Again, she could kick herself for thinking about recording too late. She pulls out her phone, opens Voice Memos, hits the button, and holds her phone near the earpiece on the handset.

"I've got eyes on your house in the night and during the day." He drinks again. "If she's in there, I'll know it."

Her voice shakes in hatred. "And do what?"

"Let her in the house and you'll find out, bitch." He ends the call.

Crystal throws the handset against the wall with a scream. She pants and turns around to see Sydney standing wide-eyed outside the bathroom wrapped in a towel, Payton and Haley right behind.

"Eugene?" asks Payton.

Crystal tries to slow her breathing, but she can't get enough air into her lungs.

Haley moves to Crystal and holds her shoulders. "Tell us what he said when you're ready. Payton, please open a beer." She meets Payton's eyes. "For Crystal." Haley steers Crystal toward a chair and sits her down. "You remember when you beat up Louis in Second Grade? The look on your face then is what we all just saw." She raises her brows and smiles. "Eugene'd better stay away from you."

Crystal takes the beer from Payton and chugs a few gulps. The alcohol burns into her chest, followed by a wave of calm. "He said Maya was in his truck when he followed us into the house. But after we left him at the school, she wasn't there. He thinks we helped her escape. Now he's super mad and drunk.

"Sis," orders Payton, "go to our room, get dressed, and bring my gun." Sydney runs down the hall.

"He thinks Maya talked to us before they drove to town. So if he's not full of shit and playing some creepy game with us, Maya left his camper when he went inside the house to get us. Her escape couldn't have been planned. She was just waiting for a chance to get away. But to where? And with who?"

"My mom?" asks Haley.

Crystal drinks. "Who else? Is there any chance Eugene knows about Maya and Holly's past?"

"I didn't know," says Haley. "Why would he?"

"If Eugene had known," says Payton, "would he have brought her back here? He couldn't have known of their plan to meet fourteen years ago."

Crystal remembers something Eugene said at the school. "After he fixed my Honda, he told us Maya had dumped us in the village to hook up with another guy. Maybe he suspects there was someone else, but it was a man, not Holly."

Haley pulls out her phone. "I'm calling Mom." She punches numbers then the speaker button, holding the phone screen up near her chest. Everyone hears the phone ring.

"Hey, honey," answers Holly.

"Mom, can you talk?"

"Sure, I can."

"In private?"

"Just a minute."

They hear footsteps and a door opening and closing.

"OK. What's wrong?"

"Maya escaped Eugene's camper this afternoon. Do you know where she is?"

Holly pauses. The three girls stare at the phone then each other. Sydney gives the gun to Payton, who holds her finger to her mouth. "Shh."

"Who told you that?" asks Holly.

"Eugene," says Crystal, standing and moving closer to the phone. "He just called, mad and drunk. He thinks we had something to do with her escape. Does he know anything about you and Maya?"

"I don't see how."

"Is it possible Maya has been communicating with another man?" Crystal asks.

"What do you mean?"

Crystal takes a sip from her beer. "Could she be planning something with a man you don't know about? Or has all her communication been with you?"

"I know nothing about another man."

Crystal looks at Haley. "What time was it when Eugene came into the house?"

Haley shrugs her shoulders. "I don't know. Maybe 4:30."

Crystal takes another sip. "Did Maya contact you about 4:30 this afternoon?"

"Yes."

"Was that a surprise or were you expecting her call?"

"She told me she'd try to get away from him," says Holly, "but I didn't know when or how or if she could do it."

Crystal thinks back to Eugene's comments in the school parking lot. At the time, he thought Maya was in the RV, maybe even listening. He admitted Maya was alive. When asked why he came to Clear, he claimed he just wanted to see his kids. Then Crystal decided he was looking for Maya. He never denied this. Like he wanted her to believe he was looking for her.

In fact, the only thing he denied was that "Maya did not run away from him."

Even though a few minutes later he discovered she had.

Crystal stares at framed photos on the walls around the table, looking for answers. "Why would Eugene want us to think he was looking for Maya when at the time, he had her in his truck? And now he's threatening us if we let her in the house?"

"He said that?" asks Holly.

"Yeah. He said he has eyes on the house day and night. If Maya comes to our house, he'll know."

"Jesus. That man is insane."

"Would he kill her?" asks Payton.

"Maybe," says Holly. "Maya told me she's been scared many times he'd do something to her."

"Then," says Payton, "we need to get him arrested while he's threatening her or convince him she's left town so he'll leave."

"We . . . have a plan," says Holly.

"Can we know what it is?" asks Crystal.

"Not yet. Soon."

"Mom," asks Haley, "will you live with Maya?"

Holly breathes rapidly into the phone like she's struggling to decide what to say. She lowers her voice, "I'd like to, but we're not sure yet."

Haley looks to the ceiling, squeezing her eyes shut. "Will I be able to see you?"

"Anytime you want, honey. I'm not leaving Clear."

"Thank you."

"Can I talk to my mom?" asks Crystal. "Please? Give me her number or give her mine."

"I will, but let me talk to her first."

Crystal grabs the phone, her hands shaking. "Where is she? How do you know she's safe from him? Is she by herself? Does she have a gun? If she comes here, we have four pair of eyes and lots of guns. She'd be safer."

"Is anyone coming to your house tomorrow?"

"JD's coming to pack his stuff, which means Gena and maybe Kato will come with him."

"In the morning?"

"Yes."

"Call me after they're gone?"

"Sure."

"OK. I'll get back to you with a number."

"Wait," Crystal says. "Has Maya seen the double exposure print and my drawing?"

"Yes. She was amazed. Just a little longer, Crystal. It won't be long."

Crystal pleads, "It's already been fourteen years. I don't want to wait any more."

"Neither do I, dear. Neither do I." She ends the call.

Everyone stares at Haley's phone, but the screen stays black. She slips it into the pouch of her hoodie.

"Why would Eugene want us to believe Maya was running away from him?" asks Crystal.

"Maybe because Mac and Summer would be more likely to take her in," says Payton. "Maya has to be worried that after faking her death, they might not accept her."

"Then why did Eugene call Mac?"

"To make sure your grandparents still hated him. And to pass on the ridiculous story that he's in town to see his kids. No one would believe that. Once you all found out she's alive, you'd jump to the conclusion that he's trying to find her."

Crystal paces. "OK. We know he's looking for her and that she escaped. She comes here, we take her in, then he finds her here. Then what? Maya runs away with Holly but somehow stays in town with her?" Crystal collapses into a chair, cocks her elbows on the table, and holds her face.

Payton fills a glass of water. "The main focus of this plan seems to be making sure Maya is accepted at this house. If she's going to leave it, why come here to begin with?"

Haley opens the freezer. "Crystal, I'm hungry. You want anything in particular?"

"Get whatever you want."

A rush of warmth rises in Crystal's chest, through her neck and into her face. She lifts her head and watches the movie in her mind of Maya and her kids coming to the village years ago. Maya had told her parents she was leaving Eugene for good even though he took her to the plane. She left her kids as planned and was supposed to return to Eugene. But Maya's real plan was to hook up with Holly. That didn't work, so she went back to Eugene.

Without her kids, Eugene wouldn't have let her go back to her parents years ago.

Then why bring her back now?

She heard a baby cry today.

Without a baby, Eugene wouldn't have let Maya come home.

Crystal blurts, "Maya has a baby and is planning to leave it here."

Haley stands, holding several frozen burritos. "A baby?"

"I heard a baby cry as I walked past the camper. I thought the sound came from one of the houses. But Maya was in the camper with a baby. Then she left." Crystal stands and paces, trying to catch up with her thoughts. "The original plan was for Maya to come home claiming to have escaped from Eugene. She'd stay a day, maybe two, leave the baby, then reunite with Eugene and drive back to Fairbanks. But Maya tricked him, and escaped for real because she wants to be with Holly. Now Eugene doesn't know what Maya intends to do."

Payton closes the microwave and punches buttons. "But if she comes here, he'll try to take her."

"Minus the baby," says Crystal. "He doesn't want it. That's why he brought her here. To dump the kid. Maybe it's not his."

Haley brings plates to the table. "Do you think Maya wants the baby? Maybe she's fooling Mom to hook up with another man."

"Then why involve Holly at all? Why escape from Eugene? If she stuck with the original plan, she'd come to the house, abandon her baby, then sneak out to someone besides Eugene. I think she wants to hide somewhere in town until he leaves."

Haley's eyes pop, and she throws up her hands. "Here. This is it. Maya comes home with her baby then 'leaves.' Eugene comes by trying to find her. We tell him we don't know where she's gone. We even accuse him of kidnapping her. He thinks she's hooked up with another guy who's heading back to Fairbanks, so he follows."

Crystal grabs forks. "But he won't find her. He'll come back. Then what?"

Payton sets the glasses on the table. "He does something stupid to get arrested or killed. Maya rejoins her baby, and she and Holly live happily ever after."

"Where?" asks Haley.

Crystal brings the hot burritos on a plate. "Here? Or maybe Lena's house. She's moving."

Everyone grabs a burrito and starts eating.

Crystal sees her reflection in the window behind Haley's head as she chews. "Eugene could be watching us right now." She shoots the finger. Then all of them do.

Haley swallows. "You really think Maya has a baby?"

Payton wipes her mouth. "It makes sense. There's no other reason for Eugene to bring her back home. I bet it's not his."

"I always wondered whether Eugene was really my father," says Crystal. "After everything Mac and Summer told me, I hoped he wasn't. And that's why he forced Maya to get rid of us, because he didn't want to raise someone else's kids. But I couldn't figure out how both JD and me weren't his. Maybe just me. Eugene was JD's father, but JD was so messed up Eugene didn't want to bother with him. Eugene seems to think Maya has had other boyfriends."

"He sounds crazy jealous," says Haley.

Sydney burps then smiles. "Maybe she did have boyfriends."

Haley burps louder. "Who would blame her?"

Sydney burps again.

Payton taps her glass a few times with a fork. "I hate to interrupt this gastric competition, but there's a big question we're not answering. Why is no one talking about the baby? Holly has said nothing. She has to know about it because she picked Maya up and took her somewhere."

Everyone pauses to think.

Haley sips her water. "If Mac and Summer were home, would they hesitate to take Maya and her baby back into their house?"

"No," says Crystal. "Summer told me this morning, she'd grab Maya and never let her go. Summer loves babies. Mac does too."

Payton stands with her plate. "Maybe because they're not here, Maya is worried about how you'll respond to her baby. After all, she abandoned you. She's got to think you have some resentment."

Yes, Crystal has felt resentment for many years but not so much for the abandonment. More for the damage Maya did to her and JD. How much different would her life have been without her mother using drugs and alcohol?

"I do resent her for leaving us," says Crystal. "But I understand the reasons better now. I want to see my mom whether she has a baby or not. Probably more if she has a baby."

"What if this baby is like JD?" asks Payton.

Crystal's heart sinks. Please not that. JD couldn't focus his eyes and seemed to live in a daze for years.

Haley grabs Crystal's hand and squeezes. "Then we'll deal with it as best we can."

Crystal meets her eyes and nods. "Yes, we will. Has your mother sent a number?"

Haley checks her phone. "There's a message: *Maya would rather call Crystal herself. I gave her the number.*"

"Ask her," says Crystal, "whether I have a brother or a sister."

Haley's eyes widen. "Are you sure?"

"Why not?"

"OK." She types out a message.

They all watch the phone.

CHAPTER 20

*a*fter staring at the phone for several seconds, Haley sets it on the table. Everyone slowly resumes eating, but Crystal can only swallow one more bite. Why can't Holly answer? Maybe Maya's told her that only she can share the news. At least now they know Maya has a baby. Otherwise, Holly would've asked what the hell they were talking about.

Or maybe Holly fell asleep? Or is in the shower.

Haley takes her plate to the sink. "Should I call her?"

"No," says Crystal, scraping the rest of her burrito into the trash. "I'm sure we'll find out soon enough."

Payton returns from her room with a sweatshirt, a flashlight, and her gun. "I'm going to walk around for awhile. Sis, can you fix our sheets and clothes and stuff?"

"Sure," says Sydney.

Payton nods and goes outside.

"She's going to vape," whispers Sydney.

Crystal smiles. "But at least she doesn't smoke cigarettes anymore."

"True. I hated the smell."

"Do you have any bad habits?" asks Haley as she rinses plates.

Sydney twists a strand of hair around her finger. "I watch too much YouTube, especially when I can't sleep."

"That's better than most of the things I used to do."

Sydney's smile puffs her cheeks out like a squirrel. "But now you can sleep with Crystal."

Haley blurts out a laugh. "True. But what if she snores?"

"Hold her nose closed for a couple of seconds. I have to do that with Payton sometimes. Or sleep back to back. We do that all the time. Then neither of us rolls over into snoring position. But you two probably don't want to sleep that way."

Haley grins and looks to Crystal. "Are you writing all this down?"

"Don't need to. I have a noise machine in my room. It kept me from hearing JD. I'm sure it'll be good enough for us." Crystal moves to Haley and pulls her close. "Besides, we have plenty to do before we even think about sleeping." Each of their mouths opens wide to caress the other's.

"And that's my cue to leave," says Sydney. "Please turn your machine on loud, Crystal. I'd like to keep what little innocence I have left." She throws up her hands. "Just kidding!" She walks back to her room.

"I love that kid," says Haley. "I wish I had a little sister."

Crystal places her palm below Haley's navel. "Maybe you'll have a daughter."

Haley clasps Crystal's hand and closes her eyes. "I just hope it's OK. I couldn't . . . couldn't take knowing I've damaged it."

Crystal leans into Haley. "Summer told me more than once that all parents damage their kids, even those most loving and careful. What matters is what the parents do afterward. Teach your child to overcome your failings and admit to them that you aren't perfect. She'd tell me this when I screamed about Maya. Summer said she never drank or smoked during her own pregnancy, but Maya still suffered from her mistakes. Summer always wanted another chance. Maybe she'll get it."

"Can you forgive Maya?"

"I guess that depends on what she does next." Crystal hugs Haley. "The past is gone for her and for you. Everything important is from now on. I'm going to take a quick shower."

"OK. I'll finish cleaning up in here." Crystal turns to leave, but Haley grabs her hand. "I know that others have labeled you special, like that's a bad thing. But you are truly special, Crystal Rose." Haley's face flushes with a radiant glow, her eyes bright and glossy.

Crystal's entire body tingles. "That's how you make me feel."

"Don't take too long. I'm serious. Just wash and dry and come get me."

Crystal nods her head and takes a few steps backward, unwilling to break the spell Haley has put her under. She reaches backward for the bathroom door, jamming her hand against the frame and tripping over the divider between the wood and tile floors.

"Are you OK?"

"Better than OK." She scrambles into the bathroom and closes the door.

Crystal starts the shower then pulls off her clothes and stares at herself in the mirror. Her hair looks like someone started making dreads and got bored. Her ribs are showing. She's hardly eaten today, actually for several days. A scattering of red bumps still appear around her pubis from when she shaved everything before sex with Kato. She turns around and notices two pimples on her butt.

Good thing Haley is the beauty in this couple.

She pulls the curtain back, steps into the tub, and finds the shower-head dangling where Sydney left it. Such a cool little girl. Forced to grow up too fast and live on the run with her older sister, yet somehow she is happy and good-natured, hiding any resentment she has every right to feel.

Kids her age and younger are entirely subject to the whims of their parents. They can be ignored, abused, even abandoned with little recourse and only a fool's hope of someone stepping up to rescue them. Sydney has Payton. She and JD had Mac and Summer.

Who will save Maya's latest child? Maya may not be able to depend on Mac and Summer a second time. Who now? Crystal? Certainly she would. How could she live with herself if she didn't? She'd feel such a connection with that baby, just like she will with Haley's.

Maybe Maya wants a new start at home, another chance to be a real parent, not only for her new baby, but also for Crystal and JD.

Is Holly willing to help her, to give up her husband and create the life she and Maya wish they'd had with each other? Or will she just be an occasional visitor and secret lover?

Crystal rinses the soap out of her hair.

Why is Maya so secretive about her baby? Is she ashamed about what she's done to it? Is she bringing home another Crystal or JD or some pitiful combination?

Crystal turns off the water and stares at the wall. No, that's not it.

What baby would Maya be the most nervous about bringing home?

The truth chills her skin.

A normal baby.

Maya must worry how this child will be received, especially by Crystal and JD. How could she have been so uncaring, so irresponsible while she and JD grew inside her and yet shown the appropriate discipline and love for their newest sibling?

How would Crystal feel?

Honestly—overjoyed. How could she wish her own misfortune onto another child? But she can understand her mother's concern. Like a parent worrying about the number and quality of presents each child gets at Christmas or on birthdays. Which parent wants to be accused of loving one child more than another?

A normal baby would be the greatest gift her mother could give her. A sign of redemption worthy of forgiveness. Of celebration.

God, she hopes this is the reason for the silence.

She squeezes and fluffs her hair as dry as she can. Her robe is in her room. She cracks open the bathroom door to see if Haley is in sight. The house seems empty. She doesn't want to call out for fear of waking Sydney, and she doesn't want to put her dirty clothes back on.

She ties the arms of her sweatshirt around her waist to cover her butt. She balls up her shirt and underwear and holds it against her breasts then opens the door and walks down the hall.

Before she opens her bedroom door, she hears Sydney giggling. Barely peeking inside, Crystal sees Haley working on the young girl's eyelashes as Sydney sits with her back to the door in front of the dresser and Haley bent over, facing Crystal.

Haley's mouth opens as her eyes roam Crystal's body.

"Toss me my robe?" asks Crystal, cocking an eyebrow.

Sydney squirms, trying to look behind her. "Hey, Crystal. Haley's making me beautiful."

"No, Sydney," Haley says, keeping her face pointing toward her. "Look at me. Crystal needs to get dressed."

Crystal blushes. "My robe?"

Haley picks up the robe hanging off the end of the bed. "This one?"

"Yes, obviously."

"Hmm. You really need this? You look covered to me." Haley holds the robe up with her left hand, her lips curled up at the corners, her head tilted to the side.

Crystal stares back at her, then shakes her head before dropping her clothes to the ground. "Do you think I need it now?"

Haley's eyes move from head to toe. "Turn around, please."

Crystal stands with her back toward Haley.

"Once again."

Crystal turns and holds out her arm, her eyes bulging. "My robe?"

Haley tosses it. "If you insist. But it's much more exciting without it, however."

Crystal quickly covers herself and ties the strap. "Let me see what's she's done, Sydney." Crystal moves to Haley's side.

"This girl has the thickest, longest lashes I've ever seen," says Haley as she holds a lash curler against Sydney's eyelid. "I've tweezed her brows and added liner and mascara. She wants you to shoot a photo and draw a picture." Haley releases the curler. "Look at yourself."

Sydney stands and leans toward the mirror. "Ooh!" She blinks her eyes. "Wow. I look like a model. Payton has the same eyelashes. She just hides them under her hair."

"Maybe tomorrow she'll let me work on hers," says Haley.

"Good luck with that. Where do you want me for my photo shoot, Crystal?"

"Stay right there. I'll move to my desk. Hold your head up with your left hand and look at me."

"Like this?" Sydney asks.

"Tilt your head just a little more."

"Should I smile or look cool?"

"Cool." Crystal takes several photos then props her drawing pad on her knees and grabs her marker. She starts with the right side of her face and draws her eye, then sweeps down for her cheek and lips then up to her nose and other eye. From there Crystal draws the outline of her face then back over to make strands of hair from right to left, ending with her arm and hand against her chin. She turns the pad around and shows her. "You like?"

"Yes! Can I keep it?"

"It's yours. Now I'm sending you the photos." Crystal works her thumbs and sends the pictures.

Sydney lunges at Crystal and hugs her. "Thank you!" She turns to Haley and squeezes her. "And you. You're the best friends I've ever had. I'm going to post everything now. Good night!" She leaves the room.

Crystal and Haley look at each other. "She makes me happy," says Haley. "I hope she doesn't have to deal with more shit in her life."

"Shit doesn't stand a chance against her."

"Now what do we do?" Haley holds the bottom edge of her hoodie tight against her skin as she raises it slowly, forcing her breasts to lift high then plunge against her ribs and jostle against each other.

Crystal gasps. "I could watch you do that a hundred times."

Haley pulls off her pants.

"Or that. Maybe you should turn on the noise machine."

"OK." Haley turns the dial until the room is filled with the sound of water gurgling. "That's going to make me pee all night." She punches a button until they hear white noise. "I can live with that." She takes two steps back and poses. "Draw me from the front. Might as well do it now before I blimp out."

Crystal stares, mouth agape.

"Draw me first. Devour me later." Haley pulls her arms behind her, pushes out her right hip and her breasts, and looks directly at Crystal. "This OK?"

Crystal inhales deeply then blows her breath out slowly. "That's perfect." Crystal sweeps her marker around the page, forming hips, breasts, and shoulders. Then she adds the face and head. Her hand stops and she gazes at her paper.

"Are you done? Show me," says Haley, who starts to break her pose.

Crystal holds up her hand. "Wait. I want to add something." She pulls a red marker out of a desk drawer and forms two hearts, a larger one on Haley's chest and another below her belly button. She turns the pad around.

Haley's skin glows pink as she gulps in a breath. Her hands touch her face then reach for the pad. "This is crazy gorgeous. I have two hearts now. I love it."

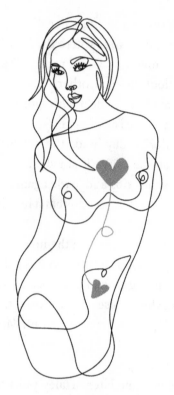

Haley lays the pad on the dresser and walks slowly toward Crystal until her breasts hug Crystal's face. "You made me feel so much better." Haley pulls the tie on the robe and gently pushes the cloth down Crystal's shoulders. Haley kneels in front of the chair. "Can I make you feel better?" She slowly lifts Crystal's left hand and kisses each finger.

Crystal's pulse quickens. "Yes, please." Crystal groans as she watches each of her fingers disappear into Haley's warm mouth then emerge slowly from a circle of thick red lips.

With her other hand, Haley softly twists and pulls Crystal's nipples.

Crystal closes her eyes. Groans rumble from her chest.

"What would you like to do with these wet fingers?" Haley purrs as she stands.

Crystal reaches between Haley's legs and pushes, separating folds in a circular motion until her fingers throb. Closing her eyes, Crystal can sense the heat streaming from throughout Haley's body to one point. Haley chugs air in spasms as she sways her hips.

Crystal stands and flicks her tongue around Haley's nipple, sucking the areola deep into her mouth. "What I want to do is show how much I love you, how much I want to make you happy, more than you've ever felt before."

"You've already done that."

"I'm just getting started."

Haley arches her back and lifts her arms above her head. Crystal guides her to the bed and pushes her back onto the covers, legs apart and draped over the edge—shimmering and luscious. Crystal places her knee between Haley's thighs and slides it up against the wetness. She leans over Haley, lifting and pushing her knee as she kisses Haley's mouth then her neck and over to her breasts.

Haley whimpers and squirms as her chest pumps breath in and out. "Oh, Crystal."

Crystal moves her knee back as she slides her tongue down Haley's stomach, twirling into her navel, meandering to her pubis, then down. The scent spanks every cell inside her nose and pushes deep into her throat—salty, rich, intoxicatingly pungent. Her tongue presses hard and stiffens against the tangy, earthy, sweet skin, lifting and swirling until Haley bucks her hips and grunts with a muffled scream.

After a few seconds, Haley lifts herself up into the bed. "Crystal, lie next to me and turn around."

Crystal climbs next to her then erupts in ecstasy as soon as she feels Haley's tongue and fingers.

Two hours later, Crystal awakes, numb and heavy, her head on one of Haley's legs, her hand nestled between her butt cheeks, and Haley's warm breath on her stomach. They breathe as one.

A vibrating sound barely distinguishes itself against the white noise. Crystal strains to listen until the urgent pulsation triggers a recognition in her brain—someone is calling.

Mom?

Crystal slides her body away from Haley's and onto the floor. Her hands push through her discarded clothing until she finds the phone, lit up with an unidentified call. She jerks it to her ear, then away to swipe, but now the screen is dark. Crystal stands, slips on her robe, opens the door, and hurries to the kitchen. After unlocking her screen, she notices a voice mail and presses the play button.

"Crystal . . . this is . . . Maya. I was hoping to talk to you. I'm sorry it's late, but Jordan took forever to sleep."

CHAPTER 21

*I*t's just after midnight. Crystal returns the call and hurries into the living room. While her phone rings, she grabs Maya's picture from the roll top desk and sits on the leather sofa, her heart thumping in her chest.

Jordan? Does she have a brother or a sister?

"Crystal?" The voice is breathy and quiet but deep like a smoker's.

"Maya?" Crystal grips the sofa arm hard, her chest tight.

"Hey. Just a minute. I need to go to another room."

Crystal hears steps and a door closing. Every one of her senses is hyperalert.

"OK," says Maya. "Did I wake you?"

"I'd just dozed off. It's fine." She swallows, trying to relax her throat. "I can't believe I'm talking to you. I've wanted to for so long."

"I'm . . . I'm so sorry, Crystal." Her voice quavers. "For everything. I don't know why you'd want to talk to me."

Crystal stands and speaks quickly. "The past is gone. Let's not worry about it right now. I've called you Maya for as long as I can remember, but you're my mom. I want you to be my mom."

"I'd like to try, Crystal. If you'll let me."

Crystal wants to leap and run. "When can I see you? And Jordan. Girl or boy?"

Maya sniffs. Maybe she's crying? "Jordan is your sister. Six months old. She looks just like you."

Tears pool in Crystal's eyes. "Can you send me a picture? Of both of you?"

"Yes."

"Is she . . . OK?"

"Yes. She's perfect. I finally did things right. Crystal . . . I wish . . ." She breaks down crying.

"I wished for a perfect sister. Thank you. Is Jordan my sister or half sister?"

"Does it matter?"

"Not to me. I just thought if she had a different father, that's why Eugene brought you back here."

"That was his reason. Not mine."

"When can I see her?"

"We're going to try tomorrow."

"OK. We'll do whatever you want us to do. Did Holly tell you . . . everything?"

"Yes. Have you heard any more about my parents?"

"Summer's on oxygen and Mac is still on a ventilator, but they both know you're alive. And Summer wants me to tell you she made a mistake with you and Holly."

Maya whimpers then takes quick breaths. "She said that?"

"Yes. I told her about Haley and me."

"Did she get mad?"

"No. She asked me if I was sure. I told her yes."

"Do you love her?"

Crystal remembers Summer's complaints about Maya keeping secrets and lying. "Mom, I don't want to keep secrets from you, and I don't want you to keep them from me. Is that OK?"

"Yes."

"I've loved Haley for years. She's asleep in my bed now. Have you . . . have you and Holly . . . since you've been back?" Crystal hears the scrape of a lighter and a draw on a cigarette.

"Yes. This afternoon."

"The first time since . . ."

"August 21, 2001." She blows out smoke. "Such a long time ago."

"Why didn't you stay with her?"

"I was pregnant with you. She was with Haley. It was a different time back then. I was messed up and couldn't figure out anything else to do besides run off with Eugene."

Crystal clutches her belly. "Will you stay now?"

"Yes. I'm not living with him any more." She puffs her cigarette.

"He sounds dangerous."

"He said he'd kill me if I left him again."

"Is he my father?"

Maya coughs. "Why do you ask?"

"I thought maybe he wanted you to take JD and me to the village because he didn't want to raise someone else's kid. Or maybe you told him I wasn't his then you'd have an excuse to come back to Alaska and see Holly." Crystal waits for a response but hears only quiet breathing.

After a full minute, Maya says, "We can talk tomorrow."

Crystal leans forward, her skin tingling. "OK. I want to see you and Jordan tomorrow, even if I come to you. I thought maybe you were in a house somewhere near the trail that Holly came down today."

"Don't look, Crystal. Please. He'll follow you. He doesn't know anything about Holly. OK? Promise?"

Crystal hears the terror in her voice. "I promise. I'll wait for you. Send me the pictures right after we hang up."

"I will. Crystal, you're better than what I deserve. I thought you'd hate me."

"I did for a long time, but I've learned a lot recently. Now all I want is to hug my mom and my sister."

"Soon. Good night." She ends the call.

Crystal breathes deep and replays her mother's voice in her head. All these years she could never remember her voice. She hugs herself and looks out a window from the living room. Lights! The aurora is out. She races back to the sunroom and looks out the windows. Vibrating streaks of green and yellow light up the east.

"They've been out for twenty minutes," says Payton from a chair in the corner.

Crystal yelps and turns. "Shit, Payton. I didn't know you were there."

"I've been keeping watch." She stands and lays her gun across the chair. "You talked to your mother."

Crystal beams with happiness. "Yes! Did you hear?"

"Just what you said. You have a sister."

Crystal's phone dings. She finds two photos—her mother's face and one of her nursing Jordan. "Look." She shows them to Payton. "Mom is still beautiful."

"Maya is breastfeeding Jordan," says Payton. "Yet the plan was to leave her here and go home with Eugene?"

"Maybe Mom's weaning her now. Or maybe she's pumped extra and saved it. Remember, all she had to do was convince Eugene she was going to abandon Jordan. If she never intended to, why would she fully wean her?"

"I heard you ask whether Eugene was your father."

"She didn't answer. 'We can talk tomorrow,' she said."

"You have doubts?"

"Yeah." Crystal watches the lights outside while she talks. "When I saw him today, he reminded me of JD. None of my features are his. They're all from Mom except my chin is sharper. Why would he bring Mom back home to abandon Jordan unless she's not his kid? Then I thought he probably did the same fourteen years ago."

"Who's Jordan's father?"

"I have no idea. Oh, look!" She grabs Payton's arm. "The lights are red." She opens the door and runs to the edge of the deck, her body light and jazzed with adrenaline. A red line glows on the bottom of the green and yellow streaks, which swarm directly overhead. Reaching into her mouth with her thumb and middle finger, she sends a shrill whistle to the sky.

From behind her, Payton asks, "Why are you whistling?"

"Mac told me the Native kids in the village would whistle at the lights to make them move." She whistles again.

Now the streaks whip across the sky then join into one dome of swirling light. "It worked!" She swears she can hear the sky hum.

Suddenly a river of purple and red splash down from the north. Crystal holds her arms and face to the sky, mesmerized. A ball of undulating red breaks away and almost bounces around the yard, changing shape continuously. She squeals and laughs, bouncing on her tiptoes. She knows these lights are sixty miles above the earth, but sometimes on a very clear night they seem to move just above the trees.

The ball dips and shimmies before bounding over the house. Crystal runs to the other side of the deck and watches it dissipate above the driveway. She turns around and the display is now just two pillars of green and yellow, which soon shrink to the horizon as a faint glow in the distance.

"I've never seen that before," says Crystal, her chest still heaving in excitement. "Have you?"

"No. That was awesome."

"Do you think it means anything?"

"Huh?"

"Like it's a sign or something."

"Some would think so, I guess."

"But not you?"

Payton shakes her head. "No. The lights are ionized oxygen and nitrogen molecules hit by solar wind. They don't *mean* anything."

"If you painted what we just saw on your shirt, that would mean something. Yes?"

"Then it's art. How I express it means something to me."

Crystal throws her arms out. "The sky is art and it just expressed a world of meaning to you. How can you not see that?" Crystal peers at the sky, enraptured.

Payton stands next to her, looking up. "Then what does the red ball mean?"

Crystal lowers her arms and twirls around the deck. "Something new, fresh, exciting, like my Mom and Jordan."

"Or it could be a foreboding of danger."

She stops and looks at Payton. "I guess it could."

A great horned owl hoots nearby, claiming its territory, warning others to stay away. This one is a monster with a six-foot wingspan Crystal saw yesterday, lurking on the woodshed, staring at her with big yellow eyes. But she felt no fear, even when it spread its wings and swooped over her head, slowly thrashing the air to glide into nearby trees. She thought it was her protector.

Now his hoots remind her of danger nearby.

Eugene.

She shivers. "It's freaking cold out here. My feet are freezing."

"Well, you *are* barefoot." She opens the door. "Come inside."

Crystal bolts into the sunroom and clutches her robe tighter. Payton takes the throw blanket off her chair and drapes it over Crystal's shoulders.

"Thank you. My brain is racing a million miles an hour. I don't know how I'm going back to sleep." She paces around the room, looking out the windows.

"She's coming tomorrow?"

"Supposed to. Along with JD and Kato and Gena and maybe Lena. And probably Eugene."

"Maybe we should wash sheets from upstairs so Maya and Jordan can stay there. Or Sydney and I can move back to our motorhome. She can have JD's room."

"I don't want you moving anywhere. We'll make room." She blows out a breath. "I could've been all alone in this house tonight."

"You and Haley have been great with Sydney. Thank you."

Crystal takes out her phone, swipes through screens, and holds it out to Payton. "Haley did Sydney's eyes tonight."

Payton takes the phone and smiles.

"I also drew a picture of her. It's in your room. She loved it."

"Thanks." Payton stares out the window and sighs.

"Why did you leave your cabin this morning?" asks Crystal. "Why not tomorrow or the next day?"

"I didn't want Sydney hurt."

"By who?"

"Bekah's father."

"Bekah?"

"She was my girlfriend. I met her at Pioneer Park this summer. Sydney and I were riding bikes and Sis saw her under a tree by herself, crying. Of course, Sis offered to help. Bekah had run away from home that morning because her father threatened to send her to a military school or a conversion camp."

"Why?"

"She's gay, using drugs, refusing to attend church, harming herself. They'd been butting heads for years, especially after his wife left him."

"She left her daughter?"

"Yeah. Seems to happen a lot these days. Bekah said her mom had a boyfriend who didn't want extra baggage."

"Sounds familiar."

"We took her to the motorhome and gave her food. She asked to stay with us, so we took her home to the cabin. Bekah's main problem had been outing herself to her Bible-thumping father. Once she was away from him, she did great. I taught her to paint. We hiked. She took me fishing." Her eyes sparkle. "We were great together."

She hugs her shoulders and bites her lip. "Evidently we went out too much because someone saw her and followed us home. Her father must've hired a private investigator."

She clears her throat and pushes her fingers through her hair. "Two days ago, she went outside the cabin to smoke by herself while Sydney and I cleaned up after dinner. I heard a scream and a car racing away. She'd been taken." Payton's lips flatten against her teeth.

"The next morning I found a note taped to my windshield, unsigned but obviously from her dad. He said he would charge me with kidnapping and I'd better keep an eye on Sydney because she might disappear too. We packed up and left, which was what he wanted us to do." She barks a harsh laugh. "Because if I'm out of town, you see, Bekah won't run away anymore, and everything will be great in the Thompson household."

Crystal holds Payton's hand. "I'm sorry."

"I kick myself for letting her go outside alone. If it was just me, I would've stayed, taken my gun, and rescued Bekah. Or tried to. But I can't take a chance with Sydney."

Crystal watches Payton move to the windows and look outside, sensing the girl's anger and resolve. Payton failed once, but looking at her now, Crystal knows there won't be a second time. "Have you heard from her?"

"No. I bought her a Tracfone. I've tried to call but I'm sure her dad found it."

"Does she know your number?"

"Yeah."

"Then maybe she'll call soon."

"Maybe. Unless they've converted her. Or she kills herself." She clenches her fist. "Why are people so fucking crazy about sexuality? Just the other day, I read a news bulletin about a second grade girl expelled from a Christian school because she told another girl in her class she had a crush on her. How insane is that? If Bekah were loved for who she is, she'd have no problems at all."

"If you come out, people hate you. If you don't, you hate yourself." Crystal hugs Payton from behind. "You should get some sleep. You can't save the world if you've been up all night."

Payton presses Crystal's hands against her stomach. "If Bekah does call, I can go get her and not have to worry about Sydney. I know you and Haley will take care of her."

"We'd love to. She's everyone's little sister now." Crystal squeezes Payton once more. "I'm going back to bed. Good night."

Crystal walks back to her room and slips quietly inside the door. Haley is on her back, snoring softly. Crystal tries not to laugh as she drops her robe and slides in next to her. She thinks about Payton's trick with the nose, but decides to gently kiss Haley's cheeks and eyes and mouth.

Haley smiles in her sleep, makes cute sounds, then rolls over on her side. Crystal scoots in to spoon her, holding her stomach with her left hand—her skin soft and warm. Heaven could not feel better than she does now. She and Haley cradle each other in a cocoon of trust and peace. She would die if anything happened to Haley.

Or JD. Mac. Summer.

Mom and Jordan.

Payton and Sydney.

Holly.

So many more people to love.

So much more to lose.

CHAPTER 22

*a*fter what seems like a few minutes of sleep, Crystal hears noises in the hall. Haley is gone.

"Hey, Crystal," yells JD. "You need to get up."

Crystal jerks upright and finds her phone. It's not even eight yet. *What the hell?* She finds boxer shorts and a t-shirt, puts them on then opens her door.

JD is standing near the bathroom door, eyes wide open. "Haley's puking."

"Shit," says Crystal. She knocks on the door. "Haley?" More retching. Crystal turns the knob and slips inside.

Haley kneels on the floor naked, her arms on the toilet seat, retching brown liquid into the water. Crystal holds her hair and kisses her back. "I'm here, Haley." She flushes the toilet.

Haley leans back, snot oozing out of her nose, face puffy, struggling to breathe. "I was hoping to get up early and bring you coffee in bed. I wanted to look sexy for you." She bends over and retches again.

Crystal grabs some tissue and wipes Haley's nose and mouth when she leans back again. "Did I ever tell you I love the sight of snot and spit? I'm very turned on right now, I might attack you on this floor." She cocks a brow.

Haley coughs a laugh. "You wouldn't even kiss me."

Crystal holds Haley's face and presses her lips to Haley's. "Don't ever dare me." She kisses again. "You will always lose."

"Good to know." She sits on her butt and pulls her legs to her chest, shivering.

Crystal drapes the robe around her. "Are you through?"

"Maybe."

Crystal flushes the toilet. "Have you peed this morning?"

"Not yet."

"I'll get your cup and a test strip. Be right back." She opens the door and sees JD sitting at the table eating cereal from a bowl. Kato drinks coffee.

"How is she?" asks Payton as she stirs cream into her coffee.

"Fresh out of bile. JD, where's Gena?"

"She's puking too. This morning was pretty bad."

"Will I see her before . . ."

JD shakes his head. "Maybe not."

She nods then hurries down the hall, grabs what she needs, and comes back to the bathroom door. Kato stares at the cup containing the test strip. She turns her back to him to hide it and walks inside.

Haley stands at the sink, splashing water on her face. "Who's here besides JD?"

"Kato."

"I'm sure I flashed JD running to the bathroom."

Crystal leans against the vanity. "He covered his eyes, didn't he? Then he apologized."

"Yes."

"He always does that."

"My brothers would've whistled and clapped. JD is a sweety."

"Yes, he is. Always has been. Here's your cup."

"OK," says Haley. "Are you watching or leaving?"

"As long as it's only pee, I'll stay. Unless you insist I leave."

"Girlfriends who pee together, stay together." Haley sits on the toilet and holds the cup between her legs. "Someone described an orgasm as dying to pee then finally being able to let it go." She locks eyes with

Crystal then sighs when the stream hits the plastic. "That description doesn't even come close to last night."

Both girls blush. "I love it when you look at me like that," Crystal giggles.

Haley hands her the cup. "Stick it and time it."

Crystal opens a strip, dips it in for five seconds then lays it across the cup. She sets her phone timer to five minutes. "Can I get you something? Clothes, coffee?"

Haley wipes, flushes then stands. "A hug?"

Crystal reaches through the robe to pull Haley's bare skin to her.

Haley clutches Crystal's back. "You made me feel so good. A new orgasm would start before the last one ended. Over and over."

A wave of warmth rises from Crystal's toes to her chest, cresting through her throat as a groan. "Over and over and over. I might want to take a nap before lunch." They lick each other's lips.

"And maybe one after lunch." Haley reaches her hands down Crystal's boxers.

"Then we'll be so tired, we'll have to go to bed early." Crystal holds Haley's breasts. "We're going to need energy for all this sleeping. Payton's in the kitchen. What do you want for breakfast?"

"You." Her fingers move down Crystal's legs.

"Later. We need to put something besides each other into our mouths or I'm going to fade away. Besides, we have guests."

"Oh, OK." She removes her hands. "Pancakes. Coffee with cream and sugar. And my makeup pouch on the dresser."

"I'll be right back." Crystal exits the bathroom. "Payton, can you make Haley a coffee with cream and sugar?"

"Sure."

"Have you eaten?"

"Not yet. What do you want?"

"Pancakes!" yells Sydney from behind her.

Crystal laughs. "Pancakes are good. There's a bag of Krusteaz in the pantry." Crystal goes to her room, pulls on sweatpants and throws her arms through a flannel shirt. She finds the pouch then heads to the kitchen where she pours her own coffee, adds cream, and takes a few sips.

"Is she pregnant?" asks Kato.

"Are you nosy?" answers Crystal. Payton hands her Haley's coffee. "Thanks." She returns to Haley and drops off the coffee and pouch. "How much time left?"

"Thirty seconds." Haley sips her coffee as both girls stare at the strip, which already shows two lines.

"I talked to my mom last night. I have a baby sister named Jordan."

"Really? That's my mother's maiden name."

Both girls look at each other. Crystal's scalp tingles. "She named my sister after your mother." A shiver of realization flutters in Crystal's chest. "Mom planned this whole thing. She got pregnant from another man and told Eugene so he'd send her home. She's coming over later today."

The phone dings. The strips haven't changed.

"What a surprise," says Haley dryly. "I'm pregnant."

Crystal rubs Haley's tummy. "Congratulations. We should send out announcements. Who's first?"

A tear rolls down Haley's cheek. "I'm not sure. Probably Dylan. He'll be ecstatic."

Probably? Crystal swallows her question then pulls Haley in for a hug. "We're doing this together."

Haley nods, lips pressed tight.

Crystal wipes her girlfriend's cheeks. "See you at breakfast."

Crystal goes into the kitchen where Sydney is mixing ingredients in a blue plastic bowl. The boys are taking empty crates back to JD's room. Payton is outside vaping.

"Hey, Sydney, how many are we making?"

"Payton says thirty-six. The boys aren't staying."

Crystal reaches inside a cabinet for vanilla and sugar and opens the butter dish. "When Summer makes these, she always adds extra ingredients. Add two teaspoons of vanilla, two tablespoons of sugar, and a half stick of melted butter."

"OK." Sydney frowns. "How much vanilla?"

Crystal remembers Sydney's short-term memory problem. "I'll write it down. I've seen Summer do it so many times, I don't even have to think, but it's brand new to you." She finds a sticky note and a pen and writes the instructions. "Once you mix everything, let it sit in the bowl for about ten minutes before you start cooking."

"OK, but Payton's going to cook them. I'm just the prepper."

Crystal wipes batter off Sydney's face and twists her hair into a knot to keep it out of the bowl. "She told me about Bekah last night. Do you miss her?"

Sydney tilts her face down. "I try not to think about her because it makes me sad. We both love her."

"Maybe she'll find a way to call you."

"She probably will. Her father will make a mistake, and boom, Bekah will be out of there in a flash."

"Is she eighteen?"

"Almost. Haley's pregnant?"

"Yes. Why?"

"Kato and JD were talking about it in the kitchen."

Crystal nods and walks away. *Great*, she thinks. What will Kato do with that information?

When Crystal enters the room, both boys are taking clothes out of JD's dresser and stacking them into the crates. "Will everything fit?"

"Whatever doesn't needs to stay," says JD, sweat dripping off his forehead. "We only have room in Lena's truck for what I can stuff into these crates."

"I can mail boxes to you," says Crystal.

"Oh, yeah. I didn't think of that," says JD. "Are Payton and Sydney going to stay here?"

"Yes."

"Are you gay now?"

Kato flashes an angry look at JD, who realizes he made a mistake.

"Oh, I'm sorry."

"No need to be sorry, JD. I've always been gay." She glances at Kato and sees him sucking in his lips. "But I wasn't sure until yesterday."

"Oh." JD pushes clothes down in one crate and snaps a lid on it. "What happened yesterday?"

"I kissed Haley and then we slept together last night."

"Is she gay?" asks JD.

"Yes," says Crystal, waiting for Kato to erupt.

"Then why is she pregnant with Dylan's baby?" Kato throws a wad of clothes into the other crate.

"The baby is Haley's," says Crystal. "It's growing inside her body."

"Is she going to tell him?" Kato grabs more clothes out of a drawer.

"That's her decision, not yours."

"Doesn't he have a right to know? I'd want to know."

"Having a *right* to know and *wanting* to know aren't the same, Kato. He treated Haley like crap. Just used her to get himself off. He doesn't have a *right* to anything with her."

Kato shakes his head. "He should know. If you got pregnant, wouldn't you tell the guy?"

Crystal sees pain and anger in his eyes. He doesn't care about Dylan. In his own way, he cares about her and hoped he wouldn't be leaving her here while he flies to the village. "I didn't get pregnant, so I don't have to worry. How long have you known Lena was going back?"

Kato diverts his eyes.

"Weeks, maybe months," says Crystal. "Long enough for you to get me pregnant and follow you. Like Gena did with JD?"

Kato breathes more rapidly and glances at JD who scratches his head.

"Like Gena did what?" asks JD.

"Nothing to worry about," says Crystal. "Brothers and sisters talk and make plans, just like you and me. Except," she snaps her eyes toward Kato, "there was another way. Like talking and asking openly and honestly. Not give some bullshit reasons for not using a condom." She didn't have to throw that last line at Kato, but she couldn't help herself. She realizes now why Gena made sure she and JD had time alone every day this past summer. All she had to do was ask him, and he would've said yes. He didn't have to be forced to become a father before he's ready.

"I don't know what you're talking about, Crystal," says JD. "But you're hurting my brain."

"I'm sorry. I didn't get much sleep last night." Her eyes meet Kato's. "I wish it didn't have to end this way, Kato. Maybe after you're in the village for a while, we'll be able to talk like we used to. And you need to think real hard before you tell Dylan about Haley. All he'll do is harass and hurt her. She doesn't need more of that."

She locks onto his eyes, trying to see inside Kato's mind. Will he want revenge or forgiveness? He turns away from her. She knows the answer.

"JD, I want to talk to you alone before you leave," says Crystal. "OK?"

"Sure."

Crystal meets Haley as she exits the bathroom. "Do I look better?"

"You're beautiful," says Crystal. "You're always beautiful." She squeezes Haley's hand.

"I'll be there in just a minute." Haley goes to their room.

Crystal finds Payton cooking pancakes in the kitchen. Sydney has two on a plate covered in butter and syrup.

"These are *sooo* good, Crystal." Sydney folds a big bite into her mouth then takes her plate to the table.

Crystal stands next to Payton. "You've done this before."

"I usually make them like half dollars because Sydney loves them that way, but she was hungry and couldn't wait."

"We're going to have more trouble with Dylan today."

"Yeah? Why?" She pours more batter on the griddle.

"Because Kato will tell Dylan about Haley's pregnancy."

Payton flips a pancake. "Of course, he will. Guys don't like the idea that a woman's body is hers and not theirs. Get a plate." Payton lifts a stack of pancakes on her spatula.

Crystal grabs a plate from the cabinet and brings it over. "Did you get any sleep?"

Payton slides the cakes. "A little. The guys woke me up at seven when they pulled up. They brought a truck and a Honda."

Crystal butters her pancakes at the counter. "Probably Lena wants to leave her Honda with us. She has no way to take it to town with all her luggage."

Crystal takes her pancakes to the table and covers them in syrup. Sydney leaps up to ask her sister for more. Haley walks in wearing her own leggings and a sweatshirt. Soon her plate is full. Finally Payton is able to sit with them and eat at the table.

"You must have three large bags of pancake mix back there," says Payton.

"At least," answers Crystal. "I told you, Mac and Summer are ready for the apocalypse. We've got another freezer and fridge full of food in the garage. No one will go hungry in this house."

Kato and JD lug their crates into the kitchen and set them on the floor. Kato pulls a key out of his jeans and flips it onto the granite island underneath the pots and pans hanging from the ceiling. "Mom said you can use her Honda."

"Tell her thanks," says Crystal. "Are you leaving now?"

"Yeah," says Kato.

Crystal finds her pack, unzips a compartment, pulls money out, and follows the boys outside. Once they load the crates in the back of the truck, Kato climbs into the driver's seat.

"JD, walk with me." They go around the house into the back yard near one of the planter boxes. Leaves swirl lazily around the grass in the breeze. An angry squirrel chirps and barks from a nearby tree. "You better get your fill of trees, JD. There aren't any in the village."

JD gazes around the yard, frowning. "None?"

"Zero." She hooks his arm. "Maya will be here later today."

"When?"

"I'm not sure." She shows him photos on her phone. "She sent these to me last night. We have a little sister named Jordan."

His eyes bulge and his mouth hangs open as his chest pumps air into his lungs. "I want to see her."

"Then you'd have to stay."

He wails. "I can't."

Crystal hugs her brother. "I know. We'll call you as soon as we can." She holds his face. "Now you need to listen to me. Yes?"

He nods.

She speaks slowly, looking directly into his eyes. "If there are any problems in the village that make you feel sad and you want to come home, you can. I'll buy a ticket for you and even for Gena. You can always come back home. Always."

"I'm not going to leave Gena."

"I know that. But if something happens and both of you feel like leaving, you can both come home. Do you understand?"

He nods quickly. "What about Mac and Summer?"

"I'm going to call the hospital just as soon as you leave. I'll text you."

"Are you going to marry Haley?"

"I don't know."

"Do you love her?"

"Yes. But getting married is very serious. It's for life. You have to love someone as much as Mac and Summer love each other. Then you don't leave just because you're mad or hurt. You have to be totally honest with each other and not be afraid to talk to them about anything. Make sure you feel that way about Gena before you marry her. OK?"

"Yeah."

"And promise me you won't tell anyone about Mom until I say you can. Eugene is trying to find her. He wants to hurt her."

JD scrunches his eyebrows. "Why?"

"Because he's mean. Everything Mac and Summer told us about him is true."

JD tightens his mouth and eyes. "Where is he? Maybe I should find him first. Maybe someone ought to hurt him."

"We have a plan to keep Mom safe, but if something happens to your flight, like it's delayed or anything, then you can come home and help us." JD nods. "Summer said sometimes they had to wait a few days to get into that village because of the weather."

"I remember."

"If that happens tomorrow, then maybe you can drive back. I'd like to see my brother again, and you could be a real help to our Mom. You might also consider flying up there a few days later and give Lena and her kids time to get settled in."

Crystal watches JD's face, sensing the war going on in his mind—shake his head and say no or nod and say maybe. Crystal holds his shoulder. "Whatever you decide."

He grabs her in a hug and lifts her off the ground like he's done for years because he could. "I love you, Crystal. You're my favorite sister."

Crystal laughs at their old joke. "Maybe not. Maybe you'll like Jordan better."

"Jordan? Is that her name?"

"Yeah."

"Well, you're still my favorite sister. For now anyway."

"And you're my favorite brother, even if I had a choice."

He sets her down.

"Remember, JD. Don't tell anyone about Mom." He nods. "And you can come home any time you want. Just call me." He nods. "And here's some cash." She hands him a hundred dollar bill. "I know you're always short of money. If you need more, call me."

His eyes widen at the bill in his hand. "Where'd you get this?"

"It's my birthday money."

"Thanks." He shoves it into his pocket.

"You better get in the truck." She holds his hand and walks him back around the house. As JD climbs into the truck, Crystal says, "Kato, take care of my brother."

"Sure thing." He starts the engine.

"And remember what I said about Dylan."

Kato shifts gears and backs up, not looking at her once.

As she waves to JD, she wishes she could've been honest with him about why Gena got pregnant and what she fears will happen to him in the village. He should stay here with Gena. He'll miss his home and grandparents too much. He won't be able to stand seeing his mother or his sister only through a phone.

How will she stand seeing JD that way? She won't. They'll watch each other cry through the screen, unable to speak.

But she can't tell him. He always had to learn things for himself, always had to make his own mistakes and then fix them.

She hopes the weather is particularly shitty in the village tomorrow.

CHAPTER 23

*C*rystal clicks on the phone number the nurse sent her yesterday. Someone from a nurse's station answers. "Hello, I'm Crystal Rose. I want to know about my grandparents, Summer and Mac Rose."

"Please wait."

A gray rabbit with white feet and ears emerges from behind the woodshed and pauses on the trail, sniffing the air. It turns its head toward Crystal, then back, and is just beginning to push off its hind legs when a blur of wings and talons each as big as Crystal's head crashes in from behind and grabs the rabbit. She watches her monster owl fly toward her, the rabbit punctured by bloody claws hanging two feet below its body. The wings flap only three times before it flies over Crystal, pushing waves of air into her upturned face.

Astonishment pulls air from her lungs and blood into her neck where it throbs, almost drowning out the words squeaking from her phone. "Hello? Are you there?"

"Yes, I'm here." Crystal sucks air into her chest now tingling with wonder. "I'm sorry. An owl . . . just took a rabbit . . ." She closes her eyes and slows her breathing. "How is Summer?"

"Hello, Crystal. She's still on oxygen, but her fever is gone. Mac is still on the ventilator, but his vitals are improving."

The nurse's voice is kind. "Can I speak to Summer today?"

The nurse sighs. "I'm sorry, dear. More likely this evening."

"Can you give her a message? It's very important."

"Certainly."

"Tell her I spoke to Maya last night. That's Summer's daughter who's been gone for years. Maya has a six-month-old daughter named Jordan who is a normal baby. They're both coming home. You got that?" Crystal wonders how that message sounds to a stranger. A daughter gone for years? And a *normal* baby? How many people have to add that tidbit of information?

"Yes, I do."

"That news will make them very happy. Please tell Mac and Summer, even if they're not conscious. Just tell them."

"I will, dear. I'm sure this will cheer them up."

"Thank you." She ends the call and looks back where the attack occurred. Blindsided in death, the rabbit had no time to run. It knew to stay in the trees and under the willows, but everyone's attention wavers sometimes.

Except for the owl. Or the virus.

Once she saw an owl rip away the kill of another owl. Part of it, anyway. She found bloody pieces after the owls had moved on.

Another time she saw a rabbit escape from the talons before it was lifted more than a foot off the ground.

She hopes the news of Maya and Jordan will help her grandparents struggle to live. No matter how long a separation or how deep, a reunion of lost love can make life worth living again. Crystal will never forget the fierce clutch of Haley's fingers against her mother's back.

Hope keeps people alive and willing to wriggle or run out of harm's way. It can blunt the depression and misery and provide some energy to continue moving, to find a different life.

Hope keeps Payton strong and ready for Bekah.

Keeps Crystal from collapsing to her knees at the loss of her brother. He will return. She knows it.

Keeps her from running through every street in town, banging on doors, asking for her mother. She must wait and be prepared lest she lead Eugene to her. Her mother will come to her.

Hope is what kept her mother scheming all those years, despite the drugs and alcohol, looking for an opportunity to come home, whether to Holly or her parents or her kids. It didn't matter. The desire to change, to live again and not become a lethargic rabbit, tired of being wary, standing in a clearing, waiting for the talons.

She needs to prepare for her mother. Bedding needs to be cleaned. When her mom arrives, everything must be ready for her.

Crystal goes to the garage, finds the gun boot JD uses when he hunts, and pulls out his .22 rifle and an extra clip. Before she leaves it in the mudroom, she checks the chamber and engages the safety then hangs it on a coat hook.

She finds the other girls in the sunroom with their computers, logged into their classes. Shit! She's supposed to be in school. "I need to get Mac and Summer's room ready for Mom. I don't have time for classes."

Payton looks over her screen. "Bring me your computer and log in. I can fake it for you."

"Thanks." Crystal runs back to the kitchen and pulls her computer out of her pack. Soon it's open next to Payton. "Remember, I'm supposed to be dumb. Just use a quarter of your brain."

Payton laughs. "In many ways, you're the smartest one in this house."

Haley grabs Crystal's hand. "Do you need help?"

"If you can."

"Hey," says Payton, "I can't fake both of you."

"Sure you can," says Crystal. "Both of our cameras are off so all anyone will see are our portraits. Type some comments in the chat room and throw in a few emojis and thumbs up. No one will know the difference. Oh, remember to misspell lots of words for me."

"If you need to," says Haley, "just say I'm puking in the bathroom. I'm sure everyone knows by now anyway." Haley stands. "Let's go."

Haley follows Crystal upstairs. At the door to the bedroom, Crystal stops. "I haven't been up here in a while. Not since I climbed in bed with them after nightmares." She opens the door. As always, the bed is made and extra pillows are stacked neatly against the headboard. Summer left windows cranked open two inches to let the virus escape, but the chill of evenings in the 30s and 40s has seeped in. A stack of books sits on each nightstand. Mac and Summer always read before sleeping, a habit they'd hoped to pass on to their kids and grandkids, but Maya wasn't interested, and reading is too much work for Crystal and JD. Besides, they have phones.

"Do you want me to strip the bed?" asks Haley.

"Yes. I'll check the bathroom." Crystal clears off the vanity counter and sprays it with Lysol. She pours a little bleach into the sink and the shower drain to fill the p-traps, plus the toilet. Then sprays the shower stall and curtain with a cleaner.

"What about the quilt?" asks Haley.

"Too big to wash. I'll just spray it with Lysol. Take the sheets and mattress pad downstairs, and I'll spray everything before I leave."

A few minutes later, Crystal descends the stairs, carrying Mac's shotgun and bear pistol. She finds Payton and Sydney in the kitchen. "How am I doing in class?"

"Great," answers Payton. "We're on a break." She takes the shotgun. "You expecting trouble?"

"As long as Eugene is in town. Sydney, can you shoot?"

She smiles, takes the pistol, flips the barrel out, and thumbs the hammer back and forward. "I'm not as good as Payton."

Payton removes a chambered shell from the pump shotgun. "Not yet, Sis, but you will be soon."

Haley enters from the utility room. "Ooh, are we choosing weapons? I'll take the shotgun. Hard to miss a target with that one."

"Have you used one?" asks Payton.

"I've hunted ducks a few times. Besides, a free gun range is no more than two miles from anyone in town. Who could grow up here and not shoot?" She takes the shotgun from Payton.

"OK," says Crystal, "the shotgun is yours. I'll take the pistol. Sydney, there's a .22 in the mudroom."

"Mine's in the sunroom," says Payton. "Let's try not to shoot each other, ladies."

"Or anyone else," says Crystal. "Unless a fool won't back down and leave."

The wall phone rings.

"Speaking of fools," says Haley.

Crystal takes two steps toward the phone then looks back at the girls. "Do you want to take bets?"

Payton raises her brows. "We're supposed to get back to class."

Haley grabs Crystal's arm. "I'm staying here."

"C'mon, Sis. Leave the pistol on the table." Payton and Sydney head toward the sunroom and the computers.

Crystal looks at Haley and answers the phone. "I am definitely changing this number."

"Good morning, Crystal," says Eugene. "Then how would your mother call you, unless she already knows your cell number?"

"What do you want?"

"I'll take that as a yes, she does." His tone turns somber. "She had me fooled, Crystal, and I'm afraid you're going to be next."

"Oh no, Daddy," says Crystal with feigned distress. "Whatever do you mean?"

Haley applauds slowly.

Crystal gives a thumbs up to Haley, then says sweetly, "Was that what you wanted me to say, Eugene?" She barks, "Well, that's too bad. Don't call back." She pulls the phone from her ear.

Eugene shouts, "Has she told you about Jordan yet?"

Crystal holds the handset a foot away from her ear and stares at Haley. She expected another threat. At least another lie. But she didn't expect him to mention Jordan. *What's his plan now?*

Crystal brings the phone to her ear. Haley huddles close to listen, both of them half sitting on the table.

"Yes, she did," says Crystal. "I'm looking forward to meeting my sister." Now he knows, Crystal realizes, that Maya hasn't come over yet. Should she have said otherwise?

"That's what she hopes for," says Eugene smugly. "That's her key into your door."

"She doesn't need Jordan to come into my house."

"Maybe not. But Maya wouldn't have come home without her."

"Because you don't want to raise another man's baby."

He harrumphs. "Is that what she told you? That I'm not Jordan's father?"

"Are you? I noticed she had blonde hair in a photo. You and Maya have dark hair. If Jordan is yours, why would you bring Maya back here? Seems like you'd want to raise the perfect daughter you and Maya made together."

Eugene chuckles. "Jordan was conceived during Maya's sixty-day court-ordered rehab treatment. Go figure. Maya found herself a young, curly-headed blonde counselor to screw. He got fired. She got pregnant. But I didn't know that when she came home. She claimed I got her pregnant before going to rehab. Which I believed until she pushed out a blue-eyed, blonde baby. Imagine my surprise."

"Why are you telling me this?"

"Because your mother is a liar."

"Says the pot to the kettle."

Eugene chuckles. "Oh, she's way better than me. She convinced me she would come home with Jordan, and if things worked out between her and her parents, she'd try to talk them into giving me another chance. If not, she'd leave Jordan with them, and we'd go home. But then she took off, as you already know, so she's got someone else she wants to run off with."

Crystal watches Haley mouth, "Mom."

Crystal rolls her eyes. "Why do you think she wants to run off with someone else? Why couldn't she live with us? We can help her with Jordan. If you'd leave town, all her problems would be solved."

"Really?" he snaps. "If it weren't for me, your mother would be dead in a ditch or some hooker on the street. I've saved her ass too many times to count."

"I'm sure she'll be eternally grateful." Crystal tightens her eyes. "Leave town, Eugene."

"Don't you see?" As if talking to a child, he says, "Whether I go away or not, she's still going to abandon Jordan. She'll tell you she needs to leave her with you so I'll think she's run off with someone else. Then I'll try to find her. And that's when it's safe for her to return. But she won't come back. That's what I'm trying to tell you. She won't ever come back."

The two girls frown at each other. Haley rolls her eyes and signals Crystal to hang up. Maybe Eugene is crazy. What's the point of telling Crystal her mother will abandon another baby? To make her suspicious of Maya? What will Eugene gain from telling her this?

Crystal stands. "And where would she go exactly?"

"With someone named Jack."

Both Haley and Crystal freeze. Haley's dad? Crystal tries to think of anyone else she knows named Jack. No one comes to mind. She pulls out a chair and flops into it.

"Who's he?" asks Crystal, her heart pounding. He's lying. He always lies. Why is she even listening to him?

"I thought you'd already talked to him."

Crystal thinks he's fishing. "I've talked to no one named Jack."

Haley scoots another chair near Crystal, sits, and leans toward the handset.

Crystal hears Eugene light a cigarette. "Or maybe someone else is helping Maya now, but there's a Jack waiting for his chance."

Crystal's brain races. Where is he going with this? "How would she know someone named Jack who lives in Clear or even close? She hasn't been back here for eighteen years."

"Exactly. Not since he got her pregnant."

Haley's face drains of color. Her body shakes. Crystal grabs her hand. "Maya told you this?"

Crystal hears him take a drag and blow it out. "Yes, she did."

"She told you when? Fourteen years ago, before you sent her to the village?"

"What difference does that make?" he scoffs.

"Because, you idiot, she knew you'd tell her to dump me and JD if you weren't my father. She could've made up any name, and you would've reacted the same way."

He inhales another drag. "Except I remember meeting a Jack at the music festival. Does Clear still have one?"

Crystal squeezes her eyes shut. "Not this year."

"But normally they still do. You know what it's like. Lots of people, lots of drugs and beer. I got there on a Saturday and met your mom that evening. She was flirting with a tall, skinny dude in the beer tent. I figured they'd hooked up, but another girl came in right after me, and he got out of there pretty quick like he didn't want to be seen with Maya. Then I bought your mother a beer, and the rest, as they say, is history." He puffs again. "That dude's name was Jack. Maya told me later they'd been hooking up for a few days, and that's when she got pregnant with you, Crystal."

Crystal shakes her head, still clutching Haley's hand. Tears drip down Haley's cheeks as she stares at the floor. How many Jacks could've been at that festival? People come from all over the state to the Clear Music Festival.

"You still with me, Crystal? I hope this news isn't too much of a shock to you because the best part is still to come."

She can hear the evil delight in his voice, like he's watching the train bear down on her car, stuck on the tracks, eager to see the big explosion. Now she's scared, because she can see the same train. She knows what's coming to her. She wants to stand and walk the phone back to the wall before he can say it, but her legs won't move.

"I couldn't remember his last name until a while ago when I noticed all the talk on Facebook about Haley being pregnant."

Haley groans.

Eugene spits. "Someone asked if Jack knew. Someone made a joke about whether the kid would look like Dylan or Haley. Someone wondered about the last name, whether it'd be Carson or Rose if you and Haley got married. But what none of them are talking about *yet* is that you and Haley are sisters. Imagine what they'll say then." Eugene laughs. "Hope you have a good rest of your day, Crystal."

He hangs up.

CHAPTER 24

*C*rystal tries to swallow, but her throat is too tight. Haley weeps into her hands. Crystal throws her arm around her girlfriend's back and pulls her close. "It's not true, Haley. He met Mom on a Saturday. There's no way they weren't screwing that night and after. No way for Mom to be sure she got pregnant from Jack. She just told him that to rile him up and send her to the village."

Haley looks at Crystal, her chin quivering. "But what if it's true? That we're sisters."

Crystal remembers the long pause after she asked her mom about a different father. "We can talk tomorrow," she said. Why wait? Because her mom knew how devastating the truth would be? Or maybe her mom sensed she didn't want Eugene to be her dad and if her mom told her he actually is, Crystal might not be as willing to help her? She clenches her jaw.

All these questions are the result of one man's lies. He could've played this ace during his earlier phone call. It would've been much more effective than screaming "bitch" and making threats.

Crystal stands. "We're acting exactly like he wants us to. That bastard got an idea because he was looking through Facebook pages. He wants us to believe Mom plans to dump Jordan regardless of whether she lives with him or not. Then he wants to split us up so we don't try to help Mom."

Haley flinches. "Is he splitting us up?"

Crystal sits by Haley and wipes her face. "Not a chance."

"But what if everyone talks about it?"

"Eugene's not telling anyone. Who is he to them? And besides, you think your father would let that story fly?"

Haley pushes her hair back. "But he's tall. And he was skinny years ago."

"Maybe Eugene met him. Holly knew Eugene. Why couldn't your father?"

Hailey breathes quickly, staring at the ceiling. "You don't think it's true?"

"No possibility."

Sydney clears her throat standing in the doorway to the kitchen. "What did we miss?"

Haley turns her face toward the girl.

"Are you crying? What happened?"

Haley wipes her cheeks. "I'm fine. I'll wash up. All I'm doing today is puking and crying." She closes the bathroom door behind her.

Payton holds her sister's shoulders. "What did Eugene say?"

Crystal decides the topic of being sisters stays between Haley and her. At least until after she talks to her Mom. "Eugene claims my mom will abandon Jordan even if she doesn't go back to him. He thinks there's another man waiting to take her away."

Payton shakes her head. "How does telling you that help him get your mom back?"

"I'm not sure. Maybe if we're suspicious of Mom, we won't let her leave or call him to stop her? The man's crazy. Every time he talks, he lies. I don't think he knows the difference any more."

Sydney finds a bottle of tea in the refrigerator. "Why doesn't he try to be nice to your mother? Why would she ever want to stay with him?"

"Maybe he's tried in his own way to be nice," says Crystal. "But she doesn't love him, and he knows it. I don't think she ever has."

"Is he more obsessed with loving her or losing her?" asks Payton.

"Mom said he threatened to kill her if she left again."

"That's sick," says Sydney.

"What class am I in?" asks Crystal.

"We have art in a few minutes," says Payton, "but you need to check your email. Some kind of legal document came in."

"You'll have to help me," says Crystal as she walks toward the sunroom. After a minute she opens an email from a retirement consulting firm in Fairbanks. She is supposed to click all the yellow boxes before returning it. "What is this, Payton?" Crystal turns her computer toward her friend.

Payton scans through a page or two. "It's setting up a living will. You'll be a co-owner of your grandparents' mutual funds and stocks. Which means all their savings are now yours." She points to a paragraph and turns the screen so Crystal can see it. "If Mac and Summer die, you have immediate access to the money. You won't have to wait months for probate."

"What's that?"

"Legal stuff that takes time and keeps you from using the money in their bank accounts. By signing this, you won't have to worry."

"How do I sign?" asks Crystal.

"I had to do a few of these when I became a foster parent to Sydney. Just click where every yellow box is. When you do, your signature is automatically entered."

Crystal clicks every box, worrying whether each one brings the reason for this document closer to reality. She hesitates before clicking the last button, but this is what Mac and Summer want her to do. She hits Submit.

Payton points to several attachments. "This is their will, a list of links to their investments, title information about the house, life insurance policies, a financial advisor to call, and more. We don't have to open these now." Payton gazes into Crystal's face and pushes hair behind Crystal's ear. "Your grandparents have taken care of you and JD."

Crystal's breath catches in her chest. "They always have." Her eyes swell and the back of her throat tightens into a knot. She grits her teeth but can't keep the wail inside her. "I don't want them to have to do this. I want both of them home."

Haley hurries in and sits next to her. "What is it?"

Crystal buries her face into Haley's shoulder.

Payton holds Crystal's hand. "Legal and financial stuff in case Mac and Summer don't come back. They've given her everything they have."

Crystal gulps air. "Summer told me they'd been saving money for a long time for JD and me. She was worried about us." Tears stream out of her eyes as she chokes out words. "She thought maybe JD could drive a truck or be a heavy equipment operator. Maybe even a hunting guide. But what if he couldn't, she said. What then? And me. What was I going to do? She didn't want me to just be a housewife and raise kids. She knew I wanted more than that, but what could I do? I promised her I would work hard at art and photography. Maybe I could sell some. She said that's a difficult way to live, and I'd have to move. I knew I couldn't go to college, but I had to go somewhere. And she said, 'No, you don't. If you and JD need to, you can stay here. Mac and I have put enough money away.'"

Crystal balls her hands into fists. "I know if it weren't for JD and me, they would've traveled. Summer said she always wanted to see Scotland and New Zealand, but they never did. They wouldn't spend money unless they had to because they needed to take care of us. She said she couldn't stand leaving us, worried we'd end up on the street. I promised her I'd make her proud, that she wouldn't have to worry. I'd find something . . ."

She covers her face and coughs out sobs. All the self-doubts and fears about her future she'd held pent up inside her now surge in full view. All the weakness she'd kept hidden behind a veneer of spunk now feels raw and exposed.

Her one source of confidence—controlling a single line through her will and imagination—had kept her anguish and despair at bay. But she always thought deep down this wouldn't be enough.

As did Summer.

Crystal is not ready to be on her own, and she knows it. Mac and

Summer are supposed to be with her for many more years. Now they're dying in a hospital a hundred miles away, and she can't even see them.

Through swollen eyes she sees her friends crying beside her, touching her. "I can't do this by myself," she whimpers.

"You won't have to," says Haley, kissing her head. "You saved me. I'll do my best to save you."

"And me," says Sydney, holding Crystal's hand.

Crystal squeezes Sydney's hand and watches Payton wiping her eyes.

Payton grabs Crystal's shoulder. "I told you yesterday that people would pay lots of money for our first collaboration." She smiles. "I wasn't joking. I have ideas. Everything is online now anyway. It doesn't matter where your business is. You can be a gig worker from anywhere. We can do t-shirt designs and business logos and temporary tattoos. We can turn any photo into a line drawing or watercolor or both. We can do it all from here. We're not helpless. Together we can all make something of ourselves."

Crystal wipes her face. "You sure?"

"Yeah, I'm sure." She laughs. "We just have a few minor dramas to deal with first."

"Minor?" blurts Haley. "Let's see." She extends one finger. "I'm pregnant. Crystal's mom has a new baby living in an abandoned house, scared of her husband killing her." Second finger. "Then there's Dylan." She extends her middle finger on the other hand.

"And JD's gone," says Crystal.

"So is Bekah," adds Sydney.

"And don't forget the pandemic," says Haley, extending five fingers of one hand and the middle finger of the other.

Payton stands. "OK. Maybe not minor, but still ones we can deal with if we take them one at a time." A timer dings on their computers. "And if we allow our teachers to give us authentic, useful information which can improve our everyday lives."

Everyone looks at her like she's an alien.

"Tell you what," says Haley, "I'll send this question to Mr. Gilroy, my shop class teacher." She types: *How do I construct a protective bubble around Crystal's house to shield us from Eugene, Dylan, Covid, and cruel comments on social media?* "When he sends me the plans, I'll participate in his class. Otherwise, I'm watching you and Payton do art."

Payton opens the door to the deck. "I'll get my painting gear and be right back." She hustles toward the motorhome.

"Haley, will you get . . ."

"Yeah. I'll be right back." Haley heads for their bedroom.

Crystal types a note to her art teacher: *Here are three photos I'm going to work on today.* She sends pictures of her mom, the one of her nursing Jordan, and Holly.

Haley returns with Crystal's pad and pen and her latest drawings. Payton sets up her easel and paints on the deck then asks Sydney to bring the portrait Crystal made last night.

"Let's go outside," says Crystal.

Payton hands Crystal a sheet of watercolor paper. "Can you copy Sydney's portrait onto this so I can paint it?"

"Sure."

Soon, Haley's watching Payton paint and Crystal draw.

Crystal sends her drawing of Maya to Diana. "I haven't seen my mom for fourteen years, but I will soon. Here's my drawing."

A few minutes later, she finishes her drawing of her sister nursing.

"Haley, do you want me to send Diana the nude I made of you with the hearts? Everybody would love to see it."

"Maybe not."

"OK. How about one of Holly?"

"Sure."

Crystal watches her screen fill with clapping hands and various happy emojis plus lots of comments from Diana and other students. Any time she feels doubts about herself, her drawings bring such praise, boosting her confidence.

Payton finishes painting Sydney's portrait at the same time Crystal finishes drawing Holly's face.

Diana sends notes to both Payton and Crystal. "These pieces are fantastic. You are both incredibly talented. I want to send them to friends of mine in Fairbanks and Anchorage at the universities and a few art studios. Maybe something good will come to both of you."

Payton smiles at Crystal. "And so it begins."

Crystal gently bites her lip and enjoys the fluttering in her belly. "Let's hope."

A car rumbles down the driveway toward the house. All three girls look up at the black Jeep leading a cloud of dust.

"I was wondering when Dylan would show up," says Haley.

Payton ducks inside the sunroom to fetch her gun. "Sydney, take your computer to the kitchen." She turns to the window, sees the Jeep, and runs out of the room. Payton walks across the deck and steps onto the gravel below, pointing the AR toward the ground.

Haley saunters across the deck to stand behind and above Payton, holding her arm out for Crystal, who strides to her side.

Dylan glares at them through the windshield then twists the key, killing the engine. He slings open the door, steps sideways out of the car but stays close to his open window.

Payton smiles. "You want to move away from your door, Dylan?"

He sneers. "What if I don't? You gonna shoot me?"

"I might. Either close the door or move away from the car. I don't like what I can't see."

Dylan slams his door shut and takes two steps toward the girls.

Payton whips her barrel up but keeps it pointed to the trees at his side. "That's close enough."

Dylan stops.

"We practice social distancing of at least twelve feet for those outside our family unit. We don't want to spread the disease."

"That's bullshit! The school shut down because of her." He points to Crystal. "She's probably one of the a-hole carriers."

Haley laughs. "Oh, Dylan. You mean asymptomatic. I know it's a big word, but you can say it. A . . . symp . . . to . . ."

"When were you going to tell me?" shouts Dylan.

"Tell you what?" asks Haley pleasantly.

Dylan's face turns red. "That you're pregnant with my kid."

"But I'm not pregnant with your kid, as you call it. Decent people might say 'my child' or 'my baby.' I'm not a goat, Dylan."

"Don't you think you should've told me you were pregnant before everyone else in town found out?"

"Oh, no! Were you embarrassed?" Haley shakes her head in exaggerated concern. "I'm desperately sorry for the hardship this situation has caused you. Please accept my apology."

His chin juts out. "You bitch! You should've told me you were pregnant with my . . . baby. That's the least you could've done."

Still abnormally calm and composed, Haley says, "I might've told you had you contributed to my pregnancy, but you didn't, so I didn't."

Crystal can't keep her jaw from dropping. She glances left at Haley, wondering where she's going with this.

"Contributed to your pregnancy? What the fuck is that?"

Haley takes a deep breath. "Sometimes, you can be totally dense. Contributing to pregnancy means you provide the sperm. But you didn't, Dylan. You are not the father of my child."

Dylan squints his eyes and tilts his head like he's trying to see behind her. "Then who is? Who were you fucking behind my back?"

"I didn't fuck anyone behind your back. That would be very risky and immodest."

Payton barks a laugh. "That was great, Haley."

"Thank you."

Dylan balls his fists. "Well, I'll kill whoever it was."

"Which is why I have no intention of telling you anything."

"I don't believe you."

Haley jerks her arm away from Crystal and stabs the air toward Dylan's face. "Believe what you want, but you will never come near me again, Dylan Whitless, or I will call the troopers."

He kicks gravel and growls. "That's my baby!"

"When was the last time you actually fucked me? Not my face or my ass. Do you have any idea?"

Dylan's eyes roll from the ground to the house to the sky. "I don't remember."

"The middle of July. I had my period a week later. You went to

Valdez to fish for a week at the beginning of August. I'm probably six weeks pregnant. Do the math, Dylan. You have no reason to see me again. Now get out of here."

"Do you even know who the father is, or were you screwing everyone?"

"I know exactly who he is. Good-bye, Dylan." She turns and stomps across the deck, yanks open the door, and pulls it shut behind her.

Dylan breathes heavily, hangs his head, looks up at Payton and Crystal but averts his eyes, scratches his neck then turns around and walks to his car. He peers at the windows of the house as if trying to find Haley, shakes his head, climbs into his car, and turns the key.

Crystal expects him to rip a bootleg turn and churn gravel and dust, but he backs slowly then turns and drives away. "I've never seen Dylan look so deflated. Do you think he wanted it to be his?"

"No," says Payton, "but he didn't want it to be someone else's. Do you know who?"

"I have no idea."

They walk inside and find Haley in the kitchen drinking a glass of ice water.

Payton claps her hands. "That was brilliant. He didn't know what to do with himself. You really pulled his plug."

"Well, he had it coming."

"He's not the father?" asks Crystal.

"No. For a while I thought he was, because my period in July was short. I stopped taking pills the day before we had sex. Which shouldn't have been a problem according to Google. Then Dylan left for a week. I went to a party where Mike was doing his usual thing. Later we were alone, and I told him what Dylan had said. That he's gay. He swore up and down he wasn't. Then I said prove it." She drinks. "And he did. I felt weird two weeks later and took the test, but it was negative."

She takes a big breath. "If it was Dylan, there's no reason that test would've been negative. But if it's Mike, it would've been too early. Mike is my baby's daddy."

"Have you told him?" asks Payton.

"No."

"Will you?" asks Crystal.

She puts her glass in the sink. "Sure. At some point."

"How will he react?" asks Payton.

"I don't know." Haley runs her fingers through her hair. "I'll have to ask him whether he wants me to keep it secret or not."

"I don't understand," says Crystal, folding her arms. "Why?"

"Because Mike is gay."

Payton smiles and nods her head.

Crystal's mouth opens and closes. "Seriously?"

"Very. He tried to put on his act while we took off our clothes. Like he could stay hard for hours and hoped I could handle him. Shit like that." She looks at the ceiling and shakes her head. "But he couldn't. He got all embarrassed and apologized. I thought he was a virgin and how cute that was. I laid him down and got on top. We were doing OK, but he wouldn't look at me. Then just before he came, I saw a few tears. He covered his face afterward, and I said, 'What the fuck is wrong with you, Mike? Did I crush your balls?'" She sets her glass on the counter and wrings her hands. "He said, 'I'm sorry.' Then I realized he's gay. I said, 'I won't tell anyone. It's OK with me if you're gay.' Then he cried more, and I felt terrible. I cried too and held him for a long time. He's really a sweet guy. All the crap he does is for show because he's scared to death someone will call him queer. We got dressed and pretended nothing had happened. We haven't spoken since."

CHAPTER 25

*M*y mother just texted," says Haley. "She wants to know if anyone else is here. Maya must be coming soon." Haley thumbs her screen. *No. Dylan just left.*

How'd that go?

I'll tell u when u r here.

Danny's coming by in a few with some crates I packed and taped. He thinks they're for you. Doesn't know anything about Maya. K?

Yeah. When r u coming?

Soon. From a different way. I'll text when we're close.

I'm pregnant.

Oh, sweetie. We'll talk soon.

Haley puts her phone onto the counter and flashes her eyes at Crystal. "They'll be here in a little while. Danny's coming by with boxes of stuff he thinks are mine, but they're for Maya."

"Maybe for both of them," says Crystal. She's going to see her mother soon. Her toes and fingers tingle. She pulls Haley's hands to her face and imagines feeling her mom's touch. She wants to hold her little sister. Crystal has never held a baby. She's seen a few at games and events at the school, and she's made faces at them until they laughed. One held her finger and wouldn't let go.

She can still feel that little hand with the long fingers tight around her pointer.

Payton goes to the window. "Looks like Danny's here."

A yellow Mustang with the front painted like a monster's mouth parks behind the motorhome. Danny hops out and pops the trunk. He lifts three crates and sets them on the gravel to the side of his car.

Haley pulls Crystal's hand as she heads outside. "Come with me."

Danny shuts the trunk and heads back to his open door.

"Wait, Danny," yells Haley from the porch. She lowers her voice to Crystal. "He's totally different when he's not with Nick."

Walking toward Danny, Crystal glances into his car, expecting Nick to appear. Only rarely has she seen one twin without the other. Together, they pose, act cool, and seem to think everyone else wishes they could be like them. Alone, Danny seems more subdued and looks *at* her rather than down to her.

"Thanks for bringing these," says Haley.

"No problem." He looks back and forth at the two girls' eyes. "So, you're going to live here with Crystal?"

Haley crosses her arms and tightens her eyes. "After how you treated us both in that house, you'd expect me to live with you?"

Danny scrunches his brows and points his finger at her. "What did we do to *you?*"

"Did you like hearing Dylan fuck my face?"

Danny kicks some gravel. "No, I didn't."

Crystal shakes her head, disbelieving him.

"Then why didn't you stick up for me?"

"I wanted to, but Nick said . . ."

Haley scolds, "You always do what he says. You're his puppy."

He shuffles his feet and shoves his hands into his front pockets. "You should know by now what happens when you beg Dylan for something. He'll make you pay as much as he can get away with. Don't ask him for oxy. If you need something, ask me."

"OK, but I'm off everything for a long time. I guess you heard." She holds her lower abdomen with both hands, forming a shield.

Danny nods. "Is it Dylan's?"

"Nothing of mine is Dylan's. He's not the father."

He raises his brows. "Yeah? I guess you're not going to tell me."

"Nope. Not now."

Danny sucks in his lips and backs up. "Well, I better go."

Crystal refuses to let him leave without apologizing to her. "What did you plan to do to me in that house?" asks Crystal.

Danny stops. "Nothing."

"You tried to rip off my shirt."

He shakes his head. "I didn't touch your shirt. That was all Dylan and Nick."

Crystal replays the scene in her mind. She hit and stomped Nick and Dylan. She never touched Danny. "But you would've let them do it," says Crystal.

"Did you think Nick would rape her?" asks Haley.

"I don't know."

Crystal leans forward. "If he'd tried to, what would you have done?"

He scratches his head. "I wouldn't have let him."

"Really?" scoffs Crystal.

Danny throws up his hands. "Why are you both grilling me?"

Crystal shakes her head. "I'm sorry to make you feel uncomfortable, Danny. Imagine how I felt at the time."

Danny looks at her, breathing hard then drops his gaze to the ground. "I'm sorry."

Haley moves closer to her brother. "Nick has always been more of a bully than you. He'd take my bikini top and you'd laugh. He'd 'accidentally' open my door without knocking to find me undressed, and you'd laugh. But you never did anything to me on your own. Why is that?"

Danny clears his throat and frowns. "Because you're my sister, and I didn't think it was right."

Haley blows out a breath. "Why didn't you say anything to him or to me? All those times."

The tops of his ears turn red. "I should have. I'm sorry."

"Is that a 'let's change the subject' I'm sorry or a real apology?"

Danny locks eyes with Haley. "It's real."

"I wish you would've said that a long time ago, but thank you."

He nods. "I don't blame you for leaving. Kinda surprised you're here with Crystal. But whatever."

Crystal feels Haley's arm move around her waist and pull her closer.

"Nick doesn't like having a gay sister," says Haley. "He thinks it affects his reputation."

"Some guys worry about rumors starting."

"Because if your sister is gay, then you might have the gay gene too?"

"I didn't say that."

"Are you worried?"

He laughs. "About a gay gene?"

Crystal tilts her head as she watches him. That laugh sounded forced. What's going on in his head? "Do you think people are born gay or decide one day to be gay?"

He averts his eyes from theirs and rubs his neck. "Probably born gay."

Haley side-glances at Crystal. "Do you think someone can be gay and try to hide it by acting straight?"

Danny tightens his jaw as he meets Haley's gaze. "That probably happens a lot."

"Do you know anyone like that, besides me?"

Danny takes a breath, lifts his brows, and shrugs his shoulders.

"Well," says Haley, "I think it happens more than people realize."

He nods. "You don't care if you're called names?"

"Like dyke?" laughs Crystal.

"Or queer?" asks Haley.

Danny forces a smile. "Yeah."

"I'm proud to be a dyke," says Crystal. "It's liberating. You should try it."

"Try what?"

"Being honest and not give a crap what others think."

Danny clears his throat. "That's . . . hard to do sometimes. I was surprised Mom didn't seem upset when she sent me here. She knows?"

"Yeah." Haley reaches for Crystal's hand. "She knows lots of things."

Danny squints his eyes and shows a half smile. "That sounds mysterious."

"It's supposed to. Do you still see Mike off and on?"

He flinches ever so slightly, but Crystal catches it.

He takes a quick breath. "Yeah."

Haley tightens her eyes. "Do you have to tell everything to Nick or can you keep some things to yourself?"

"I don't tell him anything he doesn't already know. I never tell him private stuff."

"When you see Mike," says Haley, "tell him to come over when he has a chance. And if you ever want to visit without Nick, that'd be fine."

He nods. "I'll do that. Well, I better be getting back. And . . . I am sorry about what happened yesterday."

"Thanks." She reaches out with one arm. "A little hug?"

He smiles and leans toward her, clasping her arm and touching heads.

Crystal watches Haley move her lips close to his ear. Did she kiss him?

Danny backs away quickly, eyes fixed on Haley as he stands still. He inhales suddenly and nods at both girls. "Well, I'll see you around."

The girls watch him back up then return his wave as he heads down the driveway.

"That was an interesting conversation," says Crystal. "He's hiding things."

"Ya think? 'Cause he's scared."

"Of Nick?"

"And others."

Crystal touches Haley's cheek. "I thought I saw you kiss his ear."

"No. I whispered, 'Your secret is safe with us.'"

The realization electrifies her skin. "Oh, my god! Is he gay?"

"I think so. Which is why he never crosses Nick, why he always laughs when Nick puts on his macho show."

The hair on Crystal's neck bristles. "Maybe your mom sent Danny on purpose."

"Wouldn't that be amazing?"

The door opens behind them, and they see Payton holding Haley's phone. "It's your mom."

236

Sydney ducks under her sister's arm. "Are they here?"

Both girls bolt toward Payton. Crystal leans over Haley's shoulder as she pulls up the message: *In five minutes look to the East.*

"What the hell does that mean?" asks Crystal.

Haley checks her compass app. Crystal's house is aligned on a north-south line, the deck on the southern end. The girls walk quickly around the house.

Haley points toward the pond in the back yard. "East is that way."

"They're coming over the bridge," says Crystal, her heart leaping in her chest.

Behind the pond is a wall of spruce and poplar trees, sheltering blueberry bushes, which extend from the water to the forest. A utility easement cuts through the woods about a hundred feet back from the bridge. A car can turn off Third Street and go through the passage quickly then find a gap to park unseen.

Crystal turns to Payton. "Maybe you should get your gun and keep an eye toward the driveway."

"On it." Payton disappears into the sunroom.

Crystal grabs Haley's hand. "How do I look?" She tries to keep from blinking as she stares into Haley's eyes.

"You, Crystal Rose, are beautiful." Haley smooths Crystal's hair and picks a little crust out of the corner of Crystal's eye. "Maya's going to be thrilled to see you."

A flood of emotions races through Crystal's body, pushing tears into her eyes. She blinks before they drip. "I can't breathe. I'm so nervous."

Haley kisses Crystal's forehead. "Just imagine you're waiting for the moose like yesterday morning." She kisses one cheek. "You were calm and brave." She kisses the other cheek. "Even though a thousand pound seven-foot-tall moose was standing right in front of you."

Crystal closes her eyes and sees the fog from yesterday morning dissolve into a cow and calf. Her breathing slows.

Haley gently kisses her lips. "Your mom is so much smaller, and she's bringing you a baby sister. She'll be nervous. You need to be calm for her."

Crystal sees the photos her mom sent as they float inside her mind.

Her tension drifts away. She opens her eyes and finds Haley's lips stretching into a smile.

"Go into the grass and wait for her. I'll take a video."

Crystal nods and turns. A breeze sighs against the leaves, scattering some across the grass as she walks out into the yard. Some are dark green with black spots. Others orange and brown, brittle to her step. She hears leaves clattering against tree limbs as a gust pushes from the south, bending the spruce tops swollen with caramel-colored pinecones.

As if responding to a secret cue, hundreds of leaves release from every tree around the yard, swirling suspended in the air above the bridge. Crystal raises her arms and opens her hands, feeling the leaves dance against her skin before rising up again in another puff of wind.

Then silence. Utter stillness.

Leaves flutter and spin downward, some drifting along tiny currents only they can feel. Crystal's eyes follow a blur of colors as they descend into the pond and onto the bridge. In seconds the water disappears underneath a veil of dappled orange, red, green, and yellow.

As the last leaves settle on the red-stained planks of the bridge, a woman emerges from the trees and strides through the blueberries and Labrador tea. Her head is enclosed in a dark green hood, while a multi-colored blanket stretches from her left shoulder, across her chest, where she must be carrying Jordan. She keeps her gaze down, watching her steps over the boards. Reaching the grass, her mother walks up the shallow rise from the water toward her.

A warmth blossoms from Crystal's feet, winding up her legs, filling her stomach with such a longing to run and clutch before her mother can vanish. But she worries about hurting Jordan. So fragile, so little.

"Mom?"

Maya reaches for her hood and pulls it back, revealing haggard eyes but a soft smile of unpainted lips. "Crystal," she sighs with such pain and hope and longing. "I remember when I used to look just like you." Maya turns slightly, offering Jordan. "Would you like to hold your sister?"

Crystal aches to touch her mom. "Yes, but first you. Can I?"

Maya lifts her right hand. Crystal presses it against her cheek, feeling the chill of her mother's skin and the hard bones underneath.

"You're cold. Are you sick?"

Maya shakes her weary head. "No, just worn down."

Crystal moves closer and wraps one arm around Maya's back, reaching with fingers of her other hand to touch her mother's lips and chin. Crystal stands on her toes and kisses Maya's cheek. Her skin and hair smell like milk and butter and vanilla.

Maya pulls Crystal closer. "You are so warm. Are you too old to snuggle with your mom?"

Crystal's heart skips. "No. I'd love to." Her mother's skin is cool. "Let's get inside."

Maya pulls the blanket down to Jordan's neck, revealing Maya's left breast, and a single drop of milk hanging on the nipple. "She's been feeding off and on for an hour and finally crashed." She extends her arms, lifting Jordan toward Crystal. "Hold her for me. I left my carrier in the camper when I took off. My arms are tired."

Crystal takes in a breath and holds it as she maneuvers her right bicep under Jordan's head and slides her left hand under her sister's back and bottom. When Maya pulls her hands away, Crystal feels Jordan's full weight. "Oh, my gosh, she's heavy."

"Yes, she's a tick." Maya pulls her shirt down and pulls the edges of her cloak tight.

Crystal touches Jordan's round cheek and marvels at the ripples of flesh between her chin and upper chest. "How much does she weigh?"

"Seventeen, maybe eighteen now."

Crystal sees Haley with her phone on the deck, recording everything, and wide-eyed Sydney, holding her hands beneath her chin.

"You got her, Crystal?" asks Holly from behind.

Crystal stops and turns her head. "Yeah. I'm good."

Holly carries a large, zippered cloth bag and something else with a handle—plush and bulging. Maybe a portable bed?

"This grass is lush," says Maya. "My feet sink inches with each step."

"Hey, Sydney, come help," shouts Crystal.

Sydney leaps off the deck and runs to Maya. She reaches for the woman's arm. "Can I?"

"Sure, Sydney. Gosh, you are cute."

"Thank you. You're gorgeous."

Maya laughs. "Flattery will get you everywhere, even when it's obviously false. I haven't washed my face or put on makeup for two days."

They walk toward the deck. Just before Crystal steps up, Haley stops her camera.

"Hi, I'm Haley. Holly's daughter."

"I know. Your mother showed me pictures. You are prettier in real life."

Maya steps up onto the deck. "I used to run around this yard like lightning, and now I have to trudge." She looks around. "Daddy's done a lot of work."

"You called him 'Daddy'?" asks Crystal.

"When we weren't fighting. Mom and Daddy." She clears her throat. "How are they doing today?"

"They're better but still serious. I couldn't talk to Summer this morning. We can try later today."

"I want to see Jordan," Sydney blurts.

"A little less enthusiasm, Sis," says Payton as she leans her gun against the house and moves toward Crystal. "A sleeping baby is a gift. When you were Jordan's age, I spent a lot of time trying to get you to sleep."

"How?" asks Sydney.

"I sang to you."

Sydney grimaces. "No wonder I couldn't sleep." She faces the others. "Singing is not on Payton's list of talents, just so you know."

Payton nods to Maya. "I'm Payton, Sydney's sister." She opens the door. "It's a little warmer inside."

Everyone gathers in the sunroom. The girls migrate to Jordan, still in Crystal's arms.

Haley touches the baby's cheek, her eyes shining. "Velvety soft. God, she's cute." Haley looks at Crystal. "You're not going to share, are you?"

"Not yet. My arms ache from holding her, though."

Payton steers Crystal to the love seat against the wall. "Sit."

Crystal does.

Payton wedges a pillow under Crystal's right arm. The girls kneel on the floor, their faces inches from Jordan's, listening to her soft little snores.

"Look at those lashes," says Haley. "And that cupid bow mouth. How could she be cuter?"

Sydney giggles. "She has three chins and I think she's hiding nuts in those cheeks."

Dark memories flicker in Crystal's mind. When she arrived in the village, according to Mac, she was half-starved and way too skinny. Maya claimed they had eaten before boarding the plane from Fairbanks to the village, but when Summer offered Crystal food, she gobbled it up and asked for more. Why? She could never understand why her mother wouldn't feed her. Mac claimed Maya had bought vodka and run out of money. An addict can't help but love her bottle more than anything or anyone else.

Should she ask her mom or just let it go?

Crystal closes her eyes and shakes her head—she would not allow herself to feel jealousy or anger. She had been bitter for too much of her life, and though the past two days had yanked her emotions every which way, what she feels now—among her friends, holding her sister, near her mother who wants to be with her—has to cancel what her mother did or didn't do years ago. It must, or what could their future be?

She bends down to rub her nose over Jordan's cheek, inhaling her scent of lotion and milk and sweet contentment. Soothing, like a bubble bath. She realizes she's been clenching her right arm muscle under Jordan's head and relaxes. The release sends tingles through her shoulders and neck but now she feels all of her sister's warmth and total relaxation. Crystal kisses her plump cheek.

Maya reaches for Holly's arm. "Show me the photo."

Holly sets her bags down. "In here." They walk into the living room.

The girls hear laughter from the women in the other room. After a few minutes, Holly returns and sits with Crystal. "Maya's in the bathroom. She had a rough night."

"Because of Jordan?" asks Crystal.

"Jordan is what keeps her sane. She's terrified of Eugene. We had planned for her to stay in the house I found for a few nights and hope he'd give up and leave. But the place is cold with no working plumbing. I brought food and water, an ice chest, camping toilet and heater, but she had to get out of there. She thought she heard footsteps outside her window this morning. She's a nervous wreck."

Crystal forces her arms to stay relaxed even as her stomach roils. "Eugene told me he's watching the house. He'll know she's here. What are we going to do?" asks Crystal.

"I told her I'd shoot him. Who'd know or care?"

Crystal sees Holly's hard eyes. She's not kidding. "What did Mom say?"

"If anyone was going to shoot him, it'd be her."

CHAPTER 26

$\mathcal{A}$s Crystal vacuums the floor in the upstairs bedroom, she sees Haley and her mother stretch the top sheet over the king-sized bed. Payton continues the online charade downstairs as Sydney works on her science lesson. Maya is feeding Jordan in the living room. No one bothered to clean up after lunch because Jordan was hungry, and Maya's bed was still unmade.

"Can you come back later?" Haley asks her mother, tucking the sheet under the mattress.

"That's my plan. I'll go home soon, then after Jack leaves for work, I'll return." She pulls one side of the quilt while Haley pulls the other. "Nick and Danny have dates tonight, so they'll be home late."

"How'd you ever have kids with him working nights?"

Holly laughs. "Did you notice you have no little sisters or brothers? He took the night shift just after you were born."

Haley glances at Crystal. "Did Daddy know Eugene?"

Crystal turns off the vacuum. Both girls watch Holly.

"That's an odd question." Holly leans pillows against the headboard. "Why do you ask?"

Crystal thinks Holly is purposely averting her eyes. "During one of

Eugene's rants to me, he mentioned someone named Jack. He saw this man in the beer tent during the music festival."

"OK." Holly unzips Jordan's portable bed and sets it on the quilt.

"The man was talking with Maya before he left quickly. Was there another Jack in town back then?"

"Actually there was. John Whitley, Dylan's dad. We called him Jack back then. But after he started his restaurants and brewery in Healy, he wanted to use his full name—John Douglas Whitley." She chuckles. "And now everyone is supposed to call him Douglas. I guess he thinks that sounds more impressive."

"Did he know Eugene?" asks Haley.

Holly shrugs her shoulders. "Not that I'm aware of."

"Did Mom have a relationship with him?" asks Crystal. *God, is Dylan my half brother?*

Holly's eyes blink quickly. "Wow. Wasn't expecting that question. It wouldn't surprise me. After Maya and I split, she had several relationships, especially after I got pregnant with the twins then married."

"And she left town in late August with Eugene?"

"Yes. August 23rd."

"Did you know she was pregnant with me?" asks Crystal.

"She told me. I was pregnant with Haley. We both had a good cry." She straightens a portrait of Maya as a young girl near the nightstand. "Haley, I don't want you to take this the wrong way, but I don't want you to make the same mistakes I did."

Haley puts her hand on her hip. "Getting pregnant then marrying a guy you didn't love?"

"Yeah." Holly blushes. "Have you always known?"

"No. I finally realized I never saw you two touch each other except by accident." She crosses her arms and sits on the bed. "And your drinking got worse."

Crystal sits with Haley, thankful she never had to doubt Mac and Summer's love for each other. Haley must have felt so alone in her house.

Holly clenches her hands. "I'm trying to stop. Notice I haven't had a beer since I've been here. If Maya can do it, so can I."

"You probably should see a doctor. I don't think it's good to just stop."

"I will. What about Dylan?"

Haley grabs Crystal's hand. "He's not the father."

Holly's mouth drops open. "Really? Who?"

Haley pulls Crystal's hand to her chest. "Mike, but he doesn't know yet."

Crystal watches Holly sigh and close her eyes. She drops to her knees in front of her daughter. "Are you going to keep it?"

Haley's heart pounds against Crystal's hand.

Haley closes her eyes. "I don't know. I'm worried about my drinking and . . . using drugs. Maybe I've already hurt it too much." She bites her lip.

Crystal reaches her other arm around Haley and squeezes. "What you've done and what you will do from now on are totally separate. You'll have support from all of us."

Haley leans her head against Crystal's. "Thank you. I know." Haley looks at her mother and swallows hard. "Did you ever consider aborting the twins?"

"Yes, I did. But I didn't." She flashes her eyes and half-smiles. "Though there've been many times I wish I had."

Haley looks away. "Did you ever with me?"

"No." Holly holds her daughter's knees. "What would've been the point? I was already married with two sons. I hoped for a girl. And then I had such a beautiful girl. I don't know if you remember, but we had gobs of fun until . . ."

"Fifth grade?"

"Thereabouts."

"Did you ever know about me and Crystal?"

"Yes, Ms. Cline told me."

All that time, Crystal believed only she and Haley had known their secret. But many had. No one told her. Once again, everyone kept secrets.

"You never said anything," says Haley.

"No, and I've regretted that. I didn't know what to say. 'It's OK if you like Crystal because I liked her mother?' I was too afraid." She stands and walks toward a window. "Then you started chasing boys, and Ms. Cline and other teachers told me about that too, but guess what?" She turns toward the girls. "They just laughed. I drank more and more because I saw you doing the same thing I did. I got depressed." She leans against the dresser. "I should have talked to you, but I thought if I did, I'd have to reveal my past and then what? Be the local lesbian? Maybe if Maya had been alive, I might have . . . but she was dead, or so I thought. Such a sad fucking story." She blows out a breath. "God, I could use a beer."

Haley rises and goes to her mother. "No booze in this house. No more regrets. No more 'what ifs.' We're going to love who we're meant to love and not take crap from anyone."

"That's easy to say, but I still have a job."

"Why do they need to know about your sex life?"

Holly shakes her head and moves away. "All news travels around here, as you well know. There is no legal protection in Alaska against gay discrimination except in Anchorage and Juneau."

Haley follows her. "Rumors of your sexual preference are not proof. As long as I'm here with Crystal, your visits here are for me. I'm pregnant, after all. And then I'll need help with my baby."

"That will work for now."

"Only if we keep hiding," says Crystal. "And I'm not hiding anymore."

"No, we aren't," says Haley, fist-bumping Crystal. "We have raised our dyke flag."

Holly smiles. "Well, then, all the more reason for me to visit my very confused daughter and her dyke friend." She hugs Haley. "I wish . . ."

"No more regrets. We are going to look forward, not backward."

Holly holds her daughter's face. "OK, looking forward, what are you going to do about Mike?"

"Mike will have no interest in marrying me."

"You sure?"

"He's gay."

Crystal expects Holly to be surprised, but all she does is breathe in slowly with a tiny smile on her face.

Haley holds her mother's hands. "Please don't tell anyone until he comes out. If he wants to participate in my baby's life, that's great. I hope he does. And he can certainly help support him or her."

"Did you suspect Mike was gay?" asks Crystal.

"I wondered." Holly sits on the bed. "I told you Nick and Danny have dates tonight. Nick's girlfriend is Laura. Has been for two years. Sometimes they double date with Danny and Paige, but they're just friends. Danny claims he dates other girls. There's a Sabrina on Kobe Road. And a Lisa off the highway going toward Nenana. Which is very close to where Mike lives. One night last week I called him because he was late getting home. I heard him laughing, obviously high on something when he answered. I told him to get home. He said OK and must've tossed his phone on the dashboard. Then I heard Mike's voice and what sounded like kissing. Mike said, 'Dude, you didn't end the call.' Then Danny said, 'Shit!' and hung up. I heard no girls. Neither of us said anything about the call. A few days later, he left his room to drive somewhere, and I checked his computer. He uses the same password on everything— DannyC, then his birthdate. His history was full of gay porn sites."

Crystal folds her arms. "Is that why you sent him to bring Maya's clothes?"

"Partly. Also, Nick made a big deal about never coming back here again."

"Haley figured it out," says Crystal, "and let Danny know he has a safe place to hang out when he wants to."

"Won't that be interesting when he finds his mother here too?" Holly stands and looks around the room. "Are we done in here?"

"Yes," says Crystal as she grabs the vacuum cleaner and carries it downstairs to a closet. When she comes back through the kitchen, she finds Holly and Haley at the refrigerator.

"Before I leave," says Holly, "I want to show you the extra milk Maya has collected."

Crystal's muscles tighten. "Why does she need extra? Is she leaving?"

"No, Crystal. Why would you think that?"

"Something Eugene said this morning."

"Stop listening to him. Pumping keeps her breasts from swelling too much and keeps the flow high to meet Jordan's needs. I've put six bottles in the fridge. If you ever need to use one of these, set the bottle in a bowl of hot water for about ten minutes. Then put a few drops on your wrist to make sure it's not too warm. Just needs to be room temperature. Jordan will drink it cold if she has to. OK?"

The girls nod. They move into the living room and find Maya feeding Jordan. Holly sits next to Maya and reaches for the baby's feet. Crystal catches her mother's smile and sits near Jordan's head. Haley sits on a coffee table directly across.

"How's she doing?" asks Holly.

Maya smiles. "On her second boob."

"I've got to go. I'll come back before nine."

Maya turns her head toward Holly. "Can you sleep over?"

"Yes, but I'll have to leave early."

"That will be heaven." Maya leans toward Holly until their lips meet in a long kiss.

Warmth spreads in Crystal's chest and her eyes well up. She reaches out to Haley's hand.

"Damn, Mom," says Haley. "That's the first time I've seen you kiss anyone on the lips."

"It won't be the last." Holly touches Maya's cheek. "I think you girls should have a turn watching Jordan sleep tonight." Holly kisses Maya again.

"We'd love to," says Crystal.

Holly stands. "Call me if you need anything."

Haley hugs her mom. "Love you."

"And you. Bye." Holly walks onto the deck then quickly across the yard to the bridge before disappearing in the trees.

"Haley," says Maya, "since you're up, can you bring me some water?"

"Sure." Haley goes to the kitchen.

Crystal touches Jordan's cheek. "How does it feel to feed her?"

"Wonderful. Tingly and warm. When she latches on and sucks, it's such a relief. It's like a quivering sigh after holding your breath."

Haley returns with the water.

"Thank you." She drinks the entire glass. "I get so dehydrated."

Haley takes the glass and sits next to Maya.

Crystal watches her mother's face as she gazes at Jordan—peaceful, softly smiling. Jordan sucks a few times then stops. A smile starts to stretch across her face and the nipple escapes. Maya squeezes her breast while rubbing her nipple across Jordan's lips. Crystal follows a milk drop from her mom into her sister's mouth. Jordan suddenly burrows her face against the breast and sucks hard.

Maya winces then laughs. "She does that all the time. Her little sneak attack." She touches her finger to Jordan's cheek.

"Did JD or I do that?" asks Crystal.

Maya's smile disappears. "I never found out. As soon as you were born, the nurses took you away because of the drugs in your system. And in mine. You and your brother were fed formula. Didn't my parents tell you?"

"Some of it." Crystal closes her eyes and pushes the sadness and bitterness welling up from her gut, burning her chest. She looks at Jordan and tries to feel only happiness for her, ignoring the aching, choking knot in the back of her throat.

"Eugene and I had to go to classes to learn how to be parents before we could be with you. He finished before I did and took you to his aunt's place in Mississippi. I never finished, so technically I wasn't supposed to be with you unsupervised. But I went to Mississippi soon after and hooked up with you at his aunt's. Child Services in Mississippi never knew about our problem in Texas. We weren't bothered any more. I couldn't be a real mother until I got sober. I fucked up with you and JD. Where is he?"

"He left for Fairbanks this morning," replies Crystal. "I'm trying to talk him into coming back." Crystal realizes what might persuade her brother to come home. "Haley, send me the video you took of Mom and me in the yard."

Haley pulls out her phone and sends the clip.

"I'll forward this to JD, then maybe we can Facetime him later. He needs to be here." She sends a note to JD. *Watch this then tell me why u cant get your butt home. Bring Gena w u.*

Now she finds the number for the nurse and presses it. When

someone answers, she says, "Hey, I'm Crystal Rose. I called earlier about my grandparents, Mac and Summer Rose. Can I send you a video that they'll want to see? It's of their daughter coming home. Please?"

"Hello, Crystal. Not to this number, but I'll give you my cell number. I'll make sure Summer's nurse gets it."

"Thank you."

After Crystal receives the number, she sends the video with a message. *Your daughter and new granddaughter are here, and they want to see you.*

"Do you want to burp her?" asks Maya.

Crystal's eyes widen. "Yes. How?"

Maya lifts the milk-drunk Jordan to her shoulder and gently pats her back. "Like this." She hands Jordan to Crystal. "She's good about holding her head up, but keep your hand or finger on the back of her neck just in case."

Crystal relaxes her arms as she guides her sister's head to the side of her cheek. Jordan is amazingly warm. She tries to pat her sister's back, but one hand is on her bottom, and the other is holding her head. "I need another hand."

Maya chuckles. "Just lean back a little so she falls against you then use your head hand to pat."

After five quick pats, Jordan burps. "Whoa," says Crystal. "You're louder than Haley and Sydney."

"I heard that," shouts Sydney from the sunroom. "And I'm way louder."

Payton laughs. "No one would disagree."

"Shoot some photos for me," says Crystal. "My phone's by my leg."

Sydney runs over and picks up the phone. "Code?"

"4,3,2,1,2,1"

"Ooo, a backward sequence," says Haley. "No one will figure that out."

"Like who wants to break into my phone?" asks Crystal. She lifts Jordan off her shoulder and holds her level with her chest. Jordan's eyes open. "She has eyeballs. They're deep blue! Shoot this, Sydney." Crystal blows between her lips and shakes her cheeks until Jordan cracks a smile. The baby's arms reach out, fingers splayed wide. Crystal lifts her knees and lays her sister against them then claps and makes goofy faces. Jordan laughs more. Crystal places her pointer fingers in both of Jordan's hands, which immediately close and grasp. "Shoot this, Sydney. Quick."

Sydney takes several photos.

"You have to share," says Haley, standing next to Crystal. "I've held lots of babies." Haley bends over as Crystal lifts Jordan to her girl-friend's arms. "Oh, my God, you are precious." Haley nuzzles Jordan's neck. "I love how babies smell."

Jordan rips a very wet fart as she holds her finger in her smiling mouth.

"How's that smell now?" laughs Payton.

"God, that's worse than JD's," exclaims Crystal as she stands.

Haley holds Jordan out to Crystal with a mischievous grin. "You should learn how to change a diaper. I already know how."

Maya stands. "Where's my bag?"

"We left it upstairs," says Crystal, taking Jordan from Haley.

"Come on. I'll show you." Maya moves toward the stairs with Crystal following.

Maya finds a towel in the upstairs bathroom and lays it on the bed. "We're going to need a trash can with a lid and a plastic bag up here."

"I can get something from the garage."

"Lay her down." Maya finds wipes, a new diaper, and a clean onesie.

Crystal lowers Jordan to the towel. Her eyes are bright, and all her limbs are moving. "She seems pretty happy with herself."

"She's like a pig in a mud trough, 'cept it's slimy brown poop. She always does this. OK, unzip her clothes. I'm sure the poop is up her back."

"Oh, the smell!" Crystal chokes as she lifts Jordan's legs out of the onesie. Maya is ready with a wipe to clean the baby's back. Crystal takes off the diaper, rolling it up while trying not to touch it. "What do I do with this?"

"Put it in the trashcan in the bathroom, plus these wipes. Twist the bag closed or the room will stink. We can wash our hands later."

"A little shit never hurt anyone." She grabs them and drops them into the trash then ties the bag closed.

A few minutes later, Jordan is kicking her clean legs in the air, freshly diapered and dressed. Crystal shoots a picture of her.

Maya rolls the dirty onesie in the towel. "These need to go in the wash."

Crystal watches in amazement as Jordan flops over onto her stomach. "Look!"

"She's been doing that for two weeks. And she's starting to crawl."

Jordan scoots her knees under her stomach and rocks back and forth on all fours.

"When did I start crawling?"

Maya holds Crystal by her waist. "Honey, I know you're curious, but you're not going to be happy with the answers, and I'd rather not remember. I was a horrible mother to you. Every milestone was later than it should have been. I'm trying to do better this time, and I need your help." She pulls Crystal hard against her.

"I'll do anything for you and for her." She wraps her arms tight, feeling both their hearts beating together.

They hear stomping up the stairs before Payton stands in the doorway. "There's a camper truck coming down the driveway. Haley says it's Eugene's."

Maya pulls away, shaking, her mouth wide open, whimpering.

A tongue of fear rises in Crystal's throat before she clenches her jaw tight. She will not allow Eugene to hurt her mother anymore.

"I know what to do." She grabs Maya's arms and holds her up, looking hard into her eyes. "You have to trust me. I'll get rid of him. You leave out this door," as she points to the back corner of the room. "Go down the steps and run across the bridge. Just wait in the trees. I'll take Jordan downstairs with me."

"And do what?"

"Scream at the bastard. Don't worry. I can do this. He'll leave in a few minutes. I promise. When he's gone, Payton will come get you. OK?"

Maya gasps for breath. "Why do I have to leave?"

"Because that's what you've done. Run away and left Jordan with us. Just like he said you would. If he doesn't believe me, I'll let him look around the house. But he won't come in. He'll be in too much of a hurry to find where you've gone. OK?"

Maya nods, opens the door, and runs off.

Crystal picks up her smiling sister. "C'mon, Jordan. It's showtime." She hurries downstairs.

CHAPTER 27

*H*aley and Payton stand on the deck holding their guns as Crystal opens the sunroom door while carrying Jordan across her right arm. Eugene glares through his windshield as he stops his truck about twenty feet away from the girls.

"I have a plan," says Crystal, offering a bottle to Jordan. "Just follow along. Where's Sydney?"

"Behind the side porch with the .22," says Payton.

Barely moving her lips, she quietly says, "You guys need to trust me." She steps off the porch and pushes anger into her face and voice. "Where's Maya? Is she with you?"

Eugene tightens his eyes, opens his truck door, and hops out. "What are you talking about?"

"The bitch ran off. Just like you said she would." Crystal tries to get Jordan to suck the bottle, but the baby moves her closed mouth away. "Damn it, Jordan. Why can't you eat?"

"Maya was here?" asks Eugene, tilting his chin down so his eyes glare from beneath his bushy eyebrows. "When?"

Crystal notes the skepticism in his voice. "Thought you were watching the house, Eugene," she taunts. "But you missed her entrance and her exit. You'd make a great private detective. Did you think she'd

254

come down the driveway? Walk right in front of your rented truck hiding in those trees? How stupid is that?"

Eugene jerks breaths into his lungs. "How did she get here?"

"We heard a car last night on the other side of that pond in my back yard. Then she walked across that bridge carrying Jordan and a couple of bags. She wore a headlamp. Did you give her that lamp?"

He grits his teeth then barks out, "No."

"Oh." She holds Jordan against her chest, facing out, as she shakes her right arm. "God, Jordan, you weigh a ton. Then that headlight must've come from that counselor dude she talked about. Did you ever meet him?"

His eyes roll. "The counselor? From the rehab place?"

"Yeah. Jordan's daddy. I think he dropped her off last night and then he picked her up this morning. I heard Jordan crying upstairs and found her covered in shit from a blowout in her diaper." Crystal sticks the bottle nipple into Jordan's mouth, but she spits it out. "She's barely eaten all day because she's not used to bottles. And Maya left only four!"

"I think you're lying. I think Maya's inside right now." He takes a step forward. Haley pumps the shotgun to chamber a shell.

"No, Haley. If he wants to go look, he can look." Crystal sweeps her left arm back toward the house. "If you find her, please take her and this spoiled brat with you, and get the fuck out of my life."

Eugene starts to walk then stops, clenching and unclenching his fists.

"Even if you don't find her, you're taking this kid with you." She takes three quick steps toward him before he raises his hands as she holds Jordan away from her chest.

"I'm not taking that baby. It ain't mine."

"None of your babies were yours. That's what Maya said last night. Not me, not JD, not Jordan. Why do you think that is, Eugene? Maybe you should get checked out. Maybe your balls don't work."

"Shut up, bitch! We couldn't get you and your drunk-ass brother out of my house soon enough. What did she say about the counselor?" he bellows.

Excitement and fear swirl in her stomach. She feels like hurling, but she has to stay strong. "She said he loved her but didn't want to be tied down with a kid yet, that he was too young to start a family. She showed me a picture of him. Real cute." She smiles and wiggles. "Maybe twenty-five. Nice body. I can see why Maya likes him. According to her, she told him she loved Jordan with all her heart and couldn't bear to leave her. She passed on the counselor, she said, and brought Jordan home." Crystal quickly lays Jordan down on her right arm. "Yeah, so she could breast feed her right in front of me, and show us her fat cheeks and triple chin, and brag about how *Jordan* is hitting all her milestones on time, and how *Jordan* is so different than me and JD because we were so fucked up. By her! And how *Jordan* can already roll over and crawl. I wanted to puke." Crystal growls and kicks the gravel.

"And then the perfect mommy left her perfect daughter who I guess now is going to lose some weight because she won't eat!" Crystal pushes the bottle nipple into Jordan's mouth, but she waves her arms and jerks her head back and forth until she starts crying. Crystal holds the baby toward Eugene again. "You take her."

"Not a chance in hell, Crystal," he snarls. "When I find Maya, neither of us will want a crying baby. What else did she say about the counselor?"

Jordan is bawling with clenched fists. Crystal knows she cannot flinch or try to comfort now. *Just a little longer, sister. Almost done.* "She told me the blonde stud wanted to fly to Fairbanks, rent a car, come down here, and take her home with him to Washington. But she'd told him no. Obviously, he didn't listen because that's where she is now."

"Where?"

Jordan's face is purple, vibrating in misery before she gulps another breath and screams again. "At the airport or already on a plane. Maybe you should check what flights are available today from Fairbanks to Seattle. Maybe you're too late."

Eugene turns and hustles back to his truck.

"Hey, Eugene," Crystal spits.

He stops and glares at her.

"You know what will happen if either one of you shows up again."

He looks above her head toward Haley and Payton. "Not if I shoot first," he sneers. "Have fun with your sister." He snorts a laugh, climbs into his truck, and backs all the way down the driveway.

Crystal stands totally still as Jordan screams, gritting her teeth, trying not to wipe the tears streaming down her cheeks. As soon as she sees the truck race down D Street, she pulls Jordan close. "I'm sorry, Jordan. I'm so sorry." She pats her back and shushes slowly, softly.

Haley lays the shotgun on the table and races toward her. "How did you do that?" She wipes Crystal's eyes and helps her back toward the deck.

"Payton," orders Crystal, "run over the bridge and bring Maya back. She's hiding in the trees."

Payton nods and takes off.

"Let me take her," says Haley as they walk inside the sunroom.

Crystal gives her Jordan then collapses on the sofa, holds her head, and cries. Will Jordan ever forgive her? Or will she cry whenever Crystal tries to hold her? She can't stand the thought.

Jordan begins to calm down in Haley's arms. "You scared the shit out of me, Crystal. I believed you. I knew you were lying, but I couldn't help but believe you."

Crystal breathes slow and deep. Jordan's crying is nothing compared to what she must have done at that age. Summer said the nurses had to give her a sedative along with food through an IV. Crystal had hit her "crying-like-you're-dying" milestone sooner and more often than her new sister. But listening to someone else cry is much harder than shedding her own tears. She realizes there is nothing more debilitating, more painful than hearing a baby cry. She hopes Jordan will forgive her. She swears she'll never hurt or shout at her again.

Silence.

Crystal opens her eyes as Haley sits next to her with Jordan sucking on her bottle.

"You want her?" asks Haley.

"If she'll let me."

Haley passes Jordan, who doesn't notice the change.

Crystal sees her sister's cheeks crease with each pull from the nipple. She had summoned her resentment and all her anger, spewed their ugliness out loud to save her mother, and expelled them from her mind and soul. She won't let herself think of them anymore. Jordan's cheeks are beautiful, and Crystal is lucky to watch them fill with her mother's milk.

Payton opens the door and brings Maya inside. Her mother hides her face while she cries in spasms.

"I heard . . . you. I'm so ashamed." She falls to her knees.

"That was an act, Mom. I love you and Jordan and will do anything to protect you. You'll never hear those words from me again. And I'll never think those thoughts again. I promise."

Maya lifts her wet face toward Crystal, still choking in breaths. "But . . . what you said is true."

Crystal scoots off the sofa onto her knees, facing Maya. "Not anymore." She holds her sister higher, between their chests. "Jordan is true. All that matters now is that we're together."

"He's gone?"

"To Fairbanks," says Crystal. "Maybe he'll get on a flight to Seattle." She watches Jordan sleep in her arms. "You want to take a nap with her?"

"Yes."

They both stand. Crystal and Jordan follow their mother up the stairs and into her room. Crystal lays Jordan into the bed then places the noise machine on the quilt and turns it on low. Maya raises a brace from the front of Jordan's bed and zips a mesh covering around the raised bumper pads.

Crystal wipes tears from her mother's face. "I don't want to talk about the past anymore, but I have to know one thing." She can barely swallow and dreads the answer. "Is Eugene my father?"

Maya's eyes twitch as she looks at Crystal. She opens her mouth a few times as if to speak then turns away. "I don't know. I'm sure that sounds awful."

"I'm not going to judge you, Mom."

Maya turns to face Crystal. "I didn't want to stop being with Holly, but she graduated and went to school in Fairbanks. She'd come home on weekends, and we'd sneak off. Rumors got started. Someone said they saw us kissing." She takes deep breaths. "We stopped seeing each other. Then Holly brought Jack home to meet her parents. Soon after, she was pregnant and married." Maya swallows and wipes an eye. "I fell into a dark, dull hole. I'd used alcohol and weed like everyone else before that, but afterwards I couldn't stand not being drunk or high. I went to parties and found some guy to fuck every time."

She hugs her shoulders. "I was miserable but couldn't stop. Of course, my parents heard about everything. They were teaching at the school, and that made it worse for all of us. We fought all the time." Maya covers her face, her hands shaking.

"When Holly had the twins, I went to see her. I asked her if she was happy now, being a mother and a wife. She cried on my shoulder as I hugged her. I wanted to take her out of that house and run away with her, but we couldn't do it. We'd always ask, 'How will we live?' And, 'What will everyone say?' If I was a man trying to steal Jack's wife, things would've been easier. Some people may not have liked it, but it's happened a million times before and people accept it. But two women in our situation? In Clear, Alaska? No way. No how." She collapses into a chair against the wall.

Crystal shakes and she can barely breathe. "What did you do?"

Maya raises her brows and makes a crooked smile. "I seduced her husband during the music festival."

Crystal's pulse throbs in her neck.

"Holly stayed home because of the babies, and Jack went by himself." Her lips tighten around a cold laugh. "It was easy. The first night we kissed. The second we went a little further. My head was messed up with crack and oxys and anything else I could find, so the plan I had might make no sense to you, but seemed brilliant to me at the time. Holly would leave her husband for cheating, then I'd beg for forgiveness and offer to help her raise the twins. I'd move in with her, and life would be great."

Crystal's hands tremble. "Was he the only one besides Eugene?"

Maya leaps out of the chair. "Oh, Lord, no. I was on a tear. Any man with a wife or girlfriend was fair game." With such bitterness, "After all, a man who can't be seduced by a hot, begging female is suspect. But two

259

women who simply want to love each other and only each other? Man, that's sick."

Chills crawl down her neck. "Who else?"

She shakes her head and scoffs. "I don't remember all their names." She squeezes her arms and stares at the ceiling. "I hope that doesn't lower your image of me even further."

Crystal takes a step toward Maya. "The fact that you're still alive after everything you've been through, and you found the strength and intelligence to make him bring you home with a perfect baby is beyond amazing. You never gave up. I'm proud of you."

Maya covers her eyes. "I almost did a few times."

Crystal holds her mother's hand. "But you didn't, and here you are. Surrounded by women to protect you from him."

"Thank you."

"You told Eugene I wasn't his so he'd let you fly to the village fourteen years ago. Holly told me what happened in Fairbanks and what was supposed to happen. Eugene said my father was Jack. That he met you in a beer tent after you talked to a Jack." Crystal's heart pounds. "Is that Holly's husband?"

"No. I meant Jack Whitley because I'd screwed him too." A bitter laugh escapes her chest. "Of course, I probably could've said Sam or Terry or Stuart for the same reasons."

Crystal slows her breathing. "You don't know who my father really is?"

"I'm sorry, honey. There are a lot of possibilities. All I know is I discovered I was pregnant with you in mid-August."

"I've been worried that Haley . . .that Haley and I are sisters." Crystal's shoulders curl forward, caving in her chest.

Maya grabs Crystal's arms. "I never had intercourse with Jack Carson."

"But . . ."

"We only kissed and touched. After that second night, he didn't come back."

Crystal's legs wobble as tears well behind her eyelids. She can't get enough air into her lungs.

"Crystal, are you OK?" Maya pulls her against her chest. "I don't know who your father is, but I know it's not him."

"Does Holly know about you and her husband?"

"Yes. Before I left town with Eugene, I was broke. I went to a few of my married conquests and told them I would expose them to their wives if they didn't give me money. They all did. By that time, Holly was pregnant with Haley. We met to console each other. I showed her what Jack had given me."

"Was she angry at you?"

"Some. I explained to her why I did it. She asked why I didn't follow through with my plan. I told her it was because of Eugene and his magic drugs—all I wanted for free. I was such a fool. Holly and I had one more fling on this very bed when Mom and Daddy went to town to shop."

"August 21, 2001."

"Yes."

"And you left two days later."

"The biggest mistake of my life." Maya strides across the room.

"No. The biggest mistake was not raising your dyke flag when Summer caught you and Holly." Crystal goes to her mom. "People have to change. Too many teens suffer because of idiot opinions. And that's all they are—opinions."

"What about Mac and Summer?"

"Summer already realizes she made a mistake. Every one of those girls downstairs is an amazing human being, and they've all been hurt because of someone else's version of what sex should and shouldn't be. They are safe here. And so are you."

Maya nods and hugs herself. "I hope at some point I can forget the past."

"I think the past should be like an old movie you find hidden in a box. You remember it made you sad or happy or afraid, but it's old and there are much better movies to see now. Then you close the box and put it away. Pretty soon you forget where you put the box and stop caring that you lost it."

Maya smiles. "That would be nice."

"I love you, Mom. Thank you for coming home and sharing Jordan with me."

Maya holds her daughter's face. "I'm very proud of you." She kisses Crystal's cheek then her lips. "I love you too." They hug. "I'll try hard to never let you down. Ever again."

"Get some rest. Sleep as long as you can."

They separate. Maya slides under the covers, facing Jordan. Crystal backs away, her mind filled with an image she never thought she'd see— her mother sleeping in this house with her baby sister. Regardless of what happens in the future, this picture will never leave her.

As Crystal descends the stairs, the other three girls stand and applaud.

"Shhh!" whispers Crystal. "They're sleeping."

"Only because of you," says Payton. "That's the strongest, bravest thing I've ever seen."

"What would you have done," asks Sydney, "if Eugene had taken Jordan?"

Crystal shakes her head. "I knew he wouldn't, but if he had raised his arms even a little to take her, I would've kicked him in his nuts."

"Which don't work," laughs Haley.

"Do you think he'll come back?" asks Sydney.

"Yes," says Payton. "He won't give up. And when he does, if he sees Maya, there will be a war."

"What do we do?" asks Haley.

"Keep our guard up and be ready," answers Crystal.

A phone rings. Everyone checks theirs.

"Shit," says Payton. "It's an unknown caller. It has to be Bekah." She swipes her screen and runs out onto the deck.

CHAPTER 28

*A*fter five minutes, Payton opens the door, red-faced and breathing quickly. "I need to drive to Fairbanks. Bekah's at Fred Meyer, hiding on the upper deck above the deli and hot food. She's afraid her father will find her."

Crystal pulls out her phone. "Let me call JD. Maybe he can pick her up."

Payton nods.

Crystal rings JD's number and waits for him to answer. When he does, the first thing she hears is a long sigh.

"Hey, Crystal. How's your day been going?"

His long sad breaths fill her ears. "What's wrong?"

"Maybe I should've stayed with you."

"I tried to tell you. Did you see the video?"

"Yeah, it was so cool," he exclaims. "She's beautiful. I want to see her."

She hopes none of them have been cruel to JD. "Tell me why you're sad."

"We went to the airport, and they asked us questions about Covid. A woman asked me whether I had been in close contact with anyone who had Covid, and I said yes. Then we had to get tested, and we can't go to the village until our results come back in three days. Everyone's mad at me."

"Did they say that?"

"No, but I can tell."

"Where are you now?"

"Back at Lena's friend's house."

"Do you have any money beside the $100 bill I gave you?"

"Yeah."

"Enough to buy gas for Lena's truck?"

"Yeah."

"OK. Go to Lena and tell her you need to drive home to see your mother. Offer her the hundred to use her truck. You'll be back before they fly out. Got it?"

"OK."

"And, JD. Once you have the truck, go to Fred Meyer West, the grocery store closest to the airport. Park then call me."

"Is Mom OK?"

"Yes. She's taking a nap with our little sister. You're going to love her."

"Cool beans! I can't wait." He ends the call.

Crystal stands and faces Payton. "We'll know in about ten minutes whether he can pick Bekah up. How'd she get away?"

Payton leans against the door. "Same way as always—out her window, onto the roof, and down a tree. Except this time her father had installed an alarm system on her window. All she did was peel off the part on the glass and tape it to the part on the frame. When she cranked open the window, the alarm didn't sound." She laughs. "The system is made to keep people out, not in. She bummed a ride across town and spent her last thirty dollars on a phone."

"She sounds very resourceful," says Haley. "Is she cute?"

"Yes," Payton smiles and wags her finger playfully at Haley, "but don't say anything about her looks."

"Bekah is beautiful," says Sydney. "Just keep that to yourself."

"OK," says Haley. "Is she an artist?"

"No." Payton's face beams. "She writes and is a wicked debater." She shakes her head and grins. "Don't even try to argue with her. But she's also silly and funny and loves to act."

A timer dings on Payton's computer. "Classes start in two minutes," says Payton. "This time you guys fake me. I need to fix the roof on my motorhome. Where's Mac's caulk?"

"Just inside the garage door," says Crystal. "On the right on one of the shelves."

Payton goes outside. Haley and Sydney sit at their computers while Crystal brings the art supplies on the deck back into the sunroom.

After logging in and responding to the teacher a few times, Crystal opens her drawing pad on the table and finds the photos Sydney took of her and Jordan. While she draws, she forgets about all the drama of the day and concentrates on Jordan—something new and fresh in Crystal's life. When Jordan responds to her expressions and noises, Crystal feels thoroughly jazzed and alive.

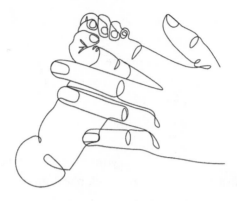

How could anything in her future be more fulfilling than helping her mother raise this precious little girl? And being with Haley as her child grows. These babies would be just over a year apart, as close as siblings.

With a chance to be raised in a safe house without secrets, where any opinion can be shared without fear, where sexuality is not hidden or forbidden. Where discovering each person's special needs is life's purpose and fulfilling them for oneself and others is a life goal.

Crystal's teacher asks for a thumbs up or down to indicate understanding.

Crystal clicks on the up icon. She understands more about herself and her family and what's important and what's not than she ever has before.

Her phone rings. "Hey, JD. Where are you?"

"In the parking lot at Fred's."

Crystal leaves the sunroom, looking for Payton.

JD chuckles. "Lena was being stubborn until I asked her what would happen to her truck after they flew to the village. I told her maybe we could rent it or even buy it. She wants you to call her sometime about that. OK, why am I parked here?"

Crystal sees Payton on top of the motorhome and calls out to her. "JD's at Fred's."

Payton pulls out her phone and punches numbers to make a call.

Crystal puts her phone to her ear. "Are you listening, JD?"

"Yes."

"You're going to pick up Payton's girlfriend from the store and bring her home. Her name is Bekah. Where exactly are you parked?"

"Just outside the exit closest to the gas pumps."

"OK. Stand next to the truck, facing the store. We'll tell Bekah where you are. Her name is Bekah. Got it?"

"Yeah. Bekah."

"And don't get gas at Fred's. Drive down the highway to Ester and get it at the new station. Call me back when you're there."

"OK."

Crystal ends the call. She shouts up to Payton. "Tell her what JD looks like. He's wearing a gray Henley shirt and driving a red Ford 150 truck. He'll be standing against it outside the west entrance."

Payton nods and talks into her phone. She calls down to Crystal, "She's walking through the store now." She pauses and locks eyes with Crystal. "She's exiting the doors." Payton talks on her phone then shouts down to Crystal. "She sees JD. She's running toward him." Payton thrusts her fist into the air. "They're on their way out of the lot."

Crystal raises her thumb and smiles then Payton blows her a kiss. Crystal heads back to her computer and sits.

"JD's bringing Bekah," says Crystal.

Sydney flings her arms into the air and kicks her feet. "Yes!"

Haley types on her keyboard. "We're running out of rooms."

Sydney writes some numbers on a paper next to her. "That's why Payton's fixing the motorhome. We can sleep there tonight."

Crystal clicks a thumbs-up emoji on her screen. "There's another room behind the pantry. Summer uses it to grow her seedlings and make her quilts. We can move the shelves outside and bring in another bed from the shed." Crystal's chest thumps with excitement. "It has windows and a heater. It could actually be two rooms if we add a wall."

"Who's moving into it?" asks Haley.

"Payton, Bekah, and Sydney. JD can have his room tonight."

"Is he still leaving for the village?"

"I don't know. I think once he's here with Mom and Jordan, he won't want to leave."

Haley counts on her fingers as she says names silently. "OK, that's eight, including Maya and Mom, and not including Mac and Summer."

Crystal stands, her chin thrust out. "Well, they're coming back, so that's ten. It will work. It has to."

"If you say so."

"Who should I send away or say no to? This is the only safe house for all of you."

Haley nods. "Safe except for Eugene."

"This house is not safe for *him*. He has one more chance to give up and leave." Crystal answers JD's call to her phone. "Hey, how is she?"

"Good. She's real nice."

"Great. Do you have enough money for gas and snacks for Bekah?"

"Sure. I still have your hundred."

Crystal frowns. "What did you give Lena?"

JD laughs. "You have to haggle with people, Crystal. I offered her twenty to use the truck. She said forty. I gave her thirty-five, which was all of my own money."

Crystal laughs. "You should be a businessman."

"Maybe. The tank is full. We're going inside now to get drinks and snacks. See ya later, alligator."

"In a while, crocodile."

He laughs and ends the call.

"Sometimes JD surprises the hell out of me. But he can always make me smile."

Payton enters the room, her eyes shining. "Bek called. She likes JD. He laughs at all her jokes."

"He always laughs at jokes," says Crystal. "Even the ones he doesn't understand. He likes to laugh. You coming, Haley?"

"Where?"

"To fix up the back room. Thought we already decided."

Haley stands.

Payton sits at the table. "This is the last class I'm faking, just so you know."

"Of course," says Haley. "It's the last class of the day." She stretches her arms above her head. "My brain is so stuffed with knowledge, I'm afraid to sneeze."

"That's a Bekah joke," says Sydney. "You two will be a riot together."

"We only have an hour, Haley," says Crystal. "Come."

"I'm coming. I'm coming." She stops and looks back toward Payton with an innocent look on her face. "I remember saying that a lot last night, but I can't remember why." She turns to Crystal. "I'm coming! Oh my God, I'm coming."

"Another Bekah joke," says Sydney, grinning and shaking her head.

Once they enter the back rooms, Crystal closes the door to the pantry.

"What do we do first?" asks Haley.

Crystal opens the side door, which exits to a small porch at the back of the house. "Wrestle these metal shelves to the garage."

For the next fifteen minutes, they haul the three units outside. Crystal brings a dolly, and both girls push and balance the large, awkward beasts around the house, over the gravel driveway, and into the garage.

They sweep the vinyl floors, push the sewing machine cabinet to a corner where they stack all the pieces and bolts of material, and move the folding table against a wall.

Inside the storage shed, they find a full mattress and box spring, a bed frame, a rolled up area rug, and a crib.

"Was this yours?" asks Haley.

"No. It must have been Mom's. Maybe she'll want this upstairs."

They carry the pieces inside and lean them against a wall. They find bumper pads, a quilt, and a bag of nuts and bolts stuffed into crates. And a wooden high chair behind an old door.

"Where do you want the bed?" asks Haley, wiping sweat off her forehead.

Crystal lifts her shirt and wipes her face. "Between the windows?"

"That works for me."

After the bed is fixed, Haley collapses flat on her back onto the mattress, arms and legs spread. "I'm pooped."

"You're also very vulnerable to attack," says Crystal, crawling on all fours, her hands on either side of Haley's waist, both knees inside Haley's legs.

"I'm stinky and sweaty. Don't you want me to wash up?"

"I don't want to smell soap. I want to smell you." She pushes up Haley's sweatshirt, exposing her stomach then presses her cheek against Haley's skin. "Jordan and your baby will be like sisters, or brother and sister. They're going to grow up together and love each other. That will be amazing." Crystal places her elbows on either side of Haley's hips and kisses her skin. "You'll make a great mommy."

"I hope so. You'll help?"

"Always." Crystal pulls Haley's pants down, exposing her panties. "No commando today?"

"I'm sure I will be in a few seconds."

"Yes, you will." Crystal presses her open mouth between Haley's legs and breathes hot air through the pink cotton.

Haley squirms and gasps. "Probably better to breathe out than in. How bad is it?"

"Overwhelmingly sultry." She presses her mouth and breathes out again. "Intoxicating." She slides her fingers up Haley's legs underneath the panties then rubs her thumbs lightly up and down in the middle.

Whimpers escape Haley's mouth.

"Maybe we have time for one ravishing orgasm," says Crystal. "What do you think?"

Haley's chest heaves more quickly. "Are we sisters?"

As Crystal slowly pulls down Haley's underwear and pants, she says, "Nope. Mom had sex with lots of men around that time, but not your father. One of them, however, was Dylan's dad. Maybe I'll call him 'Bro' next time I see him." Crystal drags her tongue from the inside of Haley's right thigh upward then across to the other thigh. "Probably half the men in this town are my fathers." Crystal moves her mouth back up Haley's thigh. She kisses and slides her lips in circles. "I'm likely illegitimate. Does that bother you?"

Squirming, Haley pulls off her top. "I go from one bastard to another. Story of my life." She pushes her breasts together and squeezes.

"Yeah. You have this weird attraction to all things Dylan." Crystal pushes Haley's legs farther apart. "But he never did this." She scoots her hands beneath Haley's bottom, lifts, leans forward, and connects with every nerve in Haley's body—feeling them spark and throb with heat through her lips. In her mind Crystal sees and hears the surging waves, all crashing against her mouth. Just as one threatens to crest, she lightens her touch. Before it subsides, she pulls it back to a higher peak. Like a conductor, Crystal manipulates Haley's groans, pounding the grunting bass and flicking the highest squeals. Their dance is both guttural and ethereal, a twisting transformation into one spirit.

Soon, every one of Haley's muscles strains to hold in her gasps. Crystal clutches Haley's pelvis as it vibrates hard against her mouth. The sucking and smacking sounds fill Crystal's brain until Haley's long, torturous, loud release bursts through, sending wave after wave thundering against Crystal's tongue and lips.

Crystal gently lowers Haley's hips to the mattress.

Haley flops her arms across her face, gasping for breath.

Crystal wipes her mouth across Haley's stomach then spreads the juices with her hands over Haley's breasts. "You won't have to buy that new perfume you were wanting."

Haley laughs and coughs. "I can't move."

Crystal lays her face between Haley's legs. "It's like you and I become a single person. I feel everything you feel. I could eat you all day."

"If you did, I'd be nothing but a puddle on the floor."

"Actually, on the mattress. You left your mark."

Haley tries to laugh. Her arms drop to her sides. "I can't even laugh. I'm gonna pay you back later."

"Promises, promises."

They hear a knock.

"Crystal?" says Maya. "Are you decent?"

Crystal hops off the bed and runs to the door. She cracks it open. "I am. Haley's indecent."

"I heard that," shouts Haley.

Maya's eyes widen as she inhales. "Maybe you should crack open the windows."

Crystal nods and stifles a laugh. "We fixed up the room and added a bed. We found a crib and a high chair."

Maya raises her brows and smiles. "Really? Everyone was wondering what you were doing. They heard such sounds."

Crystal knows she's blushing. "Is Jordan awake?"

"Yes, I fed her upstairs. Now Payton and Sydney have her in the sunroom."

Crystal grabs a pack of baby wipes from a nearby shelf in the pantry. "OK. We'll be there in a second." She backs into the room and shuts the door. She pulls a sheet from the pouch and wipes her face. Turning around, she finds Haley pulling up her pants and opening the windows. "Here." She tosses the wipes. "Use these then come to the living room."

Haley's eyes widen in mock shock. "But I thought you liked my new perfume?"

"I love it. Maybe wipe the mattress." Crystal leaves the room and tries to walk casually toward the other girls.

Payton folds her arms and tightens her eyes. "We thought someone died."

Crystal strains to keep from smiling. "We were moving a bunch of stuff, and Haley got a cramp. In her leg."

"Then you rubbed it out?" asks Payton, stifling a laugh.

"Yeah. Just rubbed it on out. It took a while."

"Sounded like sex to me," says Sydney with Jordan lying on her lap. "But I'm only twelve. What do I know?"

Payton and Crystal crack up as Jordan waves her arms and legs.

Haley enters the room. "Hey, everyone. What's up?"

"Is your leg feeling better?" asks Payton.

Haley squishes her eyebrows together. "My leg?" She catches Crystal's widening eyes. "Oh, my leg. Yeah, it's much better, thanks to Crystal's . . . magic fingers."

"There's a red truck coming," says Maya, looking out the window.

"That's JD," says Crystal.

"And Bekah," says Sydney. "Somebody take Jordan."

Crystal picks up her sister as everyone runs out to the deck.

CHAPTER 29

*J*D smiles and waves through the windshield, pushing his horn several times as he parks. Bekah flings her door open and runs toward Payton, squealing, leaping up to her, wrapping her legs around Payton's waist then pulling her face to hers for a long kiss. Bekah's ash blonde hair is streaked with rainbow colors. She sports rings in her lip, ears, and eyebrow, and a ruby stud in her nose.

Sydney runs over and wraps her arms around Bekah and her sister.

Crystal glows in the excitement of those around her.

JD walks slowly around the truck, his back straight, trying very hard to minimize his limp. Crystal and Maya stand together on the deck watching him approach. His cheeks swell as his mouth stretches into a wide smile beneath glistening eyes. He stops a foot before the deck, his eyes level with Maya's.

JD clears his throat. Crystal can see his eyes are about to flood. "Thanks for coming home, Mom. I missed you." He lifts his arms to her and moves forward.

Maya clutches her son's back and pulls him to her. "I've missed you too, JD. I'll never leave you again."

JD's back shakes as he cries into her shoulder. Crystal bites her lips and blinks tears away.

Maya rubs his broad back then holds his face in front of hers. "What a man you've become. You're so handsome and strong. Yet so sweet." She wipes his face.

JD smiles and rubs a thumb under her eye. "Think we both sprang a leak."

She laughs. "Yes, we did. Meet your sister."

Crystal steps down and lifts Jordan up against her brother's chest, the baby's eyes fixed on JD, brows furrowed, hands flailing. Crystal knows that despite his size, JD can be gentle and careful. He slowly lowers his face closer until Jordan grabs his nose and hooks a thumb in his nostril.

"Oh, Jordan," says Crystal. "I wouldn't stick my finger in there for anything."

But Jordan clenches tighter.

JD opens his mouth, "Ouch, ouch, ouch." He turns his head, bringing his ear closer to Jordan's other hand.

"Gotta be tough, JD," laughs Crystal. "Don't you dare deny your sister what she wants."

"I'm trying. Aargh."

Haley moves next to Crystal. "Ooh, Jordan look at that big, floppy ear. Wouldn't you want to grab it?"

Jordan kicks her feet, scrunches her brows with more determination, and grabs JD's ear.

Crystal snorts a laugh.

"Oh, that is so sweet," says Haley. "Jordan loves you, JD."

JD clenches his fist and whimpers. "Ouch, ouch, ouch."

"Don't you dare pull away from her," commands Crystal. "She'll think you don't love her."

JD squirms. "I do love her, but she's strong!"

"Girl power!" exclaims Haley. "And don't you forget it."

Crystal gently pulls Jordan away until she releases JD's nose and ear. But the baby still stares at her brother until her mouth spreads into a smile. She snaps her arms down with a laugh.

JD rubs his ear. "That is the cutest baby I've ever seen. And the strongest."

"Hold out your finger, and she'll grab it," says Crystal.

JD does and Jordan grabs his pointer. She fixes her eyes on the massive digit, pulling it closer and closer, her eyes crossing, until she opens her mouth.

"That finger better be clean, JD," says Crystal.

Jordan clamps her gums down on the fingertip then starts sucking. Crystal and Haley blurt out a laugh.

"She thinks she's hit the mother lode," says Maya. "What a big nipple!"

Jordan grimaces and turns her mouth away.

"Nope," says Crystal. "Just a big, dirty finger." She holds Jordan's back against her chest, with an arm under her bottom allowing her sister to look out. Jordan's eyes open wide, her lips pucker, then she waves her arms.

"She's funny," says JD. "I can't believe I have another sister."

"We've got you outnumbered, Bro."

Bekah approaches and extends her finger to Jordan, who grabs on. "Who's this?"

"Jordan, my little sister. Hey, Bekah. I'm Crystal and this is my mom, Maya."

"Hi, Bekah," says Maya.

Crystal throws her arm around Haley. "And my girlfriend, Haley."

"Hey, Bekah," says Haley. "I love your rings."

"Thanks." She looks at Crystal. "This is your house?"

Crystal switches arms for holding Jordan. "Yes, and you're welcome to stay as long as you want."

"Do you have any idea how special you are?"

Crystal's mouth falls open. "Why would you say that?"

"To open your house to a bunch of lesbians in the middle of Alaska is very rare. Lots of gay kids have nowhere to go. Yet you send your brother to pick me up, feed me, then bring me here."

"But you're Payton's friend."

"Whom you didn't know before yesterday. If another girl walks down your driveway looking for a place to sleep, what would you do?"

Crystal shrugs. "Let her stay. I know what happens when parents reject their kids because they're gay. If I can help, I will. I wish someone could've helped my mom and Haley's mom when they were our age."

Bekah nods, her face flush and radiant. "Thank you. I wasn't going back home. If I couldn't find Payton, I . . . would've died."

Crystal clutches Jordan to her chest with one hand as she reaches toward Bekah with her other. Bekah slides under it and the girls embrace. "We're all glad you're here." Crystal feels too many bones under Bekah's shirt. This girl is way too skinny. She catches Payton's eye.

"Payton," says Crystal, "why don't you and Bekah look through our food and find something you want for dinner. We should cook something special tonight."

"I can cook," says Maya. "And I'm sure Summer has homemade marinara sauce. She makes it with her own tomatoes. I could make spaghetti and garlic bread."

"Summer just made a batch this weekend," says Crystal. "It's extra good this year."

"We have salad stuff," says JD. "I always help make the salads."

Maya grabs her son's hand. "Great. You can show me where everything is."

JD looks back at Crystal, beaming a smile, as he limps after his mother.

"Do you like spaghetti, Bekah?" asks Crystal.

"It depends." She folds her arms. "I don't eat food blessed by a god who punishes homosexuality as a sin. Which was all the food in my father's house."

"Our food is blessed by the lesbians who cook it."

"Then I love spaghetti. I'm very hungry."

Crystal flicks hair out of her eyes. "If you want something now, look in the fridge and grab anything. Payton, check out the room behind the pantry. You all can sleep back there tonight. Sheets are in the hall closet and there's a twin mattress in the outdoor shed for Sydney."

"Thank you, Crystal." Payton blows her a kiss as she opens the door into the sunroom.

"You might want to flip the mattress over," says Haley. "Just saying."

Bekah frowns. "Why? Did something die on it?"

Haley laughs. "Died. Went to heaven, and came again!"

Payton whispers in Bekah's ear.

Bekah's face cracks into a smile. "We'll leave it as is. To set the mood." She closes the door behind them.

Sydney tickles Jordan's neck. "JD's really nice. And he's cute. How old is he?"

Crystal side-glances at Haley who raises her brows. "He's seventeen."

Sydney offers her finger to Jordan. "Oh. Does he have a girlfriend?" She glances at Crystal then looks back to the baby.

"You met her yesterday at school. Gena. She's pregnant."

Sydney's eyes open wide.

"She's supposed to fly to a village 450 miles away."

Sydney blows out a breath. "Is JD going?"

"I don't know. Maybe you can ask him later."

Sydney smiles and nods then runs inside the house.

Haley takes Jordan. "This will be interesting. How old is she?"

Crystal shakes out her arms and shoulders. "Twelve. JD will never leave Mom. If Gena cares about him at all, she'll realize that and stay here."

"I think Jordan needs a diaper change." She lifts the baby up to rub noses then blows strawberries on her tummy. Jordan giggles and sticks her finger in her mouth.

Crystal opens the door. "Diapers are upstairs. I think Mom has some toys."

"We can play with her on the floor."

After thirty minutes they hear JD calling everyone to dinner. Haley and Crystal bring Jordan into the sunroom and find Sydney and Bekah trying to fit seven plates and as many chairs around a table meant for four. The aroma of oregano, garlic, and onions saturates the air and makes Crystal's stomach beg to be filled. Her mouth waters over the platter of buttery garlic bread and a large bowl of salad with garden-grown tomatoes, radishes, and lettuce sitting on the table. Payton brings in the high chair and puts it beside the end seat closest to the living room.

JD carries two large bowls full of pasta sprinkled with shredded Parmesan and steaming sauce. "There's no room for these," says JD. "We've never had this many people at our table before."

"But isn't it amazing!" says Crystal. "If only Summer and Mac could see this."

Haley pulls out the table on the high chair then Crystal puts Jordan on the seat. They buckle her in.

"Here," says Payton. She pulls out the keyboard bench. "Set them here. We can pass them around after everyone is seated."

JD puts the bowls down. "Good idea."

Maya strides in with a ladle, pasta fork, and food for Jordan. "Are we ready?"

"This looks delicious, Mom," says Crystal. "When's the last time you cooked for this many people?"

"I never have." She wipes her forehead with her sleeve. "Unless you count making Thanksgiving dinner at the school for the community in tenth grade." She places a bowl with infant cereal mixed with breast milk on Jordan's tray and offers her a little spoonful.

"Crystal and I have done that," says Haley. "Last year before the plague hit. Won't happen this year, though."

Crystal takes the baby spoon from Maya. "Can I?"

Maya nods. "Do you think there's enough for everyone?"

"Plenty," says Payton. "Everyone sit, and I'll bring the spaghetti and sauce."

Sydney sits next to JD on one side while Bekah, Haley, Crystal and Jordan sit on the other. Bowls are passed and plates are filled. Payton sits at the end nearest the windows.

All faces turn to Maya.

"I don't want to pray," says Maya, "but I'd like to hold hands before we eat. Crystal, do you all still . . ."

"Every dinner," says JD, tilting his head down and trying to hide his smile. "Sometimes I think it's silly."

"You think it is," says Maya, "until you never do it again because there's no one at your table except . . . your asshole husband and maybe one or two of his disgusting friends." She wipes her eyes. "And there's never anything to celebrate. Then you miss it a lot."

Crystal reaches for Maya's hand.

"I loved cooking for all of you. I want to do it every night. I missed being with my family for so many years . . ." She touches a napkin to her eyes then reaches for JD's hand. "And JD is the best helper in the world. Summer must love you to pieces. I used to help her all the time until . . . until . . ."

"Holly?" asks Crystal.

Maya nods. "You don't miss things until they're gone, and by then it's too late. I'll cook dinner for all of you, and when Summer comes back, we'll both cook together. And I'll love helping her. But we won't do the dishes."

JD laughs. "Summer doesn't do dishes either. 'Cooks cook and eaters clean.' That's what she says."

"She's exactly right," says Maya then holds out her hands. "Everyone."

Hands are raised above the table and clasped.

"If anyone wants to say something, you can. Otherwise . . ."

Bekah stands, still holding Payton and Haley's hands. "I'd like to say something. For most of the past two years, my father gave me prayers for those trapped by their homosexuality and Bible verses telling me I could not love God and a woman at the same time." She bites her lips and looks to the ceiling. "He told me many times that I fell into lesbianism because of the media and popular culture and I could choose to climb out of my well of despair by finding a good man of the church." She blinks and pushes tears onto her cheeks. "But what lifted me out of depression and probably suicide was Payton and Sydney taking me into their home and now Crystal taking me into hers, accepting me as I am, without asking me to change anything . . ." She offers a wry grin. "Except my clothes every so often."

Payton's smile spreads from ear to ear.

JD laughs then looks around sheepishly. "Sorry."

"No," continues Bekah. "Your laugh is precious because it is absolutely real. The world needs more of your sweet laughter." She smiles at each one of them. "I do have a prayer. You may have heard a version of it before. *Grant me the serenity to accept the things I cannot change, such as my queerness, and the courage to change the things I can, by speaking out against injustice and intolerance, and the wisdom to know the difference.*" Her voice becomes solemn. "Thank you for this food, Maya. Thank you all for accepting me into your family today." She thrusts Haley's hand into the air and shouts. "And thank you to Haley and Crystal for christening our bed. Now Payton and I don't have to worry about messing it up."

Haley chokes on her laugh while Crystal slaps her back. Jordan grabs her bowl and throws it onto Maya's plate, plopping onto a mound of spaghetti. Payton and Maya applaud and laugh. Crystal notices Sydney still holding JD's hand while her brother looks embarrassed and averts his eyes. She will have to talk to him later.

"Let's eat before it gets cold," shouts Maya.

Everyone eats. Including Jordan after Crystal salvages some of the cereal and wipes marinara off the bowl.

Twenty minutes later only JD still manages to put food into his mouth. The rest lean back in their chairs, full and comfortable. Sydney and Haley burp a few times, but they run out of energy and declare a tie.

Crystal's phone rings. She groans, pushes a yawning Haley off her shoulder, and tries to decipher the number on her screen. Someone wants to Facetime. Who? Summer! A slug of heat shoots through her veins. She swipes to accept.

The image is shaky and blurry. A nurse's face behind a mask and shield finally emerge.

"Is this Crystal Rose?"

"Yes." Her heart pushes into her neck. "Is Summer OK?"

Everyone stares at Crystal, eyes wide open.

"She wants to talk to you. Give me a second."

The image jerks and blurs until finally Crystal can see her grandmother's pale face with cannula tubes in her nostrils.

Summer smiles then coughs. "Crystal." Her voice wavers. "How are you?"

Her heart racing, Crystal's voice surges through her throat. "Summer! Are you better?"

"That's what they tell me. I saw the video. Is Maya there?"

Crystal jumps out of her seat, stumbles around the high chair, and leans close to Maya so Summer can see both their faces. Both women cry immediately.

"Mom. I'm home."

Crystal's hand shakes holding the phone. She grasps it with the other hand as whimpers escape her mouth.

"Maya, my Maya." Tears trickle down her face. "I'm so happy you're back. I've missed you every day." She coughs and pauses to take breaths.

"Don't strain yourself, Mom. We have all the time in the world."

Summer nods and wipes her cheek. "I knew that one day you'd walk down our driveway, and I'd rush out to hug you. I never gave up hope. But I didn't think to look toward the pond. Or the bridge. That was such a beautiful video. I've watched it over and over."

Maya's chin quivers, her eyes brimming with tears. She taps the screen and flips the image to show Jordan, who holds the spoon against her gums. "Here's your new granddaughter. Jordan, say hi to . . . What do you want Jordan to call you?"

"I feel like a granny right now and look like one too, but when I come home, I don't want that beautiful little girl to think I'm an old lady. She can call me Summer, just like JD and Crystal."

Jordan bangs her spoon onto the tray.

Crystal moves the phone closer to her sister. "Summer, she can crawl a little, but she goes backward. It's the cutest thing. And she grabs my finger and won't let go. She's totally perfect."

Haley reaches in to wipe cereal off Jordan's face.

"Who's that?" asks Summer.

Haley leans into the frame. "Hey, Summer. It's Haley. I'm very glad you're feeling better."

"Where's JD? Did he leave?"

Crystal swings the camera toward her brother. "No, Summer. I'm right here." He waves and smiles. "Mom made your spaghetti. And we made a salad."

"Who are all the others?" asks Summer. "I saw a table full of people."

Crystal moves around introducing Sydney, Payton, and Bekah. "You'll love them all when you get to meet them in person. And Holly will be here later." Crystal takes the phone back to Maya and flips the screen.

"Holly?" asks Summer.

Maya nods, a new stream of tears gathering in her eyes. "I came back for her too, Mom."

Summer tries to speak but can only breathe quickly, her face straining. After a few seconds, she wipes an eye. "I'm sorry about . . . how I treated Holly. I didn't know how much I hurt you."

"I hurt you more. But we're not going to drown in the past, Mom. We're going to make a new life together. I want to be with you and Daddy. How is he?"

"Mac is still on a ventilator, but they say he's doing better. Where's Eugene?"

"He left Clear this morning." Maya glances at Crystal. "We think he's going to fly back to Washington."

"Good riddance." Summer looks up to her left then back to the phone. "I need to go. I love you, Maya. And Crystal and JD. And I want to be with all your friends. And I do want to apologize to Holly. You tell her that. OK?"

"Yes. I love you too. We'll call you tomorrow."

"Yes. Tomorrow."

The two women gaze at each other, smiling. Maya blows her a kiss as the screen turns black.

Jordan slams the spoon onto her tray, startling herself, then cries. Haley pulls out her tray, unbuckles the straps, and lifts her up. "I'll walk her around." She takes Jordan into the living room.

"When is Summer coming home?" asks JD.

"We don't know," says Crystal as she rubs her mother's quivering back. Maya weeps into her hands.

Sydney stands. "C'mon, JD. Let's do the dishes." She picks up a few plates and heads for the kitchen.

JD gathers the bowls and stops near Crystal, head hanging down. He whispers, "What do I do?"

"The dishes," says Crystal.

He blushes. "I think she has a crush on me."

"Then she has good taste in boys," says Crystal. "Just be sweet like you always are and remember she's twelve."

"OK." He walks away.

Payton and Bekah stack plates and gather silverware. "We'll clean up," says Payton.

"Thanks," says Crystal. She scoots a chair close to Maya and sits. "Summer is getting better. She'll be home soon."

Maya leans back and wipes her eyes. "Maybe. But what then? Is she going to want all of us in her house? Years ago, she didn't want one lesbian, much less six."

"She realizes she was wrong about you and Holly. You heard her."

"OK, but what about Payton, Bekah, and Sydney? And jokes about sex? How will she react to that?"

Scenes flash through Crystal's mind: "Why aren't you wearing a bra?" Sydney taking a shower. Bekah's dinner speech. Impulsive sex with Haley in the back room.

Crystal holds Maya's hand. "She'll change because you're here with Jordan. She wants you to be happy."

"'My house. My rules.' How many times has she said that to you and JD?"

"A few times. This will work out. I promise."

Haley returns with a fussy Jordan. "Maybe she's hungry?"

Maya stands. "I'll feed her." She sits on the sofa and pulls her right arm out of her sleeve, baring her breast. She reaches for Jordan. Haley kneels on the floor in front of Maya and hands the baby over. Maya guides her nipple to Jordan's mouth.

"Can I watch?" asks Haley.

"Certainly," says Maya.

"I'm pregnant, by the way. I haven't seen a doctor yet, but I'm probably due in April."

"Are you happy?" asks Maya.

"Scared, but excited after seeing Jordan."

Crystal sits next to Maya and holds Jordan's foot.

"Does it hurt?" asks Haley.

"Only sometimes. But overall, it's the most wonderful feeling in the world."

Haley touches Jordan's cheek. "I love the sounds she makes."

"Will you breastfeed your baby?" asks Maya.

Haley grins. "If Crystal will share my breasts." She flashes her eyes at her girlfriend.

"You've got two," says Crystal. "And they're pretty big. There's enough to go around."

"Unless I have twins. Mom did."

"In that case, we'll have to do rock, paper, scissors."

Maya laughs and Jordan loses her latch. Milk squirts onto Jordan's cheek until Maya can guide her nipple back into the baby's mouth.

Both girls hear the distinctive sound of a Mustang and stand to look out the window. Danny and Mike have arrived.

CHAPTER 30

*H*aley and Crystal wait on the deck as Danny and Mike walk over. Both wear tight jeans, bulging at the crotch, compression t-shirts revealing their tight pecs and abs, and shades. Their long sleeve shirts are open. Mike's sleeves are rolled up to show off his muscular forearms. Both are sporting scruffy, short beards and gelled hair. Crystal has seen this look for months and thought nothing other than they are both handsome guys who know girls stare at them. Now she realizes they dress for each other's gaze.

Haley blocks the sun shining in her eyes with her hand. "Are there two better looking guys in Clear?" asks Haley.

"Hell no," says Mike, "but why limit the comparison to Clear? At least extend our range fifty miles along the highway."

"I would extend it a hundred miles for you, Mike. But if I include my brother, people might talk."

"We wouldn't want people to talk," says Danny with a knowing look at his sister. "No sense giving them more ammunition."

"Join us," Haley gestures for them to walk onto the deck.

"Hey, Mike," says Crystal. "Welcome to my house."

Mike whips off his shades, smiles, scans the house then looks her up and down. "Hey, Crystal. Nice place. I'm still waiting to see those boobs."

Crystal smiles too sweetly. "You have as much interest in seeing my boobs as I do in seeing your cock. We can be honest with each other here. My house is safe."

Mike shakes his head and shrugs his shoulders. "Safe from what?"

Crystal fixes her eyes on his. "Intolerance. Harmful labeling."

"Like?"

"Twig, for example. Or dyke. Or other anti-gay slurs."

"There's a lot of them online," says Danny.

"About me and Crystal?" asks Haley.

Danny nods and takes a seat at the deck table.

Haley sits next to him. "Anyone else?"

"Not yet."

Crystal sits next to Danny. "It's better to claim your own labels rather than let others make you fear theirs."

"Meaning?" asks Mike as he sits between Haley and Crystal.

"If you fear being called a lesbian," says Crystal, "you call yourself a dyke. If you worry about your friends realizing you're not straight, you call yourself gay. Take away their weapon."

Mike's eyes shift back and forth between Crystal's eyes. "That's easy to say." He swallows. "A lot harder to do."

"Harder than lying all the time?"

Mike pops his knuckles. "Aren't you and Haley hiding? I mean, you haven't defended yourselves."

"What have we done wrong?" asks Haley.

"People are saying all kinds of things," says Mike.

"Like?"

"If Haley's a dyke," says Danny, "then why is she pregnant?"

Haley places her hand on top of Mike's. "You can answer that one."

Crystal watches the battle between denial and realization spread over Mike's face, forcing him to breathe heavily and sweat from his hairline to his eyebrows. She feels his struggle and hopes he can get through this.

Haley grips his hand. "You're the father of my baby. I'm happy it's you and not Dylan."

"How . . . how can you be sure?" Mike glances at Danny's cold eyes and tight mouth.

"Because Dylan hasn't cum inside me for almost two months. My first pregnancy test, a month ago, should've been positive if it was Dylan. I took another test yesterday, six weeks after you and I had sex. It was positive."

Danny clenches both fists. "You screwed my sister? When was this?"

Mike drags his fingers down his face.

Haley swallows, her chin quivering. "When Dylan went fishing in August. I told Mike that Dylan accused him of being gay. Mike denied it. I told him to prove it." She takes a breath and slowly blows it out. "I know you're upset, Danny. I'm sorry."

Danny tightens his eyes. "I'm upset because my supposed friend screwed my sister behind my other friend's back."

"Then that would be the first time you cared whether anyone screwed your sister," says Crystal, catching Danny's eyes.

He looks away.

Mike squirms in his chair. "Dylan will kill me if he finds out."

"Not if both of you tell the truth," says Crystal, slowly, gently. "Haley, did you suspect Mike was gay?"

"Yes."

"Maybe you wanted to see if it was possible for a homosexual to have straight sex."

Haley nods.

"Because you'd been doing it for years, and you weren't sure why you were unhappy." Crystal grabs Haley's hand.

"What do you want me to do?" asks Mike, staring at the table.

"You don't have to do anything," says Haley. "I'm staying with Crystal. You can visit any time you want, and after my baby's born, you can be part of its life. I'd like that. Kids need fathers too." She grabs Crystal's hand. "But we're not pretending we're a couple just so people won't call us names."

He looks at her with red, puffy eyes. "You're not going to tell anyone about me?"

"No. That's your job. But Crystal and I won't hide the truth about us."

"Mike," says Crystal, "you're welcome to come here and hang out when you want. You don't have to hide who you are at my house. And, Danny," she holds his shoulder, "that goes for you too."

Danny jerks his shoulder away. "What are you talking about?"

"You can love who you want however you want while you're here."

Danny forces a laugh. "Hey, I can bring Paige over here, and we can get naked in your living room. Cool!" He smiles at Mike, expecting him to laugh with his joke.

Mike shakes his head and covers his face.

"Have you ever gotten naked with Paige?" asks Haley. "Stop pretending, Danny."

They all hear tires biting gravel from a distance. Haley and Crystal stand.

"It's Mom," says Haley.

Danny jumps up. "What? Why is she here? Shit!" He seems unable to decide whether to run to his car or go inside the house. Instead, he stands as still as a rabbit, holding his breath.

Crystal checks the trees for the monster owl then realizes truth can be as life changing as an owl attack.

Haley walks toward the door. "Stop freaking out, Danny." She opens it halfway. "Maya, my mom's here."

By the time Holly exits her car, Maya stands on the deck, still nursing Jordan.

Mike's eyes bulge when he sees Maya's exposed breast. He turns his head.

Crystal laughs. "That's how I thought you'd react when you saw a boob." She hugs a very surprised Mike. "I'm glad to know you're really a nice guy, even though you called me Twig for years."

He nods. "Hey, I'm sorry."

"Thank you." She hugs him again.

Maya offers a sleeping Jordan to Haley. "Will you take her upstairs and put her to bed?"

"Sure." Haley nestles the baby in her arms and goes inside.

Maya puts her arm through her sleeve as she watches Holly approach with a small suitcase.

"Hi, Danny. I'll bet you're surprised to see me." She laughs. "Hey, Mike." Holly keeps walking until she and Maya are nose to nose.

"I missed you," says Maya.

"I couldn't stand to be in that house for another minute, so here I am."

Maya's fingers touch Holly's neck and cheek. Holly pushes her hands under Maya's shirt. Their lips open as they touch; their tongues dance with each other, just like the drawing Crystal made at school yesterday.

Crystal watches Danny's eyes and mouth fall open. She moves closer and whispers. "Like I said, you are safe at my house. You and Mike don't have to hide your feelings here."

Without turning to see her son, Holly says, "Danny, are you still standing, or did you faint?" She strokes Maya's hair.

"I'm standing. But barely." He swallows hard.

Holly turns around. "Maya was my first love twenty years ago. Danny, how do you feel when you have to hang out with Paige to double date with Nick and Laura? Is that fun for you? Because I felt the same way when I dated your father. And every day since. Do you want to feel like you do with Paige for the rest of your life?"

Danny blinks and breathes for several seconds before he answers, "No."

"Then don't."

Payton and Bekah come out to the deck. "Hi, Holly," says Payton. "Meet Bekah, my girlfriend."

"Hello, Bekah," says Holly.

"JD brought her here from Fairbanks."

Crystal approaches. "How are JD and Sydney doing?"

Bekah smiles. "I didn't know washing dishes could be so much fun. They've been laughing and splashing water at each other for the past ten minutes."

"Payton," asks Crystal, "should I send JD on an errand?"

"And incur the wrath of Sydney? No. You don't want to experience that. JD's acting as best he can under the circumstances. They'll be fine."

Haley exits the house and goes to her mother and Maya. "Jordan's asleep."

"Thank you," says Maya.

Haley catches her mother's eye. "What did you tell Daddy?"

"That I needed to be with you tonight and not to expect me home until some time tomorrow afternoon."

"What did he say?"

Holly rolls her eyes and holds Maya's waist. "Neither of us should be at this house of queers. We're going to ruin our reputation."

Haley shakes her head. "What will you do?"

"I'm not putting up with it. Too much of my life was ruined trying to hide. I don't want Danny to have to do the same. I will confront him and the rest of this town tomorrow."

Haley grabs her mother's hand. "We'll do it together."

"All of us," says Crystal, wrapping her arms around both moms.

Sydney pulls JD out onto the deck with one hand while the other carries the .22. "We are going to the shooting range. I have been challenged."

"Excuse me?" asks Payton.

JD sucks in his lips and shakes his head slowly. "I didn't challenge you. I just said I'm a pretty good shot."

"Exactly," says Sydney. "After I said I was a good shot. Now we have to see who's better."

Crystal knows Sydney wants to ride with JD on the Honda. "Do you think you can settle this feud in thirty minutes?"

JD nods his head. "Maybe less."

"It depends on how many times I have to beat you before you give up," says Sydney with a big smile.

Crystal glances at Payton who shrugs her shoulders. "OK, but bring back the targets so we can add up the points. We want this to be a fair contest."

"Fair would be if I shot with one eye closed," scoffs Sydney as she runs toward the Honda and jumps onto the back.

"Targets and the boot are in the garage," says Crystal. "Only you can decide whether you should let her win or not."

"Should I?" JD asks, scrunching his eyebrows and scratching his head.

Payton laughs. "Just do your best, JD. She's very good."

JD widens his eyes. "Well, this is going to be fun."

After a few minutes, they head down the driveway, Sydney grinning from ear to ear, barely touching JD's sides, back straight, a good ten inches of space between her body and his. Crystal figures that space will disappear as soon as they turn down D Street.

Haley hugs Crystal from behind. "Sydney's got it bad. Poor thing."

"Only in Alaska would a first date happen at a shooting range."

"Well, they can't go to movies or a restaurant. Or a school dance. Remember those?"

"I never went to one."

"Oh, my god. Can't you dance?"

Crystal shakes her head.

"I can fix that." Haley hurries to the door.

"Where are you going?"

"To get my speaker." She disappears inside the house.

"What's Haley doing?" asks Holly.

Crystal tries to stop her stomach from flipping. "She wants to teach me how to dance."

"You have great dancing genes in you, Crystal. You should see your mother shake her booty." Holly thumbs through screens on her phone until she finds "Physical" by Dua Lipa and hits play. Holly's hips start bumping. "Maya, you want to show these kids how to do it?"

Maya smiles and raises her arms above her head as her body undulates.

Soon the two women mirror each other. Danny claps to the beat and yells, "Go, Mom!"

Mike puts his hands on the back of his head and thrusts his pelvis.

Crystal laughs. "I thought you could only dance in a thong."

"If that's what you want to see, I'm wearing one." He unbuttons his pants and starts to pull his zipper down.

Crystal shakes her head. "Please no! Once is more than enough."

When Haley walks onto the deck, her eyes widen in surprise. She turns on her speaker, finds her mother's phone on the table, and turns on Bluetooth. Soon the bass vibrates in Crystal's chest, and she can't help but move. Haley fixes her ravenous green eyes onto Crystal's as if she is stalking prey. Haley snaps her hip three times and invites Crystal to do the same. Then she slides to Crystal's side and shimmies down four beats then up. Crystal tries to copy her.

Haley wipes her hands across her breasts then thrusts them down between her legs. Crystal tries to keep pace as they repeat the series of moves.

She sees Payton and Bekah slow dancing to their own music, kissing and sliding their hands under clothes, oblivious to anyone around them. Danny and Mike dance sideways to each other. Anyone looking would think they're with the girls, but she catches their side-glances and smiles.

Maya and Holly join their daughters in a circle, each taking turns showing a move for the others to copy. When the song ends, Haley and Crystal hug their mothers.

"Another one!" shouts Haley.

"Something slow," says Maya.

"I got it," says Holly scrolling through her songs. "Our old love song." The two women smile at each other as "I Don't Want to Miss a Thing" begins.

Haley and Crystal watch them hold each other and sway to the music, whispering comments and laughing. Payton and Bekah never stopped their previous dance. Danny and Mike stand awkwardly, watching everyone else.

Crystal goes to the boys. "Have you ever danced slow with each other?"

Danny looks down. Mike shakes his head.

"Now's your chance. No one will say anything." She takes Mike's hand and puts it on Danny's waist. Haley guides Danny's arms from behind until they wrap Mike's shoulders. "It's OK." Crystal pulls them closer to each other and feels proud of them and happy she can give them this opportunity.

Haley taps Crystal's shoulder.

Crystal turns, "Yes?"

"Is this dance taken?"

The lowering sun makes Haley's eyes sparkle and glow. "Not yet." She reaches for Haley's butt and moves closer. "God, I love your ass."

"Only my ass?"

"All of you. I love all of you, Haley Carson."

"I love you, Crystal Rose."

Just before Crystal's lips meet Haley's, they hear the sound of a shotgun pumping a shell into its chamber. "Hands up! Everyone put your hands up! Now!"

Crystal turns and sees Eugene walking from behind the garage.

CHAPTER 31

*I*n a panic, Crystal turns to watch her mother nearly faint before Holly catches her. Bekah screams as Payton pushes her behind her back. Haley digs her nails into Crystal's arm. "He's going to kill us!"

"I want to see your hands!" He moves closer. "Line up so I can see all of you. God, you're a bunch of fucking queers! Maya! I want you up front!"

Payton whispers, "Start recording. Hold your phones up so he can see them."

Before Crystal moves to the edge of the deck, she texts JD. *Come home. Eugene here. Now.* She slides her phone into her pants, the camera just above her waist. "We're recording everything you say and do, Eugene."

"That's great, Crystal. Now toss your phone to the gravel."

She shows her empty hands and keeps her eyes steady on his, forcing herself to focus, to keep her breathing steady. "They'll still record, dipshit."

"Not when I shoot them." She watches Eugene move within five feet of Danny, who's trying hard not to squirm. "Toss your phone, boy. Or should I say girl? I could make you one real quick." He levels the barrel

CRYSTAL'S HOUSE OF QUEERS

at Danny's groin. "Toss it!"

Danny drops his phone on the driveway.

"Now you, girly." He points his gun at Mike's crotch.

Crystal watches Mike breathe quickly, flexing his arm muscles.

Eugene's mouth twists into a lopsided sneer. "You think you can get to me before I pull the trigger? Go on. Try."

"Who the fuck are you?" yells Mike.

"Maya's husband. Maybe Crystal's daddy. Your grim reaper. Toss it."

Mike throws his phone to the ground.

"Maya get up here!"

"What do you want, Eugene?" asks Maya from behind the others. "I'm not leaving with you."

"One way or the other, you will. When did you turn gay?"

"I never loved you," shouts Maya. "I came back to be with my family and Holly. There's no other man. Just leave us alone."

"Find yourself another woman," says Crystal, quickly glancing over Eugene's shoulder to the driveway. She needs time. JD will come back. They need to distract this asshole. She moves slowly away from Haley to her left. "Shouldn't be hard for such a hot man like you."

He swings the gun toward Crystal. "Where are you going?"

"The sun was hurting my eyes. I don't want to miss the show."

"What show?"

"When the troopers come."

He laughs. "No troopers in this town. Maya, let's go!"

Holly moves up until she stands behind Danny and Mike. "You've always been scum, Eugene. And stupid. Even if you forced Maya back in your truck, do you think for one minute she'd stay? As soon as you turn your back, she'll leave."

"Who the hell are you?"

"Maya's lover, which you could never be."

"Really? Maybe Maya's dead lover."

Her heart pounding, Crystal watches Eugene point the gun toward Holly's face. Danny steps sideways, placing himself between the gun barrel and his mother.

"Back off, asshole. You couldn't kill all of us before we take you down."

Eugene sneers. "So says the faggot."

Danny glares at the man. "That's right. I'm the faggot who's going to rip you a new one and fuck it with that barrel."

Mike steps closer to Danny. "And I'm the faggot who's going to help him."

Haley moves near Mike and grabs his hand. "And the dyke."

Eugene shakes his head. "Your mommies must be real proud of you girls."

Payton's phone rings. Everyone turns their heads. For a brief second, Crystal thinks about charging him, but hesitates. What could she do to him?

Payton accepts the call. "Hey, Sis."

"We're almost there!"

"Toss it, freak!" yells Eugene.

Payton smiles. "But they're almost here. I want to shoot the video of my sister sending a bullet through your eye."

Eugene moves toward her. "Where's your gun, freak? It's a little different when you're not the one holding the rifle. Isn't it?" He levels the barrel at her face. "Isn't it?"

Bekah cowers behind Payton who keeps her pinned against her back with an arm.

"Yeah, Eugene," says Payton. "It is different when I don't have a gun. But they do." She looks over his shoulder.

Crystal hears the Honda before she sees it. JD whips into the turn onto their driveway, sending his back wheels skidding toward the trees before his tires bite enough gravel to straighten out. JD leans forward, his face just above the handlebars, lips pulled back from his teeth. Sydney supports the rifle on his back, aiming it at Eugene.

Eugene backs away, pointing the shotgun toward the deck while he twists his head around.

Payton lowers her voice. "When he turns around, all of you run into the backyard. Go around the house. Get out of Sydney's line of fire."

JD speeds down the driveway, kicking up a huge cloud of dust that glows bright orange against the sun, shining directly behind him.

Crystal watches Eugene whip his head back to the deck then back to JD, growling in frustration. He can't seem to decide which direction poses the most danger. The Honda is fifty yards away. Eugene turns toward it, aiming his shotgun.

"Go!" yells Payton. "Move!"

Eugene whips around to the deck, starts to level his gun, but the Honda screams toward him. He jerks his gun back, fumbling with his weapon.

Crystal hears shoes pounding on the wooden planks behind her. She pulls her phone out of her pants, aims it at Eugene, and runs directly left toward a tree. In her periphery she sees Payton run in a curve toward the man's side.

A shot is fired.

Payton launches a flying kick into his knee.

Eugene grunts and spins to his left.

Payton's kick crumples his right leg. In a second she's on her feet, grabbing the shotgun before it hits the gravel. She jabs the butt into Eugene's face. He groans and lies still.

JD brakes, skidding the Honda to his left. Sydney hops off the back, keeping her .22 barrel pointed at Eugene.

Crystal sucks in a breath, still holding her phone toward the scene.

JD stops the Honda ten feet from an unconscious Eugene and climbs off. "Did he hurt anyone?"

"No," says Payton. "That was a good shot, Sydney."

Sydney gulps air. "I was aiming for his gut, but it was hard to hold the gun steady."

Crystal runs over to them. "Is he dead?" Her voice quakes, and her head spins.

"No," says Payton. "Sydney hit him in the hip, and I knocked him out. He's still breathing."

Crystal tries to catch her breath. "Where'd you learn to kick like that?"

"Taekwondo lessons when I was twelve. I'll call 911." She goes back to the deck to find her phone.

Crystal hugs JD. "Thanks, Bro. I knew you'd get back in time." She goes to Sydney. "Girl, you're brave as shit. Are you OK?"

"Yeah." She bends over like she's going to throw up but just burps. After a second, she stands up straight. "JD beat me."

Crystal holds her, not believing what she's hearing.

"We only had time to shoot twice," says JD.

"Yeah, but both of yours were closer to center than mine."

"We can go again tomorrow."

"Promise?"

JD shakes his head in amazement. "Anything to keep you from being angry with me. You're really something."

Sydney smiles.

Haley runs to Crystal. "Are you OK?"

"Yeah." She holds Haley's face. "Pretty brave with that 'And the dyke' bit."

Haley smiles. "Just trying to keep up with you."

Crystal sees Payton holding Bekah against her with one hand and her phone against her ear with the other. Holly and Maya clutch each other as they walk across the grass toward the driveway. Mike stands on the deck with his arm around Danny's shoulders. "Everybody OK?" asks Crystal.

"Yeah," says Haley. "Is your house safe now?"

Crystal looks at Eugene sprawled on the gravel and feels a cold knot of anger in her stomach. "As soon as the troopers take him away."

They hold each other. A siren wails in the distance.

"Must be the ambulance from the fire station," says Crystal. She moves closer to Eugene and sees a bloody hole in his left hip, oozing blood. A large purple and red bruise extends from his lower right jaw across the bridge of his nose. His chest slowly rises and falls.

Maya walks to within ten feet from Eugene and stops. "Is he dead?"

"No," says Crystal. "He's going to a hospital and then to jail. I have video of the entire thing."

"Where's Mom?" asks Haley.

"Checking on Jordan."

Crystal goes to her mom. "You're rid of him. He won't bother you again."

A tear rolls down Maya's cheek. "When I was in rehab and finally got clean, I realized how he had controlled me. Anytime I got angry or frustrated, he'd give me something to make me feel better. He convinced me he was my only friend, the only one looking out for me. But the truth is he's full of anger and pain. Only when he believed I cared about him could he live with himself. I wanted to die many times. He couldn't decide between suicide and murder when he sensed the truth. I knew this time if I went back, he'd kill me then himself. Sometimes I thought that would be the only way to leave him."

Crystal lets out a huge breath. She holds her mother's face. "We found another way."

"How can you be so brave?"

"I don't know. Maybe because I'm not scared of dying to get what I need. I just never knew what that is until now."

"What do you need?"

Crystal kisses Maya's cheek. "You, Jordan . . ." She reaches for Haley. "My girlfriend, my brother, Sydney—all my friends. Mac and Summer, but I can't figure out how to save them. I don't want to lose any of you. I need all of you happy and safe."

Maya wraps her arms around her daughter, her hands spread wide to touch as much of her back as possible. Crystal knows her mother loves her and won't leave her.

Holly exits the house and wraps her arms around Danny and Mike, kissing both of their cheeks. Payton walks a still shaky Bekah toward Crystal.

"Troopers will be here soon," says Payton.

"Speaking of brave," says Crystal. "Payton never flinches. I've got that kick on video."

"I want to see it," says Bekah. "I'm ashamed of myself, whimpering and cowering like a puppy."

"Your weapons are words," says Payton, kissing her head. "They don't fare well against a twelve gauge. And don't tell anyone, but I was shitting a brick when I charged toward him."

An ambulance turns off D Street onto their driveway. In a few minutes, two EMTs work on Eugene. Soon after, Brian exits his car and asks lots of questions while taking notes in his flip pad. Crystal shows him the video. Brian's eyes widen, he whistles, and he blows out his breath a few times. When he watches Payton's kick, he exclaims, "Whoa, girl. That's wicked. I'm going to post a bulletin warning any and all assholes to stay away from this house. There's too much girl power here."

"Gay power," says Crystal.

Brian nods. "All right then. Gay power."

Before he leaves, Crystal airdrops him the clip.

Danny and Mike approach Brian.

Mike clears his throat. "Who's going to see the video?"

"The DA, some others in my office. Why?"

Danny scratches his neck, glances at Brian then looks to the ground. "Because anyone who sees it will know about Mike and me," says Danny.

"You've got nothing to be ashamed of, Danny. You boys held your own pretty well. I don't know what I'd do with a twelve gauge pointed at my balls, but it wouldn't be any better than you. Probably worse. You should tell your own story. Stop allowing the likes of Dylan to bully you. I've got a gay nephew. He's a great kid. Doesn't take shit from anyone. Just be who you are. If people don't like it, they can go to hell." He touches the brim of his hat and climbs into his car. "I'll be in touch."

The EMTs close the back doors of the ambulance. Soon, both vehicles are driving away.

Once they're all back inside the house, Crystal watches her friends and family try to regain some normalcy. Such a heavy load has been lifted from each of them.

Sydney calls dibs on the shower. Payton and Bekah take theirs together as soon as Sydney leaves. JD finds a little respite from adoring Sydney when he uses the upstairs bathroom for his shower. But evidently he didn't want much private time because within ten minutes he's downstairs in the kitchen, licking Holly's cookie dough from a glass bowl and frequently glancing through the pantry toward Sydney's new room. Holly pulls out one pan of cookies then slides in another to bake.

Crystal walks toward JD, carrying her drawing pad and pen. "Who are you waiting on?" she teases.

"No one. I'm just eating dough. It's good. Do you want some?" He holds out a fingerful of beige goo.

"No thanks. But maybe Sydney will, though not off your finger." She laughs and starts to walk away.

"Gena called."

Crystal stops and turns. "And?"

JD smiles. "Lena's thinking she might want to come back to her house. The last whale was caught, and there's no space on a plane for another week."

"So that's good." Crystal feels such relief. "That solves a lot of problems."

"Yup." He nods and scrapes another fingerful of dough into his mouth. "I think Gena and Sydney will be good friends."

God, I hope so. "I'm sure you're right." She notices JD's eyes widen. "I know. How many times have you heard me say that? Sydney will be happy you're not flying away." She smiles and walks through the living room. Haley, Danny, and Mike wait for her at the table. Haley wants the boys to watch Crystal draw, and she can't wait to show them.

"Who are you doing first?" asks Haley.

"Bekah. Payton sent me her favorite photo of her." She unlocks her phone and finds the picture.

Maya smiles at her as she feeds Jordan on the sofa. "Show me when you're done."

Crystal nods at her then moves her magic pen across the paper. After ten minutes, she turns her pad toward her mother who shakes her head in amazement.

"How do you do that?" asks Mike.

Crystal removes the page and puts it on the table among her huddled friends. Danny and Haley try to follow the line shaping her face and hair.

"I fucking watched her do it," says Danny, "but I still can't trace her lines."

Haley points to where a line stops in Bekah's hair. "This is where she started from."

Maya still smiles at Crystal.

"Don't look at me, Mom. I want to draw your profile."

"OK." She turns her head. "Tell me when I can move."

"You are totally beautiful," says Crystal. She turns her pad around and shows Maya her drawing.

"Oh, Crystal." Her eyes glow with pride. "You left out all the wrinkles and bags under my eyes."

"I'm drawing what's inside your soul, not just your face. All I see is perfection."

Maya chuckles. "I hope your eyes never fail you."

Payton and Bekah enter the sunroom with wet hair and Payton's school computer. Payton shows Crystal's drawings to Bekah.

"Ooh. Thank you, Crystal," says Bekah. "I love it."

"I want to paint that," says Payton, pulling her easel from the corner. She hands Crystal a sheet of watercolor paper. "Will you?"

"Sure."

Bekah, Haley, and the boys watch Crystal draw a duplicate portrait of Bekah.

"That is amazing," says Bekah. "Maybe I can use this for the post I'm writing."

"Post? For what?" asks Crystal.

"Our response to the community on Facebook."

Danny and Mike's heads snap up to her.

"Don't worry. I'll get everyone's approval beforehand."

Holly walks in with a tray of cookies. "They're still warm." She offers them to everyone.

Sydney stomps into the sunroom, JD hobbling behind her. "Holly said you danced while we were gone? Why didn't you tell us you were going to dance before we left?"

"Number one," says Payton, "we didn't know we were going to dance until it happened, and number two, if we had told you, we all would've been caught on the deck unarmed against Eugene. I still kick myself for leaving my AR inside."

Crystal finishes her copy and hands it to Payton. "Do you like to dance, Sydney?"

"I love to dance."

"So does JD," laughs Crystal.

He shakes his head and waves his arms while mouthing, "Noooo."

"You're good, JD," says Crystal. "You always do that robot move."

"Cool!" Sydney retrieves her phone and pulls up her playlist. Haley hands her the speaker.

Holly pulls the two boys into the living room. "Yes, I'd love to dance with you too good-looking guys."

Lady Gaga's "Stupid Love" pounds out of the speaker, startling Jordan.

"Down just a little, please," says Maya.

Sydney carries the speaker into the living room, sets it on the coffee table, and starts flailing with her arms and legs, shaking her body furiously. JD's eyes bulge.

Haley extends her hand to Crystal. "My love?"

"Yes, I'm coming."

"I've heard you say that before." Haley shimmies and shakes.

"And will again." Crystal tries to copy Haley, but she has trouble focusing on her own movement as she watches Haley's body. Truthfully, she'd just like to gawk. "C'mon JD. Do the robot."

"OK." He jerks his arms into angles while his body bends and leans.

The contrast between him and the blur of Sydney forces Crystal and Haley to laugh, but JD is enjoying himself. Holly bangs hips with Mike and Danny. At the end they all cheer and applaud Sydney. She grabs JD's hand, and they both bow.

"This old woman is tired," says Holly as she moves to sit with Maya on the sofa.

"I'll put on a slow song," says Sydney. The soft guitar plucks the beginning of Jason Mraz's "I Won't Give Up." Sydney approaches JD, who raises his hands.

"I don't know how to do this."

"Then I'll teach you." She puts JD's hand on her waist, and she holds his other hand out from their shoulders. She holds his waist. "Now just a little step, then a shuffle, bend at the waist, and sway back. We'll just go in a circle." They start. When Mraz starts the chorus, Sydney begins to sing along, looking directly at JD.

Crystal has to bite her tongue to hold her laugh. Haley holds her waist, and she starts singing with Sydney.

Crystal's heart seems to freeze then pounds. "I didn't know you could sing."

"One of my few talents."

"I love it!" Crystal floats in Haley's voice, eyes fixed on her lips, breathless, every nerve tingling. JD stares transfixed at Sydney as she pours her heart into the song. Danny and Mike hold each other close, watching Sydney and Haley sing.

Holly stands in the sunroom recording the event.

When the music stops, Haley and Crystal kiss. Sydney smiles at JD, holding herself back from hugging him. He claps his hands and nods. Mike and Danny whistle. Haley holds her arm out to Sydney, who leaps toward her.

"We sound good together," says Haley. "We should work on some songs tomorrow."

Sydney radiates happiness as she nods.

Bekah holds Payton's computer as she stands between the two rooms. "Thought you might want to know about the latest comments on the community Facebook page. A few people saw JD racing down the streets on his Honda with a young girl carrying a rifle. Others heard a shot and saw the ambulance and trooper leaving Crystal's house. Someone named Dylan claims the house is full of dykes. He hopes his girlfriend wasn't shot by the crazy girl with blue hair. And on and on. We have to respond before a bunch of fools with torches and pitchforks march down the driveway."

Holly flops onto the sofa with Maya. "We get rid of one menace so others can take his place. Why can't people leave us alone?"

CHAPTER 32

*B*ekah clears her throat. "I've written something I'd like to read to you."

Everyone turns to her and listens, except Payton who continues her painting. "I'll hear every amazing word."

Bekah reads off her screen. "Maya's husband, Eugene, came to Crystal's house this evening to kidnap or kill her. The man had a pump shotgun and threatened to shoot us all. JD and twelve-year-old Sydney raced to their aid from the shooting range. From thirty yards away in a speeding Honda, Sydney shot at Eugene who had aimed his shotgun and was ready to fire. She hit him in the hip. Her older sister, Payton, then knocked him out. The entire episode was filmed and given to a state trooper. Eugene is a homophobic, hateful man who wouldn't allow Maya to come home to her parents and children."

Bekah continues, "That explains the siren and the gunshot. But what about the rest of us? The queers now residing in Crystal's house?"

"Think of someone you love outside of your family and ask yourself why you care. Make a list of reasons. Try to explain why your heart pounds when she is near or aches when she is away. Why your nerves tingle and you groan inside at his touch. Why you can't stop seeing her face in your mind. Why you'd risk anything to save him. Then after all that, try to convince yourself not to love her. Not to yearn for him. Try as hard as you can, but you won't succeed. You know this is true.

"Then why does any parent or minister or fellow human being think they can simply tell you to stop loving another person because he's a man like you are, or a woman like you are? Did anyone in your life succeed in forcing you to stop loving anyone? Or did that effort cause you pain, make you depressed or angry, push you to self-harm, and make you wonder why life is so unfair as to punish you for something you can't control?

"Holly and Maya loved each other as teens. But they weren't allowed. Now they are together and relish every moment they can share. Crystal and Haley have loved each other for years. Now they don't care what others think, and they are happier than they've ever been. Bekah and Payton fell in love the moment they met. Why should they have to hide that love from anyone? Danny and Mike would have taken a twelve-gauge slug today to keep the other alive long enough to kill their assailant. Can anyone convince either of them to stop loving each other? We dare you to try.

"Crystal Rose has opened her house to save all of us because she knows the pain of intolerance, of being ridiculed and rejected because of who we are. She welcomes any other gay teen who needs shelter and safety. We will love you and defend you.

"Our queer flag is raised. Bigots be warned. Please do your part to add more love to this world, not hate."

The only sound is Maya's light patting of Jordan's back and then a tiny burp. Crystal grabs the top of a chair for support, as her legs feel wobbly. They've raised their flag—finally.

"Yes or no?" asks Bekah. "Anything you want to add or take out?"

"I think it's beautiful and true," says Holly. "Post it."

Haley hugs Crystal from behind. "I agree."

"Yes," says Maya.

"Danny, Mike?" asks Bekah. "I don't have to mention you."

Mike raises his eyebrows at Danny who then nods. They bump fists.

"Why the hell not?" says Danny.

"Any additions?" asks Bekah.

Sydney raises her hand. "Tell them we have guns, sharpshooters, flying kickers, daredevil Honda drivers, and some of the best dancers, artists, and singers in town."

"Noted," says Bekah.

Payton holds her painting for everyone to see. "This is for you, Bekah."

"I love it!" Bekah and Payton press their lips together for a long kiss.

Crystal stretches her back and neck and feels taller than ever, proud of herself and all the others. They will not hide any longer.

"I think we should post some of our drawings and paintings along with the message," says Payton. "People need to see we're human beings, not labels."

Bekah opens the camera on her phone and shoots her painting and Haley's. "Take pictures and send them to me." After a few minutes, Bekah is ready to post everything. With finger poised above the keyboard, she says, "Speak now or forever hold your peace."

"Do it," says Crystal.

Bekah presses her trackpad. "Done. I think we should carry on with our lives and not watch the screen. I'll check back in an hour." She closes the computer lid.

Holly brings Jordan's bed from upstairs and hands it to Crystal. "Maya and I are going to take advantage of Jordan's nap and go upstairs for a while. Would you mind?"

"Not at all," says Crystal. "Haley and I will fix her bed in our room and keep an eye on her."

Maya gives Jordan to Crystal. "If she wakes up before we come back down, just bring her to me. Thanks." She holds Holly's hand as they make their way to the stairs.

"Bring her bed," says Crystal to Haley.

They walk back to their room and set the bed along the headboard then place pillows along the other side. Crystal fills Jordan's cheeks with butterfly kisses before laying her down. She turns on the noise machine before they leave the room and find Danny and Mike rummaging in the kitchen.

"You hungry?" asks Crystal.

"A little," says Mike.

"There's leftover spaghetti in the fridge. Get what you want."

"Thanks."

Danny folds his arms and leans against the counter. "Hey, Crystal. We don't want to go home tonight. I don't feel like dealing with my father and Nick. Can we crash here?"

"Sure. Either in the living room or ask Payton about using her motorhome."

"Thanks."

Mike puts bowls of spaghetti and sauce into the microwave.

Payton and Bekah walk into the kitchen holding hands. "Think we're going to our room for a bit," says Payton. "Sydney's talking to JD in the sunroom. They'll keep an eye out for visitors."

"I hope we don't have to worry about who comes to our house anymore," says Crystal.

"You just posted an invitation to any queer needing help. You'll have replies."

"I want those." She shakes her head. "Just no more haters."

Crystal and Haley walk toward the sunroom where they find Sydney and JD sitting together on the little sofa.

"Payton and Bekah wanted private time," says Sydney, very seriously. "We're on watch duty."

"We both feel safer already," says Haley.

"And you don't need to worry about JD and me doing anything we shouldn't, especially now that Gena is coming home. He's a very respectful man, and I just like being with him. I love Payton, but sometimes I need a break."

JD raises his brows, smiles, and puffs his chest just a little.

Crystal presses her lips against her teeth to keep them from spreading into a laugh. She nods. "Good to know, Sydney. Haley and I will go outside for a bit."

Crystal hustles Haley onto the deck then toward the woodshed. When they are out of sight from the sunroom, Crystal stops and barks a laugh. "Can you believe that girl? She is amazing."

"I want to squeeze her I love her so much," says Haley. "She's so fucking cute."

Crystal watches the sky change colors through the trees. The sun set a few minutes ago, but it will still paint the clouds and the horizon for another hour and a half. The season rushes toward winter, losing six minutes of light every day until December twenty-first. But beauty demands to be seen and admired even so. She remembers the fall into cold and darkness as depressing, fostering only a longing for spring and summer seven months hence. This year, however, an abundance of friends and purpose and love claw back at the death march. She feels no melancholy, no dull apprehension, only hope and desire and a confidence she is doing right—for herself and others. Crystal has never been happier.

She pulls a shivering Haley close to her, slipping her hands up her shirt. "How can your skin feel so warm when you're shivering?"

"Because you touched it," says Haley.

Crystal opens her mouth and sucks Haley's bottom lip toward her tongue. Haley licks Crystal's upper lip. Then both girls tilt their heads and push their tongues deep into each other's mouths. The rhythm of their exploration is hypnotic and engorging and feels so hella good, Crystal has no doubt she can climax just from Haley's kisses.

"Are you getting warmer?" asks Crystal, gulping for air.

"Yes. There is no comparison between kissing you and kissing a boy. Even in fifth grade, our kisses were juicier, softer, and more luscious than anything I felt from any boy."

"We shouldn't have stopped."

"No." They kiss. "We'll never make that mistake again."

They both see the lights turn on inside the motorhome.

"Good," says Haley. "Danny and Mike will have one peaceful night before the shit hits the fan tomorrow."

Crystal hears a murmur in the trees and feels an oddity in the air. She separates her mouth from Haley's and turns her head toward the trail.

Something moves.

A breeze stirs the leaves, but a few crunch under hesitant steps.

Crystal separates from Haley and walks onto the trail. She sees the girl now. Tall, long legs, straight black hair, thin, oversized glasses.

The girl stops.

"It's OK," says Crystal. "You're welcome at my house."

Haley moves to Crystal. "Who?"

"Ainsley. Freshman."

"Her father is Robert Boyd," whispers Haley. "He's crazy."

The steps continue until the girl stands ten feet from Crystal.

"Do you need help?"

The girl nods.

"Come with us, Ainsley. I'm Crystal and this is Haley." Crystal holds out her hand.

The girl breathes deeply while staring at them, her eyes wide with fear. She looks over her shoulder.

"Do your parents know you've left?"

"I don't think so."

"Come," says Crystal. "Let's get inside. You're safe now."

Ainsley walks forward. Crystal puts her hand on the girl's back. Ainsley whimpers and squirms.

Crystal removes her hand. "Are you injured?"

She nods.

"Did someone hit you?"

"Yes. My father whipped me with a rod."

Haley covers her mouth with her hands. "Tonight?"

"Yes. For days."

"Why?"

"Because I kissed another girl . . . at a sleepover."

Crystal's face tightens as she grabs Ainsley's hand. "Inside. Let's hurry."

They move quickly around the swingset, onto the gravel driveway, and up onto the deck. Crystal opens the door and finds JD and Sydney in the sunroom. "JD, take Payton's rifle and stand guard on the deck."

He pushes himself up stiffly. "Hey, Ainsley. What's wrong?"

"Her father beat her. If you see or hear anything, call me."

He nods, picks up the AR leaning against the corner, and exits the house.

Sydney stands. "Can I help?"

"Yes. Check on Jordan then see if you can interrupt your sister."

She nods and takes off.

"Haley, contact Child Services . . ."

"No." Ainsley pulls her hand away from Crystal's, her eyes bright with panic.

"Her father is anti-government," says Haley. "He got into a big argument with Rathbone last year about how he taught his classes. He's complained about how girls dress at school, including me. He's going to freak if he gets a visit from Child Services."

Ainsley nods frantically.

"Then don't use names," assures Crystal. "We just want to know what our options are. Once we know, we'll all talk, and you can decide what we do. OK?"

Ainsley nods.

"Haley . . ."

"Got it. I know what to do." She pulls out her phone and sits at the table.

"Let's go to the bathroom and have a look," says Crystal, extending her hand.

Ainsley holds it and follows Crystal into the kitchen.

Sydney meets them. "Jordan is asleep. I called Payton, but she didn't answer, so I'm going to knock."

"Good luck."

"It'll be fine. It's nothing I haven't seen before." She walks away.

Crystal guides Ainsley into the bathroom and closes the door. "Can I see? I have all kinds of medicine here if you need some."

Ainsley's face is red. She wrings her hands.

"Has anyone put ointment on your back or given you anything?"

She shakes her head quickly.

Crystal reaches for Ainsley's buttons. "No one will hurt you any more. Ever." She undoes each button then stands behind the girl who hangs her head, breathing rapidly. Crystal removes the shirt and has to close her eyes for a few seconds before she can face the crisscrossing red welts on Ainsley's back again. Before opening her eyes, she steels her nerves, but still the web of torture—freshly raised pus-filled lesions over older, purple bruises—makes her gasp. "Oh, Ainsley, I'm so sorry. You must hurt so much."

"I'd gotten somewhat used to the pain. But when he hit me tonight, I snapped. I screamed at them both. Said I hated them. I found your post before they took my phone and computer. Later I snuck out." She looks at Crystal with wet eyes. "I can't help it. I've tried . . . very hard, but I keep staring at other girls. Lucy invited me to her slumber party last weekend. Lots of girls were in their sleeping bags on the floor. Lucy and I were talking softly late at night, our faces close together. We had a flashlight between us. I couldn't stop staring at her lips, and then I kissed her. She kissed back but then turned over and went to sleep. She must have told her parents because they called my father. I couldn't help it. What am I supposed to do?"

"There's nothing you can do. Every time I see Haley, especially from behind, I gasp and gawk." Crystal finds a Tylenol. "Do you want one?"

Ainsley nods and takes the pill. Someone knocks on the door.

"Can we come in?" asks Payton.

"Yes."

Payton's eyes tighten as she stares at Ainsley's back. Bekah gasps and turns away.

"Who did this?" asks Payton.

Crystal tightens her lips. "Her father."

"Well, he sure didn't spare the rod." Payton pulls out her phone and snaps a quick picture of the girl's back.

Ainsley turns, her eyes pleading.

"The photo just shows your back, not your face. We need evidence of abuse."

"But . . . they'll . . ."

"Your father committed a crime," says Payton. "I've dealt with child services many times. They won't let you back into that house."

"Send the photo to Haley," says Crystal.

Sydney sticks her head around the jamb and looks in. Her mouth drops open.

"Sydney," says Crystal. "Go get my mom and Holly. They'll know how to treat this."

She takes off.

"Do your parents know you're here?" asks Payton.

"No," says Ainsley. "They ordered me to get to bed early. I put pillows and clothes under my sheets. If they look in my room, they'll think I'm sleeping."

"But they'll know in the morning at the latest."

Bekah slides by everyone until she faces Ainsley and holds her hands. "You did nothing wrong, Ainsley. You're not evil or aligned with Satan or going to hell. You're just like us. And we're going to get you through this. We promise."

Ainsley tries to smile.

"Let us in, girls," commands Holly.

Payton and Bekah move to the hallway, giving room to Maya and Holly, both wearing thin robes.

"This is Ainsley," says Crystal. "Robert Boyd's daughter."

"Jesus Christ," mutters Holly. "Hey, Ainsley. My name is Holly, and this beautiful woman next to me is Maya, Crystal's mom. We're going to take care you. Would you like that?"

Ainsley smiles and nods.

Holly looks at Crystal and nods her head toward the exit. Crystal leaves, and the door closes behind her.

The other girls have gathered in the sunroom. When Crystal arrives, Haley is still on the phone, and Bekah is reading replies to their Facebook post.

Beautiful artwork!

Don't think Mac will be happy about a queer flag at his house.

Or Summer.

Bless you girls. You are all God's children.

Think I'll take this up with the City Council. Are queer houses allowed in Clear? When did we vote for that kind of zoning?

I moved to Alaska to get away from liberals and communists and gays everywhere. Where do I go now?

This is what happens when the schools are allowed to spread their liberal agenda of tolerance for everyone, no matter how sick they are!

"That, by the way, was from Robert Boyd."

Payton shakes her head. "And he calls us sick."

I wish all of us could be as accepting and brave as you. Alaska girls kick ass!

Can a bunch of us come over to watch you all make out?

We need more love in the world. Thank you!

"Better or worse than you expected?" asks Payton.

Bekah closes the lid. "Actually better."

Haley ends her call. "They'll want to talk with Ainsley tomorrow morning."

"Did you give names?" asks Crystal.

"Just ours. I sent the photo. They said they would likely get involved and keep Ainsley from going back to her parents. And we should call the troopers."

Payton stands. "I think we need to make a decision about Ainsley and what will happen in the future." She opens the door and signals for JD to come inside. "Everyone should have a voice in this."

JD comes inside, rubbing his arms and shivering. "I forgot to wear a jacket or something heavier."

Sydney offers him a throw blanket from the sofa arm.

"Thanks," says JD.

Payton continues. "We got rid of Eugene, so we could stay here in relative peace. May have to deal with stupid comments on Facebook or at school or the post office, but otherwise we'll be fine."

"Until Mac and Summer come back," says Bekah. "Like the man said, 'Don't think Mac will be happy about a queer flag at his house.'"

"They'll change," says Crystal. "They'll do anything to keep Maya and Jordan here. She'll help them understand. I promise."

"OK," says Payton. "That's option one. Option two is we deal with Ainsley and all the other Ainsleys who will come our way. And there will be more if we keep our invitation up. But that means we're always on our guard. Mr. Boyd will raise a big stink, but he'll probably be charged and legally restrained. What do we do when another minor girl comes knocking who hasn't been beaten? And her parents show up because everyone within a hundred miles will know where their gay kid has run to? Then we have problems. We can't stand on the deck with our guns and tell them to go away. We can't be kidnappers."

"Aren't we kidnapping Bekah now?" asks Crystal.

"Not after Monday when she turns eighteen."

"What's your question?" asks Sydney. "Are we supposed to tell other girls, or guys, to leave because we want a peaceful life?"

"That's option one," answers Payton.

"I don't like that option," says Sydney. "We can't just save Bekah and say to hell with everyone else."

"I agree," says Crystal. "Ainsley's crime was kissing her friend. An impulsive kiss because she couldn't help herself. That can't be a crime or reason to beat your child or make her feel like crap. We know what that leads to."

"What do we do?" asks Haley.

Crystal moves to the center of the room. "We educate people. We post, we publish our art, we invite people to have their portraits drawn and painted. We host events online. We show people we're not freaks. We're loving, caring people, just like they should be. When those parents come to our door wanting their kid back, we'll talk to them. Maya and Holly will tell their stories. We are not all the same. We all have special needs. Society cannot deny me an education because I don't learn like most others. They have to accommodate me." She can't stop the tears from rolling out of her eyes. "Society cannot deny queers a normal life because they don't act like everyone else. Everyone needs to hear that message. I want to help. I don't want to hide." Crystal wipes her eyes and reaches back for Haley's hand.

Haley squeezes and kisses it. "You're the most amazing human being, Crystal Rose. I'm always on your side."

"I agree," says Sydney.

"I do too," says JD.

"You already know where Bekah and I stand," says Payton. "Ainsley can sleep with Sydney in our room. I'll take watch, JD, and wake you up later."

JD nods.

Jordan's cries drift toward them.

Crystal's heart swells as she looks at her friends. "I love all of you. Thank you."

Louder cries pull every face to the other end of the house.

"I'll take care of Jordan." Crystal runs to her room where she finds her little sister flailing her arms and legs. Crystal unzips the cover and checks her diaper, which is sopping wet. Haley walks into the room as Crystal lifts her sister's legs with one hand and pulls the diaper away with the other.

"I'll take that," says Haley, grabbing the diaper.

"You think she's hungry or just uncomfortable?"

"Or wants to be held and loved like we all do?"

They lock eyes. "Why is that so hard for people to understand?" asks Crystal. "We all need to be held and loved. Why do people take issue with who does the holding?" After a good wipe of her sister, Crystal attaches a new diaper, and lifts Jordan to blow strawberries on her bare tummy. Jordan laughs. Crystal blows more until she squeals. "Why is happiness so much easier for a baby to feel than for a teen or an adult?" She lays Jordan down in the bed and makes faces at her.

"Because people stop blowing strawberries. I know where I'd like you to do that to me," Haley purrs, sliding her hand over Crystal's butt and straddling the girl's hip from the side. "That would make me very happy."

Crystal leans against Haley and momentarily closes her eyes. "OK, but blowing strawberries doesn't fix Ainsley's situation and wouldn't have fixed either of our Mom's lives. In fact, Payton and Bekah had to stop making love because that doesn't fix abusive parents or the community's bigotry. Ditto for Mom and Holly. Even us kissing outside."

Haley slides her hand under Crystal's shirt and strokes her skin with her fingertips. "To every thing there is a season. A time to be born, and a time to die; a time to plant strawberries, and a time to blow them."

"I don't remember that last part."

"It's there. I promise you." She flicks her tongue into Crystal's ear.

Crystal squirms. "I think you lie, but I love you anyway." Crystal breathes more rapidly. "All I can think about now are strawberries. But first we have to feed Jordan and put together her crib and figure out how to make Ainsley's life better, and make a plan for how we'll respond when other teens come knocking."

Jordan grabs her toe and tries to pull it to her mouth.

"Yes, all that is important," says Haley, "but remember, the issue we're fighting for is sexual preference. Without the sex, we're just a bunch of girls living in your house. Everyone in town would call us future spinsters and try to hook us up with eligible men. And all the intolerance and bigotry would continue. We can't forget the strawberries." She rubs her lips along Crystal's neck.

"A time to plant," Crystal bends her head back, exposing her throat.

"A time to blow, a time to love." She leans against Haley's wandering hands. "And a time to fight."

"Because we love."

"Because we love."

THE END

ACKNOWLEDGMENTS

I have known many teens like Crystal and JD, who despite their traditional academic challenges, discovered and shared other talents, including in art, music, dance, and athletics. Their needs are no more special than mine or yours. They are basic needs, which must be addressed. As Payton declares, "We all have special needs and special powers, don't you think? Finding out what they are has to be our life's mission." And the schools' mission for every student, which can't happen when arts and elective programs are cut. Thankfully, Crystal has Diana two days a week. So many kids like her, especially the younger ones, have no one outside their core teachers. I am grateful to have known many youth who were able to discover their passions, often despite their circumstances.

Once again, I am fortunate to have great beta readers and editors, several long-time friends and some refreshingly new. Jerrica McDowell somehow keeps her eyes, and mine, fixed on the forest and the trees and every little plant in between. She is my special spirit guide through the dark and often lonely journey from initial idea to completed manuscript.

I can honestly say that *this* story would not have been possible without the passion and enthusiasm and honesty of Ruth Torrence, who graduates high school this year, ready to add her amazing talents to UCLA this fall. She has a great future ahead of her, and I hope to send her my future novels for her wise critiques.

Emily Wright, Biancalice, and Gennifer Ulmen gave me so much actionable feedback. I can't imagine writing another book without their help. Jessica Scurlock and Ashleigh Bilodeau, once again, helped me tremendously.

Once again, Cherie Chapman (www.ccbookdesign.com) designed my cover. She continually amazes me. I could say I keep writing books just so I can enjoy the covers she creates, but you might not believe me.

No, I did not create the art. I found a wonderful artist at Dielyn_lineart who worked very hard to translate my ideas and photographs into Crystal's continuous line drawings. She is amazing. And thanks to Arju for the great watercolor paintings.

Last but not least, I wish to thank the moose cow and calf, which have visited my house many times since last summer. And I really did see them emerge from a trail near my house, though during an early snow. Book ideas often begin from such chance, close encounters.

ABOUT THE AUTHOR

Brooke Skipstone is a multi-award winning author who lives in Alaska where she watches the mountains change colors with the seasons from her balcony. Where she feels the constant rush toward winter as the sunlight wanes for six months of the year, seven minutes each day, bringing crushing cold that lingers even as the sun climbs again. Where the burst of life during summer is urgent under twenty-four-hour daylight, lush and decadent. Where fish swim hundreds of miles up rivers past bear claws and nets and wheels and lines of rubber-clad combat fishers, arriving humped and ragged, dying as they spawn. Where danger from the land and its animals exhilarates the senses, forcing her to appreciate the difference between life and death. Where the edge between is sometimes too alluring.

Crystal's House of Queers is her third novel.

Visit her website at www.brookeskipstone.com for information about her first two novels, *Some Laneys Died* and *Someone To Kiss My Scars*.

instagram.com/brookeskipstone

CPSIA information can be obtained
at www.ICGtesting.com
Printed in the USA
BVHW071001150521
607358BV00004B/164